Too Far Gone

also by Chadwick Ginther

Thunder Road
Tombstone Blues

Too Far Gone

By Chadwick Ginther

Too Far Gone

Published by Ravenstone
an imprint of Turnstone Press
Artspace Building
206-100 Arthur Street
Winnipeg, MB
R3B 1H3 Canada
www.TurnstonePress.com

Turnstone Press gratefully acknowledges the assistance of the Canada Council for the Arts, the Manitoba Arts Council, the Government of Canada through the Canada Book Fund, and the Province of Manitoba through the Book Publishing Tax Credit and the Book Publisher Marketing Assistance Program.

Printed and bound in Canada by Friesens for Turnstone Press.

Library and Archives Canada Cataloguing in Publication

Ginther, Chadwick, 1975–, author
Too far gone / Chadwick Ginther.

(Thunder Road trilogy)
ISBN 978-0-88801-541-9 (paperback)

I. Title. II. Series: Ginther, Chadwick, 1975. Thunder Road trilogy

PS8613.I58T66 2015 C813'.6 C2015-906070-2

For the Inner Circle:

You know who you are, you know what you've done.
Thanks for sharing stories and games for over 25 years.

Roll initiative.

Too Far Gone

1. Comin' Home

"I'm comin' home."

Ted Callan ended the call. It was a hell of a message to leave on the machine after not talking to his parents in months. But the whole story would do more than eat up their answering machine's memory, it'd also put their lives at risk. He was coming home to Edmonton. That's all they needed to know.

He lit a cigarette, inhaling the mixture of butane and burning tobacco. Ted held it in, savouring the smoke, eyes closed. Expelled it in one long breath through his nose.

Whenever Ted saw fire, he heard the giant Surtur's laugh, "*Lock, lock, lock.*" He still dreamed he was burning alive. If he turned northwest, Ted could almost hear the crackle of flames.

Going back to Edmonton wasn't safe for Ted. Wasn't safe for anyone. But it had to be done. Even if Edmonton wasn't home—couldn't feel like home, not ever again—speaking the promise made it real.

The wind scattered grit over the parking lot of the greasy spoon. Its egg-shaped mascot grinned down from the sign with its empty grin, giving Ted a thumbs-up. Hardly the greatest endorsement of his plan. But the franchise had begun in Alberta, and that seemed a good omen.

Though there was more on Ted's plate than greasy eggs and

bacon. The *dvergar*, the *álfar*, the *jötnar*, the Norns; his friends and his enemies. They'd all settled their hash at the "Council of Humptys," and he felt he could leave Winnipeg in their hands. They'd promised to come when he called and in return he'd given each a token. Vera had scoured the Gimli beaches to find all those lucky stones. Each with a natural hole through its surface that Ted had run a cord through. On each stone he'd carved *Raidho*, a rune in the shape of a stylized "R." A rune of travel. If shit hit the fan, he'd have backup. *If* they had his back.

They'd agreed to his treaty. But Ted had also had most of their blood on his knuckles before.

There was someone else, someone Ted had half-expected to crash the council, whom he'd bought some insurance against. He didn't want to think of the fucker's name. *Speak of the devil, and all that.*

Ted's insurance was two thin golden chains around his wrists. Chains that were shards of something once used to terrify and bind him. Now they were a gift from Andvari's dwarves and Youngnir's giants. The dwarves had taught him Gleipnir's song. He sang to the chain—the tune reminded him of The Flys' "Got You Where I Want You"—and the chains separated, slithering around his forearms, and then rejoined, looking as if they'd never been broken. Better to have insurance, hoping you never need it, than not having it when you do.

He'd have to suss shit out quick and get out quicker. Pulling off this expedition into the lands of the enemy would take every bit of deception he'd ever learned from Loki.

Never thought I'd stop thinking of Edmonton as home.

Things change. Kick the asses of a few valkyries and a dragon, throw in the god of thunder and the goddess of death, and word gets around. Winnipeg wasn't a big city, and it hadn't taken long. Winnipeg became more—if not completely—normal. But after Hel's invasion, the city would never be the same. Ted's presence brought enough danger all on its own. Maybe today would be the beginning of the end of that. *If* Ted could pull it off.

Big fucking "if."

But Ted also knew there was no way he'd be able to deal with Surtur—once and for all—from Winnipeg. Not with the fire giant squatting, brooding back in northern Alberta. Those fires had grown against nature or logic, but for the first time since Ted had put boot down on his weird road through the Nine Worlds of Norse mythology, the fires had receded. This lull in the giant's advance might be Ted's only chance to find out what the goddess of death had meant when she'd told him how to kill Surtur.

Build a cage from Surtur's Bones.

Only then will the Bright Sword appear.

None of his plans had worked. Hel had also warned him Surtur's death was only for Ted, and he'd believed her. Tilda could've helped, but the last of the Norns was long gone. And while she'd said she'd see him at the end of the world, she never said she'd help him.

How can I build a cage out of his bones until I fucking kill him? How can I kill him without the fucking sword?

When Ted's buddy Ryan had told him he was getting engaged last November, the wedding had seemed so far off. They'd left their friendship on a knife's edge, and if Ted didn't stand up for Rye, they'd be done. Another part of his old life—another part of Ted Callan—the Nine Worlds would have stolen.

So he'd said yes.

His monkey suit fitting was done. He'd pick up the finished product in Edmonton. Knowing his luck, the suit wouldn't survive the trip.

Ted didn't want to go back to Alberta without knowing how to kill Surtur, but he'd promised, and he wouldn't renege. Hell, if he did, Rye's mom Gloria would find a way to kill him, if Surtur didn't.

He hoped there was a home left when he was done.

He passed by Gaol Road and the correctional institute there. Correction. Jail didn't *correct* anything. Go inside, get punished, become a better criminal. Not that Ted had done much better at rehabilitating the monsters he'd battled. He'd tried, though. A little mercy could go a long way.

Ted squinted against the sun. Sweat ran down his face, getting caught in his beard; pooling in the small of his back where his bag was slung over his shoulder. He wondered whether he could still get sunburned. He'd always had fair skin.

It would be utter bullshit if his dragon-scale tattoos would protect him from an inferno, but leave him pink and blistered by the sun.

Ted stuck out a few tentative thumbs to hitch a ride, but there were no takers. One vehicle slowed down as it passed him, but that was all. It was pretty much what he'd expected. When you're 6'4" and covered head to toe in tattoos, the families and farmers see you with a different eye. Maybe when he got a little further away from the jail, he wouldn't look like an ex-con on his first day out of the clink. *Or on the run from it.* Just an unkempt hitchhiker with more grey in his beard than red, and a bag slung over his shoulder, endlessly walking.

Ted checked his wrist by instinct, looking for the time, forgetting his watch had been trashed. He reached for his phone, but it hadn't worked for shit since Loki had stolen it on their way up to Flin Flon. Ted barely trusted the thing to tell time. His stomach growled, threatening to chew a hole in his belly. Whatever the o'clock was, he could eat.

If his phone was accurate, it had been a long ten hours to Portage la Prairie, the August sun beating down on him the whole way. Ted needed a hot meal and a cold beer. He settled into a franchise pizza place. If you're going to be overcharged and mildly disappointed, you may as well know that going in. After arguing all the previous night, and walking without sleep through the day, a full belly did him in. Ted found a hotel room and slept through the night.

He was back to the road with the dawn. He'd never been a morning person, but he'd woken up needing to piss, and decided on an early start. A couple hours beyond Portage, and at the beginning of the Yellowhead Highway, he felt oddly like his journey was beginning here at that prosaic set of lights and gas station. While he was on the Trans-Canada, he could fool himself into thinking he was going to Regina. To Vancouver. Anywhere but Edmonton. But here he was. Angling north. Saskatoon, and then Edmonton. He hadn't heard of monsters in Saskatchewan.

Don't tempt fate.

Fate. Doom. Destiny.

Words that had meant nothing to him before he'd met Tilda.

He left the town of Neepawa behind him. Sparks danced over the tattoo of Mjölnir on his right hand, though there wasn't a cloud in the sky. A convoy of concert trucks rushed past, trailers plastered with the face of some teen pop sensation he'd heard of but never consciously listened to, buffeting him with displaced air and kicking up dirt and grit from the highway shoulder. Miles up the road, he came to a dead stop.

Here.

He knelt and touched the pavement. As if it were happening again, he could hear the wipers squeal trying to keep up with the pounding rain, feel his car hydroplane on the rutted, shitty road and slide to a stop on the soft, unpaved shoulder. This was where he'd almost run over Tilda on a rainy night in September. From here and back to the Trans-Canada intersection they'd joked and flirted for the first time. Where she'd explained that doom wasn't necessarily a bad thing.

There was no one to hear. No one to judge him now. And so Ted said, “I miss you, Tilda.”

Saying it aloud made it harder. Made it real.

His phone chirped in his pocket and an electronic voice said, “Calling. Tilda. Eilífsdóttir.”

“*Gah!*”

Ted didn’t have his voice dialing turned on. Didn’t have Tilda programed into the phone. As far as he knew, Tilda didn’t *own* a phone. Another of Loki’s tricks. Ted fumbled his cell from his pocket and ended the call before it connected.

He breathed a relieved sigh, but it didn’t last long. In the glare of headlights, Ted’s shadow grew long in front of him. Tires squealed. Burning rubber filled his nostrils. Someone laid on the horn. Ted realized he was standing in the middle of the highway.

Ted had an instant to wonder whether this was how Tilda felt when she’d been caught in *his* headlights. He scrambled to the shoulder of the road. His shirt and hair whipped in the wake of an Econoline van. The brake lights flared red as the van stopped. The reverse lights kicked in and the van backed up, gravel spinning under its tires. The side door slammed open. Ted caught the telltale “One-two-three-four” that could only mean The Ramones blaring from inside the van.

An Aboriginal man leaned out from the open door and shouted, “What the hell, man?”

“Sorry,” Ted said, hitching his backpack over his shoulder.

The man’s head craned up and down, taking in Ted’s every detail. He asked, “Looking for a ride?”

“If you’re offering.”

The man got out of the van and motioned towards the interior. "Get in."

Ted hustled over, climbing in past the big stocky guy who'd called to him. He slid towards the driver's side as the man got in. The van smelled like old socks and fresh cigarettes and had neatly stacked musical equipment cases and haphazardly piled duffel bags behind his seat.

"Leon," the man said, offering his hand.

Ted shook it, introduced himself. In the dim illumination of the interior light, Ted saw two women in the front seats, also Aboriginal.

"Angela," the driver said, not offering to shake hands.

The woman riding shotgun leaned around the seat and said, "Chris."

"Thanks for stopping," Ted said as Leon slammed the van door shut.

Tires spun gravel as the van pulled back on to the highway. Angela said, "It was that or run you over. What the hell were you doing standing in the middle of the road?"

"Trying to get us to stop, what do you think?" the big guy said with a laugh.

"No," Ted said, "but I'm glad you did. No luck today."

"Where are you heading?"

"Edmonton."

"Lucky you," Angela said, glancing back.

"You too?" Ted wasn't sure whether this was good luck or bad—he'd get to Edmonton earlier than he'd intended, and that meant he'd have to stay there longer than he'd like.

"Eventually," Chris said. "Saskatoon next, Edmonton the day after. Inaugural tour of No NDN Princess. Leon's drums—" at this, Leon patted his bicep—"Angela is words and bass. I'm guitar. We can take you all the way there, if you don't mind spending a night in Saskatchewan."

Leon gave a fake shudder that elicited a laugh from Chris and Angela.

"Thanks," Ted said.

The Ramones were replaced by Dead Kennedys. Stiff Little Fingers. Good stuff. No Green Day, thank Christ. So far, so good with their taste in music at least.

"Mind if I smoke?" Ted asked, holding up his cigarette pack.

"Not if you're sharing," Angela said, holding a hand behind her. "Road tax."

Ted coughed up a smoke to the driver, who put it to her lips, but made no move to light it. He passed one to each of the other two band members, they lit theirs and then Ted lit his own. He was getting low. He figured this pack would last him longer, which might have been the case if he'd been driving. But his cravings didn't care that he was on foot. He should've bought another pack back in Neepawa.

"What takes you to Edmonton?" Leon asked.

"My buddy's getting married."

"Hitching to a wedding?" The drummer nodded, as if that impressed him.

"I met a hitchhiker on this highway. She changed my life."

"Better or worse?"

That was a good question. Ted still wasn't entirely certain of the answer. "Better. Worse. Both."

"Sounds like a woman."

"Watch your fucking mouth," Angela said, tossing a crumpled paper bag at Leon.

Chris laughed. "Good luck."

She'd turned the music down, enough that Ted had noticed it. Enough for her and Angela to join the conversation.

"It seemed fitting, that I walk back to that old life."

Chris asked, "Where is she, this woman that changed you?"

"Don't know. Wish I did."

Leon laughed. "Screwed up, didn't you?"

"I did."

Ted could try and blame Loki. Try to hold on to the fact Tilda had been acting out of hurt, but the simplest answer was that things weren't great before the trickster had impersonated Tilda—*and done such a good job that I couldn't tell the difference.*

It was simpler to believe everything had been the trickster's fault. His first marriage should've trained him how to live with a woman. *Evidently not.* All the women he'd shared a home with, whether for years, or for weeks, had left him.

It's not Loki. It's me.

"You think going home will win her back?"

"Not the way I screwed up."

The drummer laughed and held up his cigarette as if he was giving a toast and said, "To winning back crazy broads, even when it's our fault."

Angela gave the drummer the finger.

"Okay," Leon said. "*Especially* when it's our fault."

Ted looked at her eyes in the rear-view mirror. They flickered between him and the drummer. He wondered whether those two had a history. If they did, it was none of his business.

Ted also wondered when the drummer was going to give up with his questions. The lights of Russell—Ted remembered the town from his drive out, he'd topped up The Goat's gas tank there his last time through—were brightening, and the relentlessly chatty man still hadn't let up.

They talked music. No NDN Princess was a punk band, but that wasn't all they liked to listen to, and as the klicks rolled on, Ted felt as if they could've plugged his iPod into the stereo and he'd never have known the difference. A little more country. A little less metal. But he knew most of the songs.

When they stopped for gas, Ted got a better look at the band. And they got a better look at him. They all had tattoos, but nothing like Ted's. When they asked who did his work, Ted said, "A guy from Flin Flon."

They couldn't see the majority of his tattoos. The storm on his chest, the tree that ran up his spine, the four horse legs that ran down the inside and outside of each leg, terminating in four horseshoes on the soles of his feet—all were hidden by clothing. He'd never be able to explain why he'd gotten those tats. Of course, the *why* definitely hadn't been his call.

Chris was the shortest of the three as well as the thinnest. She let her hair fall over her eyes like a mask. Her nails were long, hard. Her jeans had more holes than denim.

Leon had an open, round, friendly face. At least he did after three hours of talking. The guy would be intimidating if you didn't know him, with his barrel chest and a belly that didn't look like flab. He had "kiss" and "kill" tattooed on his knuckles. Some mostly healed scabs above the tattoos told Ted he'd been in a fight not too long ago.

Angela had shaved the sides of her head, and tied her hair back in a scalp lock. She wore a Tank Girl t-shirt and snug red jeans.

Ted felt a tingle run up his back, as if a wind had fluttered the runic leaf branches of his Yggdrasill tattoo. He knew that wind was carrying his ravens Huginn and Muninn home. Once they had scouted for Odin, had been the All-Father's *Thought* and *Memory*. Now they were Ted's.

Together, the ravens said, speaking in Ted's thoughts, **We have news.**

Obviously, Ted shot back.

The blank spaces over Ted's ears itched, anticipating the ravens' return to their roost. Huginn and Muninn landed at the entrance to the gas station's convenience store and Ted knew they wanted back in his head. They stared through the glass door, cocking their heads at him. If they wanted to, they could ditch their flesh and feathers and turn to mist, passing right through that glass.

Now is not the best time.

Soon, Huginn said. **We have much to share.**

Can you wait until Saskatoon?

That would not be wise.

I'll try to find an excuse to get alone.

Good, Muninn said.

"Ravens," Chris said, looking out the door. "That's a good omen. My *kookum* always said ravens set things right."

Huginn and Muninn preened themselves, pleased as beetles in shit.

"Sometimes," Ted said.

Ravens were trickster figures too, and Ted knew how tricksters liked to "set things right." Loki had tried to do that for the gods, and for Ted. It had worked great, until everything went wrong. The two ravens took to arguing over a discarded bun from a nearby Subway and danced around it, flapping their wings.

The clerk behind the counter watched them. He could feel her stink-eye from across the store. Angela went towards the washroom, which Ted figured wasn't a bad idea. Ted grabbed himself a cup of coffee and some road snacks: beef jerky; and a bag of Doritos. He asked for a pack of Canadian Classic and then paid for their gas.

"I'm gonna hit the head, and I'll meet you out there," Ted said, handing the spoils to Leon.

The men's room smelled of a mixture of urinal cake, piss, and the after-effects of someone who'd been on the wrong side of truck-stop chicken. Ted sidled up to a urinal that looked like it had more piss on the floor than it had ever caught, and let fly.

Now? Huginn asked.

Never *talk to a man while he's pissing. Bad etiquette. How many times do I have to tell you that?*

Muninn asked, **Would you like the running total?**

No, I would not like the running fucking total. And you're still talking to me. Stop it.

If that is your wish, both ravens said.

Ted would have said that it was, but that would have kept the uppity birds talking. When he was done, he gave himself a quick two shakes, washed his hands and headed out.

The ravens' croaking cries sounded a lot like laughter as they sloughed off their flesh and feathers and misted back under Ted's skin.

It had been months since the ravens had first left his body, and Ted still hadn't grown accustomed to the sensation. It felt like sandpaper running over already raw skin, beneath his beard, grown to better hide his raven tattoos. If anything, the new facial hair had made this part worse: it felt as if someone had grabbed a fistful of hair and yanked. But at least the raven tattoos were harder to see, which made their absence in the daylight hours easier to explain.

He asked, *Okay, what's the news?*

Finally, Huginn muttered.

When the ravens finished, he wished he were dreaming.

2. Burning Inside

Someone in Saskatchewan was trying to summon Surtur from the patch.

When the giant had followed Ted to Flin Flon, he'd managed it because of a stray lightning strike in a dry wood. Ted's carelessness had started a forest fire, and Surtur had felt it. It had only taken every drop of rain Ted could summon to push the giant back, and the deluge wouldn't have been enough without Loki's help.

This will, by necessity, require a change in your plans, Muninn said.

I'm aware of that.

The ravens snickered, and Muninn chirped in with, Forgive me, but that has seldom been the case.

Yes, Huginn added. I am anxious to hear this new plan of yours.

Keeping the secret of Hel's riddle walled up and away from the ravens was tiring. One of the reasons Ted had finally given the birds their wish and let them roam around to their feathered content during the day.

He wondered whether they spent their nights snooping around in his head trying to pull the secret from his brain like a nightcrawler stuck fast in the earth. He wondered what would happen if they did find out. W*ould it invalidate what Hel had said?*

There were probably magical ways to ward his dreams and thoughts from the ravens, but Heckle and Jeckle were a part of Ted now. He figured any supernatural defence he could put up, their sharp beaks would be able to slice through in the same way that dragon's-blood-tempered *álfur* dagger had cut through his dragon-scale tattoos. A dagger Ted hadn't seen since Loki'd handled it—worrisome, considering how he and the trickster had parted. A better defence against the ravens was to fill his thoughts with things they didn't care about.

Football. Whiskey. Rye's wedding.

Tilda.

Unfortunately, thoughts of Tilda had a tendency to bleed into thoughts of the Nine Worlds. And that was asking for Surtur to come up. And Hel. But there was no keeping Tilda out of mind.

He could feel her, somewhere, out in the world. His magic drawn to hers with the same insistency as a mosquito bite. The more he gave in to scratching that itch, the more he had to find her, to feel her. The exact opposite of what she wanted.

"I'll see you at the end of the world," she'd said. That time was coming. Fast. Ted's arrival in Alberta could kick off the war. When it did, his allies in Winnipeg wouldn't be able to hold back the destruction.

Muninn felt the need to remind him, **You would trust them? They tried to kill you.**

So did Urd. And the dwarves. And Youngnir. And Hel.

Ted winced. He wished he wouldn't have brought up Hel. He didn't want the ravens heading down the thought and memory path to Surtur's death. Would it do any real harm to tell them Hel's secret when Ted didn't know what Hel's words meant, let alone how he'd accomplish it?

You trust too easily. And too much, Muninn mentioned for what Ted felt was the thousandth time in the last several months.

Then why should I trust you?

Huginn snickered that Muninn had fallen for that comeback, again. But the raven couldn't help but remind Ted of things. It was in his nature. At times, particularly when they set to squabbling, the two birds were like a having a bowling alley crashing around in his head. Ted enjoyed that the ravens took the piss out of each other at least as often as they did to him.

Do you know who *is trying to call Surtur?* The ravens' petulant silence told Ted they did not. *I guess you'll have to keep looking.*

But it is evening now, we have roosted.

Do you think this will wait until the morning? This is important, unless I haven't been following what you've been telling me.

I hate you sometimes, Theodore Callan, Huginn sulked.

Now it was Muninn's turn to laugh.

Theodore used to send us out in the night all the time, Muninn said.

And you hated it more than I did, Huginn muttered.

Muninn laughed again, adding, **That is not how I remember it.**

Can you fucking go? I'd like to get some shut-eye. Lord knows I'm going to need it soon enough.

The ravens pulled free of his flesh again without answering. The more often he had them do so, the more it hurt. He rubbed at his beard to check it was still attached. In the dark of the van there was no way the band would see the inky cloud of the ravens leave his body. Huginn and Muninn drifted backwards, seeping out the not-factory-fresh seal on the rear door and zipped away faster than wings should allow, out into the world.

Finally. Peace and fucking quiet.

Ted shut his eyes, let the thrum of wheels over asphalt lull him towards slumber. He could feel his head get heavy, start to droop, when Leon yelled, "I love this song!"

The speakers crackled as he turned up "Run to the Hills" and sleep flew away faster than the ravens.

The first sign advertising the concert appeared after they skirted Yorkton. It was hand-painted and said: "Yellowhead it to a black metal show. Blucher Road." There were no bands listed. The sign made Ted curious. Not that he wanted to check out the concert. Black metal was shit metal in his opinion, but many of those bands were steeped in Norse mythology. He'd been warned about them too; how they'd kill for a taste of his power.

Killing and power, two things Surtur knew well.

It could be a coincidence. But Ted didn't think this was one of those times. He checked his phone, trying to find where the show was happening. It took a bit of doing. Even when Ted entered "Saskatchewan" into the search field, it kept showing him maps of the U.K. and New Zealand.

Fucking phone. Fucking Loki.

Ted added "please" to his search—the trickster often insisted on politeness from others—and Ted found what he was looking for. He gave his head a shake, and surprised himself by muttering a "thank you" under his breath. Loki couldn't get back into Winnipeg—Ted had seen to that—but the god of mischief could be anywhere else, or any*one* else. He could be Leon. Or Angela or Chris. No sense tempting fate. Blucher Road looked as if it were one of the roads that prairie surveyors had laid out in Manitoba, Alberta, and Saskatchewan, marking off one-mile-by-one-mile sections of land. He had a few hours left before he needed to decide whether he had to cancel this show.

The hours both flew by and seemed to drag by turns as Ted waited for news. A few more roadside signs dotted the highway, advertising the concert. The last sign had said fifty klicks. Finally, he could feel a twitch. Huginn and Muninn returning. It was fortunate the music in the van was loud enough to hide Ted's sharp intake of breath. He'd been pushing the ravens hard lately, and as they drifted under his skin, the pain of their return dwarfed any headache.

Took your sweetass time.

It is lovely to see you, also, Huginn said.

And?

Muninn affected a put-upon sigh, and then said, **Yes, it is good to be back in the roost.**

Stop calling me that. What did you learn?

That is what we are here to tell you. They are here.

Ted felt his head pulled towards the north. *Who's here?*

Those who would summon Surtur.

And those summoners are?

The ravens released a *quork* that sounded like another hard-done-by sigh. **The band. You would call them the "headliner." Surtsúlfar. The wolves of Surtur.**

Ted didn't like that name. Not. One. Bit.

It's the band?

Another sigh. **Yes.**

Fuck me sideways. Do you think they know I'm on the way?

In between songs from the van's stereo he could make out the drone of guitars and the pounding of drums being carried on the wind. A line of cars in front of the van turned down a road, on their way to the concert, Ted figured. Muninn confirmed the suspicion. Ted poked his head between the two front seats. Chris was still driving and Leon was leaning against the passenger-side window—finally too tired to talk—his mouth hanging open, his breath fogging the glass.

Ted asked Chris, "Can you let me out there?"

She gave him a surprised look. "I thought you were riding to Edmonton."

"What can I say? I'm into all that viking shit." Ted forced a smile. "Seems like too good an opportunity to pass up. Call it fate."

Chris shrugged and eased the van onto the shoulder.

Angela opened the door and slid out, waiting for Ted to grab his backpack. "We're playing the Odeon in Saskatoon tomorrow. If we see you there, you're welcome to a ride to Edmonton."

"Thanks," Ted said. "I'll keep that in mind."

Angela gave a brief nod and hopped back into the van, dragging the door shut. Leon gave Ted a wave with a cigarette burning between his fingers. The van drove off, leaving Ted at the side of the road. Bonfires dotted a farmyard not that far away.

The property was over a set of railway tracks. A single-storey farmhouse tucked into some trees at one corner of the yard. Rusty farm machinery—harrows and combines—and an old truck decorated the fallow field.

Two men in replica viking garb banged swords on their shields as Ted approached. The fires lit all over the farmyard were enough to see by, and the gathering crowd were a curious mix of historically accurate vikings and leather-clad metalheads. There were enough greasepaint-covered faces for Ted to think he'd stumbled on a Kiss tribute band, and enough vikings that he could've gone back in time.

One of the vikings asked, "What do you want?"

"I'm here for the show."

They scanned Ted's appearance, scowling.

Ted didn't know how far word of his tattoos might have spread through the gossip lines of the Nine Worlds. It seemed everybody he'd crossed paths with knew the name the dwarves had given him: Ófriður. He rolled up the sleeve of his jacket to show them his Mjölnir tattoo. It was a common enough symbol. Despite being a total dick, Thor had been a popular guy.

For a second, Ted thought they'd lay into him with those swords, until one man held out his hand and said, "Twenty dollars."

"Seems steep," Ted grumbled, fishing a bill out of his jeans.

A broad, hungry grin. "It'll be worth it."

"Fucking better be."

Ted walked past the two vikings and sidled through the milling crowd towards a stage set up out in the field. He passed duels fought with swords, axes, and daggers. Weapons clanged off each other and thudded against heavy wooden shields. Aside from the weaponry, he could have been at any small outdoor music festival. There were people fighting, fucking, drinking, and puking. Straw bales were laid out in the field as seats, but only a handful of people were using them, and they drank from horns instead of plastic cups. A dog loped through the crowd with a stolen hot dog in its jaws.

A skeletal-looking sculpture of riveted iron loomed next to the stage. He recognized some guys making their way towards it. Former patchers who'd moved on to potash after the fires didn't stop. It didn't seem like it should be their thing. But looks could be deceiving. No one would guess at first glance Ted liked Mary Lou Lord as much as Motörhead.

The sculpture was old rusted-out farm equipment, bent and welded into the shape of a giant. The metal figure loomed with one leg resting in the dirt at as if the sculpture were straddling the stage. An arm reached out towards the audience. Ted shuddered. Bonfires made the metal glow, a sharp contrast against the dark hollows of the sculpture.

Voices chanted Surtur's name.

That is not a good thing.

He felt an unwelcome pressure, as if every eye in the crowd was on him. They were.

Maybe this was not the place to be flashing Mjölnir around and calling lightning. It would be overkill to use his powers on a bunch of obsessive twats who wished they were the Crow. There were some big guys in the crowd, and Ted wouldn't be able to wade through them without it being obvious he was something a little more—a little less—than human.

There was no defence in the Canadian Criminal Code for being Ófriður. If the dwarves wanted him to be their "Un-Peace" they'd better be prepared for some bad press.

Remember, whatever the dvergar might want of you, you are supposed to be flying under the radar, Muninn said.

I'm fucking trying.

A couple of larger guys, shouldered into Ted as they headed towards the beer tent.

"Piss off," one of them said.

The other followed it up with a muttered, "Jerk-off."

Ted clenched his fist. Mjölnir would make short work of them.

Try harder, Muninn said.

In front of the stage the crowd chanted and shoved. It looked as if a fight was going to break out at any moment. A dozen fights. A hundred. People climbed inside of the sculpture, thrusting arms between its metal ribs and screaming.

Ted's nose wrinkled.

He'd been around enough big equipment in his life that he knew the stink of diesel. He was on a farmyard, there *should* be diesel here. But this ... it was everywhere. As if it had permeated the soil. Ted dropped to one knee and dipped two fingers through the straw spread all over the yard and into the ground. Lifting them to his nose he could smell the scent more clearly.

Fuel. Fire. All it needed was a spark and the entire place would go up. These people planned on summoning Surtur, all right. They'd given some thought to how to succeed. All they needed was the right spark, and Ted had a feeling it was him.

A guitar droned from behind the curtain. A snare hit. Bass drum pounded. Ted could appreciate the suspense the band was creating, until the curtain was set afire, and the vocalist "sang."

The band dressed like the bastard kids of both their fan bases. Black leather. Studs and chains. Shit-kicker boots. Greasepaint faces. They wore black wolfskins for cloaks, the taxidermied beasts' heads more helmet than hood. Human limbs jutted from the metal giant, index and pinky fingers held out from a fist, throwing the horns.

"Surtur. Surtur. Surtur."

The chants were as loud as the music, and overtop of it all, Ted could hear the king of Muspelheim's laugh, "*Lock, lock, lock.*"

On his back, the tattoo of Yggdrasill trembled. He felt the power at play. These dumb fuckers could do it. They could bring the giant here.

It was hard to make out any individual in the swarming mass; fire and smoke obscured them.

Ted could almost understand their words. He'd been yelled at enough in Icelandic that he could make out some Nordic words. The names he understood: Thor. Odin. Fenrir.

Surtur.

The chant shifted. The crowd closed in on him, every lip speaking, "*Fehu, Fehu, Fehu.*"

He knew that name too. It was the rune of the primal fire. Of creation. Of destruction. *Fehu* was the rune of Surtur.

Everone in the crowd held lighters. Not unusual for a concert. Not a great mix for a venue doused in diesel.

"I see you, Ófriður," they all said in one voice, flicking their Bics.

Flames jumped from the lighters and into their eyes and Ted smelled something like caramelized jelly. Thick, black smoke emanated from their mouths. A choking stink that took Ted's mind back to the patch, and Surtur. To the day he'd been confronted by something beyond reason. Something that viewed human life as meaningless.

Now that Ted's life *did* have meaning for Surtur, the giant wanted to end it.

From the stage, the band intoned, "Surtur. Surtur. Surtur," followed by, "We *all* see you, Ófriður."

Screams rose from inside the metal giant as those within burned alive. The crowd poured towards him like ants hunting sugar. A wall of humanity. Fire-eyed and angry as sin.

He never should have left Winnipeg. He hated proving people right.

3. Paper in Fire

Ted had burned himself before, welding. But there was no comparing that with what was coming from the metal giant: agony and ecstasy melted together as bodies that had once been human reached through the metal of the giant statue, clawing for him. Somehow still alive. These sacrifices would scream after their lungs were gone. When their tongues had cooked. Until there was nothing left of their bodies but ash. Ted would hear those screams for the rest of his days. He couldn't forget if he wanted to.

Vikings and metalheads wore flames for hair. The fires guttered and swayed in the growing winds as they closed on Ted, encircling him. Ink slid under the skin of his chest; the storm trapped inside his chest wanted freedom. Mjölnir hummed in answer, electricity dancing over Ted's forearm, reaching for the clouds.

If Ted gave in to that feeling—much as he dearly wanted to—it would not be a good thing. He'd done so before, been careless, and if he hadn't been lucky, hadn't had Loki on his side, things would be worse. "All of Earth on fire" worse.

"Strike!" they said, begging in one voice to be hit with a thunderbolt.

Ted wanted to fill the prairie with lightning. Mjölnir buzzed and crackled, sparks of blue electricity arced from Ted's forearm to the storm cloud tattoo on his chest. Ted didn't give in.

He wanted rain, not lightning. The storm clouds stopped flashing bright, growing so black they choked all light from the sky. A fat drop of rain slapped against his hand. The only fires left were the hatred smouldering in the crowd's eyes. A collective moan rose up from below.

Weather was changeable on the prairie. Big skies, open ground. Ted had seen a blue sky go black in no time at all. Knowing it was possible, he made it so. He found a cold, arctic wind and drew it down, howling like a fiend, to fill the sky with rain clouds.

Fingers tore at his clothes, men and women trying grab him, hold him. He tried to shake them off, but the crowd's numbers were too great. He needed some room first.

It was overcast. Dark. Clouds groaned with rain. A drop hissed into vapour as it struck the lightning sparks that traveled over Ted's hammer hand. He closed his fists around the edges of the sky as if he were wringing out a dish towel and summoned the rain.

"Suck it, Surtur."

The sky opened up and rain fell like bullets. In an instant, Ted was soaked to the skin. The din of the rain striking cars, cement, and metalheads filled his ears. Steam rose up from the burning crowd as the rain slapped against them.

Before long, the rich farm soil would be a quagmire. No traction for the metalheads and vikings, but that wouldn't be a problem for Ted. The rain sizzled when it touched the fires. The screams from inside the giant became more plaintive, more pained, if such a thing was possible. All sense of twisted joy was gone.

The front line of Surtsúlfar's roadies shrank away from Ted.

Ted took the moment's respite to kick off his boots. Then he ran, but instead of running away, he ran up. Sleipnir's hooves allowed Ted to walk on air and water as if they were solid ground. The winds picked up as he climbed. Sparks jumped from the flaming eyes of the roadies, alighting on clothes, and catching flames.

One of the roadies had grabbed hold of Ted's foot, climbing hand over hand up Ted's leg.

"You will burn, Ófriður. Burn for Surtur."

Ted grabbed hold of the metalhead's flaming hair and jerked him upwards.

Staring into the smoking cavities that had been the roadie's eyes, Ted said, "Someone should tell your motherfucking boss: I don't burn."

Ted dropped the roadie in a slough and circled back for the ringleaders. From his vantage point in the sky, the fires burned a scar on the farm, drawing a giant *Fehu* rune across the property. On Ted's back, the tattoo of Yggdrasill itched, sensing the magic that permeated the air. Ted's magic. Surtur's magic. Every leaf tattooed on that tree was one of the twenty-four Elder Runes. Two of those runes felt more insistent. Ted had never separated them out in such a manner, but now he could feel them. *Fehu* and *Kenaz*. The fire runes. Primal Fire. Tool of man. *Fehu*, Ted felt more strongly.

Whenever humanity's ancestors had first captured and

controlled fire, had learned the secret of sparking it themselves, that part of Ted told him that this fire could be mastered. Even Surtur could be controlled. And if necessary, snuffed out.

Both this fire and the giant himself would require more than a strong rain and kicking dirt over the ashes.

Ted dropped out of the sky over Surtsúlfar. He hit the dirt, his knees bending to absorb the impact, but stopping short of dropping to a complete crouch. He didn't want them to hear his knees pop and creak when he stood. Or to think they'd picked a fight with their dad.

Now that Ted was closer to the band, he had a better look at their gear. Chains that dangled teeth; big dirty cubes—giant's teeth, maybe. They pulled the wolfs' heads up over their scalps, like hoods, and the pelts bonded to their flesh, ragged edges of fur melting into their shaved bodies and pale skin.

Dead get of Fenrir, Huginn noted.

"The stones told us of your coming, Ófriður," the band said together. "Unsightly one, we want your gifts. Warbringer, we want your power."

"Is that a fact?"

All five growled at him. "You are not worthy of it."

The singer was the same size as Ted, and played at menacing. An oversized rune pendant pinned the wolf's-legs clasps of his cloak around his neck.

Surtsúlfar advanced, hunched over like movie wolfmen, growling, aping their leader and trying to look threatening. Tongues of flame flared out of the wolfen mouths like a tank fire blowing back in the patch.

"I don't have time for this, you dumb bastards."

Power called to power and Ted could feel their energy, tingling each of the tiny *Fehu* runes on the Yggdrasill tattoo running over Ted's spine. Ted let them come to him. Let them try and carve his gifts out of him. Hard nails slashed across his chest, ripping his shirt, shredding his jacket, revealing the thundercloud tattoo and the dragon-scales.

"Seems like you can't hurt me after all," Ted muttered as he held up his hammer hand. "You wanted a gift? This one's my favourite."

He lashed out with a jab, Mjölnir cracking in to the leader's jaw. There was a lupine whine as the singer tried to retaliate. Ted swung his arm and connected with the back of his hand, and the singer hit the ground. Ted stomped on his belly as he leapt over the prone singer to get at the others. He felt nails catch his pant leg, shredding his jeans.

Goddammit.

Take them out. Don't kill them.

Huginn asked, **Why ever not?**

I have an idea.

There is a first time for everything, Huginn said, feigning awe. To Muninn he said, **I expect you to remember this date, brother.**

The ravens snickered together.

Pipe down, Heckle and Jeckle.

It was a short, dirty, ugly fight. All elbows to chins and knees to nuts, with a headbutt thrown in for spice. Ted finished the last two off by picking up one and swinging them into the other. He counted four. One of them had got away.

The rest of the wolfen lay unconscious, still gasping flaming breaths. Ted went to work. He pulled out his Zippo, running his thumbnail over the *Kenaz* rune scratched onto its surface. With a snap, he opened the lid and ignited the lighter's flame in a single, smooth motion.

"*Fehu*," he called to their fires. The singer's flame jumped from his mouth, and eyes, flaring hot and bright. "*Kenaz*," Ted said, and the fire shot like lightning to marry the Zippo's flame.

The flame guttered wildly, then rose over a foot from the lighter, then shrank into a normal size for a lighter's flame. It felt as if he were taking a long drag from a cigarette, but the smoke in his lungs was hot as a steaming kettle. The sensation reminded him of Surtur's vapour ghosts. They'd been able to burn him the first time Ted had tangled with the fire giant. He snapped the Zippo closed, snuffing the flame. He repeated the exercise for each member of the band. It became easier to take their power each time. When he was done, the lighter was hot to the touch, but no more so than if he'd let it burn for a good long while.

Ted stood in the rain, breathing hard. The deluge had drowned the fires. There were moans and cries. But the wailing and screaming had ceased. Ted tilted his head back and let the rain wash the mud and blood and beer from his body. He slicked his hair back with his fingers and sighed.

"No one will give me a ride now."

A slow clap sounded from behind him, and Ted didn't have to turn to know who it was.

"Hello, Loki," he said without looking.

4. When the Trickster Starts A-Pokin'

Loki.

Ted had thought he'd been done with the trickster when he'd hurled him out of Winnipeg. He should've known better. He'd crafted a fence that not even the shapechanging God of Mischief had been able to slither through, and yet, here Ted was, not out of Manitoba for *one fucking day*, and who'd come calling?

A thunderhead stood out white with flashing lightning from the dark clouds and rain. Its shape had the flared head of a warhammer—like Mjölnir. The clouds twisted, and Ted felt the storm on his chest mirror the happenings in the sky. Loki twisted everything up. It would take more than a bolt of lightning to stop the trickster. But Ted had an entire sky's worth.

When he spoke, he managed to sound calmer than he felt. "You have got a brass-plated pair of low hangers, to show your face to me."

"You noticed," Loki said, adjusting himself. "I'm touched." The trickster looked up at the sky and a nascent funnel cloud and said, "Do you want to do this? Here? Now?"

What Ted wanted was to wipe the smirk off Loki's smug face.

A deep breath. Rain aside, this whole farm was still a powder keg of spilt diesel and rune magic. If Ted let himself go—and he'd need to if he wanted to take down Loki—he'd end up starting the fire that he'd fought so hard to keep Surtsúlfar from igniting. Much as he wanted to sock the king of Muspelheim in the jaw, tonight wasn't the time to ring his doorbell. Not when Ted wasn't ready to kill him.

I am grateful that you appear to be learning some sense, Huginn said.

Because he listened to me, Muninn said.

Ted released the building storm. He unclenched his fists, pumping fingers to get blood flowing to white, numb digits. Pounding rain eased to a gentle mist.

"So you *do* remember what happened last time."

Ted glared at Loki. The trickster may have found a new outfit, and a new face, but Ted knew it was him. Or should he say *her*.

Loki was female today. Wearing tight jeans, shitkicking brown boots and a scarf tied around his neck. Light brown or dark blonde hair—it was hard to tell in the dark and the wet—was plastered to a face with intense blue eyes and a smile that would wake a dead man.

"Who are you supposed to be?"

Loki smiled. "Judging from her Facebook profile, my biggest fan." Loki padded to Ted's side, rain plastering a comic book shirt to his chest. Ted looked away. "Where'd you come from?"

"Same place as always," the trickster said.

"Fine, be that way."

"You know I've always said, 'Nothing good comes from

Saskatchewan or goes to Alberta.'" The trickster paused, as if trying to remember. "Or is it the other way around?"

"You've been in Winnipeg too long."

"I haven't been in Winnipeg *at all* lately," Loki said acidly. "As I'm sure you're well aware."

"Kind of the point of my kicking your ass out of my city."

Loki's lips twitched. Not quite a smile, not quite a grimace.

"Nice work," the trickster said, gesturing to the path of destruction and the band Ted had left in the farmyard. "You haven't lost your touch."

Ted muttered, "Thanks."

"Why are you hitching?"

"You know damn well why I'm hitching. My fucking car is rusting in Hel."

"Get Moustache and his army of Beards to make you a new one. I'm sure the dwarves would love the challenge." Loki's eyes sparkled with mischief. "And if they won't, you know I'm always happy to offer you a ride."

Ted snorted. "I'm aware of that."

"And yet you never call, never write."

Ted could feel Loki affecting a hurt pout. Just because the trickster was good at getting his way with the face didn't mean Ted had to look at it.

Loki nattered on anyway. "First I was pissed, but whatever, you know? Your loss. Then I figured, it's perfect. The bad guys'll think you've kicked me out and they'll try to recruit me to come after you. We could use that."

"There's no 'we.' Not anymore. We *were* friends, you son of a bitch, but you ruined that."

Aloud, Muninn said, "**You ruin everything.**"

Ted turned from Loki to the band. Surtsúlfar was heaped in a pile where he'd left them. Their greasepaint devil faces smeared with rain and struggle. Moans and whimpers escaped from the jumble.

The singer was on the top of the pile. Ted grabbed him by his wolf pelt and dragged him to his feet. The singer managed a weak snarl and clawed at Ted. Ted headbutted him, and the singer's lupine snout cracked. Ted tore at the pelt. There was resistance, as if the pelt were a part of the man, and not something he wore. With a sound like denim tearing it ripped free. The skin left behind took on a raw look, like he'd picked a scab off, and oozed blood. He couldn't help but notice their tattoos had come away with their skin—what they'd wanted to do to him.

Tyr would be pleased, Muninn said.

"I'm not done yet."

When he'd stripped each of them bare, Ted piled their skins and giants' teeth, rune stones and instruments, and everything else he could find that looked Norse, in a heap.

"What took you this long to track me down?"

"I've been waiting for you to cool down. I figured I'd respect your wishes."

Ted barked a laugh. "You've got a funny fucking way of showing it."

Loki pointed at the band and said, "I came looking for *them*. Seeing you is a happy accident."

Yeah, right.

Ted snorted, regarding his shredded clothing and the pile of moaning, wannabe Kiss members. "Could've helped me."

"What makes you think I didn't?" The trickster stepped aside, gesturing with a flourish at the fifth member of the band. The one Ted thought had escaped. "You missed one."

"Thanks," Ted muttered.

Voice full of false graciousness, Loki replied, "You're welcome."

"Don't stand there with your thumb up your ass, drag him over."

Loki gestured at the body he wore. "But he's so big. And you're stronger than me."

"Jesus Christ."

Some things would never fucking change. The trickster would do anything to get out of an honest day's work.

Ted strode over and dragged the stray over to the rest of the band by the wolf's tail connected to his belt. Stole the woman's flame, and piled her skin with the rest. He snapped the Zippo closed. The lighter felt warmer. He tucked it into his shredded jeans.

"What are you going to do with those clowns?" Loki asked.

Ted shrugged. He hadn't thought that far ahead. Not like he could drop them off at the Saskatoon RCMP detachment and say they'd been trying to summon a fire giant.

"They're kids with toys. I'm grounding them and taking their toys away."

Loki tapped at his teeth. "They're still a threat."

"I won't murder them."

Loki pursed his lips and let out a slow exhale. "You're going to let them go."

In the time it took to blink, Loki had interposed himself between Ted and the band. The pretty face he wore twisted. It looked old. Powerful. Full of hate.

To the band members, Loki said, "You stole their skins."

He stepped on one set of outstretched fingers. They cracked over the sound of the flames.

"They had to be *alive* when you did this, or you couldn't have taken their power."

A kick to the chin. Ted winced. A kick to the singer's balls. Ted felt himself subconsciously covering up.

"They were my grandchildren."

Ted wondered how many "greats" might be hidden in that descriptor, but from Loki's voice, the trickster didn't care. Another kick. A stomp to one of the women's temples. Whoever those dead wolves had been, in his eye, they were his family, and that's all that mattered. He considered stopping Loki, but realized he didn't care what the trickster did to the band.

That's what you get for siding with the walking end of the world.

"Maybe I'll skin *you*," Loki said, holding up who Ted thought had been the bassist, and dragging a fingernail from temple to jaw. "Wear you to a concert."

Or maybe Ted *did* care. That's what happens when you fuck with a trickster. Mischief can turn to mayhem, to murder, on a dime.

"Loki. That's taking it a bit far."

Loki's eyes flashed, bright as lightning, hot as a prairie grass fire. "An eye for an eye, tooth for a tooth, Ted."

Ted didn't want Loki to turn on him—

Again, Muninn reminded.

But Loki also wanted Ted's friendship. Loki wanted to be on Ted's side. If Ted intervened to stop him, he doubted that would be the case. But he had to intervene. Laying a beating on someone was one thing, especially when they had it coming. Ted had done that more than once, and long before he'd had Thor's hammer backing him up. Torture, that was something he couldn't abide. Loki should know better—given how the Aesir had tortured him. Ted had seen those scars when Loki had fought at Ted's side in his true form. Loki also knew how Thor had tortured Ted.

Huginn said, **I hate to say it, but with the Odin cloak destroyed–**

I need the sneaky fucker to get me into Edmonton without Surtur noticing.

"Do what you have to." Ted turned his back and walked for the road. "I thought you were better than this. Better than what Odin did to you."

He felt a twinge between his shoulder blades. Turning your back on Loki was never a smart thing to do. He made it a nervous nine steps before the trickster called out after him.

"Wait. They'd probably like that. I won't do the bastards any favours by giving them the street cred of being scarred by Loki."

Ted let out a breath he hadn't been aware he was holding and turned around. Loki was right behind him.

"Can you get rid of the skins, Ted?" Loki looked sadly at the pile. "I don't … I can't."

He hadn't expected he'd be doing Loki a favour today. But this was something Ted would have done anyway.

A slippery slope, Huginn said.

Muninn added, **That is how he extorts further help from you.**

It needed to be done, regardless.

"*Fehu*," he said, and the flame shot up from the lighter. "*Kenaz*."

This time, when Ted spoke the rune of controlled fire, fire harnessed by man, he didn't wish the flame to be snuffed, but instead, he directed it at the pile of bloody wolf skins. As much as Ted would like to call the lightning and blast these filthy trophies to ash, he couldn't risk it. But the band had held Surtur's power. Maybe the giant wouldn't notice Ted using that same power. Surtur burned everything. He'd see little difference between his own servants and Ted's friends.

Holding the fire rune in his mind and watching the symbol flicker and glow in front of him, Ted said, "Burn."

As if it had been shot from a flamethrower, a tongue of fire arced from Ted's Zippo to the wolf skins.

The flame burned hot and fast, and stank worse than if a giant had taken a shit to top off the smelly skin sundae. He looked down at Surtsúlfar. They cried, and feebly dragged themselves towards the fires.

"How many distant thunderstorms can you sense right now?"

Ted had never thought to check before, but the storm cloud in his chest and the hammer in his hand could feel them. "Thirty-seven. Scattered over North America."

"Drop them in the middle of one. Or in the middle of all of them. Bounce them around like skipping stones and scatter them. Make a stopover in Winnipeg."

"They're powerless, not harmless."

"So send your buddy Robin a text. Do I have to think of everything?"

Ted grimaced. He'd already asked a lot of Robin. In hindsight, leaving a tattoo artist in charge of the mystic defence of Winnipeg might not have been the best idea.

"Surtur will think you came to deal with them and after you won, you went home. Meanwhile we keep going."

"Not bad."

Loki nodded. "Get them out of my sight. Or I *will* kill them."

With a nod, Ted patted his pockets for his phone. Loki passed it to him with a sly grin. Ted rolled his eyes and sent Robin a text.

—You free?

Ted's phone buzzed within a second. —Yeah? What up?

—Incoming bad guys shortly. I declawed them for you.

Ted walked back to the band. Surtsúlfar turned as one and Ted smiled.

"Go home. Or next time I won't play so nice."

Empty eyes stared at Ted. Their fires might have gone out, but they still smouldered.

The singer spoke through a mouthful of broken teeth and blood. "You think this means anything? How will you breathe when the world burns? All the fires of Muspelheim come. I will destroy your city. Destroy you. Destroy everything."

Ted ticked off his middle finger. "You want me to kill you. Loki wants you dead. You're goddamned lucky *I* don't give a shit about you."

"Kill me," another band member wailed.

Ted didn't kill them. He could have. But they were human once, whoever they'd been before Surtur hijacked them.

Ted had been practising since he'd ridden a lightning bolt part of the way from Niflheim to Earth, but he'd never tried to do it with someone else. If he fucked this up, he wasn't sure what would happen to them.

Ted clenched his fist, as if he was grabbing the singer's shirt. *Only his shirt. Only his shirt.* Sparks danced over the man, like he was a living Tesla coil. Clouds gathered and the sky rumbled. Ted's Yggdrasill tattoo burned hot, tiny pinpricks of mixed pain and exhilaration. *That's new.* Ted didn't move his arm but he felt as if he were jerking the man upward. Ozone burned his nose as Ted squinted against the glare of the lightning strike. The bolt couldn't touch the ground, not here. Mjölnir completed the circuit, tiny lightning sparking all over Ted's body.

In a flash, they were gone.

Loki stared at Ted from between his fingers. "What did you do?"

Ted was breathing hard. His chest tingled. The storm wanted to join those other storms, to form one supercell; one giant storm that could swallow the entire continent. Ted let go and popped the band into Winnipeg. Loki put a hand on Ted's shoulder, and Ted shoved it free.

Ted reached for his package of cigarettes and tapped one out. He held it up to Loki. "You have until I finish this to convince me why I shouldn't also beat your ass." Without checking his pocket for his Zippo, Ted added, "And I'll be needing my lighter back."

He reached into his pocket, and sure enough his lighter was there. He flicked the lid open with a snap of his fingers, shielding the cigarette from the rain. Ted ignited the lighter and breathed in the butane and burning tobacco. He held the smoke in his lungs, eyes closed, before pushing the smoke out through his nostrils in a slow steady stream. The wind died. Stars peeked through the clouds.

Loki produced his own pack of smokes, evidently smart enough not to try and bum one off Ted. He held out his hand for Ted to pass him the lighter. The trickster could take it any time he wanted, and *that* little violation was not the one worth fighting over.

Another power drag. Ted regarded the orange cherry of the smoke.

"Talk fast, Loki. You're burning daylight."

The trickster nodded. "You need me."

"You should have considered that."

"I did." Loki hung his head. "Things weren't supposed to turn out the way they did."

Ted exhaled smoke in Loki's face. "They never are with you.

Baldur wasn't supposed to die. It was a prank. One of the million you played on your family."

Loki's faced twisted. The trickster hated the Aesir being given that designation.

Sue me, I feel like being a bit of a prick tonight. "Actions have consequences, *kemosabe*."

The trickster's voice was small when he responded. "I know. Believe me, I know."

"You've got a funny way of showing it."

"You can't beat him without me, Ted."

No need for Loki to specify who "him" was.

"Maybe." He thought of the Bright Sword, whatever the fuck that might be, and added, "Maybe not."

"Ted, I will get down on bended knee, I will suck your cock, I will apologize. But what I will not do is let you go at him alone. Because Surtur is most definitely *not alone* out there. You know he has help. Fire giants. Vapour ghosts, who could burn you even through your dragon-scale armour, and I'm sure he's got more than that. You have no one. Where are the Norns? Where are Robin and Aiko?"

"I wasn't planning on starting the war today."

Loki laughed at that. "It started a long time ago. And you never should have left Winnipeg if you weren't ready to finish it."

Ted hid his grimace with another drag. He hated to think that Loki might be correct.

"Winnipeg being safe doesn't matter if the Nine Worlds burn, Ted."

"I'm only concerned about one world."

"You don't have that gods-damned luxury. Not anymore. You've made treaties with Jötunheim, Alfheim, Niðavellir." Ted was surprised that Loki knew. But then, Loki was Loki. "Oh yes, I've heard all about your 'Council of Humptys.' You may not care if what's left of their homes is destroyed, but the *jötnar*, *dvergar*, and *álfar* do. And if they find out you don't care, how well do you think they'll look after Old Peggy?"

Ted had to admit that he hadn't considered that.

"They didn't sign on because they like you, but because they want to live. That's why I'm here too, yes, but I want everyone to live." He paused, a small smirk. "Sorry, almost everyone."

"I appreciate your honesty."

Loki snorted. Ted fought a smile. The trickster probably hadn't heard that statement too often.

"Careful, you throw that accusation around too much, you'll give me a bad name." The trickster's face grew probing, curious. Huginn and Muninn would hate the comparison, but Loki's eyes looked much like the ravens' as he regarded Ted. "You know something. Something big."

Ted didn't answer. Three could keep a secret if two of them were dead.

"'Fess up, man. It's me."

Exactly why not to say anything. Ted knew he didn't have much of a poker face when it came to the trickster. But he didn't want to talk about it. Ted also knew that Loki would happily make his life miserable if he kept stonewalling.

"Ask your daughter if you're curious."

Loki grimaced. "Low blow, Ted."

He held up his hammer hand, lightning arced over the tattoo of Mjölnir. "Metaphorical punch in the balls, or a real one. Take your pick."

Loki pulled a serious sulk. "Fine, be that way. I think I have something that will help you start to trust me again."

The trickster held out the *álfur* stiletto. Tempered in dragon's blood, and full of dragon's venom, the blade had slid through Ted's protections once already. Hurt him so badly, Huginn and Muninn had needed to trick him into using the powers of his sun tattoo to heal himself. Ted still hesitated to take the weapon from Loki.

Especially when he was presenting the weapon with its blade pointed at Ted.

5. Why Does It Always Rain On Me?

Loki smiled and flipped the stiletto so he was holding the blade and its bone hilt faced Ted. "I'd hate for you to cut yourself on this. Again."

Ted took the stiletto gingerly.

"What? Not enough? Odin's balls, Ted. What'll it take for you to trust me again?"

What, indeed? Loki's gesture was meaningless. The trickster could steal back the knife anytime he wanted to. He was like a negligent parent, showing up with an extravagant gift to make up for months of absence and inattention.

"You can't buy my trust. Gone is gone."

"Anything lost can be found, Ted."

Ted thought of his and Tilda's daughter. Erin wasn't coming back.

Loki rolled his eyes, managing to look disgusted and bored. "I could have killed you any time I wanted. *If* that was what I wanted."

Ted was well aware of that. Still curious, and knowing he'd regret the question, Ted asked, "So why didn't you?"

"I like you, Ted," Loki said. "No lie. No trick. We're friends."

Ted snorted. Loki's "friendship" had cost him plenty. His old life. Tilda. Erin. But losing the trickster's friendship had cost the Norse gods more. Vili had said that only after Asgard stopped laughing at Loki's jests were they doomed. There was a threat that hung over Loki's friendship that was hard to forget. Sometimes those jokes weren't necessary, but maybe if Odin had treated the trickster like the brother he'd named him instead of a tool, Ragnarök wouldn't have happened.

Unsure what to do with the stiletto, Ted tore off the remnants of his shirt and wrapped the blade in the fabric so that he didn't accidentally stab himself. When he was satisfied the knot around the hilt would hold, he slid the knife between his belt and jeans.

With the knife was safely tucked away, he pulled up his jacket sleeve, revealing a thin golden chain. "I've got a little something for you too."

"Gold. You shouldn't have. Are we going steady now?"

Ted smiled and held up Gleipnir. "Take a closer look." Loki's eyes went wide. "I want you to wear it."

You should have forced him, Huginn said.

So he'll work against me the entire time?

Eyeing the chain as if it were a snake, Loki said, "If I'm to put that on, I've got a condition of my own."

"You're in no position to argue."

Loki barked a laugh. "I'm in the *perfect* position to argue, *kemosabe*. You *need* my help now. I *want* to help you." He smiled. "Maybe you need the ravens to explain it to you."

He's not wrong, Huginn said.

Muninn added, **Damn him.**

Ted sighed. "What's your condition?"

"How's Hel?"

"Still alive," Ted said. "She calls herself something else now."

Loki waited for Ted to offer the name. When he didn't, the trickster asked, "You kept her safe?"

Ted nodded. "It cost me, but yeah, I did. Urd wanted me to name you outlaw, whatever the hell that means."

Loki sulked. "It would have meant everyone would be free to kill me and take what's mine."

"So I should've said yes to shut her up. Everyone wants to do that anyway."

"You *didn't* name me outlaw?" Ted shook his head and Loki breathed a sigh of relief. "Thanks for that."

"She gave me this," Ted said, handing Loki a folded, sealed parchment. "It's for you."

Loki tucked the letter into his pocket without reading it. He smiled when he said, "Obviously."

"I didn't lie about your daughter," Ted said. "I wouldn't bullshit you on that."

"I know." Loki eyed the chain, and let out a resigned sigh. "Putting that on…. It's a lot to ask. How do I know you won't screw me over the same way the Aesir did to Fenrir?"

Ted shrugged and held up Mjölnir. "You can try to bite my hand off, if it'll make you feel better."

Loki snorted. When he glared again at the chain, still hurt, still angry, the trickster nodded. "If I let you bind me, what then?"

"I let you help me."

"Will you bitch about how I choose to help?"

Ted snorted. "Probably."

Loki's eyes glittered at that, and his lips twitched into a half-smile. "Not enough."

"What do you want?"

"Forgiveness. A clean slate."

"Fine. A clean slate." Ted wanted to tell Loki that forgiveness wasn't a bargaining chip. Instead, he pointed at Gleipnir. "But if you fuck with me this time, I'll kill you."

"Trust me."

The last being, man or god, Ted was inclined to believe when they said "trust me" was Loki.

Loki exhaled a long, slow breath and held out his right hand as if he wanted Ted to shake on the deal. "Okay, let's do this."

Ted clasped Loki's hand, and the golden tether around Ted's wrist slithered on to Loki's, clasping shut with a soft "click," binding the trickster. He stared at the golden chain as if Ted had pressed dog shit into his hand. Gleipnir *had* been made by the *dvergar* to hold Loki's son. Ted wasn't fond of the thing either: the dwarves had used a shard to bind Ted when they'd empowered him. The *jötunn* had a fragment as well. They'd used it to bind Loki in Flin Flon. Youngnir had given that piece to Ted. Muninn had heard Mustache and Urd sing the binding song and he'd taught it to Ted.

"So are you going to compel my obedience?" Loki asked, giving the chain a little shake.

"No. But if you don't give me a reason to trust you, I'm going to stake that cord to the ground and call Tilda."

Loki seemed much more worried by *that* threat than Ted's promise to kill him. "You've grown hard."

"I've had to. The two people I leaned on the most to get me through this nuthouse are gone. You fucked me over and the other fucked off. If I can only have one of you back on my side—"

"You'd choose Tilda."

"Surprise. You're not as charming as you think."

Loki winked and cocked a hip. "You haven't seen me try to be charming."

That statement was scarier than anything the trickster had promised to do to Surtsúlfar.

Ted sighed. "This fight has taken everything from me, Loki. Friends. Family. My daughter. Tilda."

"You wanted a life that mattered, Ted." Loki gestured at the wreckage of the farm. "Now you've got one."

"If you say, 'Careful what you wish for,' I swear to Christ I'm going to kick your ass."

"Tilda was going to leave you, anyway. Don't worry, she won't know I'm helping you now if I don't want her to know."

"She can read the future, numbnuts. The present. The past. She'll see that. She's probably already fucking seen it."

Loki picked at a fingernail, the chain of Gleipnir dangling from his wrist. "Then I guess it's already too late for you guys, because here we are."

"Yeah. Here we are."

"I could sever that connection of yours, you know."

Ted didn't want what Loki was offering. With Tilda gone from his life, that thread of feeling between them was reassuring. She'd been the first good thing to come out of his association with the Nine Worlds.

"Cut the cord, *kemosabe*."

Ted winced at the trickster's choice of wording.

"You'll never have the same connection again."

Ted grimaced. It was true. They weren't meant to be together. Fuck destiny. It still didn't feel right to pull the plug. "It stays."

He has a point. Damn him, Huginn said.

Loki smiled, and then in a sugary voice added, "So, that's decided at least. I realize that what happened in November.... It was your *Empire* moment, Ted."

"If you tell me that Tilda's my sister, I'm going to rip your dick off through your mouth."

Loki appeared to consider the logistics of that, looked down at the crotch that probably didn't have a unit attached to it, and rubbed at his jaw as if it were tender.

"Time's long past for that joke, I'm afraid. Wish I would have thought of it when I caught you both with your pants down." Loki screwed his face into a surprisingly serious visage. When he spoke, it was in a deep, measured baritone. "What if I told you: I am your father."

He did do a fine James Earl Jones impression. Ted squinted at Loki, who seemed ready to flinch away from a strike and was glancing at the sky. Little fucker knew damned well that Ted had a temper. Which buttons to push to bring out that temper, Loki knew better.

It would feel good to shove Loki. To beat him into the rain and diesel-sodden earth. That momentary good feeling would accomplish nothing in the long run. Where Ted was going he needed to *not* resort to busting chops at the slightest provocation. Even with Loki doing the provoking. While Ted knew turning the other cheek was the right thing to do in theory, putting that into practice was harder than he'd have liked.

Ted realized he'd already given Loki more time than the one cigarette he'd promised. He supposed the point was moot now. He dropped the spent butt and lit another.

"You look like shit." Loki wrinkled his nose, regarded Ted. "And smell worse. *I* wouldn't give you a ride in your current state."

"Thanks." Nonetheless, he gave himself a sniff. Loki wasn't wrong. Maybe he only told the truth when it allowed him to be a dick. "You mind scoring me some new clothes?"

"Mr. Law and Order giving me permission to thieve in his name?"

"Go," Ted said. "You'll do it anyway, and I may as well not roll into Edmonton looking like I went ten rounds with a werewolf."

"You *are* scruffy looking."

He disappeared.

When Loki had gone, Ted ran a finger over the second string of Gleipnir wrapped around his left wrist. He felt it slithering in his hand, trying to rejoin the one tied around his wrist.

Good. Like would call to like.

Ted could call Loki back if he needed to. The trickster would have as much freedom as he could earn. Ted hoped

Loki didn't kill him in thanks. Ted lit another cigarette. Stared at the flames.

Ted turned the flames on his own clothes, they were shot to shit. No saving them. He waited for his body to be wreathed in flame. And it would burn until it consumed everything he wanted burned. And only that.

A good idea, Huginn admitted.

I liked it.

Is it wise to hold Surtur's power so close to you?

It might hide me.

It might reveal you, also.

Loki should be able to solve that.

For one blessed, fucking time, the ravens didn't object, nor complain about the folly of trusting the trickster.

The fire wouldn't burn him. He knew that much. As Surtur's stolen power covered him, Ted caught a glimpse of the giant, squatting on a throne built from the wreckage of Ted's old work site. He knew what the giant could do.

The vision did nothing to convey the giant's immensity. But Ted knew. He'd seen the bastard first-hand when Surtur had erupted from an explosion at his worksite on the oil patch. Surtur looked like a two-legged volcano, his body basalt black, except for wherever he shifted, and the stony exterior cracked. Lava seeped from those cracks, dripping to join and intensify the flames. He smiled as if he'd seen Ted, each jagged tooth in the giant's mouth a broken knife.

It had been nearly a year since Ted had last seen the giant, and despite pushing Surtur out of Flin Flon, the creature had starred in too many nightmares since. His laugh. The destruction that Surtur was capable of.

Edmonton in ruins. Winnipeg in ruins. The world burning.

Jenny and Ryan dead. His parents dead. His niece and nephew. Dead. Everyone he loved, catching fire like paper.

Ted stared at Surtur's gaping mouth. Beyond the sharp, white teeth was glittering black rock, and a flame burned bright yellow and orange. That maw reminded Ted of a crater on the other side of the world. Darvaza. He remembered reading about it in school, and the site popped up from time to time in his online feeds as "The mouth of Hell." Place had been burning since 1971, so it had a few years on Surtur's recent appearance, but then, the geologists who'd tried to set fire to the natural gas in the cave had thought it would burn out in a matter of days. Surtur was just warming up, too.

Was Ted any less arrogant than those men had been? To think he could stop a force of nature?

The giant laughed. *Lock, lock, lock.* Ted couldn't see at what. At him. At everyone.

It was mesmerizing. As if Ted were staring at the end of time. He reached out for that end.

"Ted!"

Loki shouted his name, sounding as if he was at the other end of the field. Huginn and Muninn joined in, sounding no closer, despite being locked inside Ted's skull.

"*TED.*"

Their combined effort shook Ted from his reverie. He could still feel Surtur's presence, but it was distant now, and fading fast. The ground was smouldering. He gave the rain clouds another squeeze.

Joke'll be on you.

He took a deep breath, and aloud he said, "I know how to kill you."

Loki wiped a slick of sweat from his brow. "You made any headway on what she told you?"

Numb, Ted said, as if by rote, "His death belongs to me."

"Then I guess it does. You'd better figure that out."

"I got it."

Ted wished he felt half as confident as he sounded. Or sounded half as confident as he was trying to. He was pretty sure Loki would be able to tell the difference.

Loki smiled and knocked the ruin of Ted's jacket off his shoulders. "Fine, I'll drop it. I suppose having Mjölnir beats a pair of antlers."

The remnants of his clothes ran off his body with the rain. The farm was soaked enough Ted didn't expect the fire would spread.

Loki wore a different shape: tall, blonde, and stacked, with fingernails like talons. The trickster had a shopping bag in hand; a Harley-Davidson rested on its kickstand behind him, leaning towards Ted. Loki let out a wolf whistle and hurled the bag at Ted's feet. Ted couldn't help but wonder what bad clothing choices the trickster would force upon him as punishment for Ted throwing him out of Winnipeg and separating him from the daughter Tilda had vowed to kill.

"Looking good, Teddy Bear. You've been working out."

"Not as much as you've been working your mouth," Ted said. He pulled out the first shirt and pair of pants, and got dressed. As he buttoned up the fly of his jeans and pulled the green T-shirt over his head, he noted Loki had showed a surprising level of restraint in the clothes he'd brought back. "You know, I trust you less when you do that."

"Trust *me* less or yourself?"

"You. Definitely you."

"I'll dress how I want, Ted. You need to deal with it."

Deal with it. Ted was a little tired of "dealing" with Loki. But he had no choice, and arguing only ever egged the trickster on. Instead, he asked, "Who are you supposed to be now?"

The form looked familiar, like something out of a dream.

"Freyja," Loki said, alongside Muninn. "I find she helps things go my way."

"I'm sure she'd be as pleased as Tilda was to know you're borrowing her body."

Loki waved off Ted's concern. "Haven't seen her since Ragnarök. I doubt she'd going to show up and complain."

Ted pinched the bridge of his nose. With his luck, Loki may as well've sent her an engraved invitation.

When Ted looked up, Loki was wearing a different shape. Still female. Still beautiful, though slim and boyish rather than stacked.

"You said you knew how to hide me from Surtur," said Ted. It had been one of the last things that the trickster had said before Ted had banished him. That Surtur would never expect him to roll into Alberta powerless. "Let's get on with it."

"You're ready?"

"I suppose that depends on what you plan on doing."

"I'm going to lock you up in your old self. Same idea as how I put myself so firmly in Tilda's shape." Ted must've scowled, because Loki flinched; and when he spoke again, it was at a rapid-fire pace, as if trying to forestall any angry interruptions. "You'll be the old you. Your old body before the *dvergar* gifted you. Your powers will be locked away, like you're two different people."

"So Ted Callan never got any magical gifts," Ted said. "But Ófriður did?"

"Now you're on the trolley," Loki said.

"And in my old body, I've got no tattoos," Ted said. He'd gotten used to them, but it would be nice to not have to try to explain them to his family.

"Sorry, big guy. Your tattoos can look different, but they need to be there."

"Why?"

"Too many people *know* that Ted Callan got tattooed all to Hel. The disguise won't take as well if we give you your baby-fresh body back. Nothing I can do for you there."

Ted squinted, searching the trickster for a lie. *Pointless*. Loki would help as he pleased. "Fucking magic."

Loki asked again, "Ready?"

Was he ready? To hide his powers? To allow Loki back into his life?

The trickster could get Ted into Alberta without Surtur crawling up his ass the moment he hit Lloydminster. But it was more than that. It was to keep his family safe. His friends safe. To allow him to be Ted Callan one last time before Ófriður was needed again. Before there was nothing left *but* Ófriður, the herald of war.

Loki asked, "How were you going in?"

"Odin's cloak," Ted said. "Vera turned it into a leather jacket."

"A good start." The trickster nodded appreciatively. "Anything else?"

"Rungnir's son is using his illusions to keep up appearances that I'm still in Winnipeg. In case Surtur has eyes on me."

"Not bad. Might've worked."

"Might've?"

"If it was anyone other than you executing the plan."

"What the fuck does that mean?"

"Your plan would've worked for a time. And then you would've been tempted. 'I can kick this guy's ass. I can lightning-bolt this. Hailstorm that.' And then Surtur would find you. To say nothing of the thousands of ways your powers would kick out without you thinking. What if some jackass runs you over? Guaran-damn-teed when you stood and dusted yourself off, people would notice. My work is all or nothing. You're in hiding or you're not. Vulnerability will keep you honest. Once you blow it, I won't have a chance to reinstate it."

"All or nothing, eh?"

"Ninety miles an hour, Teddy, only speed I'll drive."

"You're certain your plan will hide me from Surtur?"

"Nothing's certain, *kemosabe*."

"Except death and taxes."

"And me. I'm a sure thing, baby." Loki smiled, a thousand-watt come-hither look, and gestured at the motorcycle. "Let's hit the road."

"I haven't driven one of these in years," Ted said.

Loki shrugged. "I can drive if you're nervous."

"I'm not nervous," Ted said, straddling the bike, and drawing up the kickstand.

He'd mostly ridden dirt bikes, not road bikes, but the principle should be the same. It was an old bike Loki had swiped, with no electric starter. He kickstarted the Harley and felt the rumble of its engine thunder through his body.

Loki hopped on, nestled in behind Ted, and clutched him tight. "Hi-yo, Silver. Away!"

6. At Home He's a Tourist

Loki made the turn into the Edmonton International Airport in their stolen—"borrowed"—Bentley. They'd had to ditch the bike outside of Lloydminster, because Loki had gotten distracted by a squirrel or some fucking thing, and threw Ted off balance and off the road. Neither of them got hurt, but the Harley wouldn't start when they'd gotten it upright. Ted assumed because she'd been bored of the thing.

Despite him long ago vowing always to think of Loki as "he" regardless of the shape the trickster wore, their sustained travel together, Loki being in the same female form, and not—thank Christ—constantly hitting on Ted, Ted found he couldn't help himself. It was easier.

Ted lit a cigarette and rolled down the window. There was a hint of smoke in the air. Distant. But it was impossible to ignore. *As if I needed to be reminded of Surtur squatting up north.*

Nine months since the dwarves had made him into their weapon. Their Un-Peace. Ófriður. Before Ted had been invulnerable, he'd often felt invincible. He didn't feel that way now. Loki had buried Ted's powers so deeply it was as if Ófriður had only been a dream.

Freaky.

Ted poked at his face, reflected in the vanity mirror. "I look the same."

He was still getting used to his new appearance. Or rather, his old appearance. Loki had moved Ted's tattoos around like they were iron filings in that beard toy from when Ted had been a kid. His entire body itched and ached, as if the replacement tattoos that Loki had placed in his skin were real—and fresh. The sensation was similar to the first time he'd put on Odin's bum cloak. But Loki's work went deeper. The changes were more complete.

"Your parents would be surprised if Harrison Ford walked through the door saying he was Ted. And Surtur expects Ófriður, not Ted Callan."

"We're the same fucking guy."

Loki turned towards Ted and arched one of her eyebrows theatrically. "Are you?"

Ted tapped his chest where Loki's work had replaced his storm cloud tattoo. "Did you have to put your name over my heart?"

Loki pouted as if he'd hurt her feelings. "I thought it was a nice touch. It was your dog's name. You loved your dog. *Totally* believable."

The scroll with the trickster's name on it wasn't his only questionable tattoo. Where Ted's Mjölnir tattoo had been was a naked lady—one who looked remarkably like Tilda—winking as she straddled a rose stem like it was a stripper's pole. "Every Rose Has Its Thorn" was written in flowing script beneath her, forming a stage.

None of his new ink looked Norse. Some of it looked as if he'd tried to cover up his old tattoos. Others, like the spider's webs of blue lines sleeving his arms in barbed wire, looked like a blind epileptic had been holding the needle.

Ted still had Huginn and Muninn tattoos, on the back of his neck now, instead of his temples, but done in Haida style, not Norse. Ted still hadn't seen what the trickster had done to his back. *Probably two horses fucking.*

"I still think your disguise would have been better if you'd let me dress you in drag."

Ted shot Loki a dirty look. "I have a beard."

Loki shrugged. "Didn't stop Thor."

"I'm 6'4" and 240 pounds—"

"More like 220, these days. Good work."

"I'd make one godawful-looking woman, Loki."

Loki continued as if she hadn't heard Ted. "I'll get you a hat with a veil to soften all those wrinkles. You should have moisturized more, with all that time you've spent outside. You're like a walking callus. We'll tart up your neck with some fancy jewelry…"

Refusing to engage Loki or the cross-dressing subject any further, Ted focused on another source of irritation. "I still don't know why you couldn't drop me off in the city."

The trickster looked at him as if he were clueless and held up the wrist bearing Gleipnir. "And I don't see why, after I returned a weapon forged specifically to kill you, that you don't trust me to help you without shackles."

"Then you haven't been paying attention."

"Neither have you. Thousands of people leave and enter Edmonton from this place every day. What better way to slide in unnoticed?"

It made sense, but Loki was probably fucking with him.

"Whatever."

"Here's a few bucks for the shuttle," Loki said, passing Ted a roll of worn fives, no doubt lifted from Ted's stash in his backpack. "Don't use your gold card. Svarta spending coin here might raise a few eyebrows."

"They have offices here. What's the big deal?"

Loki smiled. "Svarta has *many* offices, Ted, but only one of you."

Ted asked, "What're you going to do with the car?"

"I'll leave it in short-term parking. The owner will find it. Eventually."

"Along with one hell of a parking tab."

Loki laughed. "He's earned it."

Maybe Loki was being a white knight, crusading against some injustice, but more likely, the Bentley's owner had looked at the trickster sideways.

Ted sighed. "I hope I'm making the right call."

Loki asked, "What's not right?"

"Maybe my best friend deserves to *not* have his wedding invaded by monsters?"

"Seriously, Ted, as for monsters, I've seen worse than you. And as for best friend? Ouch, man. That's *low*. I'd expect that from your birds, not from you."

"Ha fucking ha."

"Besides, I doubt the king of the fire giants is concerned with the wedding ceremony of a pipefitter."

"Maybe. But the fires are receding, he's got me back here and—"

"It's a trap!" Loki yelled in a croaky voice.

"You're one *Star Wars* reference away from getting my boot up your ass.

"Promises, promises."

Loki slammed on the brakes. Some asshat in a Cavalier had darted into their lane, cutting them off, and Loki had barely avoided getting clipped. The trickster leaned on the horn as if she owned the stolen car, all the while reciting the Cavalier's licence plate number and muttering under her breath.

Ted wouldn't want to be them. Not for all the dwarves in Flin Flon.

Loki drifted to a stop at the passenger dropoff. "What's the plan, *kemosabe*?" When Ted didn't immediately answer, Loki doubled down and asked, "You *do* have a plan, don't you?"

"Get the lay of the land. Maybe grab a beer with an old friend."

"Can I come?"

Ted considered how poorly that could go. Also the new form Loki was wearing. "Rye's getting married on Sunday, and I'd rather you didn't fuck the groom a few days before the wedding."

Loki feigned offence. "He's not my type."

"He's exactly your type."

Loki cocked his head.

"Unavailable," said Ted.

The trickster smiled that shit-eating grin of hers. Ted wasn't sure if it was more, or less, unsettling than the first time he'd met Loki. "Sounds like he'd make himself available if I was there."

"What'll you be doing?"

Loki rolled a long-suffering look at Ted. "What you asked me to."

Yeah, right.

"Go have some fun," Ted said. "Let me know what you find out."

Ted grabbed his bag and hopped out of the vehicle, slamming the door. Hard. The car rocked a little bit. Ted wasn't sure why he'd done it. It wasn't as if this was Loki's car. Loki smiled. The trickster had made a habit of slamming the doors on Ted's GTO before it had ended up smashed by Thor. Petty revenge. Loki understood that better than anyone.

Ted might pay for it later, but for now, he felt the trickster approved.

A chorus of loud caws made Ted jump. One of the floors of the parking garage was lined with ravens. He wondered if Huginn and Muninn were among them, watching him, watching Loki, before leaving to scout the city proper.

Ravens in Edmonton.

There'd been ravens out the ass when Ted had been up in Fort Mac.

When there still was *a Fort Mac.*

Ted had usually fed them. He couldn't be certain, but he'd always suspected that it was the same birds who followed him around camp, begging for more. When guys were coming off shift and getting trashed, they'd throw rocks at birds picking through garbage. The ravens remembered *that* too. Toss a single rock at a single raven and the rest would divebomb the hell out of you.

Thought and Memory, Ted mused. *The vikings sure as shit got that right.*

He imagined the ravens of Fort Mac were too smart to get consumed when Surtur destroyed the city. Maybe some had come this far south, evacuating with the other residents. As irritating as he found Huginn and Muninn at times, Ted found himself hoping that was the case.

Ted took the airport shuttle to the Century Park station. On his way into Edmonton he noticed the city's welcome sign had been changed; instead of saying "City of Champions" it now read: "Suck it Calgary."

He had to laugh. It had been a long time since the glory days of Wayne Gretzky and Warren Moon and someone must have thought "Champion" no longer applied. Everyone thought the sign referenced the championships of the Edmonton Oilers and Eskimos, not the response to Black Friday and the tornado that had ripped through Edmonton in '87. The only thing he would have found funnier was if the sign had mentioned construction or speed traps. He wondered whether Loki had made the switch, but he supposed if he couldn't blame her for every bad thing that had happened in his life, he didn't need to credit Loki for the awesome things either.

Thanks to Loki, he was in Edmonton a couple days earlier than he'd expected. He'd hoped to spend the bare minimum amount of time in Alberta to meet his commitment to Ryan, so he could snoop around, see his parents, and then leave without endangering anyone. Now he had more time for his family and what remained of his old friends to grill him. He did want to see them all, and yet … he wasn't ready. He'd been gone too long. Seen too much.

What the hell would I tell anyone?

Uncertain where to go, he bought a ticket and rode the LRT towards downtown. Ted got off at the U of A. He wanted to get the lay of the land. To feel like he was home again. Walk across the High Level Bridge and feel the air and listen to the North Saskatchewan River compete with traffic. He wound his way along side streets towards the Bridge. His mouth watered a bit, as he passed the High Level Diner. He slapped at a mosquito buzzing him. They were bad. The cloud of bugs around him seemed big enough to carry a guy away.

At least they hadn't filled up on *jötunn* blood—those little biters had not been fun to deal with. Those fuckers *could* carry a grown man off.

It was also damned hot in Edmonton for August. Ted should be wearing a hoodie or a light jacket at this time of night. Instead, he was sweating through his T-shirt, and walking around in ball soup.

Ted didn't need to calm the buried storm in his chest to know a real one was coming. This heat, humidity, the wind. He looked at the sky. He hoped it passed over. Hoped he wasn't the one to bring it—but it felt reassuring to think that as bad as a storm could get, once it broke, the weather was usually smooth sailing.

For a time.

He hoped this storm didn't break everything.

Wind whipped at him as he crossed the bridge. The Perseid meteor shower was supposed to peak tonight. It would be great to get out of the city, away from the lights, and watch meteors die. There was a crane atop a tall hexagonal tower near 120th avenue. Something new was going up. A few more gaps in his presence here, and it wouldn't feel like home at all. But for now, looking up at the familiar buildings and breathing in Edmonton's stink, it was as if he'd never left.

On the other side of the North Saskatchewan, the Valhalla condos overlooked the High Level Bridge and the river valley. The name Valhalla hadn't meant anything to Ted the last time he'd seen them. But he'd considered buying there. He snorted. Tilda probably would've found that hilarious. *Loki definitely would've.*

Once he was off the bridge, Ted wandered towards 97th Street and the hard line that separated downtown Edmonton's business towers from the peepshows and bums. Ted missed his favourite donair place. That food hadn't caught on in Winnipeg, and Ted hadn't found one that compared to the joint on Jasper. There was so much of this city he'd missed. So much he hadn't missed at all.

According to the GPS on his phone, Ted neared where the Church of the Eternal Flame was supposed to be.

A bum leaning against an empty storefront looked familiar. It wouldn't be the first time a down-on-his-luck patch employee became homeless. Ted imagined there were more of them now, with the fires up north slowing production, and competition for the remaining work fiercer. Overtime dried up and so did the money that came with it.

"Spare change?" the man asked as Ted approached him, holding out a hand without looking up.

He recognized the voice and was able to place the man's face when the two were added together.

Corey Toews. He'd worked in the patch. Crazy as a shit-house rat, but a hard worker. He was lucky he was still alive. Ted couldn't remember whether Corey had been on site when Surtur escaped, but knowing the coke habit he'd cultivated, it was only a matter of time before he ended up out of doors.

Ted passed Corey a bill and he tucked it into his dirty jeans without looking. "Thanks."

When he showed no sign of recognizing him, Ted asked, "You okay, Corey?"

He looked up, then and smiled. He'd lost a tooth since the last time Ted had seen him.

"Hey, T-Bag."

"You need anything?"

Corey shook his head and patted his jeans. "Nah. How're you and Suze?"

"We're not," Ted said flatly.

"Shitty." He pursed his lips as if considering something, and asked, "Got a smoke I could bum?"

Ted nodded and passed the man a cigarette. Corey fished in his pocket as if hunting for change. Ted waved him off. He pulled out his Zippo, and then thought better of it. Corey was watching it a little too closely.

"Out of fluid," Ted said, procuring a Bic from his pocket.

"Thanks for stopping." He lit up, and so did Ted. "Seen other guys from the patch. Walked right past me."

Ted wasn't terribly surprised.

"What made you stop?"

"A guy, down on his luck, like you. Saved my life last year."

"*Hmmphf.*" He exhaled smoke through his nose, and let out a relaxed sigh. "Thought you moved. What brings you back?"

"Rye's wedding."

Corey muttered something Ted didn't quite catch, forced a smile, and added, "Congratulate the prick for me."

Ted nodded and gestured down the street towards where the Church of the Eternal Flame was supposed to be. "Know anything about those guys? That new church?"

Corey looked at Ted's rumpled appearance, nodding slowly. "They find work for guys like us."

"Guys like us?"

"Yeah." Corey gestured north with his chin, towards the fires. "Patch orphans."

"Why haven't you gone?"

"I'm not down with the whole religion thing."

"Normally I'm not, either."

Corey took two deep drags of his cigarette. He stared down the street a long while, watching the exhaled smoke drift on the wind before asking, "You heading down there?"

"Maybe," Ted said.

Corey plucked the cherry off the tip of his cigarette without hissing, and tucked the half-spent butt into a jacket pocket. "Watch your ass, man."

"Always," Ted said, and passed him a twenty.

He watched Corey's reflection in the windows until the man was out of sight.

Ted passed the Church of the Eternal Flame. It didn't look like much. The thought of people unknowingly putting their faith in Surtur made the hair on his arms stand straight up. There was no sign above the door, but the candle glow inside was a dead giveaway. Lights were off, blinds were drawn. He wasn't getting a better look short of busting in.

He kept walking.

The Hotel MacDonald looked down at him. Looking at the place felt different now—Ted could afford to drop the coin. He'd never thought it was worth the price to stay in the old railway chateau, but he'd stayed in a sister hotel in Winnipeg for the last several months and it did have its perks. He'd never felt it worth the indulgence while he'd lived in Edmonton, not when he had a perfectly good bed to crash in at home. While he may not be wearing his filthy coveralls and rolling up in a muddy pickup, Ted still felt they'd smell the stink of the patch on him.

He was home, but not quite ready to go home. He decided to call anyway.

He pulled out his phone and wondered whether it would cooperate.

Dial tone. That's a good sign.

There was no answer at his parents'—they weren't expecting him yet—and Ted hung up before he got the machine. Ted's dad didn't have a cell. He hated them. "I have a phone," he always said. "It's in my house. If I'm not there, I'm too busy to talk to you." Ted's mom did have one—for emergencies—despite his father, a.k.a. the Sergeant, being convinced of his own invulnerability.

Ted had given his parents enough notice to change the locks on the house. His father had threatened to do so shortly before Ted had left for Winnipeg, after one too many drunken nights, one too many fights. He wasn't sure whether his coming home would be a pleasant surprise or not.

He scrolled down to Rye's photo in his contacts, pressed the image of his best friend passed out with a cock drawn on his cheek, and waited.

The call connected. "What up?" Rye asked.

"I'm in town."

"Already? I thought you were coming a few days from now."

"Got lucky on a ride out."

"Ah. Wait. Ride? Since when do you catch a ride anywhere? I thought you had The Goat out of storage?"

"Totalled."

"Motherfucker." A disbelieving pause. "Really?"

"Really."

"You kick the guy's ass?"

Ted supposed that beating Thor with his own hammer until the thunder god's half-dead lover, Hel, decided to consume him to save herself counted as an ass-kicking.

Not wanting Rye to dig too deeply into the destroyed car, Ted told him what he wanted to hear. "Yeah, I kicked his ass all over Winnipeg."

"That's the Ted I fucking miss, man. There's hope for you yet."

Ted asked, "What are you up to tonight?"

"Nothing important," Rye answered, quickly following with a guilty-sounding, "Wedding shit."

"Want to grab a beer?"

Ted could almost feel Rye's nod through the phone, then he said, "Or ten. Yeah, I've got some time. Should I call the guys?"

Ted wasn't sure he wanted to talk to the old gang. Wasn't sure they'd want to talk to him either. "Save it for the stag."

"See you at the 'Wolf's then. I'll get you home when we're done."

Howling Wolf's. A bar in Edmonton's north end. It had been too long since Ted had been there. "Done."

Ted ended the call and looked for a spot to drop his cigarette, surprising himself at the muscle memory. It was a $250 fine for littering in Edmonton, and the streets were relatively clean as a result. In Winnipeg, you could hide a body under the spent butts—at least until the wind picked up, which it had a tendency to do while Ted was around. The sidewalks here seemed all the cleaner by comparison.

He didn't need to walk far. There was a butt stop that had a concert poster for Raygun Cowboys taped to it. Ted had missed the show. A damn shame. They were great live. Cigarette discarded, Ted hit the closest LRT station before he felt the urge to light up again.

Rye lived a ten-minute walk from the last stop on the north end of the LRT line. Not that he ever *walked* when he did need to take the LRT. It was convenient to live out there if you worked in the trades. You had a straight shot to any yard, plant, or job from your apartment—and Rye's was also stumbling distance from 'Wolf's. Ted and Susanna had lived out there too, before they'd bought their house.

There was a 7-11 near the LRT station, and Ted needed more smokes. He bought a couple packs of Canadian Classic, and then headed underground.

Shiny silver plates lined the vaulted ceiling over the dual tracks, positioned on either side of a centre platform. The tiled cement circular benches spread across the platform were mostly empty. A couple women, one in a suit, the other with dreads and her head down while she fiddled with her phone, stood by one. Three guys having a conversation sat at another, one over. It was stuffy in Bay Street station, but it was cool, and a welcome relief to sweating his bag off. Staccato, static-y pops echoed over the intercom in the station.

Mjölnir wasn't visible, but Ted felt his hammer hand twitch, and the storm cloud tattoo stir on his chest. They fought against

Loki's enchantment. Ted was reaching, involuntarily, towards one of the train lines. He could feel that current—six hundred volts per line—feel Mjölnir quivering, wanting to steal that man-made lightning.

Someone bumped into Ted and he felt the spark discharge, like a static shock.

"*Ow*," a woman's voice said.

Her voice sounded familiar. Ted mumbled a "sorry." She took a step back at first, and then said, "Ted? *Ted Callan?*"

He recognized her now that's she'd spoken his name. He never would have by appearance alone. Eva. She'd dyed her hair. Cut and styled it differently. And the clothes. Jesus. His first day back in the city and he managed to bump into his high school girlfriend. He wondered if it was Loki's work. More likely she *was* Loki. But coincidences do happen. Such as the fact that Cheap Trick's "The Flame" was playing. Ted and Eva had danced to that song—and more—many times in the past.

A couple of passengers, one of the guys, and the woman with dreadlocks, looked up and over at Ted and Eva, before going back to their phones and copies of the *Metro*.

"Hey, you look great."

She did. Although considerably more … adult was the word to spring to mind. She was wearing dress slacks, a matching jacket, and a black shirt completely bereft of any band logo.

"You too. Pretty hardcore."

Her voice told him that she didn't mean it. That seeing him travel-worn and needing a shower, carrying a duffel over his shoulder, she probably wondered whether he were homeless. Or on drugs.

Ted *told* himself he didn't care. He'd hardened himself to what strangers thought of him at first glance back in Winnipeg. But seeing an old flame, hearing her disapproval, the unspoken *thank God I had the good sense to dump his ass,* gave him the first hint of what he'd be facing when he got home. Jenny had been surprised, but not horrified. Had taken him at his word that someone else had done this to him. She'd been horrified at it, but not horrified of *him*.

Waiting long enough for the silence to grow uncomfortable, she asked, "What are you up to these days?"

"I'm a consultant for a mining company in northern Manitoba," Ted lied.

Her eyebrows rose in disbelief. "Oh. Last I heard you were—"

"In the patch."

"Yeah."

"You could say I had a couple of life-changing events. I got headhunted and the company wouldn't take no for an answer. At least things are never dull. You?"

"Financial planning."

Ted pursed his lips and gave a short nod. He never would have believed that in a million years. When they'd dated, her going into finance had seemed as likely as finding out magic was real.

"Hard to believe, right?"

"You were the most metal chick in the school."

Ted worried that he'd pissed her off by calling her a chick, but before he could apologize, she smiled warmly, as if reminiscing, and said, "You can't listen to Iron Maiden forever, Ted."

"We'll have to agree to disagree," he said, throwing the horns.

More silence.

Fortunately, the sharp steel-on-steel sound of the approaching southbound train cut the catching up short.

"This is me."

"Take care of yourself."

She looked at him, as if trying to decide how to take the statement, and then said, "You too."

The few other people who'd been in the station followed Eva onto the southbound train. The dreadlocked woman reconsidered getting on the train, and stepped back onto the platform. He didn't know if he should know her, but he felt like he should. Probably because he was home. He expected everyone from his past to jump out around every corner. Seeing Eva had spooked him a little. The dreadlocked woman ignored him, preoccupied with her phone. Texting, by the look of it.

Ted never thought he'd be nostalgic for the LRT. He'd spent more time yelling at trains than riding them. He was a driver by nature, and trains always seemed to conjure themselves up in his way right when he needed to be somewhere. If it weren't for the fact that problem affected everyone, and had begun long before Ted had been exposed to magic or the Nine Worlds, he'd blame Loki. Now that he didn't have wheels, it sure made it easier to get from downtown to Ryan's place out by Clareview.

The northbound train approached. The sign lit up.

When it came to a stop, he boarded and slumped into the

blue upholstered seat, smiling at the pleasantly bland announcement voice on the train. He'd always figured that announcer was chosen so drunks on their way home from Oils and Eskies games didn't want to pick a fight with the disembodied voice. Lord knows he and Rye had got their blood up for stupider reasons back in the day.

The train emerged from the tunnels and was running on street level. Near the tracks, a heavier train carried a load of oil cars. The woman with the dreadlocks sat nearby. She was only paying attention to her phone. Maybe she was watching a video. Didn't look like she was texting. He looked away.

The train stopped at the Stadium Road-Commonwealth Stadium stop. Seeing the home of the Eskies, Ted felt Rye could have at least had the decency to plan his wedding so Ted could have taken in a football game while he was in town. Ted had checked, but the Eskimos were on the road this week.

Before the train could head off to Coliseum and the home of the Oilers, a guy rushed onboard, narrowly beating the closing doors. He plopped himself down, breathless. There was a gaping hole in the crotch of his jeans, and his shirt and left hand were stained, like he'd been doused with fluid. He smelled sharp. Might've been a sniffer. Given how sketchy the guy looked, maybe it was blood on his clothes. He fumbled for a copy of the *Metro*, and held it up an inch or so from his face, sliding his head around the paper every now and then to give Ted the stink-eye.

From a seat behind him, Ted heard, "I'm telling you, the fires in the sands are a secret society. They're trying to break the unions."

Ted watched the weirdo in the reflection of the train window. Open staring tended to aggravate the crazies. Not all that long ago, the way the guy was looking at him would've been enough for Ted to have wandered over and offered to tune him up. The hot, hungry look still bothered Ted, but he reminded himself he wasn't in Alberta to fight.

"Next stop, Belvedere."

As the train approached the Belvedere stop, the weirdo got up from his seat, still holding the *Metro* over his face, and walked past Ted. He dropped the paper and hurled himself at Ted.

The fucker landed three or four shots before Ted got his guard up. Surprised by the intensity of the assault. And that he could feel it. The storm wanted to move. Mjölnir wanted to fly. Dragon-scale wanted to grow in response. If his powers came out, everyone could die. A punch glanced off Ted's forearm and slammed into his throat. Ted crushed down his body's instinct to defend itself with the return of his tattoos. But he needed to not die himself until his gifts could come back safely. The train lurched to a stop, throwing the weirdo off-balance. His punch hit the edge of the seat instead of Ted. That gave Ted time to recover, and using only natural strength and size, he shoved him away. The guy tried to slide a hand into Ted's pocket, where he'd stashed his lighter. Ted slapped the man's arm away. At that, his assailant dashed out the open door and away down the Belvedere platform.

Ted stood, breathing hard, his knees wobbly; but adrenaline pushed him to give chase and finish the fight. A bunch of passengers had their cellphones trained on him. All the more reason not to pound the guy into paste.

Ted unclenched his fists.

A woman asked him, "Are you okay?"

It was the dreadlocked woman from the Bay Street Station, she had her cell out too, but that seemed to be a natural state for her, and since she also appeared to be the only one on the train who gave a shit about him, he let it go.

Ted rubbed his jaw, strangely finding that he'd missed the sensation of a good noggin-rattler. Of being hit, and feeling it. One hell of a welcome home. The desire to unleash hell on the prick had been intense. He patted his pockets. Wallet, phone, and Zippo were all accounted for. Good.

"I'm fine," Ted said, wincing a bit as he forced a smile and felt his lip split. He licked at the blood. "Surprised."

She stared at him for a long time. Everyone else on the train had gone back to their own seats and their own business. She passed him a bit of Kleenex from her purse, and joined them.

7. Old Haunts

Despite Howling Wolf's name, Ted doubted he'd be treated to any Chicago-style blues while he was there. Nothing had changed since the last time Ted had been in there except for the staff. Wood panelling with an island bar jutting from the wall like an oaken peninsula. Neon beer signs: Canadian, Kokanee, Bud Light, Keiths. Oilers and Eskimos flags hung with equal reverence alongside the Maple Leaf.

Opposite the bar on the right side from the entrance was a brick wall lined with bookshelves. For some reason, Rye had always liked the books. He'd never been a reader to Ted's knowledge, but they did give the place a homey atmosphere. There was a raised deck of seats and booths immediately to the right of the entrance and up two steps by an ATM.

There were a few folks in the bar that Ted remembered, but they either didn't recognize him or didn't want to talk to him, so he sat alone. There were *dvergar* in Howling Wolf's, three of them, which made Ted start. They glanced up at him, but went immediately back to their pitchers of beer. He breathed a sigh of relief. Loki's disguise did work. He hoped they didn't start anything. He rubbed his jaw. It would be nice if his anonymity in Edmonton lasted more than an hour.

His old regular table was vacant. There was a seven-foot

statue of a knight, still wearing a *Scream* mask, post-Halloween two years ago, its sword bent in the middle of the blade. Ted remembered tossing Rye into that statue when they'd argued over Warren Moon's NFL versus CFL career.

No one was at the pool tables past the booths on the way to the can. Maybe if Rye had time they'd get in a game or two. Ted sat with his back to the wall, facing the door. Shitty protection if any of his enemies found him, but he found he wanted to see who was coming into the place.

A waitress dressed all in black, tight t-shirt, mini skirt, fishnets, and hideous Ugg boots came by his table. Other than the clothes, she was a dead ringer for the actress who played that psychic chick with all the vampire troubles. She talked fast, breathlessly, as she offered a menu and recited the beers on tap. Those hadn't changed since Ted's last visit.

Ted didn't recognize her, and if she didn't recognize him from last time, all the better. He ordered a Pilsner, a Jim Beam chaser, and a rare steak that, if past experience was still true, would probably arrive medium-well, and waited for Rye. The music at 'Wolf's was in a heavy '90s rotation: Pearl Jam, Mudhoney, Temple of the Dog—all Seattle, all the time. When the satellite station had exhausted the Seattle scene, it moved on to the fakers that had followed, aping the grunge sound.

The waitress was quick on the draw with his bourbon and beer, and Ted's steak arrived in time for whiskey number three. By his fourth bourbon, Ted was starting to wonder whether Rye had stood him up. He stared up at the green steel bare roof frame with its exposed ductwork considering whether he should ask for a fifth, when Ryan finally strolled into the bar. Typical. He lived down the street and he was still late.

Ryan was half a foot shorter than Ted, and almost as wide as he was tall. Neither of them were in their old game shape, but after Rye had stopped being a running back, it was as if he'd never ran again.

Ted waved him over, Rye squinted in the half-gloom of the bar's houselights before yelling out, "T-Bag!"

The dwarves looked up briefly and went back to their beers.

"Took your sweet fucking time," Ted said, throwing up a middle finger.

"What can I say? The female was wanting my company."

"There's something you don't hear too often."

"Jesus. Jenny told me you had tats, but, *shit*. That is a metric fuckton of ink you've got."

"That it is," Ted said, wondering what Rye would think of Ted's *real* tattoos. "The monkey suit you're cramming me into will hide them, don't worry."

"Oh, I'm not worried. It's Randy and Gloria you'll need to worry about."

"Ah, your mom loves me, and you know it. She may love you more, but she likes me better."

"Well, there's no accounting for taste, is there?"

"Guess not, someone willing to marry you proves that."

Rye laughed. "Guess so."

"How're things?"

Rye screwed his face up like he was getting ready to hock a gob on the floor. "Things have gone to shit ever since we lost

Fort McMoney," Rye said. "Guys who could have left for the States and the shale fields in North Dakota. Some moved into potash in Saskatchebush."

"Fuck."

"Yeah. I saw Corey—what the hell was his last name? You know, the big, bald bastard."

Ted nodded. "Ran into him tonight. He's homeless now."

"Not sure if it's the drugs or lack of work. That fire made him weirder than it did you."

"That so?"

"Keeps hanging around that weirdo church."

Funny, that wasn't how Corey had described the situation.

"I saw the place on my way in. It looks like it should be a bus depot or something."

"No doubt," Rye said with a nod.

They sat in silence, sipping their drinks. It probably wasn't a good idea to bring up Rye's sister, given how their last conversation regarding her had gone down, but Ted was worried.

"How's Jenny?"

"You're asking *me* that?"

"She hasn't taken my calls, man. Every time I swing by, she's not home. I want to know she's okay. A friend of mine works with her, but she's not talking either."

Ryan exhaled, a long, hard breath, from his nostrils. "She's okay," he said finally. "All that weird shit last November rattled her. She hasn't been the same since."

"Rattled me, too."

"Sorry man. I forgot."

Forgot. Even without Muninn in his skull, there was no forgetting Hel showing up for Ted. He put on a smile. It felt weak, but it was enough, to make Ryan appear a bit less guilty.

"How's your girl?"

"Gone."

"She split?"

"We had a rough go after we lost the baby."

"Must've been meant to be, then, you know."

A bullshit platitude. Meant to be. For the best. God has a plan. Fate. *Doom.*

Hardly comforting. But at least Rye had tried. The way they'd left things, Ted had been surprised an invitation had showed up, let alone that Rye still wanted him to be a groomsman.

"So you're single is what you're saying."

"I guess you could call it that."

Rye inhaled through his teeth. "Don't go getting any ideas, but—"

"But what?"

Ted waited for Rye to use the opening to say something like "butt sex." He didn't. Ted was surprised. Maybe he had grown up.

"Susanna's going to be at the wedding."

Ted's knuckles tightened as his hands clenched the table's edge. In a flat voice, he said, "You invited my ex-wife to your wedding."

Rye wouldn't meet his eyes.

"What the fuck? Why are you only telling me this now?"

"Would you have shown up otherwise?"

"Yeah, but I would've brought some incriminating pictures of you to pass around."

"Like what?"

"Mexico. Folk Fest. Fringe. The time you shit your pants in the McKenzies mosh pit. Pretty much every time you put a beer bottle to your lips."

"Easy, big guy, no need to go nuclear." Rye threw up his hands like he was getting ready to block a punch. "*I* didn't. Lisa did."

Ted shook his head, muttered, "Godammit."

"You gonna be cool with this?"

Ted wasn't sure. He should be. Their life was long in his past, but they'd spent more time married than they'd been separated and divorced. He didn't want to see her happy with her new guy. He didn't want her to be unhappy, either. He thought they'd said their goodbyes. Her last words to him were a harsh message left on his phone. The last time they'd spoken to each other in person hadn't been much better.

He forced a smile. "I guess I have to be, don't I?"

"I'm glad to hear you're not gonna piss in the punch at my wedding."

"No promises. I'm assuming it's an open bar."

Rye smiled. "Seriously. Are we cool? Because I can—"

"What? Piss off your fiancée by saying her friend can't come because your deadbeat buddy will be put out?" Ted remembered the *negotiations* that went into planning the guest list for his and Susanna's wedding. Inviting *this* friend means she gets to invite *that* aunt. He shuddered. "I'll be fine."

"Funny, you don't look 'fine.' You look like you wanna punch me in the dick."

"Later."

Complaining aside, Ted was glad for the heads-up. It beat the hell out of being surprised.

"Knowing you two, you'll end up having a tumble anyway"

"Doubtful. I heard she's seeing someone else."

"Oh, yeah," Rye said.

Ted wondered whether that part of the negotiations had already been forgotten. Or how often Rye and Lisa saw Susanna.

"Don't worry, you can take him."

That made Ted laugh. Louder and harder than might have been appropriate.

"Of that I have no doubt. But don't worry. I have no intention of starting a fight at your wedding."

"Thanks."

Ted joked, "Still can't believe you finally got caught. Or did you get too fat to keep running?"

Ryan took a sidelong glance at Ted's own midsection. "I doubt Coach Dean would be happy with your time in the forty these days either."

"No shit."

"Got something serious to bring up with you. I've been talking with the female, and you've been coming up. I wanted you up there," Rye said. "But, you know how it goes. Weddings man, it's all about the dress."

Ted nodded. Weddings were a master's program in Compromise, with a minor in No One Gets to be Happy. He remembered that well enough from his "involvement" in planning his own wedding.

"Who's the man?"

"Her brother. I wanted you up there, but she said if you were my best man she'd have met you by now."

Hard to argue with that. "I'm sorry—"

Rye waved him off. "I did manage to pair you up with Jenny."

That surprised Ted.

"Devil you know, brother, devil you know. Her bro's a good guy, but I don't like him so much that I'll be letting him that close to my sister."

Ted narrowed his eyes, chose carefully what to say next. "So Big Brother is your best man?"

"Yeah." Rye hung his head, like he was embarrassed. Which would take something. Rye wasn't shy. "You okay with that?"

"It's your wedding, not mine. So I guess I have to be."

"If it's any consolation, the Maid of Honour is a total dog."

"That so?"

"Dude. Not with my eyes gouged out and eight rubbers on. Not if I wanted to get back at you for that business with my cousin, I couldn't do that to a brother."

"But a brother-in-law is fine?"

Rye laughed.

Ted let out a low whistle. "Me and Jenny. That is going to be interesting. What's Jenny think of having to walk down the aisle with me?"

"You two need to sort out your shit," Rye said.

"I've been trying."

"Try harder."

"She doesn't want me to." Ted rapped his knuckles against his forehead. "I'm thick, bro, but I can take a hint."

"Well since you two will be a pair going up the aisle, and people will be taking pictures, I'd prefer if you didn't look like someone pissed in your mouth in my wedding photos."

"I'll do what I can."

"Do better." Rye sighed, rubbed at the bridge of his nose as if he were trying to explain something to an infant. "My sister's had a wide-on for you since the seventh grade. You're single. She's single." He waved his hand. "Love is in the air and all that bullshit. Take a run."

"How many times have you said 'hands off'?"

Rye took a long pull on his beer. "I don't want to know what you two do. I don't want to think about it. But I do want Jenny to be happy. And I'd rather have you for a brother-in-law than Tyler."

"He'll already be your brother-in-law."

"Details. What I'm saying, is this is your one-time get-out-of-ass-kicking, free chance to hit on my sister. Choose wisely."

Ted didn't hate Rye's plan. He didn't think it was much of a possibility, though. And Rye's opinion wasn't the one that mattered.

"Pretty sure Jenny gets a vote, too, Rye. And after the way her and I left things, I doubt she's going to choose to get involved with me."

"That could change," Rye said. "You two have never danced

together. By the end of 'I Don't Want to Miss a Thing' you'll be together. I guaran-fucking-tee it."

Ted muttered, "I fucking hate that song."

Rye smiled. "No more wedding talk. It makes my head hurt."

"Suit yourself," Ted said. "How's the patch?"

"What patch? Nothing but fire."

"Thought it stopped spreading," Ted said, wanting to tread carefully.

"Stopped *spreading*, yeah. But half of the north's still burning. Some smaller jobs going on, but it's not like the old days."

"You'd think they'd be going balls-out on the other sites."

"Oh they are. They need welders and fitters, but they also want to pay them ten bucks an hour. Bringing them over by the boatload, but no work for us. I'm ready to give it up, man," Rye said. "No more shutdowns. No more trips up north. It's family time, you know."

Ted nodded. He did. He'd said the same thing, many times. He hoped Rye had an easier time following through. The money that came with the overtime hours was as addictive as cigarettes.

"You sure you don't want to move back here?"

Ted shook his head. "Not gonna happen."

Rye grimaced. "I got nobody, you know. Everyone I know is from the patch. It's boring as shit at home. They're never around when I want to grab beers."

Ted remembered. He also remembered Rye not being around when Ted had wanted to grab beers.

"You bailed on the life," Rye said. "So I was hoping you'd come back."

"I didn't bail on it, it blew up in my fucking face. I'm not moving back."

Rye nodded. "I know."

"You going to be okay?"

"Yeah. So long as the new house doesn't bankrupt me."

"You've got a new place?" Ted asked. "When? Where?"

Rye hesitated a long time before he answered and then it was obscured by a cough.

"Could you repeat that?"

"You're going to make me, aren't you?"

"Yes. Yes, I am."

"You're a bastard, Callan."

"True."

"Sherwood Park."

Ted couldn't help it. He burst out in a braying laugh that he couldn't stop. Other patrons in the bar looked over. It was too funny. His parents were ready to disown him. He had to fight a fire giant. *The* fire giant. The world might be ending. But the idea of Ryan living in Sherwood Park would be funny until the day Ted died. As funny as Ted trying to blend in in Wolseley in Winnipeg.

"So how's Jimmy?" Ted asked.

"Dead."

Ted blinked. "When?"

"Couple months ago."

"How?"

"Suicide."

"You're shitting me. Jim Allen did himself in? I can't believe that. He was more Catholic than the fucking Pope."

"You think that's crazy, you should hear how he did it."

"How?"

Rye leaned in, said the words quietly, "Lit himself on fire."

Ted shuddered. An unpleasant way to go. Whether Surtur was responsible or not.

"And he's not the only one."

"What?"

"Jimmy. Danny. Billy. All fucking topped themselves man." He drained his beer. Motioned over at the waitress with two fingers raised. "Bryan was murdered."

Ted shuddered. "Jesus."

Rye nodded. "They never caught whoever did it. You and me, brother. We're an endangered species."

"Last of the greats," Ted said.

Rye didn't laugh. Only snorted. "I gotta take a piss."

"Don't have too much fun without me."

"You'd have to work out for a year to be able to hold my dick."

"As soon as someone's able to find the thing we'll discuss holding it."

Rye left the table and Ted drained his whiskey as the waitress rolled by with Rye's beer and another bourbon for Ted. More dead. Suicide by fire. Murder by arson. Church of the Eternal Flame. More to lay at Surtur's feet. Ted couldn't wait to collect on the tab the giant had racked up.

Ted's phone rang, playing the opening bars of The Who's

"Who Are You?" Whoever was calling, it was an unknown number. Alberta area code. Ted didn't pick up.

Some guys had taken up at the pool tables. They were doing more leaning on cues and staring than sinking balls. Fuckers leaned like professionals. You'd think they worked for the city. Once he'd have gone over there. Got in on the game. Maybe share beers. Maybe start some shit. He could fight them, take them all on. The mood he was in, he'd be happy to, but then he might as well slit their throats. The smallest slip-up, the tiniest glimpse of his real power, and that would be it.

They'd be dead.

No sooner than Rye came back and sat, his phone buzzed on the table. He glanced down at it, picked it up and shielded it from Ted as he checked the incoming message.

"Lisa," he said, not able to hide a smile. His entire face brightened. For all Rye's bluster, Ted knew he was happy. Good for him. "I gotta take this."

"No worries. I've gotta break the seal anyway," Ted said and headed for the can.

The washrooms still had the signs that read "Dawgs" and "B*tches." Ted didn't understand the point in trying to confuse folks who've had (more than) a few.

When Ted got back, Rye said, "Love you too," and ended the call. He looked embarrassed that Ted had caught him being sentimental, and put his phone in his pocket. He covered the flush on his face by draining his beer.

"Duty calls, T-Bag. Time for me to be hitting that old dusty trail."

"I thought you were going to run me to my folks."

"You know how to use the train."

"Jesus, man. That's cold."

Rye smiled. "Ah, I'm just fucking with you. I've got a ride sorted out for you." He paused only an instant before saying, "You're welcome."

Ted snorted. "Thanks."

Rye gestured for Ted to look over at the bar. Somehow he missed her. Maybe she'd come in while he'd been taking a piss, maybe while he was watching the waitress. But there, by the bar, was Jenny. She looked leaner—not diet-thin, but as if she'd been exercising hard. There was power in her walk. She looked harder, wilder, than Ted remembered.

Rye said, "There's your ride. Play nice."

"Easy for you to say," Ted muttered.

Jenny walked over to the table. Ted kept an eye on the trio of dwarves, and followed their gaze to Jenny. Her, the dwarves *did* watch. Ted wasn't sure whether it was because of something that had happened to her the night Hel came to Winnipeg, or simple lust. Either way, he didn't like it. Rye noticed too, and gave their table a stink-eye that Ted doubted frightened them. She seemed hesitant at first. Rye gave her a crushing hug, lifting her off the ground, and accentuating the fact she was taller than him.

"Gotta go, sis," he said. "My old lady is on me to help. We're still wrapping party favours. Jesus Christ. I promised T-Bag a ride to his parents', you don't mind? Thanks!" Rye left, throwing a "See you at dinner tomorrow," over his shoulder to Jenny. To

Ted, he turned and pointed cocked finger pistols and fired them off. "So glad that you'll be in town for the stag!"

"Behave yourself," Jenny warned. "After Ted's stag, he was lucky to have a wedding."

She had a point: the groomsmen, too pissed to keep carrying him, had left Ted passed out with a giant condom on his head and puke for a shirt.

"Hungry?" Ted asked. "Want a drink?"

"I ate already, and I'm driving," she said. "But I'll have a Coke."

Jenny took a deep breath and then sat in Rye's old seat. She grimaced a moment. It was probably still warm from Rye's ass.

Ted put his hands up, warding off a potential protest. "Not my idea."

"I know," Jenny answered. "If Rye had been any more obvious you could see him from space."

Ted chuckled. "No doubt."

They sat in silence. It stretched out between them. Finally, Jenny said, "Sorry I haven't got back to you, it's been a weird—"

Year.

"—time since that night."

"Yeah, I know."

Jenny leaned in and canted her head to the side. "I guess you would, wouldn't you?"

"Yup. Wait? What?"

She waved her hand. "You know, the tattoos, dating a fortune teller." Jenny paused, as if unsure how to continue. Ted got the impression she was going to say something neither of them would like hearing. "Aiko told me—losing the baby, and Tilda splitting. I'm so sorry, Ted."

It wasn't what Ted had expected to hear. Nine months gone, and it still hurt. He wondered what Erin would have looked like now. Tilda had seen her in her Norn visions. Ted never had. He wasn't sure what was worse, a memory of loss, or imagining what could've been.

Unlike Rye, who'd only heard that Ted had got a bunch of ink, Jenny had seen the work. It had been a year. He hoped she hadn't been paying too close attention.

"Your tattoos look different," Jenny said.

Shit.

Ted nodded. "I had some of them removed. Had others worked over to look different." Hoping she'd drop it, Ted added. "I don't need a reminder of that night."

Jenny pursed her lips over the straw in her drink and took a long sip. "Not surprising, I guess. You're growing your hair out to hide them, but I can still see some of the ink on your scalp."

Ted smoothed his beard. "Didn't think two giant birds on my face would fly in Rye's wedding photos."

Jenny smiled. "You know, they weren't so bad. After I got past the shock, I liked them."

Ted hid a grin of his own behind a sip of bourbon. He was glad the ravens hadn't been in his skull for Jenny's praise. They'd never let him hear the end of it. Especially if they figured out he felt the same way.

Ted finished his drink and they left the bar. The air was humid and the sky clear. The first few stars of evening shone. The parking lot was filling up.

"I'm not ready to go home yet."

"Well you bailed on my offer to stay with me last time I made it, so you can't crash in my hotel room."

"Hotel? Not staying with Randy and Gloria?"

"I want to have some fun while I'm out here. What if I meet a guy at the wedding? I'm *not* bringing him back to my parents' house."

"Fair enough."

Seeing Jenny, talking to her, lifted Ted's spirits. He'd worried about her. Worried what had happened to her the night Hel had come to Winnipeg. She didn't bring it up, and Ted didn't ask, worried the fragile peace between them wouldn't hold. She was alive, that was what mattered the most.

He felt her hand brush his forearm, not an unwelcome sensation. Her grip tightened. She jerked him back towards the restaurant.

A truck screeched past them, doing the speed limit—if it had been on the QE2.

"What the fuck?" Ted yelled. "That asshole's gonna get someone killed."

"He almost killed you," Jenny said.

Ted shook his head, trying to appear shaken. Normally, it might've knocked him ass-over-tits, but it wouldn't have hurt. With Loki's disguise in play, Ted wasn't sure what would've happened. The dragon-scale tattoos had tried to come out when the guy on the train was punching him. Getting hit by a car would definitely pop his power back into play. It would be inconvenient trying to explain why he hadn't been killed. It would be worse when he dropped a storm on the city that made the Black Friday tornado look like Family Day.

"Yeah. Thanks. I owe you."

"You owe me plenty."

The truck's brake lights flared red, and Ted smelled rubber on asphalt as it came to a stop. His first instinct was to go and tune the driver up. Jenny still had her hand on his forearm.

"Don't," she said, as if sensing his desire. "It's not worth it."

Ted grimaced, but she was right. The guy still might kill someone else.

"I'm getting his plate number."

She rolled her eyes. "Why don't I believe you?"

"Why would I lie?"

Ted scowled at the words. Loki had said them to him once. Damned if the trickster hadn't managed to insinuate herself back under Ted's skin in a hurry.

"I've already picked you up from the cop shop once, don't expect me to pay your bail if you get arrested. Again."

"I'm *not* going to fight him."

The guy stumbled out of his truck like he was drunk. Another car pulled into the lot behind Ted, and as it turned the headlights caught the drunk driver's eyes and they flashed like tiny candles. The wind was behind the guy. He didn't smell like he was soaked in beer or whiskey.

He reeked of diesel.

He lit his cigarette. The fumes coming off him caught the flame, igniting with a soft *whump* and he was engulfed. The man didn't move as the fires caught, and the fuel smell became the scent of cooking meat. Hair sizzled and fat crackled, lost in screams from elsewhere in the parking lot.

For a brief, horrified moment, there was nothing Ted could do but watch. His left hand twitched. Using *any* of his powers would probably alert Surtur and his forces that Ted was behind enemy lines.

Weird to think of his old home that way.

And Jenny was with him. She'd come out of Hel night okay, but she was still vulnerable to the Nine Worlds. Ted whipped off his jacket and ran towards the man. It was a decidedly low-magic solution, trying to knock him down, and pat out the fire.

Only the fire wouldn't stop.

Jenny yelled to a 911 dispatcher. Help wouldn't get here in time. Not for this guy.

The man fought Ted's efforts to help. Not actively. He stood stock still, as if every joint was locked. Ted tried to bear him to the ground. He could feel the fire burning through the leather of his coat.

Crying out, Ted jumped back. His jacket went up in flames. He whipped it to the ground and let it burn.

The man's clothes were gone.

Flesh seared, caramelizing, and fat popped and hissed. The simultaneously mouth-watering smell of meat cooking and the revolting realization of what that meat was. His eyes were gone. He kept walking. With every step the fires grew more intense.

His arms made no effort to beat at the flames. Instead, they stretched toward Ted and Jenny. He wasn't screaming. Wasn't wailing.

Finally, the man sank to his knees. With one last gasp, he cried out, "*Fehu*." The oooo sound of the rune dragged out long after their life had left. A gust of smoke, like a last breath, billowed out of the man's mouth. It held the shape of the man for a moment and then disappeared on the wind.

Sirens sounded in the distance.

"That was horrible," Jenny said, looking away.

"Yeah," Ted said. He'd seen some awful shit since the Nine Worlds had come calling. But this … this was definitely up there. Magic might've saved the guy. Ted had needed to make some hard choices in the past year. But this one… Rye had called the Church of Eternal Flame "loud candles." Ted hadn't considered the meaning until today. *Jesus*.

Jenny must have thought Ted was in shock. She slid her hand into his and pulled him into an embrace.

"You did all you could."

"No," Ted said, squeezing her back. It felt good to be held. It had been a while. "I didn't."

"Don't blame yourself. I froze too. What was he yelling?" Jenny asked. "I couldn't make it out."

Ted wondered whether Surtur knew he was here. Whether this were a coincidence or a potential attack. Bringing up Norse runes wouldn't mean anything to Jenny, and her knowing wouldn't keep her any safer. So he lied.

"I think it was 'Fuck you.'"

Jenny looked skeptical, but didn't query any further. A crowd had gathered around them, gawkers from inside Howling Wolf's and the other bars and restaurants in the parking lot. The dwarves were among them, stroking their beards and sipping their beers.

Cops, paramedics, and firefighters all showed up. Ted would've preferred not to have been there when they arrived. But he had no choice. Too many people had seen his involvement. Unlike his last dustup with the cops, at least this time someone reliable had been witness to the fact it wasn't his fault. He was pretty sure when they got his name, the false accusation of murder and kidnapping from last year would follow him. The cops here wouldn't care that he hadn't been convicted. That he'd been charged would be more than enough for them to look at hanging another charge on him.

Maybe because he'd been dreading their questions, things went well with the police for a change. But it didn't go quickly. It was later than he wanted to get home, but still not an unreasonable time to knock on his parents' door.

There was a truck Ted didn't recognize taking up most of the driveway, so Jenny parked on the street.

"You want to come in?" Ted asked. "I can make you a cup of tea. Coffee. Whatever."

"Last thing I want is caffeine," she said. "It'll be hard enough to sleep tonight as is."

"Yeah," Ted said. Jenny looked wrung out. He imagined he didn't look any better. It was selfish of him to ask her to come in the house with him. His mom loved her. It would make his homecoming less awkward. Jenny should be leaning on Ted, not the other way around. Not that he'd earned the right.

"Rehearsal dinner is on Thursday, I assume you're going?"

"Rye forgot to mention it."

Jenny shook her head. "I'll pick you up."

Thursday. Thor's day. Hope that's not a bad omen.

"Thanks," Ted said, getting out of the car, and easing the door shut.

Jenny peeled out and sprayed a bit of gravel from the curbside at Ted. It stung and he relished the feeling. Even his sucker-punched jaw felt familiar. Felt right.

He stared at the house, wondering what he'd say. And why it was so hard to walk up those fucking steps *this* time. He took a closer look at the truck in the driveway. Yellow ribbon bumper sticker. Extended cab. Extended box. Dualies. Whoever owned it had something to prove.

A dog barked in the house.

No going back now.

8. This Old House

From the sound of the barking, Ted was ready for the dog to come right through the door. No point in ringing the doorbell with that monster as an alarm.

Through the door, a voice yelled, "Goddamn it, settle down!" It was his brother, Mike.

Mike opened the door enough to see Ted, but still be able to block the dog from sliding out. Mike was wearing his green army dress uniform, and it seemed as if all the hair he'd lost on his head had migrated to his moustache. He was not who Ted had been hoping to greet first.

"Look who finally showed his fucking mug."

"Fuck you too," Ted said. "And hello, by the way."

Mike always had a way of getting under Ted's skin in a hurry, and their brotherly reunion was already off to a shitty start. Mike also had coffee covering up a hint of alcohol on his breath. Probably rum, Mike's drink of choice.

To change the subject, Ted asked, "That your truck?"

Mike nodded.

"Nice."

Mike peered out and scanned the street. The dog was trying to worm its way between Mike and the door. Its brown and black colouring, along with its size, made Ted think it was a mix of Shepherd, Rottweiler, and maybe Fenrir.

"Where's The Goat?"

Smashed into the walking dead, driven through the front entrance of a train station, crushed under a dragon and hurled into Hel. "Totalled," Ted answered.

"That car should've been mine," Mike said.

Ted smiled. "Maybe if you hadn't shifted gears like a goddamned spastic, Uncle Chuck would've agreed with you."

"You only got it because you were older."

"Still burns you, doesn't it?" When Mike didn't answer, Ted asked. "Gonna let me in?"

"Have you had a few?" Mike asked. "Mom won't be happy."

Ted gave his brother a dismissive sniff. "You're one to fucking talk."

"I never lost my licence. I've never spent the night in the drunk tank."

"You never got caught. You want a fucking medal for that, too?"

"Fuck you."

"Michael John Callan," their mother said warningly.

"Sorry," Mike muttered.

Ted's mother came to the door dressed as if she were ready to leave for church, and dragged the dog away from the door. It quieted down immediately when she got her hand on its collar.

Over her shoulder, she added, "You're not off the hook either, Theodore Benjamin."

"Sorry, Mom," Ted said as he pushed past his brother and into the house.

He was surprised it didn't hurt, walking through that door. Ted had been expecting some pain. Other than Mike giving him a cheap shot in the shoulder. The family room had been moved around, but the furniture was the same worn leather sofa set and tables made from real wood that Ted's mom had inherited from her parents. Some of the photos were new, most were older than Ted.

"Michael, your wife's on the phone for you. She's coming to pick you up." The dog resumed its barking tirade, snapping at Ted. Helen Callan seemed unconcerned. "And put Samson in the kitchen." His mother looked old. Drawn. It had been less than a year since Ted had seen her, but that intervening time with no visits, no calls, seemed to have aged her more than he'd expected. A few more lines makeup wouldn't hide. Probably a few more grey hairs under her chestnut-dyed hair too.

Ted fought a snicker. His mom never referred to Mike's wife, Val, by name, if she could help it. Hammer and tongs, those two.

She must've sensed he was ready to laugh, though, because a thousand-watt angry mom stare caught him and he froze, like a stupid deer. Maybe if he was lucky Val would bring the kids. He hadn't seen his niece and nephew in ages. He knew the lie of that hope. It was way too late for them to come along.

"I'd like to talk to you, Theodore," his mom said. "We have some things to discuss."

Now it was Mike's turn to snicker as he dragged the dog through the family room and into the kitchen.

You'll get yours yet, Mikey.

"I can't believe how selfish you've been. It's been months—months!—since your last call. The CBC made it sound like the end of the world was happening in Winnipeg, and you can't call to say you're alive? I don't know you're dating again and then I hear you got some … girl pregnant."

"Who told you that?"

"Jennifer told Ryan, and he told his mother. Gloria and I still go for coffee, you know."

Ted did know, and shouldn't have been surprised. With the trouble he and Rye had been able to get into, cross-checking information had been one of their mothers' tricks at keeping them in line.

"And don't interrupt."

"Sorry." Now he knew why Jenny hadn't wanted to stick around.

"Don't say it unless you mean it, Ted. And I don't think you're sorry."

Ted closed his eyes, sighed. "I am sorry that I haven't called. Things got out of hand."

"You could have at least told me I was going to be a grandmother."

Ted felt his face crumple. He wasn't going to cry. He thought those tears had long ago dried up when Erin was gone. When Tilda left him. But they weren't done.

"I … we … lost the baby."

Helen's hand shot to her mouth, tears rimmed her eyes. Anger, not forgotten, but folded up and neatly stowed away, was gone as she pulled him into an embrace.

"Oh, Ted. I'm so sorry. I know how much you wanted to be a father."

Ted mumbled something into his mother's shoulder. It was unintelligible, but that didn't matter. His mom seemed to understand well enough.

"Is that why she's not here with you?"

Ted wondered how *that* would have gone. He extracted himself from his mother's grasp and wiped at his eyes. He shook his head. "It was hard. Tilda didn't take it well. We thought we were past it, but then there was a stupid fight, and she left. I don't know where she went. Don't know when I'll see her again. *If* I'll see her again."

"Do you want to?"

"What?"

"It has been nothing but hard times for you since you moved away and met this … woman, Ted. You've been arrested. Lost your friends. Ignored promises. Poor Jennifer was beside herself with worry." She paused, as if sifting for the correct tone. "Maybe it's better for you to be apart."

To be fair, things hadn't been so shit hot before he'd moved either. Jenny's concern was news to Ted, and welcome.

"Me and Tilda need to be together, Mom. It'll be bad if we aren't."

He wasn't sure why he was being so honest. But it was hard to lie. His mother eyed him quizzically, as if unsure what to make of that statement. She dabbed at her eyes, and put on a smile he was certain she wasn't quite ready to feel.

"Come on. I'll make some tea."

"I'd like that," Ted said. His voice sounded raw and small, surprising him.

The house hadn't changed since he'd taken what he could fit into The Goat and hit the road for Winnipeg and a job offer at Svarta Mining that had turned out to be a lie, and a lure.

His mom asked, "What's with that beard? You look like a hobo."

"I do some consulting for a mining company up north." Truth, if not the whole truth. And if by "true," he was taking Loki's idea of the concept rather than the one used by the rest of the world. "It's cold up there. And there are bugs."

Her eyes fell on the ink peering out from under the sleeve of his shirt. "I see there are tattoo parlours, too."

Ted almost said his tattoos were unrelated to his work, and had to bite back a laugh.

"I'm glad you got the job."

"I didn't," Ted said. "But a … different position opened up."

"I hope you like it better than the patch." She took a longer look at Ted. "You're sure you're okay? You've got thin."

He smiled. He wouldn't call himself thin. "Exercise, Mom. It's all good."

From the kitchen, Mike snorted. "Exercise? You mean lifting a whiskey bottle?"

"Michael! Enough."

Mike came out with a cup of coffee, looking completely unchastened.

"How are the kids?" Ted asked, trying the only subject that he and his brother could agree on. Cam and Carrie were the best things his brother had ever done.

Mike's face brightened, but that might've been the rum. "They're sleeping," he said. "Stick around and maybe you'll get to see them."

Mike's phone buzzed as headlights pulled into the driveway.

"That's Val," Mike said. He took another swig of coffee and gave their mom a half-salute on his way out the door.

"Where's the Sergeant?" Ted asked as the door clicked shut.

His mother put on a patient smile Ted knew to be false. "Your father is at the Legion."

It was a bit of a relief, not to have to deal with the both of them together. But delaying the inevitable would bring no joy either. Especially if the Sergeant had been drinking. And if he was at the Legion, that's what he'd be doing.

"What's the occasion?"

"A wake."

That explained why his mom was dressed up. She would have gone to the funeral with his dad, regardless of whether she'd known the soldier who'd passed away. But she rarely had more than a glass or two of wine, and those always with dinner.

"Want me to pick him up? I could go."

She shook her head. "You've been drinking too. I'll wait until your father calls."

She would have dropped him off at the Legion, he wouldn't

have taken a cab. Ted wondered whether his dad would drive home.

"Maybe it's better if you settle in here," she said. Her eyes ran up and down his tattoos again. There'd been no long-sleeved shirts in the stack of clothing that Loki had stolen for him, and those shirts wouldn't hide the tattoos on his hands.

Settle in.

Not likely.

But he headed into the basement towards his old room. The dog followed him to the stairs, growling. It barked his entire way down.

The basement had been tidied up considerably since Ted had left. Shelves of things his family had collected over the years weren't emptied or organized, but gone entirely. As if his mother had taken the lot and sent it by flatbed truck to Goodwill or the Salvation Army. It was, if not cold, pleasantly cooler than the rest of the house. Most folks in Edmonton didn't bother with AC. Heatwaves in the city rarely lasted more than a couple days, and this far north, summer evenings cooled off quickly. He hoped somebody knocked some sense into the weather, because he couldn't.

The door to his old room was open. Ted walked in and dropped his bag on the floor. Everything was different. A floral comforter covered the bed. As soon as Ted sat down on it, he knew the bed was new. His second-hand furniture had all been replaced with what looked like slick pieces from Ikea. A painting of a log cabin next to a lake in the mountains was hung where Ted's autographed Warren Moon poster had once resided. The only evidence Ted had ever lived in this room were the trophies from his high school football days. Those had been moved from a wall shelf that now held bookended paperbacks to the bureau, placed on either side of the oval mirror.

Ted checked the closet. Only bare wire hangers. It had been full of some clothes that had no longer fit when he'd left. Some had been there since his university days. No great losses there, he supposed.

While the rest of the room had received a serious makeover, the inside of the closet had not. Score marks from the hangers hitting the drywall hadn't been patched up.

There was a safe in that closet. It had been built right into one of the walls. No one knew the combination. At least that was the story the family told. Ted knew the combination. A stoner at school, who would end up serving five to eight for his part in some break-ins, had had a gift with locks, and could crack most old-time safes by feel. He'd done so back in junior year. Ted had been hoping for a stash of cash, or valuable coins or bonds, something that would allow him to live well and not work.

That hadn't panned out. The safe had been empty when they'd opened it. No hint remained of why it had been placed there, or what it might have held. Ted had enjoyed imagining what could have been, however, long after those first hopes had been crushed. And the safe hadn't remained empty for long. It was large enough to hide a twelve of beer, and kept it cool, if not ice-cold. And a place to keep the odd joint stashed away safely. He tried to remember if he'd left any beer in there. If he had, they'd have long ago gone skunk.

His fingers twitched as if the muscles and tendons remembered the combination. He spun the dial, smiling. *Twenty-four, nine, zero.*

He gave the safe door a tug, but it didn't open.

Ted tried the combination again. Still locked. He squinted at the lock. It was dusty, so it hadn't been disturbed recently. He could, if he wanted to, tear the door off. That would reawaken his powers. Not what he wanted while he was so close to Surtur, didn't know how to kill the giant, and was squatting in his parents' house.

There was an insistent tapping at the window that looked out over the lawn.

A raven stared through the glass at him. Ted closed and locked his bedroom door, before he opened the window to let Muninn in. The bird hopped through the gap, and there was a flutter of wings as he came to land on Ted's shoulder.

"Perhaps I might be of assistance?"

"Sure."

"You misremember. The final number was not zero, but three. The tumbler was loose, and would accept a range."

If the tumbler was loose, who fixed it?

"That is not one of the things I have learned."

Ted grimaced. Evidently the ravens could still read his

thoughts, although they had to speak aloud for him to understand. "I assume that implies that you've learned *something*?"

"I might tell you, if you learn to appreciate me."

Ted gave the revised combination a spin, listening for the satisfying click of the tumbler falling into place. He pulled the door open. Inside the safe was a squat bottle of premium bourbon and an envelope. While Ted hadn't known what he may or may not have left in the safe, neither of those items rang a bell. The envelope was sealed. It had a slight bulge and weight that told Ted it held more than a letter. Ted slid a fingernail along the edge, slicing the paper. He pulled out a folded note. It had the same handwriting as another note that Loki had made appear in Ted's wallet when he'd borrowed the *dvergar* no-limit credit card.

It read: *You're welcome. Loki.*

Ted gave the envelope a shake and a plastic baggy that held two rolled, thick joints tumbled out. The baggy had its own note: *For later.*

"If I may be the voice of caution, Theodore, I would not smoke any narcotic provided to you by Loki."

The liquor he conjured never fucked me up.

"To put it bluntly, you are well used to consuming alcohol."

Ted tucked the joints into his pocket. *I'll take your concerns under advisement. Now what have you learned?*

"I thought you would never ask," Muninn said. "There have been more assaults, more missing people, and more murders. Not noticeably so. Naturally, Winnipeg has had it worse in the last year."

"Thanks," Ted muttered.

"It was not a rebuke, merely a statement," Muninn said. "The rise is being attributed to a downturn in the economy, more homeless, more jobless, an ongoing result of Surtur's fires."

"So he's indirectly to blame as well as directly to blame?"

"Yes. He is spreading his influence across your country, and further. His fires have spread so far and so deep that in Niflheim, Yggdrasill's dead roots burn." Muninn paused. "Soon he will be everywhere."

And I'm caught in the middle of it.

"Why didn't I hear any of this?" Ted asked.

"You did not send us to Alberta," Muninn said. "As we suggested."

"We had enough business to take care of back home, and I didn't want to poke the bear until I knew how to kill him."

"Fair enough," Muninn conceded. "But while Surtur has never been subtle, it would appear he has learned something from his imprisonment. He has followers throughout the province."

"Not surprising."

"Indeed. As you suspected, this Church of the Eternal Flame is his tool."

"I'm surprised he'd bother creating a religion if he's going to end the world."

"I said it was his tool, not his creation. Mortals have never needed much to see the divine or demonic in natural phenomena. It began innocently enough."

"For a doomsday cult."

"Yes. But as they burned their sacrifices and prayed for deliverance, Surtur heard them. And realized they could be used. He calls pilgrims to the edges of the flames. Imparts them with a modicum of his power. Then sends them out to recruit more. They are able to perform small magicks. Enough to be seen as miracle-workers by the gullible. And so he grows his army beyond what waits in Muspelheim."

Ted didn't like that one bit. He'd seen Surtur use people before: the vapour ghosts who had once been Ted's coworkers in the patch and had joined Surtur's exploratory attack on Flin Flon.

"What if I steal that flame from them?"

"As you did with Surtsúlfar?"

"Yeah."

"It will not diminish Surtur, if that is what you are hoping. His power is endless and self-replenishing, tied as it is to Muspelheim, and creation."

"If I can't lessen his power, I can grow my own."

"Would you trust power stolen from your adversary?"

Ted hadn't thought of that. He didn't have any idea what he'd do with the fire he'd lifted. Hearing from Muninn that his possession of the flame would do nothing to harm Surtur made it seem all the more dangerous to be carrying it around trapped in his Zippo. He dug it out of his pocket. It was as warm as if he'd just used it.

"I did not say it would do nothing to harm Surtur, I merely stated that it would not diminish him. He could share his flame with every mortal on Midgard and still remain King of Muspelheim."

"That's a frightening thought. How'd you pick this up?"

"I read between the lines of what a particularly crafty mortal knew. That reporter who interviewed you after Surtur's arrival."

"Colour me suspicious of particularly crafty anybody. Especially her. We didn't get along."

"Wise, given your past history with tricksters. And your continuing desire to engage with them."

"Loki is going to show up whether I like it or not. And when she does, she is going to do what Loki does."

Muninn nodded in agreement.

"The best I can hope for is to direct our ends towards the same purpose. So long as Surtur wants to burn the Earth and Loki resides here, I think we can trust her to fuck with me for fun, but not double-cross me in a serious way. Besides, Huginn's trailing her."

As if conjured by Ted's thought of the raven, Huginn flew in through the open window to land on his shoulder.

"I have lost Loki."

"Goddammit!"

"Perhaps you should go back to Winnipeg," Muninn said.

Ted wasn't a "go back" guy. Eyes front, power through. Get 'er done. Winnipeg was in good hands. Or at least, in hand. Edmonton had no defence. It would be ground zero for Surtur's attack. When he attacked.

And it seemed pretty clear that "when" was going to be soon.

"Warn Robin and Aiko."

"**And the Norns?**"

Ted nodded, although he wasn't sure what they could do. Their power and most of their knowledge of the Nine had passed on to Tilda. Maybe they could get a message to her. Maybe she'd know what to do.

He wasn't sure how deep the protective fence he'd built around Winnipeg ran. Whether it could stop Surtur's fires.

Someone was coming down the stairs; the click-clack of Samson's nails followed. Ted shoved the ravens into his closet and shut the door. They squawked and fluttered.

"Ted," his mother called. Her voice was imbued with the long-suffering tone he recognized from the worst of his fuck-ups. "There's a policeman here, asking for you."

9. Same Boy You've Always Known

He wasn't in uniform, but he had cop-walk.

Ted knew that walk well. He was leaning ever so slightly, favouring his gun side, though Ted didn't see a sidearm. It had little to do with knowing the man attached to that walk was, in fact, a cop. It made Ted conscious of the fact he was carrying two joints laced with gods-knew-what. He stuffed the baggie further into his jeans.

Constable Dennis Fontaine of the Flin Flon detachment of the RCMP. Ted hadn't seen him since the events up north. Fontaine was walking around pretty good for someone who'd taken an arrow in the shoulder and another in the guts. But then, Ted had healed him of the worst of those two wounds.

Samson had been shut up behind a baby gate, and was barking his fool head off. Ted wasn't certain that gate would stop a baby, let alone 130 pounds of angry dog.

With an incline of his head, Ted said, "Constable."

"Mr. Callan."

"Mr. Callan is my dad," Ted said.

Fontaine didn't smile.

With a sigh, Helen asked, "Do I need to call him a lawyer?"

Ted looked at Fontaine. “Does she?”

The cop smiled at Ted’s mom, attempting to be reassuring. “No, ma’am. Mr. Callan spoke with the EPS regarding a fire earlier, the RCMP would like to ask some follow-up questions.”

“Fire?” She asked, sounding worried. “What fire?”

There was no point in lying, she’d find out. Still, there was no need to mention the smell. Or the screams. Or that the “victim” worshipped a giant wanting to end life on Earth.

“I met Rye for a drink at Howling Wolf’s,” Ted said. Helen’s face hardened. “Somebody lit themselves on fire in the parking lot.”

“Oh my God!”

“Mr. Callan and his companion—” Fontaine checked a notebook—“Jennifer Hildebrandt were the first on the scene. Mr. Callan attempted to put out the fire. Ms. Hildebrandt called 911.”

“Fire wouldn’t go out,” Ted said. “I couldn’t make it stop.”

“That poor man. His family will be in my prayers.” Helen reached out to touch the tips of Ted’s fingers. “Why didn’t you tell me?”

“I didn’t want to upset you.”

“Lying upsets me.”

“I didn’t lie.”

“Omission isn’t the truth.”

Fontaine couldn’t hide his shit-eating grin, as if he found it amusing that someone with Ted’s powers was still caught up in a parental scolding. Cop or no cop, if he laughed, Ted was going to slug him.

"Mrs. Callan, the sooner I speak with your son, the sooner he'll be home."

Helen nodded and said, "Of course. Ted, I'll probably be asleep when you come in. Try not to wake the dog."

Samson growled as Ted followed Fontaine out of the house.

Good fucking luck.

Fontaine gestured towards the front passenger seat of a civilian vehicle, and not the cage of an RCMP cruiser when he said, "Get in," so that was a good sign. Ted joined Fontaine in the car and they headed downtown.

"This isn't about the guy who ignited himself, is it?" Ted asked.

"Not entirely," Fontaine admitted. "I saw your name in the report, and since I moved here, I thought I'd touch base with you."

"Why would the Mounties be looking at that report?"

"We've been following the arsons for a while. With this fire cult spreading into Saskatchewan, we're taking a serious interest. I want you to come and take a look at one of the arson sites."

That surprised Ted. "I'm no detective."

Fontaine laughed. "You consult for Svarta, you can consult for me."

"They pay me."

"I won't arrest you."

"For what?"

With a smile, Fontaine turned and said, "Whatever I want to."

Ted laughed. Fontaine had him there. "Sure. I'll take a look. Why'd you move?"

"Transferred," Fontaine said.

"You're in danger here."

Fontaine shrugged. "I'm an Indian and a cop. I'm always in danger."

"The dwarves said they'd keep you safe."

Fontaine sniffed. "That's a hell of a way to keep me safe."

"So I take it you're not exchanging Christmas cards, then," Ted said.

"No." He took a sip of his coffee, and then Fontaine added, "I don't forget when someone tries to kill me."

"Good for you. I'm starting to lose track of when it happens to me."

Fontaine held up the police tape, and Ted slid under. "I could lose my job for sneaking you in here, you know, so try not to be you."

"You could lose everything if you don't."

Fontaine pulled a pissy face, but didn't say much else. The runes tattooed on Ted's back tingled as he stepped over the threshold of the remains of the building. Whatever had happened here was calling to them. They may have been hidden by Loki, but Yggdrasill wanted to emerge in response to the arson site. That told Ted enough.

In his mind's eye, ghostly echoes of future flames burned. People would keep immolating themselves, and committing arson in Surtur's name, so long as the giant lived. To Ted it felt like the magic of the giant's flames still burned here, smouldering. Waiting. He couldn't explain it, but he could feel the anticipation of the flames, wanting to cut loose. Wanting to consume all.

"Magic *was* used here," he said.

Fontaine let out a long sigh, he probably hadn't known he'd been holding in. The Mountie followed it up with a muttered, "Shit."

"Not what you wanted to hear?"

"No."

"Not what I wanted to find," Ted said. "Magic and fire. That's a dangerous combo anywhere. Especially this close to the patch." *And what was waiting there.*

"I suppose I should be happy it was monsters and not people."

"Oh, it was people. They had some help, but I think those doomsayers in the Church of the Flame are your first suspects."

"You know about them?" Underlying Fontaine's question, Ted got the sense there was an unspoken demand to know why Ted hadn't shared this information sooner.

"A buddy told me they'd popped up last fall, but I never heard anything else, and so I didn't give them much thought."

"Nothing they've done would have made national news. Hell, even the Calgary news. But we've been keeping an eye on them."

"*Hmpf,*" Ted mumbled. "And?"

"Nothing major, as I said. A couple break-and-enters. Some petty theft. A couple missing persons, who ended up being found with them. But since the persons were over eighteen and didn't want to leave, there wasn't anything to be done. I get a bad feeling about their leader."

"You've met him?"

"Her," Fontaine corrected. "Tall drink of water, blonde, with an eye patch. Would be beautiful if she didn't look like she wanted to cut you." He shuddered. "She stared at me like I was already a dead man."

He flipped on his flashlight once they were inside. "Watch where you step," Fontaine mumbled. "Floors may not be safe."

The beam cut a swath of light through the burned building, motes of dust and ash, a fuzzy snow in the narrow beam of illumination stirred by their steps. Ted thought something skittered away from the light. He strained his ears, but didn't hear anything.

Ted pulled a cigarette out and put it to his lips. Fontaine stopped him before he could light it.

"You want to be dropping butts with your DNA all over them in a potential crime scene?"

Ted grimaced, but tucked the lighter and pack away.

Fontaine sniffed the air. "Somebody's been smoking in here. And recently."

Ted tested the air, his brow crinkling. Hidden in the old smoke scent of the burnt building, was a fresher, more pleasant smell. Cigarette smoke. "You're right."

"Someone *is* here," Fontaine whispered. "I can hear them breathing."

Ted didn't argue. He'd been to enough loud concerts, and worked around enough loud machinery, that he doubted his hearing was what it should be. Being constantly trapped in a thunderstorm didn't help, either.

Fontaine scanned his flashlight towards the sound, sweeping across the ruins of the building, his hand on a knife sheath.

Ted clenched his fist, wanting to feel the rumble of storm clouds across his chest and the crackle of lightning over his fist. But with his powers subsumed there was nothing. He was vulnerable. Mortal. *If* Loki had done her work—and Ted wanted to believe the trickster had, despite the freak on the train. Whatever his connection to the Nine was, and wherever Loki had hidden it, for tonight, at least, Ted was just a man.

He'd forgotten that sense of vulnerability, had grown used to his invulnerability and power. Fear was, if not quite a thing of the past, no longer a constant companion. A shiver ran through his body at the hidden sounds, and gooseflesh prickled beneath his tattoos. Anyone—anything—could be hiding in the shadows and Ted had to rely on Fontaine to keep him safe. Or at least keep him hidden. If Ted's powers were activated by a real threat, Surtur would feel him. It wasn't so far to the northern fires where the giant squatted and fumed at his imprisonment.

Ted imagined what could be here: one of the minions of Surtur. A vapour ghost, a troll, a dragon, some monster that Huginn and Muninn hadn't thought to reveal to him. Göndul herself. They'd never found the valkyrie's body. There was still so much he didn't know.

Something squeaked. Fontaine's light caught a rat scurrying. It froze for a second, and Ted was pretty sure the fucker winked at him. A second later, the rat disappeared out of the light and a woman screamed.

She rushed out from behind some debris, pawing at her dreadlocks. It was the woman from the LRT station. *What the hell was she doing here?*

She moved slowly now, shielding her eyes from the light of Fontaine's flashlight.

"RCMP." Fontaine had a knife pointed at the woman. "Let's see the ID. Slowly."

She reached into her purse.

"Why don't you toss that over here?"

She stooped to get the purse on the ground and kicked it over with a regretful look at the filthy ground. A bunch of shit clattered out, but nothing that looked like a weapon.

Ted leaned into Fontaine's ear. "I know her."

"You would."

"She was on my train today, before that guy lit himself up."

Fontaine pinched the bridge of his nose. "Who are you and what are you doing here?"

"I could ask you the same thing. I want to see your badge. Since this is not an RCMP case, and he's *not* a cop. Are you, Mr. Callan?"

How'd she know my name?

Then it clicked. She wasn't a monster he hadn't faced. It was a different creature and no less dangerous for the fact that Ted recognized her from his mortal life. That most dangerous of Midgard threats—the reporter.

She hadn't changed much since she'd grilled him after the explosion in the patch that had freed Surtur. Her dreadlocks were a little longer. She'd changed her glasses. Might have a new piercing. He couldn't say for sure on that note. He couldn't believe he hadn't recognized her in the LRT station.

"She's a reporter. Sally Kroeger."

Fontaine mumbled a curse under his breath. "Who he is, is none of your concern, Ms. Kroeger. I'd be more concerned about your criminal trespassing."

"I'm a consultant," Ted said, trotting out his usual lie.

Fontaine shot Ted a "shut the fuck up" look. It didn't matter. Sally didn't seem concerned.

"You nearly had me fooled in Bay Street Station with the tats and the beard."

"So what gave me away?"

"That pissed off look on your face. You pulled that same face when I didn't believe your story about a giant in the patch."

Ted wanted to tell her, *show* her, it wasn't bullshit. But he held his tongue. Knowing his luck, she'd figure it out soon enough.

"Wait. Is this about what you told me after the explosion at Fort Mac? You seriously expect me to swallow your giant-monster-in-the-flames story? What a load of crap."

Ted let her talk. He had nothing to add that would keep her safe. In fact, curious as she was regarding the events surrounding *these* fires, and Surtur's arrival, Ted was surprised she was still alive.

"You think your *story* is responsible for these fires?" she said. "People would have seen a three-hundred-foot giant man made of fire. And somewhere other than the *Weekly World News* would have reported it."

Fontaine snapped a set of handcuffs on Sally. "No one is reporting anything."

She looked surprised that the cop was doing his job. Ted wouldn't feel bad if she did time. She hadn't been too sensitive to Ted's feelings when interviewing him after Surtur had blown up his work site. She'd been a bitch to some of the other survivors, too. Most of those guys were dead now. They'd survived the blast, but Surtur had picked them off one by one in the meantime. If he hadn't, some other monster had. Ted wouldn't have been surprised to learn that he was the only "survivor" of Surtur's arrival still surviving.

"You can't arrest me," Sally said. "I'll tell them—"

"Tell them what?" Fontaine asked. "That an off-duty cop saw you crossing a police line? Nothing will happen to me on your word."

That shut her up. Ted wondered how long it would last.

"You didn't listen to me before," Ted said.

He felt his tattoos wanting to come out. Mjölnir, the storm. He itched and burned for the lightning to come, and show her how fucking real Surtur was. Ted crushed that feeling down. It wouldn't help anyone. Her eyes went wide. Ted ground his teeth and took a deep breath. He hadn't meant to threaten her. Something in his stance must have come across that way.

Sally stepped back, stumbled over debris and fell. Fontaine jerked her to her feet.

"You treated me like another ignorant rig pig. Already had your story and were crossing the Ts and dotting the Is. All about the land and nothing about the men who lost their lives on it. Did you follow up on everyone in Fort Mac who lost their homes? Lost *everything*? Do you know how many of those guys you interviewed are dead now?"

She didn't look away or look ashamed, but her silence told Ted he was correct.

"Listen to me now. Stop digging. You won't find the answers you're looking for and the ones you will find won't stop with words."

"Are you threatening me?"

"Me? Shit no. I want you to live a long and healthy and ignorant life."

If Loki had been there, Ted imagined the trickster doing a serviceable Nicholson and adding, "You can't handle the truth." Or knowing Loki, he'd bust out a *Star Wars* reference to piss Ted off. "Not the droids you're looking for," to paraphrase.

"You should leave, Ms. Kroeger," Fontaine said, taking her cuffs off.

"You're not arresting me?"

"Should I?" Fontaine was calm, matter-of-fact, but no less serious as lightning when he made his own threat. "You have weed in your purse? I see your pipe on the floor there. Leave. *Now*."

Fontaine tossed Sally's purse back at her. She caught it and gathered up her belongings, stuffing them inside. Ted fell in behind Sally and Fontaine as the cop escorted her out. Ted's eyes drifted downward, watching her gait. He stubbed his toe and snapped his eyes back up. He needed to get laid. He'd been a bit busy to find dates. True, a couple of women *álfar* had hit on him back in Winnipeg, but he hadn't been certain he'd survive the experience.

Once they were outside, Ted offered her his number. "In case you won't listen to reason, give me a call if you cross anything you can't handle."

She laughed. "I already have your number, Mr. Callan. And if I can't handle something, what makes you think you can?"

They let Sally leave.

Fontaine insisted on waiting around longer than Ted was comfortable to ensure she didn't double back. Ted didn't like leaving the fire ready to ignite again, but didn't know what else to do. He could use runes to pull the flames into his lighter, but containing them would mean his hiding days were over. Surtur would know.

The tornado that had come through here in '87 would look like a fucking summer breeze next to a three-hundred-foot-tall walking volcano showing up downtown.

Ted had stolen a fair amount of Surtur's flames in Saskatoon.

The warmth of the metal felt as if Ted had left the lighter burning for a good long stretch, or abandoned it in the sun. It wasn't hot enough to burn him. Yet.

Lock, lock, lock.

Surtur was in there.

The Zippo wanted to be used. Which meant Surtur *wanted* it to be used.

Which means I'm stuck using a shitty disposable for the duration. Ted supposed he could buy a new Zippo, but it wouldn't be the same. *This* was his lighter. Scratched and scuffed; dented and old, he'd owned it as long as he'd smoked. His mother's voice told him he should just *quit smoking.*

He'd already lost The Goat. It was stupid, but he wanted to hang on to what parts of himself he still could. Sally showing up was a reminder of everything he'd lost, and everything he'd given up to come home.

Ted shook his head.

"God, why'd *she* need to be involved?"

Fontaine shrugged. "You've got a special brand of luck, Callan."

Ted sighed. He was turning into the ravens, correcting people on myth and magic. "Yeah, I believe it's called *doom.*"

10. All You Ever Wanted

Ted couldn't breathe.

There was a weight on his chest. He was suffocating. All he saw was black. His nostrils filled with an animal scent.

Mara!

Ted rolled out of bed, hurling Hel's former minion away from him. She flew through the air with an angry yowl. Ted's heart pounded as his feet hit the carpet. Mjölnir was useless against the Mara—a living nightmare. Ted opened his mouth to speak the rune that would banish the monster.

"*Mew.*"

The rune died on his lips as a cat cried.

"What the fuck?"

A cat padded back across the floor, purring, and rubbed up against Ted's leg.

Goddammit. When had his parents got a fucking cat?

He'd been ready to blow his disguise and risk the deaths of an entire city, because of a goddamned cat. He shooed it away with one bare foot, but the cat, an orange shorthair, insistently wove itself around and between his legs, tail gripping one calf and then the other.

Ted rubbed at his eyes. Fontaine had kept him out later than he would have liked and this was a hell of a way to wake up. He let his breath steady. At least he had a day to recover before he had to deal with Rye's family at the wedding rehearsal. The cat had abandoned him, only to get seemingly caught up in his pant leg.

It would be great if that reporter would let this story go, but Ted doubted she would. Even with Loki on his side, he wasn't *that* lucky.

The heavy curtains that used to block out the light so he could sleep off the night before had been replaced with ones that were light and gauzy. They let too much damned light into the basement. Probably why they'd been chosen, but it still felt too damned early to be awake. He pulled on a fresh pair of underwear and last night's jeans before digging a shirt out his bag. This one said, "Keeping it Loki."

Cute.

He was surprised the shirt didn't have Loki's grinning face on it, so he supposed he should count his blessings. Wherever she was, Ted had no doubt the trickster was laughing her ass off.

Ted opened the bedroom door and Samson was waiting for him on the rug. The dog barked. Ted had to wonder if the damned thing *was* Loki. Wouldn't have been the first time the trickster had insinuated herself into Ted's family. The possibility gave him a headache. He rubbed at his temples and then dropped his arm. Ted's motion must have been too rapid for Samson, because the dog shot to his feet and growled, tail low and flat and all his considerable coat standing out on end.

"Jesus, dog," Ted muttered, and then louder, "Give it a fucking rest."

Samson bolted forward and snapped at Ted. He jerked his hand away and the dog's teeth closed on air. Samson settled in for a good bark, inching his way around Ted, as if he were looking for that one magic spot where he could herd the intruder out of his home. Dogs were what they were. So were cats. So was Loki.

Assholes.

"I lived here first, you know."

The answering bark told Ted that if Samson could understand him, he wouldn't give a shit, he only cared that Ted didn't live there *now*.

Samson's irrational hatred drove Ted nuts. He loved dogs. He missed having one. A new pooch barking behind the door was exciting. As if the simple fact of there being a dog at his parents' house again would make it feel more like home.

But it didn't.

It wasn't home.

It could never be home again.

Not after what he'd seen, and done. Not with what he had left to do.

Even if Samson had met Ted with a wagging tail and a lick to the face, it would take more than an animal to roll back the years. But goddammit, they could help you ignore it for a time. Instead of reminding you every goddamn minute of every goddamn day.

"Fuck this, and fuck you, you grumpy bastard," Ted said.

He had to take a piss. That didn't meet with Samson's approval either. The dog followed him, growling all the way.

The cat's litterbox was in his old bathroom.

The tail end of breakfast was waiting for Ted after he'd showered and went up to the kitchen. He swore he could still smell the smoke from the crime scene on his clothes, and in his hair, lingering. Some cold but buttered toast, a jar of jam, plates that had once had sausage and bacon, judging from the grease, and a bowl of fruit that looked as if it hadn't been touched.

If Ted's mom had aged, his dad still seemed forged out of iron. Hard. Tough. He and Mike shared a love of moustaches that could stop a bullet. If anything, the Sergeant seemed in better shape than ever. Ted hoped his dad wasn't going to tell him to lace up his gloves.

"Tattoos," the Sergeant said, putting down his newspaper. "Next thing, you'll be voting for the goddamned NDP."

"Pop…"

The doorbell rang and the Sergeant got up and walked away from the table as Samson raced along, barking. There was a flurry of activity, and voices all together. Samson's barking stopped and the dog rushed away, back through the kitchen, nails skittering over hardwood.

What would spook that big, mean bastard?

"Heya, Unca Ted!" Ted's nephew, Cameron yelled.

Ah.

Cam ran past his mother Valerie and sister Carrie to hug him. His nephew had always been a tornado of energy. Loved everybody, and expected everybody to love him. Ted tried to kneel, but the boy had already latched on to his leg.

"Hey, buddy," Ted said tousling the boy's blond hair.

Carrie, the older of the two, was more hesitant. She stood behind her brother with her arms crossed, all elbows and knees. She had glasses now, and dressed as if she were already a teenager. Ted shook his head. It hadn't been that long since he'd seen them. And yet Val didn't seem happy in the least to have a full-on Callan reunion. Her frown encompassed her sensible shoes and nurse's scrubs, and ran all the way to the top of her mop of curly hair.

"My dad's mad at you."

"Carrie!" her mother yelled.

"Well he *is,*" Carrie said, her voice dripping innocence.

"Don't worry, kiddo," Ted said, smiling. "That's nothing new."

At least Mike had stopped yelling at him with the kids around. Mike looked like he'd lost weight. Ted would have thought Afghanistan had agreed with him, but he didn't look happy.

"Where you been?" Cam asked, tugging at Ted's shirt.

"Busy with work," Ted said, choosing the most comfortable—the safest—lie. "But I missed you guys."

"How much?"

Ted stretched his arms out as wide as he could, and faked straining from the effort. "This much," he said.

They smiled at that.

"Why's there a naked lady on your arm?" Cam asked.

Ted dropped his arms, trying to hide the tattoo that had replaced Mjölnir. He shrugged. "I woke up with it."

"Tattoo or lady?" Val muttered. "Probably not a first for either."

Ted did his best to keep from shooting her a scowl, and keeping his smile up for the kids. It wasn't hard. He was glad to see them.

"If you're so busy, what're you doing home now?" Carrie asked.

"Here for a wedding. But I sure am glad to see you little buggers."

"Watch your language, please," Val said, maybe mishearing him, maybe operating on instinct.

Cam's eyes glittered. Mike fought a grin too.

"You know Ted," Mike said. "That's as close as he's likely to watch his mouth."

The kids tittered.

"We brought the swear jar," Cam said, pulling a peanut butter container with a slot cut in the lid out of his backpack. Some change rattled around with each happy shake of the boy's fist.

"You did?" Ted asked, pretending surprise.

"Yup!" Cam said, serious as could be.

Ted turned out the pockets of his jeans. Some lint, a loonie, a couple of dimes, and an old washer dropped out.

"*Hmmm*," Ted said, examining the bounty. "That's not going to cover much."

Cam's face crumpled. "I was hoping to get a new game after this weekend."

Ted grabbed a few twenties from his wallet. He folded them up and stuffed them into the jar as the kids stared wide-eyed.

"How about you call it even, and I can say any damn thing I want?"

"Me too!" Cam yelled. "Shitdamnboobs!"

"Cam!"

"Uncle Ted paid for it," he protested. "I can say anything I want to."

"Sorry buddy," Ted said, pulling a twenty out of the jar. "That's not how it works. That shitdamnboobs is coming out of your share of the jar."

Cam pouted and Carrie smiled. Val still scowled, but seemed mollified by Ted's half-assed attempt at discipline. She turned back to go into the kitchen and Ted slipped another five into the jar.

"It won't cost you," he whispered conspiratorially, winking at Mike as he returned the bill. "And spot your dad a few on me too, okay, buddy?"

"No!" Cam yelled gleefully. "Daddy has to pay!"

Val went home to sleep. According to Mike she was working nights at the Cross. Playing with the kids tired him out. It was harder to watch his tongue, not about magic, but in general.

Looking into their eyes, he also saw the life he could've had. Watching the Sergeant with his grandkids, compared to how he'd been when Ted and Mike had been growing up, was like seeing two different people. The stern disciplinarian. The distance. Everything that Ted had felt growing up melted away when he was with Mike's kids.

He was playing Go Fish with Cam, for Christ's sake.

What if Erin had lived to be born? What if Tilda were here with Ted? Would the Sergeant be coo-cooing and rocking their infant daughter? Ted hoped so.

But that wasn't going to happen. He excused himself from playing Mario Kart with Carrie—she'd been kicking his ass anyway—and if he got hit by one more shell, all the gold the *dvergar* hoarded wouldn't be enough to cover his swear jar tab.

It was great to have the kids around. Samson didn't seem to mind them, but he probably viewed them as family in a way he would never see Ted. The kids wanted his attention something fierce, especially Carrie, and he was incredibly patient with her. Cam was more concerned with chasing the cat. It was smaller than him and equally unimpressed with these small interlopers. Ted smiled as Cam pulled on the cat's tail and it yowled.

Give it hell, kid.

There were pictures of dogs scattered throughout the house. A couple were from before Ted's time. His parents had been dog people before Ted had entered the picture. All the dogs had made home feel more like home. The distance of being away, of all he'd seen, made Ted nostalgic for what was, despite knowing he no longer belonged here.

He stopped short when he came to a photo of himself with his old dog, Loki.

Loki, who, for an indeterminate time, at least, had *been* Loki.

It was Ted's favourite picture of Loki, taken back when the name belonged to his dog and not to mythology. Susanna had taken the photo the day they'd brought the dog home from the pound. Something in the shepherd mutt's one flopped-down ear, and the way she'd always seemed to be laughing, the way her tongue lolled out of her mouth was all it took to make Ted want to bring her home.

Susanna had thought Loki would grow too big for their apartment. "Look at her paws," she'd said. "This dog's going to be huge."

Ted hadn't cared.

He hadn't listened to the warnings of the staff either, that the puppy was a troublemaker and prone to fight anything larger than her when the opportunity arose. She shit in the house. She ate their garbage.

God, he missed her.

Ted liked big dogs. Dogs like Samson. Dogs he could roughhouse with. If he were going to get something that could fit in his lap he'd get a cat. And he hated cats.

So they took Loki home. And she grew, and outgrew their apartment. They'd bought their first house looking for a yard.

They'd both recognized it hadn't been fair to keep an animal cooped up in that small apartment. It hadn't done any wonders for him and Susanna, but she'd loved Loki too, and once Loki had some space of her own, Ted and Susanna settled down and settled in. It was then that they'd first talked about a family.

Ted wondered whether they would have gotten married without that damned pooch.

He smiled thinking of when that photograph had been taken, and how Loki had sat perfectly still until the moment before Susanna took the picture and then lurched up and swatted Ted in the face with a paw. His surprised reaction gave the photo a *Raging Bull* look. Ted wondered how long the trickster had impersonated his dog. Or had Loki always been his dog?

That was not the best line of thinking to pursue. The god of mischief was no tame animal, trained to obey. Not that Ted's dog had been, either. He knew he shouldn't mix his memories of the two Lokis in his life. Ted should know better than to trust her. He knew what Loki had done. She was the reason he didn't have a Norn blocking for him while he was powerless. Ted could imagine Muninn's accusation: *And still you curry her favour, as if friendship ever meant anything to Loki.*

But Ted knew that friendship meant something to *this* Loki.

She could be a terrible friend. But then, so could Rye. So could Ted. So could everyone, eventually.

Ted smiled at the photo again, at the seeming joy on the dog's face, at the surprise on his own. It wasn't hard to believe, looking back on things, that Loki had always been … Loki. Ted didn't see the trickster as one to play the long con; she was more of a used-car salesman, ready to skip town before you realized you'd bought a lemon. But thinking of the two Lokis, if the trickster had been involved in Ted's life from the beginning, had directed him on this road to being Ófriður … complicating Ted's feelings was an excellent loaded die.

If the ravens were here, they would tell Ted he was being manipulated. They would rustle their feathers under Ted's skin, put out by his refusing to listen. Their voices were a hollow echo, as if Ted had gone swimming and water was trapped in his ear canal.

The ravens had told Ted not to trust Loki. And they'd been right. Some of the time, but not all. Ted could trust that he couldn't trust Loki. She rarely acted against him out of genuine malevolence. She did appear to like him.

Ted smiled. *Takes all kinds.*

He didn't believe Loki would turn on him this time. She hadn't betrayed Ted at all. She'd done things that had pissed him off. Sometimes the trickster was ten pounds of shit in a five-pound pail, but she'd walked into Hel with Ted. Had been willing to kill her own daughter for what she'd done to Ted and Tilda. *Tilda*. Loki claimed the Norn had been the one who wanted to leave. That wasn't a betrayal, either. Not anymore. Anger had prevented him from seeing that; he'd blamed the trickster for Tilda's leaving. But she'd also never see the trickster's point of view.

If there's one thing true about Loki, it was that she loved life. She'd never side with the end of all things. Not again.

I guess I'll have to be a better friend to her than Thor and Odin were. Ted chuckled to himself. *Nothing like grabbing for low-hanging fruit.*

There was another picture frame up by the mantle. Inside was a yellowed newspaper clipping from the day he and Rye and the rest of their team had won the provincial football title. It was a crowd shot. Everyone rising up and cheering. Ted smiled at the memory. It was a good one, that's for sure. There had been few thrills in his life that had compared to that day. Uncle Chuck and him in front of The Goat, the night he met Susanna, the day she'd said she was pregnant.

All of those moments were tainted now. The Goat was scrap, lost in the cold fog of Niflheim. Susanna had left him. Their child had never been born. But this, he still had this. Something from his old life that was still pure. Something that still belonged to Ted, and to Ted alone. Something the Nine Worlds couldn't touch.

In the intervening years, he'd forgotten the names of most of those people in the stands. Muninn could probably remind him if he asked, but tonight Ted wanted to test those pathways himself. There was his mother, beaming, he knew, despite the blurry old newsprint. Mikey was next to her, a hole in the crowd, still sitting, his face probably buried in one of Ted's old comic books.

Ted took the picture down and sat in his dad's old recliner, what had been his grandfather's, and put his feet up. He wanted a smoke, but didn't need another lecture. The cat leapt up onto the chair, climbing Ted. It swatted at his head, where his raven tattoos should be. Rubbed against his neck and cheeks. A fucking nuisance.

"Off," Ted said, tossing it onto the floor.

The cat landed nimbly, and circled the chair, no doubt preparing to pounce again. Ted wished the dog would do him a favour and chase the cat out of the house, but more likely Samson would give Ted the bum's rush. He sighed and turned his gaze back to the picture.

His dad hadn't been in the picture, it was still something that disappointed Ted, but the Sergeant had been to every other game. Ted knew, rationally, that his father had been there in spirit.

A few faces stepped out of the fog, becoming clearer. Amy, the first girl he'd slept with. The guy who ran the menswear shop that had been Ted's first job. Ted had never paid much attention to the man standing next to his mother, other than the fact that he wasn't the Sergeant. He was smiling. Like everyone else. His arms were raised up in celebration. Like everyone else. Ted hadn't known him at the time the photo had been taken. But looking now, he couldn't shake the feeling that he did know who he was. He knew that smile.

Despite the yellowed old newsprint, and the blurry photo, that smile leapt out of the frame white and bright as day. A Cheshire grin. A trickster's grin. Ted didn't know the face. *Fuck me sideways, I know that smile.*

Loki.

The wood cracked. The glass cracked.

How long had he been playing with Ted's life?

Ted hadn't realized he'd been holding the picture that tightly. Loki. Sitting next to his mother in a twenty-five-year-old photo.

Why was Loki at that game? With my mother?

The first time Loki had come into Ted's life was after Surtur arrived.

Loki was the God of Lies. And trickery. But why lie about that? If the fires of Ragnarök had never burned, if Asgard had never fallen, if the trickster had remained chained still to the rock where the Aesir had left him, they would still not understand why Loki did what Loki did.

Ted wondered whether Loki understood her own motives.

She'd intervened when Andvari's *dvergar* wanted Ted dead. *Made sure they turned me into Ófriður.* Loki wanted this. Ted held out his hands, staring at the new tattoos embedded in his flesh. *Loki wanted them to make me into what I am. And I doubt her reasons were the same as the Moustache's and the Beards'.*

They had wanted to bring back the old days and the old ways. Loki had had more fun in those times. Whatever Loki's motives, when she turned up again, Ted was gonna get answers.

The floor creaked in the kitchen, and Ted knew his mother had come back inside from the garden. Ted took a deep breath to steady himself. His mom walked past the living room, and then her footsteps stopped, and she backed up and came in, stopping by Ted's side.

"What's the matter?"

Ted looked up, and he couldn't lie to her. Guile had never been in his nature, and Helen Callan had a way of catching people in any of their lies, little or big.

"I knocked this old frame down," Ted said, holding it up. "I'm sorry."

She took it from his hand. "It can be replaced. You didn't cut yourself, did you?"

He shook his head, wondering whether she'd had any inkling who she'd been sitting next to. How could she? Magic, tricks, Norse gods, none of that had any business in her world. But as had been made patently clear in Ted's life since the rig fire, *shit happens.*

"I was trying to remember some of the people in this old picture," Ted said, and placed a finger down over Loki's smile. "But for the life of me, I can't place this fellow."

Helen's mouth twitched, and curved up in a little smile, as if she was remembering something—or someone—fondly. Her cheeks flushed.

"My goodness, I haven't thought of him in years."

Ted asked, trying to hide his surprise, "You know him?"

"No," she answered. "I met him that day. I never saw him again, but he wasn't the sort of person you forget in a hurry."

You can say that again.

11. Wake Up, You're on Fire

Ted walked past his dad to grab a beer out of the fridge.

The Sergeant didn't look up from scrutinizing his cards. "You didn't call."

"Nope. Things were shitty."

"Uncle Ted!" Cam yelled, shaking the swear jar.

"I already paid, kiddo."

Sergeant snorted and laid down three fours. "More reason to call."

"I needed to sort shit—stuff—out for myself." Ted paused. "I laid a wreath for Papa."

His father gave him a "least-you-could-fucking-do" look, but the Sergeant's stiff posture loosened. "Good."

The phone rang. Ted ignored it and took a long pull of his beer. It wouldn't be for him. His mother made an exasperated noise as she walked past him to grab the phone. She eyed his beer but said nothing.

"Hello? Yes. Ted? It's for you."

"Who is it?"

A shrug was his mother's only answer. He wondered why they hadn't called his cell. The cross-section of people who knew he was in town and staying at his parents' house was pretty small. Maybe it was Jenny. He hoped it was her. It was probably Loki.

Ted took the phone from his mother. "H'lo."

"Mr. Callan," the reporter said.

Fuuuuuuuck.

Now he wished it had been Loki. He considered hanging up on her, but he doubted that would keep her out of his hair. His mom looked on from the breakfast table. Ted mouthed the word *reporter*.

"You're persistent."

"You're ignoring me. I've been trying your cell since yesterday."

"Didn't see your messages," Ted said. His phone vibrated so fiercely, and in rapid succession that Ted was worried it would leap out of his pocket. He checked the incoming messages. All from Sally Kroeger. They were there now. He shook his head.

Fucking Loki.

"I'd like to meet."

Ted glanced at his parents, watching for whether they were paying attention. "I don't think that's a good idea."

"If you don't, I'll tell everyone the truth."

"What truth might that be?" Ted said, leaving the room.

"Fires that won't go out and your role in them."

If Loki hadn't hidden Ted's gifts, his grip would've shattered the phone. "You didn't believe any of that last year. Or last night."

"I believe it now."

"What changed your mind?"

"I've got proof. Proof of what you are, and what you've done."

Shit.

She might be bluffing. She was probably bluffing. Maybe she wanted him to talk to Fontaine about the investigation. But if she dug too deep, and in the wrong place, *boom.*

If Ted didn't go, she'd end up dead. She'd tip off the wrong folks that he was here too.

He sighed and rubbed at the bridge of his nose. "Where do you want to meet?"

He looked up Sally Kroeger. He'd never bothered after their first run-in. Thinking of how she'd spoken to him, and to other survivors of the fire in the patch, got his blood hot. But he'd only had their first encounter to judge her on, and coming off antagonistic wasn't going to help him any—she'd only dig in.

Sally had a blog. Her Twitter feed was full of activism. Talking shit about the oil industry, the seal hunt, the prime minister and the Alberta premier, former and current. But that was all common enough. What struck Ted were the tweets about the fires in the patch.

"Why aren't we stopping these?"

"What aren't they telling us?"

"This man was reported dead in an explosion three years ago. This picture was taken yesterday."

Ted knew him. They'd worked together. Terry Whitehorse. Surtur had turned the former pipefitter into a vapour ghost able to burn Ted through his dragon-scale tattoos. He didn't want to run into Terry now.

Cam and Carrie weren't happy that Ted was leaving. Neither were his parents. Telling the kids he had to talk to a reporter about a fire only made things worse. They wanted to come with him.

He should've made Sally pick him up, since she was inconveniencing him, but he didn't want her at his parents' place. Especially with his parents home and Mike's kids there. No telling what the chick would say. It would lead to questions that Ted didn't want to answer, and his mom was aces at catching him in a lie. He wouldn't put it past Sally to show up anyway. Realistically, if she had found the phone number, she already had the address.

As for getting a ride, he doubted she owned a tandem bicycle. Ted considered asking to borrow his mom's car. But knowing his luck, it would get trashed, just like The Goat had. It was a long walk to the LRT, but he hated the bus. And he had time. And if he was late, and made her wait for him, so be it.

He plugged the meeting place she'd given him into his phone. Goddamn it.

She'd asked him to meet her at a vegan restaurant.

Sally was waiting at Centennial's when Ted arrived. Headphones around her neck, sunglasses on, and phone in front of her face.

The restaurant was named for its owner, born in Canada's centennial year, according to the website. What the website didn't show him was a single fucking thing on the menu he'd want to eat. Ted had only walked a few blocks from the bus stop, and he felt like he was covered in a slick of sweat. He was pretty sure he hadn't stopped sweating since he'd arrived in Edmonton. He gave a tentative sniff at his pits, but didn't smell anything worse than ordinary. Despite seeming to be engrossed in a game or video, Ted caught her checking the entrance and exits. She had her back to the stone wall in a corner booth.

She smiled when she noticed him, but it wasn't a friendly smile. Probably laughing her tits off that she'd gotten him in the door. It hardly took an oracle to figure he was a carnivore. She seemed quite pleased with herself. But Ted refused to be egged on this early. They'd probably get to arguing soon enough. There was no point in doing it over something as meaningless as her poor taste in restaurants.

Ted wondered if acting dumb was the smarter play for this meeting. Loki or the ravens might've insisted that there was no "playing" necessary. Deny, deny, deny. While that might've been smarter, his showing up tacitly admitted Sally might have something on him. What mattered was that Ted didn't think she was going to give up. She'd crossed a police line. She'd tracked him down. Left over a dozen messages. No, she wasn't going to give up.

Ted sat in front of her. Music blared from the headphones. "You wanted my attention, you've got it."

Sally removed her headphones and wrapped the cord around

her fingers, before tucking them into her purse. She took off her glasses and her eyes were bloodshot from lack of sleep, tears, or hangover. Maybe all three.

"I've got photos." She watched him closely as she reached into her backpack, as if she were worried he was going to swipe her phone and run. Sally dropped an envelope on the table. Waited for Ted to open it. "Here's you before you left for Winnipeg. Your mugshot. Yesterday at Bay Street. See the differences?"

"I got some ink. Regretted it, and had it removed. Big fucking deal."

She tapped the picture of his mugshot. "You had *these* tattoos removed and then replaced with shitty-looking prison tats? Please."

"If that's all you've got to say to me, I think I'm going to go somewhere else and grab a burger."

Ted moved to stand up and Sally grabbed his wrist. She held him for a moment, her hand small where Mjölnir should be. When Ted didn't shake her off, she released her hold. She seemed surprised that she'd grabbed him.

She smiled. "I think you might find this more interesting."

Sally took her tablet out of her backpack and showed Ted a screencap. Of him. On the train before the weirdo had attacked.

"Right here is where your ink starts to change."

She tapped the screen and it replayed in an endless loop. The crazy prick who'd tried to lay a beating on him covered most of Ted's body. But not his dragon-scales appearing and then being subsumed under his skin.

"You're not a 'consultant' for Svarta Mining and Smelting,

either. You've been telling people that, but I called them, and no one in their office has heard of you. I've looked into the news from Winnipeg. Arrested for murder, charged with kidnapping—"

The waitress chose that moment to show up to take Ted's order. She forced a pleasantly neutral smile. "Coffee?"

"Yes," Ted said.

"How would you like it?"

"Black."

She turned to Sally, and asked, "And for you? Everything okay?"

Sally nodded.

"Anything to eat for either of you?"

"Shit, no. I ate before I got here."

The waitress forced another smile and walked away to get Ted his coffee.

He turned back to Sally. "Those charges were dropped."

"Winnipeg sure has been weird since you showed up. So, I guess the question is, what are you?"

Ted rubbed at his temples. She'd seen magic. It was small. Not of the struck-by-lightning variety, but he had to assume that she was a part of the Nine now.

The waitress returned with Ted's cup of coffee. He took a sip. It was quite possibly the worst he'd ever had to choke down. And he'd had some cups up north that had tasted like they'd been squeezed out of a raccoon's ass. But this, this topped all of those. Maybe vegan meant *we serve shitty coffee.* Ted dumped an ass-load of sugar into his cup, drawing stares from Sally.

"Sweet enough?" she asked.

"We'll see," Ted said, taking another sip.

It tasted like someone had rolled a turd in sugar.

"*Gah*," he said putting the cup down and sliding it towards her. "Help yourself."

She wrinkled her nose in distaste. "I think I'll pass, all the same."

They sat in silence, Ted trying to figure out how he was going to explain the Nine to her, and convince her to move to Winnipeg where she'd be safer. *And able to annoy him more frequently. Fuck.*

Sally asked, "Does your family know?"

"No," Ted said vehemently. "And they damn well better not find out."

Sally shook her head, and then asked, "Everything you told me last year is true?"

Ted looked at the reporter, nodded slowly.

She continued on, "I thought you were high. Another meth-head on the rigs. No story there. Unless you were the one who caused the explosion."

"That disbelief probably saved your life," Ted said. "If you'd kept digging into that instead of corporate wrongdoings, they'd have found you."

"And what would they do when *they* found me? And who the hell are they?"

"The arsons, the suicides by fire, they're tied to the fires in the patch, and the real cause of the explosion."

"The giant?"

From the way she'd said it, she still didn't believe him. He couldn't really blame her.

Ted shrugged. "Yes. I'm up to my balls in Norse myths, but there's no point in trying to research it. The books don't get it all right. Or if they do, there are three other versions to contradict that story. I've heard stories about wizards, indigenous peoples' tricksters, and the gods of the Greeks, that might suggest they're running around too, but they haven't crossed my path."

"So where do you get your information? You seem to know how to kill these things."

Ted tapped his temple in his mugshot photo, Muninn's tattoo. "I've got my sources."

She ignored his private joke. "If it wasn't for everything else I've seen—"

"Took me awhile to believe too."

"And if I tell people? Show them?"

"They're in danger."

"For how long?"

"Until they die," Ted said, matter-of-fact. "And that won't take long. You'd be an accessory to countless deaths."

Her shoulders slumped, but she didn't seem defeated when she spoke again. "I have to say, the more people know, the more the risk is spread around and the safer people would be. Think of it like vaccines and herd immunity. If everyone knows, we'll find a way to beat the monsters. If *everyone* knew, the odds of any one individual getting targeted and killed—"

"You want to play those odds when a dragon wakes up and firebombs the city?"

Sally blanched. "There are dragons?"

"Yup."

"Fine, so if everyone knows magic is real, we'll find a magical way to fight back. It's another tool to solve our problems."

More wizards. More magic swords. What the *dvergar* had made Ted for. He still wasn't convinced their wish was the best thing for the world.

"New ways for us to kill each other."

She didn't have an immediate answer for that. "Say nothing and people are guaranteed to be safe?"

"Nothing is guaranteed. Nothing with magic is one hundred percent," Ted said and dropped his palm down on the table. "Or this wouldn't have happened to me. Shit happens. Shit *always* happens."

She smiled back at him wanly. "Well there's your guarantee, I guess: shit happens."

"Yeah. Sorry."

Sally dropped her head in her hands. "I don't know what to do."

Ted glanced at the camera and she protectively slid it closer to her body.

"Don't think it. And if you destroy this, I've backed everything up. You'll never get every copy."

Ted couldn't help himself. He barked out a loud laugh that carried across the restaurant, drawing eyes to the table. He tried to stifle himself, for a while with no luck, before people started paying too much attention to them.

"Oh, I can get every copy. Trust me."

"What makes you so certain?"

"I've got someone who could get that video and the last apple in your crisper before you knew they were gone."

"Prove it."

"You really don't want me to do that."

She smirked. "You've got nothing. Nobody. No *tricks*. Just empty threats."

"You asked for it."

He pulled his phone out of his pocket, and went to his contacts. He wasn't surprised to find Loki in there. Or that the photo was of the trickster blowing him a kiss. He was more surprised that Loki hadn't included a dick pic.

The call connected. Loki didn't say anything. No hello. Nothing.

"I'm with someone who needs proof you can get to them." Sally didn't like the sound of his 'get to them' so Ted added: "Don't do anything serious."

Loki was never serious. But Ted was still worried about what he was asking her to unleash.

"Magic," Sally said, unsurprised. "So who's your guy?"

There was no harm in telling her. *Knowing* about Loki was absolutely no defence *from* Loki.

"Loki."

Her brow furrowed, as if trying to place the name, then her eyes widened. "But he's a bad guy!"

"In the comics, the movies, yes. But the real deal is a bit … complicated."

"Does he look like—?"

"Loki looks however the fuck he or she pleases." Ted leaned in. "As far as you know, Loki could look like me, right now." Her eyes widened, and Ted smiled. "As far as I know, Loki could look like you right now, and be taking the piss out of me."

"Hardly sounds like a trustworthy person to have on your side."

Ted shrugged. "Gets the job done. So you can do whatever you want, whatever you think is the right thing, and so will I."

"There's no one else."

Ted had thought those same words about himself.

Reluctantly, she handed over the memory card from her camera. "Fine. Here. So you don't destroy my entire damned camera."

Ted took the card and tucked it into his pocket. He'd fry it when he was alone.

"But I'm keeping my backups."

"No you're not," Ted said. "They're already gone. This meeting was only a courtesy."

She snatched her phone and did some frantic scrolling, frowning intensely.

"Sorry."

She flushed.

"What?" Ted asked.

"You bastard."

"What?" Ted asked again, confused.

She slinked down in her seat and crossed her arms over her chest. "He took my bra."

Ted tried not to laugh, all the while trying to apologize to the mortified reporter. He stopped laughing when he realized he was missing something too.

"What?" she asked.

"Nothing," Ted muttered, shifting in his seat.

"Loki got you too, didn't he?"

There was no point in denying it, with Ted's red hair came the absolute inability to hide his anger or embarrassment from the slowest observer. And Sally was far from that.

"Let's just say you're not alone in feeling draftier."

She scrunched up her brow for only a moment before bursting out in a laugh of her own. It was a musical trill that Ted wouldn't quite place as natural against her dogged demeanor.

When the waitress returned, Sally ordered some food. Ted didn't recognize the dish, but as it didn't contain the keywords to his enjoyment—"beef," "bacon," or "cheese"—he figured he'd hate it anyway. When the food arrived, Sally picked at her plate, moving the food around as much as she put it in her mouth. Ted hadn't had much of an appetite when he'd woken up to a world of magic, either.

"So what's your plan?" she asked. "To finish off that big bastard in the patch?"

"Me to know and you to find out."

"You don't have a plan."

"I know what I have to do," Ted clarified. "I don't know how I'm going to pull it off."

"That's not a plan, that's a mission." She shook her head. "We're all doomed."

"I believe the words you're looking for are, *fucking magic*."

She snorted and this time when her spoon left her plate, the food found its way into her mouth.

"Anything I can help with?"

"You can help by laying low and staying out of trouble, so I don't have to worry about you too."

And those dreads of hers would probably burn up like cordwood.

"Look, no offence, but I could probably help you out."

"I'd feel better if you didn't."

"But I've been doing some digging." She was back on her tablet. "There's been a small uptick in arsons. Not enough to raise any real flags. At least until recently. Now the RCMP are involved for some reason. And they're aware of you." She paused and looked at Ted, as if waiting for him to elaborate, or explain why he'd been at the arson site with Fontaine. Ted didn't answer her. "*I* think the arsons are linked. The deviation from the norm mostly accounts for the fires that wouldn't go out."

She passed her tablet to Ted. There was a map of downtown Edmonton, with red dots flashing over it. Sites of the fires, Ted assumed.

"One of the recent arsons took place at Svarta's new Edmonton office."

"Weird."

Sally's face brightened, as if she'd caught him in something. "Why is that weird?"

"Most of the corporate offices are in Calgary. It's the government offices in Edmonton."

She shook her head. Groaned. Ted hid a smile with his coffee cup.

"I can't find a pattern in the sites, though. Other than that the fires are strangely hard to put out. We have a restaurant. A condo tower. An old coal mine. A camping store."

Ted didn't see a pattern, either. There was a cluster of sites by the river valley, but not only there. If those buildings were important, why? He rubbed at his eyes. He tried to seem bored and frustrated. One of those was easy. He didn't have to fake his frustration. He wasn't cut out for this shit. He wasn't a detective.

Maybe Huginn and Muninn already knew. Maybe they could tell him when they got back. He'd send them chasing after her lead if they didn't. But then he'd have to welcome them back into his head for a day, and listen to them.

The peace and quiet with them out in the world had felt fucking wonderful. But they'd been replaced by someone else asking questions.

"You're not going to stop, are you?"

Sally shook her head.

Ted worried at his bottom lip with his teeth. He didn't want her getting hurt. He didn't want anyone getting hurt because of the Nine Worlds, but he could also only be responsible for his own actions.

"Be careful," he said, standing up. He dropped a five on the table and walked away.

Ted's phone rang the moment he stepped onto the street. Loki. She'd changed her profile picture. Ted answered the call.

"Her underwear is nicer than yours."

"And yet I notice you gave hers back."

Loki chuckled. "Because I know that you can take a joke, and she doesn't have an all-expenses-paid-courtesy-of-the-bloody-dwarves gold card."

"We'll see how funny the joke is when you're choking on your own cock," Ted threatened without much sincerity.

"Promises, promises."

Ted snorted. "Give me back my damn gonch."

"I don't have it *with* me."

"Oh for fuck's sakes."

"You'll thank me later."

"I'll thank you now," Ted said. "Or I'll kick your ass later."

"It's waiting for you at home."

Ted ended the call before he threw his phone under a bus.

Surtur had gotten through Odin's fence around Midgard when Ted had unknowingly called to him in Flin Flon. So it was possible to get him out of the fires. He could leave his link to Muspelheim. It was also possible to send him back. The rain and Loki's magic had made certain of that. But Loki had said she'd spent the last cold of Jötunheim to pull off that trick, so Ted couldn't count on her doing so again.

What if someone else were calling to the giant with all these fires?

Why had they chosen those particular locations?

He wished Tilda were here. She could do a rune reading and tell him what to do. Maybe he could try one himself. Except he didn't know what the fuck he was doing. He wasn't a goddamned seer. Tilda had told him once that his interpretations were too simplistic. Too literal. But casting the stones would be busy work, keeping his hands occupied and keep him downstairs at his parents' and out of the heat. *It was also a terrible idea.*

Ted lit a cigarette instead.

Only Samson and the cat were home to greet Ted when he got back. Any peace Ted had earned with the dog had evaporated without his parents there. He might as well have entered with a ski mask and bolt cutters for all Samson cared.

A note on the kitchen island told Ted he was on his own for supper. He had no idea what he wanted to eat. No idea what his parents had around the house, or where it might be anymore. Knowing his mom, she'd picked up some of his favourites when he'd called to say he was coming home, whether she'd been pissed it had taken so long or not. His stomach gurgled, loud enough to set off Samson.

That dog is going to be the death of me.

Ted went into the living room. Samson followed, barking, of course. Once in the living room, Ted darted back to the kitchen and closed the baby gate behind him. Samson was not pleased. Ted smiled and headed to the basement. If the fucker was going to bark anyway, he could do it upstairs, and not outside Ted's door.

It had been easy to choose between his new life and his old one, when the old had been 1400 kilometres away. But staying in his parents' old house, drinking with old friends, seeing his niece and nephew again, the decision was not so clear. His new life, and the adventure and power it had brought him, was equally weighted by the pain and blood, and death.

He pulled Loki's bourbon out of the safe, popped the cork to give it a sniff, and debated getting tore back.

There was an insistent tapping against his bedroom window. He jerked the curtain aside. Huginn and Muninn waited for him, shuffling from side to side and cocking their heads back and forth.

Perfect.

Ted opened the window to let the ravens in, and braced himself to have an already shitty day solidly ruined. The ravens hopped through the window, landing lightly on the dresser before vaulting onto Ted's shoulders.

The cat had slunk into the room, unseen, and darted up and onto the bed, launching itself towards Muninn. The raven took flight, his wings buffeting Ted as he flew past. Huginn fluffed his feathers, already larger than the cat, and cawed shrilly before darting out with his beak. Muninn landed nearby and took his own bite at the cat as it thought better of its decision to hunt, and bolted out of the room and towards the stairs.

Cheeky fucker.

"Okay, spill," Ted said.

"We have some idea of what Surtur's plan is," Huginn said.

"And why the flames have been retreating over the past year."

"Let me guess," Ted said. "It's not because I busted him one in the chops up in Flin Flon."

The ravens managed a chortle. "No," Huginn said. "It is not."

"The fires have diminished in the north because Surtur is seeking to expand his domain."

"That doesn't make a lick of fucking sense."

"Surtur is burning the dead roots of Yggdrasill. His fires have moved into the underworld. Muspelheim flames fuel volcanoes all over Midgard."

He could feel Muninn prodding around in his old rock-hound days, filling in the blanks that had been lost to time and bourbon, looking for potential threats. Volcanoes lit up like blinking red lights in his mind. Some brighter than others. Tendrils stretched from northern Alberta like travel lines in a movie across the globe, presumably along Yggdrasill's root system. Yellowstone was over a dormant supervolcano. It had been heating up of late too. Melting roads through the park.

There were volcanos in Iceland too. Lots of them.

Eya—Eyafuckaskull—

"Eyjafjallajökull," Muninn corrected.

Whatever.

Eyjafjallajökull. That volcano had been the first time Ted had paid any attention to Iceland. That unpronounceable fucker had grounded flights for half of Europe the last time it had got going. Iceland seemed like a great place for rockhounds. All things considered, it was probably for the best that Ted had never gone there.

The volcano reminded Ted of something else. Something scary. There was an island named for Surtur. The connection had meant nothing to Ted when he'd first heard it. An infant island had appeared in the '60s. A tumultuous series of volcanic eruptions thrust it out of the sea. He hadn't been born at the time, but he'd seen some videos of the event years ago. New earth breaching the sea. Powerful.

Surtsey might erode away, be gone, in a few hundred years. A geological instant, when one dealt with rocks. The island was one of the newest places on Earth, born well after Odin's fence had been made. There was no protection from the Nine Worlds there. Ted wondered whether that was the real reason the Icelandic government didn't allow anyone to set foot on the island, and not for reasons of geological study. They formally acknowledged the existence of elves in that country, after all.

He wondered whether the island had risen because Surtur was waking? Or did naming an island for the giant draw his attention? The why didn't matter. Names mattered in the Nine Worlds. A volcanic island named for Surtur couldn't be a coincidence. It would've been nice to fight Surtur in the middle of a deserted island. He should've fucking known better. Ted rubbed at his eyes. Only putting the giant back to sleep for good mattered.

Every volcano on the planet igniting at once. This time Surtur wasn't going to start his war on a single front, where Ted could stand and try to hold back the flames. If the giant didn't turn Earth into Muspelheim, he'd kick off a volcanic winter that would freeze everyone to death. Fucked either way.

Things had gone from shitty to shit tornado.

Samson was barking. Ted took a long pull of the bourbon. The door to his room creaked and Ted turned. There was Jenny, staring wide-eyed at him. He froze, a bottle of bourbon in one hand, a doob in the other. And a raven on each shoulder. He looked back and forth between Huginn, Muninn, and Jenny. The ravens looked at Ted and then Jenny.

"Uh, I can explain."

12. What Is and What Should Never Be

"Why don't you let them do the explaining?" Jenny pointed at the ravens. "You've got a bird on each shoulder, and your raven tattoos are missing. I'm not an idiot."

"That's a bit of a leap."

"I heard them, Ted."

Huginn and Muninn hopped from foot to foot, like they wanted to make a break for it.

You had your chance to bolt, you cowards. Do what the lady says.

"**If that is your wish**," the ravens said. Jenny eyed the birds curiously.

"**Magic is real**," Huginn said, in his slightly croaking voice.

"I know," Jenny said.

"I know it's hard to believe—wait? What?" Ted asked. "You knew? You're not freaking out?"

"Winnipeg's been weirder ever since you turned up, Ted. Your attack, the tattoos. Thunderstorms in Winnipeg in November? How often does that happen, let alone multiple times? I got over my freakouts in November."

"Yeah, November sucked."

"That's not what I meant. I saw things in that mist," Jenny said. "Things it would take more than a vicious hangover to explain away. The Leg and Union Station both trashed. The whole city going crazy and seeing ghosts. Aiko and Robin not wanting to hang out as much. And you three were buddy-buddy. No explanation makes more sense than 'magic is real.'"

"You're taking it better than I did," Ted said.

"Is this why you bailed on helping me with my renos?"

Ted wanted to protest that he hadn't bailed, but he had. He'd taken the coward's way out and left Jenny a message when he'd known she'd be out.

"Yeah," Ted said. "Magic is not only real, it's dangerous. And once you've been exposed to it, there's no going back. You're fair game for every dragon, giant, or dwarf that walked in myth."

"I've been reading up on my mythology."

"Pffah. Worthless," Huginn said. "Every book tells the story in a different way. Slight variations."

Jenny asked, "Why's that worthless? Wouldn't some knowledge be helpful?"

"The core of it is the same," Muninn said. "For instance, in the Norse myths, which are what concern Theodore—and you—at the moment, Odin is the All-Father, Loki the trickster ... those tales do not change. But it is the subtle differences that will kill you. Is that a troll? An ogre? A jötunn? It could be any depending on where your story originated. The álfar were made of sunshine and leaves, flowers and honey. Look at them now. As twisted as the dvergar."

"If you want to learn something, in this case I would suggest speaking to someone who has lived through it," Huginn said, before adding, "If you can stop them from killing and eating you long enough to wring some measure of truth from them."

"Speak to someone? Like who?"

"Me," Ted said.

"Because you're *so* reliable."

"And he only knows what we have told him."

"When he chooses to listen," Muninn sniped.

"Tilda," Ted said.

"She's in this too?"

"Oh yes, she is one of the Norns," Huginn said.

"The only Norn, now," Muninn added.

Jenny stared at the ravens blankly, then asked, "What's a Norn?"

"Fortune weaver, and doomsayer, they spin out the destinies of man. Or they did, when there were three of them."

"Like the Greek Fates?" Jenny asked. Then sheepishly added, "I taught a unit on Greek mythology in my English class. That's where I started my reading."

The ravens cawed shrilly. Evidently they didn't care for Heracles.

"None of that will help you."

"Is there anyone else?" Jenny asked. "Besides Ted's ex-girlfriend."

"You heard about that?"

"Why not Mathilda? Though she was not alive then

herself, she has all the knowledge of her grandmother, Urd, who was. Mathilda could tell you much. If the two of you can stay away from each other's throats long enough to be civil."

"Not bloody likely," Jenny said.

"There is the Norn's mother, Verdandi. Like her daughter, she did not live in the time of the Aesir. But much of what she knows would be truth," Huginn said.

"And she is of an age with you as well." Muninn cackled evilly at that.

"Jesus Christ, Ted," Jenny stopped and shook her head. "Her *mother* is my age?"

"Vera's nice," Ted said.

"I'll bet she is," Jenny muttered.

To the ravens, Ted said, "Get the hell out of here and see if you can broker a meeting with Tilda. If she's here now, it's not good, and I'd like to make sure she's here to help."

Huginn and Muninn each nodded once, and then flew out of the house.

Jenny had her hip cocked and a hand resting on it as she watched the ravens leave.

"They talk in your head too, don't they?" she asked.

Ted nodded. "How'd you know?"

"You had that same faraway look you got at the bar … that night. I could've sworn your tattoos moved, but I wrote it off as being drunk the next day."

"I was hoping you hadn't noticed."

"We're running late," she said, tapping her watch. "Tick tock."

Jesus, she still wanted to go to the rehearsal. "Okay, okay. We'll talk more in the car."

"You bet your ass we will."

Ouch.

Ted closed the window behind them and tried to give his armpit a surreptitious sniff, to make sure he wouldn't stink up Jenny's car. Not bad, but not great. He ducked behind his closet door and pulled off his t-shirt to put on a slightly less rumpled collared shirt. He wasn't sure how formal he was supposed to be tonight, but Jenny was wearing a nice skirt and blouse, so ratty jeans and a novelty T-shirt would only reinforce his reputation as a fuck-up. Randy and Gloria liked Ted, but there was no reason to push his luck any further.

Ted popped the top button of his jeans, hoping to swap those out too, but remembered that he still hadn't replaced the underwear Loki had stolen.

They were already running late.

"How bad will things be?" Jenny asked. "If your disguise breaks."

Ted clutched his Zippo as if it were a talisman. Jenny was a good driver, but she was hauling ass, and Ted wasn't invulnerable anymore. "Bad."

"How bad?"

Ted popped a cigarette in his mouth but didn't light it. Jenny shot him a look anyway. "End of days. Bad. You haven't told anyone, have you?"

Jenny shook her head. "Who'd believe me?

Ted breathed a sigh of relief. "Thank Christ for that."

"Why?"

"Once you're exposed to magic you're open to it. Open to the Nine Worlds. And there's mean things in those worlds that are waiting for a snack."

"I've fought mean things."

"In Winnipeg."

Jenny tilted her head towards him, and shot him a look.

"Are Rye and my folks in danger?"

"I hope not." Ted didn't know how to continue. "I'm probably responsible for you getting drawn into this. So be careful. On the plus side, they shouldn't go after your family."

Jenny waited in silence at a red light.

"So those tattoos," Jenny asked.

"These are fake."

"They look real enough." She poked him with a finger. Hard.

Ted rubbed at his forearm, winced. "They're real tattoos, but they're only there to hide the ones that you remember."

"Why bother?"

"I had to. Those were the tattoos that the dwarves gave me, and my enemies know to look for them."

"You?" Jenny snorted. "You have enemies."

"I had enemies long before I got tossed into the magical deep end."

"So what can you do?"

Ted told her. The highlights anyway. The strength, the speed, the storm. The ravens. The Honoured Dead he kept to himself. Summoning the dead sounded creepy, especially after Hel had come to Winnipeg, and it was personal. They were his family. Not something to be shared.

"You still have a horseshoe up your ass, I see."

"How the hell do you figure that?"

"All I got was a sword."

"Wait? A sword?"

Jenny nodded.

"You've got a magic fucking sword."

Jenny nodded again.

"Where'd you get that?"

"From the dead hand of a woman who saved my life." The words came out harsher than Jenny had probably intended. "I've seen things. You don't have to coddle me."

"Jesus."

"Haven't seen him."

"Where's the sword?" For a moment, Ted hoped that Jenny's sword was the Bright Sword. But proverbial horseshoe or not, he'd never been *that* fucking lucky. "Can I see it?"

"It's in the trunk."

"What good will it do you in there?"

"It comes when I call, Ted."

"Who doesn't?" Ted managed not to snort a laugh. Though it was a near thing.

Jenny punched him in the arm, harder than she'd poked.

"*Ow.* Jesus." Ted rubbed his arm. "That's gonna leave a bruise."

"You totally deserved it. And I've got to get my knocks in before you go all invulnerable again, don't I?"

Ted smirked. "You still walked right into it."

"I suppose I did." Jenny smirked back. "Just like you walked right into my fist."

Ted let out a long whistle. "Magic sword, eh?"

"It's got a name and everything. After the night I had last November, I never leave home without it."

For a moment, Ted really *did* hope it was the Bright Sword Jenny had found. But it couldn't be that easy. He'd made no cage for Surtur built from the giant's own bones. There was no way her sword could be the one he needed. Robin had a magic sword. Now Jenny had a magic sword.

Everyone had a magic fucking sword but him.

They made it to the rehearsal dinner at EPC with ten minutes to spare.

Ted looked at the tattoos on his arms and let out a sigh.

"What's the big deal?"

"Your folks'll hate seeing this ink."

"Why do you care? They're not your parents."

"I've already been sailing the sea of parental disappointment since I arrived, thank you very much—I'd rather find a safe port from the storm."

"It'll be fine. They'll be fussing over number one son, and quietly disapproving of their future daughter-in-law."

"If you say so."

Jenny held the door open for Ted and then followed him into the Petroleum Club. Ted shook his head. Weird coming back here, to where he and Susanna were married. He wondered if she'd find it weird too, when she came to the reception on Sunday.

It wasn't fine.

Most everyone at the rehearsal was dressed closer to business than casual, so Ted stood out, but at least no one showed up black-tie a few days early.

"Never thought I'd see the day," Randy said, shaking his head.

"Not my choice," Ted said. "I got jumped in my hotel my first night in Winnipeg by a group of punks. They thought it'd be funny to do this to me."

Mostly true.

"Why didn't you get them removed?" Gloria asked.

"They're a good reminder to be careful and make good decisions."

"You've grown up," Gloria said, laughing. "And it's *so* nice to see you and Jennifer getting along."

Her inflection told Ted that she had her sights set on another wedding.

Jenny was great, an amazing woman, but Ted doubted there were nuptials in their future.

"At least your tuxedo will cover them," she said patting his hand. She gave Jenny a kiss on the cheek and a hug. "You look lovely, dear."

"Thanks, Mom."

Ted gave the room a quick scout, and to his surprise, there was a bar.

"Thank God, there's beer," he whispered to Jenny after her mother walked away to do more mingling. "Want one?"

"No thanks, I'm driving tonight, remember?"

"You don't want to drink in front of your parents."

Jenny smiled. "Bad enough I showed up with you on my arm. If I had a beer in front of Dad, he'd have a stroke."

"Rye doesn't seem to have any difficulties."

"It's different, and you know it. I'm Daddy's Little Girl. I never drank. Never smoked. Never fooled around before I got married. In his eyes, Jim and I aren't divorced. You know he tried to invite the bastard out for Christmas?"

Ted grimaced. "That I didn't."

"What's good for that gander is definitely not good for this goose."

"That is bullshit of the highest order," Ted said. "Does Randy know Daddy's Little Girl curses like a sailor now?"

She slapped his arm and smiled. "He did *that* weekend, that's for certain."

Ted slid away from Jenny and hit the bar, hopeful that the rumpled five he had in his wallet would be enough for a drink.

He'd gotten used to throwing everything on the *dvergar's* credit card, or billing it to his hotel room, which amounted to the same thing. Scanning the bar, he could see only wine and beer, no hard stuff. Disappointing, but not surprising. No point in a rehearsal that you got too destroyed to remember.

The bartender waved Ted off when he reached for his wallet, but there was a tip jar. Ted stuffed the fiver into it, where it was lonely with only coin for company, took his Pilsner and turned around, bumping into a woman he assumed to be Lisa from the way Rye was hovering over her.

"Looking good," Ted said.

"Yes, thank you," Lisa said. "We're so glad you could be here, Theodore. *Aren't we, Ryan?*"

Rye nodded. "Absolutely. So glad you could make it. Wouldn't be the same without you standing up for me, bro."

Lisa scowled a bit at the word *bro*. Reminding Ted that her brother would be standing in the spot that Ryan wanted Ted to occupy. Her eyes dropped to the beer.

"Susanna's told me all about you."

Of that, Ted had no fucking doubt.

She dabbed at an eye. "Try to keep the fisticuffs to a minimum tonight, could you? I only have so much cover-up and Ryan does have pictures to think about." She looked at Ted's hands. He was sure that the photographer would be receiving instructions to have Ted posed with his hands in his pockets in every wedding party picture.

He plastered a grin. "No worries," he said.

He must have spent enough time with Loki for his fake-as-shit fake smile to become believable. Lisa's face brightened. Either she believed him or she thought he was too stupid to know she'd insulted him.

Jenny slid back to his side. "Hey guys. Ryan. Lisa."

"Hello, Jennifer," Lisa said. "You look lovely tonight."

Jenny did look lovely.

"Yeah, you'll be the second-best-looking couple walking down the aisle, that's for sure," Rye added.

"Oh, I didn't know you two were a couple," Lisa said, clearly addressing Jenny.

"We're not," Jenny said, a little too quickly.

Ted shook his head. "Rye has always enforced a strictly hands-the-fuck-off policy when it came to his friends and Jenny."

"Can't help but notice you're violating the letter of that policy, if not its spirit, T-Bag."

Ted hadn't realized he'd put his arm around Jenny, to reinforce the joke, but she hadn't shied away, and instead put her arm around his waist. She leaned her head on his shoulder as Rye's parents called everyone over for the first run-through for pacing and locations. It felt good, having Jenny close. Natural. It only took three tries before the minister was satisfied and they left for dinner.

It was a simple dinner, but good. The minister said grace. He was a youngish fellow, younger than Ted and Jenny; probably had some years on Tilda, though. Tyler, the best man and Lisa's brother, ended up sitting between Ted and Rye.

"You live in Edmonton," Ted asked.

"I'm not from Edmonton," he answered. "I'm from The Park."

Ted hid his grimace in a pull of his beer. The "Sherwood" that was sandwiched between "The Park" always went unspoken. Nothing to be proud of. Some of the worst air quality in the province, and an extra 100K added to your mortgage for the privilege. Its only redeeming feature was the Costco liquor store. They had good, strong bourbon there—and reasonably priced.

"So, Ted, what are you doing these days?" Tyler said.

Ted figured Tyler knew goddamned well that he did—at least in the eyes of the mortal world—nothing. He decided to tell the smug prick the truth. Not the whole truth obviously. That would only endanger him. And he hadn't quite tipped the scales to where Ted wanted him eaten by a dragon. But enough truth would shut him up and hopefully give Ted some peace and quiet.

"Until recently, I was living on the charity of my pregnant twenty-three-year-old ex-girlfriend."

Maybe he'd said that a little louder than he'd intended. Cutlery scraped over plates in the awkward silence that followed. Ted took a long sip of his beer. Jenny snickered further down the table and tried to hide a smile.

"But I've got a job now," Ted finished, before taking another bite of his prime rib. "So things are lookin' up."

Dinner was over and Ted had mostly behaved himself. Barely had a buzz from the beers he'd put back. People gathered in little groups, separated mostly along familial lines, groupings that Ted and Jenny existed outside of—for the moment.

Jenny asked him, "Remember that time you crashed at our place?"

Ted eyed her curiously. He'd stayed over at Rye's parents' place often enough.

"Maybe? Got a specific time in mind?"

Her eyes glittered. "Oh, yes. It was after Rye turned eighteen and you took him to *that* club."

Ted knew what club she meant, but smiled at his lack of memory. He could honestly say, and did, every time it was brought up, "I have no recollection of that night."

He wasn't sure who'd gotten more bombed that night, him or Rye, or who had hit harder, the bouncer or the stripper.

"You two came in like a thunderstorm that night. Good thing the folks were away."

"They were working as camp counsellors or something, right?"

Jenny nodded. "You fell down the stairs, laughing. Swearing. Woke me up. I thought someone had broke in."

"Sorry," Ted said.

She waved him off. "I'm over it. You *thought* you were being quiet. Kept shushing each other and then laughing. Since I was up, I got a glass of water, was going to prank Rye, but he'd left a note on his door: 'Jenny don't come in. Ted's in here.'"

The note maybe rang a bit of a bell.

A bit.

Maybe.

"You'd passed out on the floor. I'd already found Rye, he was in the bathroom, and had built a nest in the bathtub with all of his blankets and a garbage can."

"Yeah, so?"

"I did go in."

"Okay."

"You'd kicked your covers off."

Ted shrugged.

Jenny smiled and leaned in close, as if embarrassed to say, "You were naked. Pulled your underwear off with your jeans judging from the tangle of clothes on the floor."

Not sure how to respond, Ted blurted, "I saw your boobs once."

"What? When?" Jenny's awkwardness disappeared, replaced by indignation.

"I came over to hang with Rye, but he was stuck at work. You were doing the dishes. Your bathrobe flapped open. Just enough. From where I was standing I could see them. Well, the right one anyway."

"And?"

"And?" Ted repeated, confused.

Jenny elbowed him in the ribs. "What did you think?"

He smiled.

Jenny didn't, though Ted was pretty sure her seriousness was put on.

"Obviously you didn't think that much of it," Jenny teased. "You never did anything about it."

Under his breath, Ted muttered, “You don’t wanna know what I did.”

Jenny’s smile said she’d heard him and he flushed.

In a low voice, she said, “Let’s get the hell out of here.”

13. This Tornado Loves You

Jenny's hotel was downtown, a tall tower that connected to Edmonton City Centre Mall. The lights were all on in Jenny's hotel room and the curtains drawn when they entered. It was a nice room. More modern than Ted's hotel room in Winnipeg, larger too. They walked in and the door clicked shut behind them. King-size bed, desk, couch and chair, flatscreen television. It had its own small kitchen. The place looked more like a well-furnished bachelor suite than a hotel room.

Jenny walked into the kitchen and grabbed a couple of glasses from the cupboard.

"Drink?" she asked, holding a glass towards Ted.

"Sure."

"Take a seat, I'll be right over."

Ted plunked himself down on the couch. The bed was staring at him. How long had it been since he'd felt he'd never have a first time again. He didn't have too much time to dwell on how bad a mistake tonight might be. Jenny set a glass of whiskey in front of him.

He gave it a sniff. "Always keep bourbon in your room?"

She smiled and they clinked glasses. She slid in beside him, her hip touching his. Ted put his arm around her and pulled her closer. They each took a sip.

They sat in silence for a moment. "Why are you staying in a hotel room?"

"My folks are putting up some of the out of town guests. I offered to give up my room. Said I was fine staying in the hotel."

"Knowing your parents, I'm surprised they agreed."

"I'm an adult with my own job and credit cards and everything, Ted. They can disapprove, but can't stop me. Besides, what if I get lucky at the reception?"

Ted searched her face for a joke. He always thought he could read her, but then, she'd kept her crush hidden from him for years. She couldn't keep a straight face forever and snorted a laugh.

A sly smile. "We could always go back to your place. Give the old room a workout."

"Jesus, no. Why the hell would you want to do that?"

"We could sneak in…"

"I don't think that's a good idea." Their eyes caught as they sipped from their drinks. "Maybe I don't want to sneak."

Each knew what would happen, neither ready to initiate it. Jenny slid one of her smooth, muscular legs over Ted's, nudging his knees apart. He felt her tremble. He eased a hand over her skin, stopping under the hem of her dress.

"Slow down, cowboy," Jenny said. Taking that hand and pulling it to her mouth she kissed Ted's knuckles. "We've got all night. Nobody's coming knocking."

She climbed on to his waist and bit his ear. Jenny wriggled on his waist and Ted's jeans became uncomfortably tight.

Her hand drifted towards his crotch. "That got your attention."

He kissed her neck, and pulling back said, "This is a bad idea." Acknowledgement of that fact didn't stop him from kissing her again. Or from sliding his hands under her dress again. He squeezed her butt.

"Why, because of my brother?" Jenny ran her tongue over Ted's ear, and whispered, her voice husky, "Not his business."

"Please don't mention your brother."

Jenny let out a little trill of laughter, before covering her mouth. "Why is this a bad idea?"

"You know damn well why." He tried to turn away but her grip was too strong. His voice was a whisper. "I'm dangerous to be around."

"Because of the magic thing?"

"Yeah."

"Ted," Jenny said, pulling away from his ear, "you've *always* been dangerous to be around."

He started a bit at that, as Jenny unbuckled his belt, then unbuttoned his jeans.

"You pick fights, drink hard, smoke. You drive fast. You've been giving the finger to the Reaper as long as I've known you."

"This is different."

"Only in scale. I know who you are, Ted Callan." She kissed him. "Always knew you were dangerous. But I want this. And I want you."

"I want you too."

Jenny ran her hands over his right arm, taking in the full extent of his tattoos. "These don't suit you. This ... disguise." She pressed a hand to Ted's temples and gripped his head to turn him to face her.

"I'd never hurt you."

She waggled a finger in front of his face. "You'd better not. I've got a magic sword now."

Ted reached to unbutton her shirt, but she slapped his hands away.

"No peeking. Not yet. Well, maybe a little." She smiled and unbuttoned the top two buttons on her shirt, pulling it down and to the left. She flashed him her right breast. "To get you reacquainted."

"Like I'd forgotten."

"Flattery will get you *everywhere*."

"Promises, promises."

Her lips met his. She slid her hand into his jeans. Her eyebrows rose when she noted he wasn't wearing underwear.

"Expecting to get lucky tonight?"

"Happy coincidence. I'm not wearing underwear for reasons completely unrelated to tonight."

Jenny took in the statement. She cocked her head to the side.

That didn't help.

"Do I want to know?"

"*I* don't want to know," Ted said.

Jenny drained her drink and set the glass down on the table. She stood, and pulled Ted to his feet. Ted slammed back his drink. It was a pleasant burn as the whiskey slid down his throat, and a warm heat of confidence swirled in his belly. Jenny danced around the table, and did a little twirl; her light skirt spun up and gave Ted a peek at her ass.

"Is this present real enough for you?"

Ted smiled. He rushed around the table, giving chase. Jenny squealed a laugh and dove for the bed. Ted caught his shin on the heavy table, shoving it aside. He grunted in pain, but caught himself before he fell.

Jenny had tucked her feet under her. She stifled a giggle. "Smooth move, ex-lax."

"I'll show you a smooth move."

Ted launched himself at the bed, and Jenny. She cried out in mock terror, rolling out of his way as he thudded onto the mattress, bouncing up and rolling on top of her.

She grunted out an, "*Oof*," as his weight settled.

"I forgot how big you are," she said.

Ted pushed himself up on his elbows. "Thanks for not saying fat."

Jenny gave his belly a squeeze under his shirt. She locked her fingers in his hair and pulled him in for a kiss. She tasted of Coke. Dimly, he'd wished he'd brushed his teeth. He hoped Jenny liked the taste of whiskey and cigarettes. Their tongues met and the kiss stretched on, so she mustn't have minded.

She popped the last two buttons on his jeans.

Ted leaned back on his haunches and Jenny pulled his shirt over his head. She ran her hands over his chest while Ted finished unbuttoning her top. She hissed as his knuckle brushed the top of her breast.

"Your hands are rough," she mumbled. She undid her own

bra and pulled it out one of her sleeves. By way of explanation, she said, "You'll snag the lace."

Ted appreciated the gesture. Tilda never wore them, and he was out of practice with working the clasps. Jenny left her unbuttoned shirt on.

"Get the lights."

"Now you're shy?"

Jenny smirked as she gathered the two sides of her shirt in her hand and pulled it closed in a fist. "I can drive you home right now and leave the interior light on in my Honda if you're scared of the dark."

Ted got the lights.

He felt his way back towards the bed, only stubbing his toe once. He climbed onto the bed and could feel Jenny was under the sheets. Ted rolled onto his back, pulled off his jeans and socks and joined her. Jenny was leaning on her right side, waiting for him. Their naked bodies touched. He nudged her knees apart with his legs and pulled her closer. He throbbed against her.

"Damn it," Ted said. "I don't have a condom."

"Shit," Jenny said, sounding disappointed.

"I'll run out and grab some," Ted said. Jenny made a grumbling sound. Crawling under the blanket, Ted kissed his way down her chest. "Or there's other stuff we can do."

Jenny sat up and crossed her arms over her chest. "Nope. There goes the night."

Ted stopped his kissing. It was too dark to see, but he could feel Jenny's smile. Her stomach was trembling from holding in her laugh.

She pressed a foil package into his hand. A condom.

"I've gotta say, I can't imagine you not carrying one, the way you used to get around."

"I wasn't expecting this."

Better to be lucky than good.

Be good and you'll get lucky.

Jenny pressed her hands on Ted's shoulders, nudging him back under the blankets. "Well I like your backup plan. But the Ted Callan I knew never went anywhere without protection."

The Ted Callan she was referring to may have carried that protection, but his use of said defences had been spotty at best.

Word would get out about the two of them. Speculation was probably already rampant within the wedding party. But all consideration of what anyone else thought flew away on raven's wings as Jenny tore into that wrapper. She slid the rubber on him and he groaned.

Ted kept kissing his way down Jenny's chest. He lingered for a moment at her breasts and then moved lower, and gave Jenny what he'd promised. Ted was surprised by some of the things Jenny liked—and asked for; she was unsurprised by what he wanted. But they did it all, all the same.

They lay in bed, spent, panting, slick with sweat. Done. For now. But hopefully not finished. Ted was on his side, arm around Jenny, her hair tickling his face.

"This is gonna sound weird, but I want to see your sword."

Jenny turned on the light. "What? Now?"

"You thought going back to my old room was hot. Maybe I want to watch Jenny Warrior Princess in action."

"You've already seen her in action, mister."

Ted trailed a finger over her ribs and hip. "Humour me."

"What'll you give me?"

"When we get back to Winnipeg, and I'm off the down-low, I can show you sex magic."

Jenny sat up. "Wait. There's sex magic?"

"Oh, yeah."

Her eyes narrowed. "And why haven't you been using it?"

"I thought I was."

She put her hands on her hips. "I can't believe you're holding out on me."

"I've got to save something for our second date."

"You think there'll be a second date?" Jenny made a tut-tut noise. "Pretty cocky."

Ted shrugged.

"All right, close your eyes."

Ted did. Metal slid over leather. Sounded like someone honing a straight razor. There had been more than a few swords drawn on him lately. The sound sent a shiver up his spine.

When he opened his eyes there was a heavy-bladed sword clutched in his fist.

His arm slumped towards the ground.

"This thing is *heavy*."

"It's not your sword," Jenny said, holding out her hand.

It took actual effort for Ted to pass the blade to her and he could lift a car and punch through a wall. Not at the moment, but he got the feeling that the strength that came along with his tattoos wouldn't have made a lick of difference in the weight of that sword. Jenny accepted it back like he'd passed her a pen.

Fucking magic.

Once he would have said it like a curse, but now it was how things were in his world. Full of magic.

Holding the sword ready, her arm only quavered a little. Anticipation, though, not the weight of the sword. She worked through a series of sword forms. A slash, a thrust, a block, she even did that Conan sword spinny thing to show off. Jenny was still muscular, and lean. Her hair was down and wild, sweat-plastered strands stuck to her forehead from their lovemaking. He'd always, always remembered it drawn up in a tail. A few scars stood out that he hadn't noticed in the dark. Claw marks like coke lines, slashed across her back. What looked like a bite over her left breast. Road rash on her ribs. She'd been through the ringer in the last nine months.

"So I'm way stronger when I have this thing in hand. Could probably curl a couple hundred pounds, if I had to. I know how to fight," she said, lunging in the direction of the bed. "I've never been in a fight before, but it's so weird, now I know what to do. I'm tougher. Got run over by a car and didn't break a bone. Bruised me up for a day or two, but that's it."

"Impressive."

"Satisfied?"

Ted pulled the blankets and sheets aside and patted the bed.

Jenny smiled and sheathed the sword.

"Evidently not," Ted said.

They dozed off. Ted hadn't been sleeping well at his parents' house. All hotels have a similar vibe, and after sleeping in one for the last nine months, a hotel bed felt more homey than his old bed in the basement.

He wondered what this was going to be. Was it a fling for Jenny? Would they go back to Winnipeg as a couple? He'd joked about a second date. This wasn't a first date. Jenny seemed to have had this night planned. Or at least planned for the possibility of them hooking up at the wedding.

Ted had said "when they get back to Winnipeg" and was already thinking about what that meant. Would he finally get to help Jenny with her renovations? Was he done living at the Fort Garry Hotel?

He didn't know.

But then no one ever knew. Except Tilda.

The first time he'd met Susanna, he'd thought, *Holy Christ, look at that rack,* not *That woman's gonna be my wife.* Tilda had surprised him too. Jenny had already surprised him tonight. He'd have been happy enough that their friendship was back.

He allowed himself the luxury of dreaming for more. Jenny nuzzled up against him and it felt so good.

So fucking normal.

Ted hadn't wanted any of this for Jenny. He'd wanted to keep her safe. Tried to keep her ignorant of the Nine. He should've known better. *Shit happens.* True then, and equally so now. He hoped her enthusiasm remained, that the light of her smile never dimmed. She was in this with him now. She'd need him soon. He needed her now.

He wanted her always.

Hugging Jenny close, Ted drifted to sleep.

"Mathilda is in Edmonton."

Huginn's voice jolted Ted awake. The raven's sharp squawk was better than any alarm clock.

"Where is she?"

The ravens turned their heads toward the couch. The Norn was sitting there, back straight, falcon cloak spread over the couch like an afghan, one leg crossed over the other, a spear balanced on her knee. A halo of runes glowed a soft blue over her head, the same blue as her eyes.

"*Gah!*"

Jenny stirred, but didn't wake.

It was the first time Ted had seen Tilda since she'd left. The mother of his child. A child that would never be born. Her face was hard. Cold. She reminded him an awful lot of Hel's unburnt side, not that Ted would ever make such a comparison aloud. Especially not with his cock out, and another woman in his arms. Things had been too raw when they'd come out of Hel. The surprise that Loki had masqueraded as Tilda had been too fresh, that their reconciliation and shared grief had been false.

A lie.

No, not a lie. A trick.

When Loki took a form, Tilda's in this case, to hide within, she became it. Ted and Loki—as Tilda—had seemingly fixed things. Did that mean that Ted and true Tilda could as well? Did she want to? Did he?

Fuck.

Ted didn't know either answer. All he knew was seeing her now brought up all of that grief and hurt fresh. With Muninn in there, he'd never forget. He could revisit that moment of loss again, and again. He had done so. A weeping Tilda. That gut sense of loss, as fresh now as it had been in the moment.

The death of their daughter.

I'll see you at the end of the world. The last words Tilda had said to Ted. And now she was here. And Surtur was coming.

She hadn't killed him yet. That was a good sign.

"Hello, Ófriður. Hello, Jennifer."

Tilda had used his dwarven name. That was less good. Jenny sat up, squinted against the sun, then took in the shocked look on Ted's face. The blankets fell off her body. And then she noticed Tilda.

Jenny hadn't been lying when she'd said her sword would come when she called. The blade slid out of its scabbard and into her hand as if it had always been there. She held the short, heavy-bladed weapon out straight, point levelled at Tilda.

"Sheathe Tyrfing, Jennifer," Tilda said, her voice like gravel sliding over rocks. "Or it will be your death."

Ted believed her. He scowled at Tilda.

"Don't fucking threaten her."

The Norn smiled. It was a faint thing. Barely there. "Quiet, Ófriður. *This*, at least, doesn't concern you."

"You know the name of my sword?" Jenny asked, pulling the blanket up over her body, and reaching for Tyrfing's scabbard.

Tilda nodded. "Three wielders died with that sword in their hands before you took it up, yes?"

Jenny nodded.

"It is a cursed blade. A treacherous blade." Ted and Jenny both flinched at the Norn's pronouncement.

Jenny asked, "Cursed?"

Tilda smiled. It didn't soften her face. "At least it was. It is still powerful. But I think its hex is spent. You found it the night Hel came to Winnipeg."

Jenny nodded again.

"When it passes from your hand, to its next wielder, the curse will be reset. So I suggest you use it wisely and well."

"I'll try."

Tilda nodded. "I had hoped that you would stay safely out of the Nine Worlds. I was being selfish, of course, but now that you are one with the Nine, I will say this: if you ever require aid or information, I hope you will ask me."

Ted cocked his head at that. Jenny seemed surprised too. The Norns normally required payment for their aid. Ted remembered that from his first dealing with Tilda and her family. When Jenny didn't respond, Tilda said, "This is not a gift I offer lightly."

"Thanks," Jenny said, uncertain. "I'll keep that in mind."

"Mighty kind of you," Ted said.

"You'll both need all of the help and friends you can find in the future."

Ted asked, "Where can we find you? Should we need to."

"The ravens know where to find me. We should talk soon." One last glance at the bed, and she added, "Alone."

Tilda disappeared in a shimmering rainbow.

14. Strangers When We Meet

Tilda's appearance had destroyed any chance of morning shenanigans. Ted and Jenny took turns in the shower, and then she drove him to where the ravens had said he'd find Tilda. Given Jenny's silence in the car, Ted counted himself lucky she didn't make him take the train, or that she hadn't shown him the business end of her magic sword. Ted hoped Tilda's arrival hadn't ended whatever he and Jenny might have.

On top of everything else, it was barely noon, and already hot as balls. Friday was off to a shitty start.

With the Fringe Festival happening, Whyte Avenue was a fucking gong show of foot traffic and people trying to find parking. Jenny stopped at the corner of Whyte and 109th Street for a red light.

"Are you going back to her?"

"No," Ted said.

"She's younger than me—"

"She left me, Jenny."

"So did I, in a way."

"You came back."

"So did she."

Ted smiled. "You have nothing to worry about."

"Except the end of the world."

"You have *one* thing to worry about." He leaned in to give her a goodbye kiss. She gave him the cheek, but didn't shove him away. "I'll be back."

Ted hopped out of Jenny's Accord before the light changed, barely getting the door closed before it turned green. The car behind her leaned on the horn, and Ted flipped them off as Jenny headed down the street.

According to the ravens, Tilda had a fortune-telling booth at the festival, and was set up among the gypsy merchants. Ted shouldered his way through the crowds. He preferred hanging out in the beer tent till all hours, but he and Susanna had always gone to a few plays if he'd been in town and not in the patch.

A woman at the corner of Whyte and 106th held up a Bible and demanded, "Do you want to hear a verse that explains how we're all astronauts?"

Ted did not. "Not even if it comes with a free drink."

Winnipeg's Osborne Village reminded Ted of Whyte. Younger crowds. Eclectic businesses. Though both had seen cooler days. Whyte Avenue was always a busy street, but during Fringe you had to shoulder your way through the crowds to get to the festival. Ted was glad he hadn't driven here. Pedestrians paid no attention to the traffic lights, or the fact cars outweighed them.

He arrived at the Fringe grounds and it smelled like the city had been deep-fried. A couple of guys eyed him up; they had an aura of day-old beer and fresh-brewed hatred. Ted watched them, worried they might take a run at him like that freakshow on the train.

A woman behind him said, "That fortune teller told me I was going to die. So I told her 'no tip.'"

Someone else laughed. "What'd she say to that?"

"That I could die sooner rather than later. Crazy bitch."

"You should report her to somebody."

Their steps carried them away from Ted. Fortune teller making threats. Had to be Tilda.

Anyone who got a death fortune from Tilda would either think it was a part of the show, or ignore her as a loon. *What the fuck was she doing? Maybe she's seen something and feels this is a way to assuage her conscience.* Assuming she still had one. Ted remembered Vili's warning after Tilda had fallen into the fog of Niflheim. She was colder than she'd been when he'd met her. Harder.

She has plenty of non-magical reasons for that.

Huginn and Muninn circled above Ted, dropping in front of a gazebo-style tent with its flaps open. They gestured none too subtly towards the entrance with their beaks. Ted took a deep breath. His talk with Tilda wasn't going to be fun. Surprise colonoscopy fun. The Norn stepped out of her tent to greet him.

"You're changed," Tilda said. "Only one fate now."

Ted wondered which of the two she meant.

Tilda took a few steps closer. She wore a leather buckskin jacket that looked like it had beaded feathers on the back and sleeves. Annie Oakley and Calamity Jane's badass sister. A closer look and those beads were the same colours as the falcon cloak she'd worn into Hel—and Jenny's hotel room.

Her hair was still grey, longer than he remembered, and tied back in a braid. Her eyes were still the same intense blue. Eyes that had seen the past, future, and present with equal exposure. Her lips quirked into a smile as if she were waiting for something.

She smiled.

God, how long has it been since I've seen Tilda smile?

Muninn probably would've told Ted, if he and Huginn hadn't been occupied bullying crows away from a discarded hot dog. A few people pointed at the birds, and a few others readied cameras, which made Ted nervous, but by the time they were ready to take a picture, both crows and ravens had scattered back into the air.

"Took you long enough to get here, Callan." She looked him up and down. "You look like you've been rode hard and put away wet."

Ted searched the accusation for a hint of anger, but to him, it seemed more filled with wry humour. Huginn and Muninn had circled around, and they landed behind Ted. Both ravens sidled toward Tilda. It would be comical, watching them bob side to side, in their awkward grounded gaits, if he weren't worried this was a trap. If it was, she could've easily killed both him and Jenny last night. He hated that he didn't trust her. But who knew what she'd been up to over the last months. Huginn and Muninn would be able to suss out the truth.

Tilda arched an eyebrow at Ted.

He doubted Loki would be dumb enough to try it again. And after all they'd been through, he wanted to trust the trickster. But the fucker was a born agitator, and had made some bank from provoking Ted—and Tilda—in the past.

"Shoo, bird," she said, and both ravens shot away like an elastic band that had been stretched too far and then snapped. "Checking me out?"

"Needed to make sure you weren't Loki."

"At least you can learn from your mistakes." She paused. "Eventually."

"I didn't think you'd come," Ted said. "I wasn't sure you'd help after … you said you'd see me at the end of the world, but you never said you'd help."

She sighed. He couldn't tell if it was disappointment, or regret. "I live in this world, Ted. I don't want it burned to ash either."

"Well that's a fucking relief."

"I've reconsidered what you did back in Winnipeg."

Ted opened his mouth, ready to blame Loki by instinct. Instead, he said, "I'm sorry."

"I appreciate the sentiment. We both screwed up." She paused, as if weighing the events that led to their split. "Some of us more than others."

She seemed pretty ambiguous with the blame, but Ted let it slide. Most of their problems together came down on him, and he knew it.

"Wasn't an easy time," he said.

"No time is easy." She wiped the slick of sweat from her brow and shot a peeved look at the sky. "Come inside and get out of the sun before you look like a lobster."

One of Tilda's neighbours gave her the stink-eye from behind the relative safety of a jewellery table.

"You're going to die," Tilda called over, shaking her bag of runes. "Get out of Edmonton and keep running."

The woman dropped her head, busily rearranging pendants and bracelets.

"I've come to have a bad reputation," Tilda said with a shrug.

Ted chuckled. "You Norns never get along with your neighbours."

Tilda smiled, as if fondly remembering her youth in Gimli. It didn't take long for the cast of her face to turn sad.

"Inside." She nodded towards Huginn and Muninn. "You too."

He entered her booth. His back tingled as he stepped over the threshold. Yggdrasill reacted to a subtle working of rune magic, wanting to burst through his disguise. Ted wondered what other wards Tilda might have laid into this temporary home and what might have happened if he'd tried to enter uninvited.

There were no pests buzzing anywhere in the tent. Mosquitos swarmed around the door, but none entered. She pulled the flaps closed.

Ted rubbed at his arms as gooseflesh peppered his skin and sweat froze. He wasn't used to feeling cold. Wasn't used to the weather affecting him much at all.

The glowing symbol of a rune hung in the air: it was a single straight line, like a capital "I." After the initial rush of freezing air, Ted felt the tent cool to a reasonable temperature.

Isa, a rune of cold, of static. He knew it without Huginn and Muninn reminding him. Which they certainly would have had they been in his skull, ignoring that he'd been using rune magic for the last nine months. While he may not share Tilda's mastery, at least he knew their fucking names.

"*Algiz,*" she said, and a second rune, shaped like an upside-down peace symbol, appeared in the air, hanging next to *Isa.* A breeze circulated in the tent, coming from somewhere. Ted couldn't pinpoint it. It felt as if it blew from whatever direction he turned his head.

"Better than air conditioning," she said, a satisfied smirk on her face. "Refreshed?"

"Yeah." Ted shook his head. "Thanks."

Her eyes glittered with mischief when she said, "Any time, Callan. Any time."

Seeing Tilda now, alone, brought all of their time rushing back. *Crazy visions and sex magic'll do that for you.* Ted looked away, not sure he *should* be looking, after last night.

He pulled her into a hug. "*Goddamn.* It's good to see you."

She gave him a squeeze back and asked, "You mean it?"

"Why wouldn't I?"

"You *were* all wrapped up in a brunette."

Ted sighed. "I tried to find you. Months. Nothing. Not a word."

"I know." She lowered her eyes, shook her head. "I wasn't ready. I was too angry."

He couldn't blame her. "I can't take last night back."

She waved him off. "No, and you shouldn't need to. Jenny loves you."

Ted was taken aback by that. Like, yes. Attraction, yes. School-time crush, absolutely. But love?

He stammered out, "She had a crush," but didn't believe the statement. It struck him then, that Tilda's phrasing had implied that she did not love him. As badly as things turned out between them, as shitty as Ted had been to her when they'd grown up together, Jenny hadn't shaken those feelings. He didn't think she was the type to try to get a notch on the bedpost with an old flame. Ted lowered his eyes. "Besides, I'm hardly a trophy."

"Oh, I don't know. You have your … qualities."

Ted snorted. "Shit, yeah. Ted Callan, Gentleman of Mother-fucking Quality. Esquire."

Tilda laughed.

"I don't think you would have ended up in that bed together unless it meant something to her. The question is, what did it mean to you?"

"I … I don't know. I haven't had time to think about it."

Tilda said, "I'm happy for you both."

"Really?"

He wanted to ask if Tilda had met someone else. There was no mileage in that thought. They were talking again. Fastest way for that to stop was for him to put his giant boot in his mouth. If she'd slept with every dwarf in Flin Flon it was none of his business.

So long as it wasn't Loki. Ted would *never* hear the end of that.

"I'm glad that despite what's coming, you found some happiness. You're going to need it."

"Thanks," Ted said. The rest of her words sank in. "What's coming?"

It was a tight squeeze inside the tent. Neither of them were small and they kept bumping into one another, all shoulders, hips, and elbows. It had been a long time since they had been so close, in such intimate quarters. Intimate.

Get that thought out of your head, Callan.

Remembering the brand new bed they'd purchased when they'd bought their house in Wolseley, remembering that they'd never had a chance to break it in. Too much misery. Too much death. Ted had nearly died in that bed. Tilda had lost their daughter, Erin, that same night.

He had missed her. Missed this. He hadn't realized how much. They hadn't known each other long, but she had been such an integral part of his new life in the Nine Worlds, it was startling he believed he could keep on fighting without her.

She sat behind a folding table. It had the same embroidered rune cloth atop it that she'd used when reading the runes for him in Gimli. It looked odd seeing that cloth on a plastic table instead of the ash wood monstrosity the Norns had kept on their upper floor. But it was more portable.

Tilda smoothed the cloth and set her runes down on the table. She considered for a moment before nodding and motioning at Ted to sit down across from her. He placed his hand on the table between them. The silence lingered, threatening to drive a deeper wedge in between them. Outside, the sounds of the Fringe buzzed like a swarm of mosquitoes.

"What's this all about?" Ted asked. "Why are you here now?"

"Slow down," she said. "We're not there yet. I felt you. In that spot where we first met. And then later. You were full of power and then … gone."

The band. The concert. Loki.

"I thought you were dead. But it was too soon for that." She smiled, warmly, as if trying to soften the pronouncement. That she had seen Ted's death. *Doom.* "When I showed up to investigate I could see what happened, I could see you fighting. And then everything was gone."

Loki had done a damn good job then, if he could hide Ted from Tilda. *And if he'd been able to hide himself.*

She shook her head. "I *am* glad you're alive."

"You don't seem it."

"Don't push your luck." She took a deep breath. "We're going to lose."

Ted snorted. "So there's a 'we' now."

Tilda tilted her head down and shot him side-eye.

"You've seen us lose."

She nodded. "There's only one future left."

"I don't believe that. I can't believe that. There's got to be a way."

"I can't see it."

Ted hesitated before he told her. He knew this would be a touchy subject. If knowing he and Loki were working together irritated her, hearing that he was listening to the former goddess of death might throw her round the bend. Hel had sent the mara. Hel had sent the valkyries. Hel had taunted and teased. Ted had used Tilda's power to give Hel new life—to spare hurt to Loki—and that had hurt Tilda deeply. Hel, who'd taken Erin from them.

"Hel told me how to kill Surtur."

"What?"

"She knew his death. Told me what to do."

"So why isn't it done?"

"I can't figure out what the fuck she meant. I tried. It didn't work. I didn't know how—"

Tilda sighed. "You could've asked me."

"Hel said his death was for me alone. I didn't know what else to do. I was worried if I told anyone, it would change fate. It was my hope. My only hope."

She looked deadly serious, when she said, "No, there is another."

Ted scowled. *Why the hell would she say that.* "Did you say that to fuck with me?"

"You got me."

Ted faked a chuckle. He was glad his tattoos were hidden. The weather did have a tendency to follow his mood. Wasn't hardly fair that his emotions would manifest visibly all over his body like a god damned roadmap to what he was feeling, when she got to be a cipher. She could see the future, and while she might not be able to read his mind, peering into the future would show her what he'd do. Nearly the same thing. He was glad she *couldn't* read minds.

"Maybe you'd be further along if you had told someone. You and your gods-damned pride."

"Who was I supposed to tell? You were gone. I'd banished Loki."

"Have you considered maybe that was Hel's plan all along? Give you knowledge you couldn't share or figure out alone?"

That stung. Ted knew he was no riddle master. But it still stung.

"No. She seemed grateful for her new life. I think she meant it." He paused, watching Tilda's face—with the passing of a year, the hurt had not lessened. She still had her visions. Still remembered every moment of a life that their daughter would never have.

"I'm still going to kill her, Ted." Like she killed Svipul, and Kára, and Mist. All he'd seen her do, and he still had difficulty seeing Tilda as a killer.

"She said there was hope—"

"There's no hope for her. I'll find her. And end her once and for all. With or without your help or blessing."

"I said I'd keep her safe."

Tilda brushed a strand of hair away from her face. "And you're okay with that? You're okay with trusting Loki again."

"I had to trust somebody." Ted measured his next words carefully, running his fingers through his beard, as if that would help him think. He'd thought about this, since they'd split. Wondered if it was true. He hadn't wanted to believe it was. "Loki said you were going to leave me. That you'd left a note for me at Robin and Aiko's, when Hel came to Winnipeg. I didn't want to believe him. But then—"

"I left."

"Yeah."

Tilda nodded. "He was right. Things got hard and I was going to bail."

Nine months gone, that truth hit him in the gut. He let out a short grunt and muttered, "I need a smoke."

"So have one. Cigarettes aren't how either of us die."

Tilda struck a match, lit her cigarette, cupped her hand over the flame as Ted leaned in to spark up his. He took a deep drag and held the smoke in his lungs. Such a simple thing, enjoying a cigarette with someone you know. It had been one of the first things he and Tilda had done together.

After exhaling, he gestured at her braid. "Christ, you let your hair get long."

"That happens," Tilda said, giving Ted's beard a tug. He winced. "When you don't cut it. You've gone a little shaggy yourself."

Ted raked his hair back behind his ears with his fingers. "It helps to hide Heckle and Jeckle when they get to yapping."

"**Yapping**," Huginn said, peevishly.

Muninn added, equally disgusted, "**Honestly**."

Tilda nodded towards the ravens knowingly. "And how's that working out for you?"

"They pull my beard something fucking fierce every time they leave or come home to roost."

Tilda laughed. "Yeah, you're real hard done by. Invulnerability, strength, walking on water. Those are some terrible burdens to bear. Maybe the *dvergar* left you with these little trials to remind you of your humanity."

Ted snorted with disbelief. "Yeah, maybe. Or maybe Andvari is a big bag of pricks."

People in the Nine Worlds had a tendency to hold grudges.

Something we have in common, I guess.

Tilda smiled a mysterious smile and patted where Mjölnir should be. There was no reaction. The hammer tattoo should have buzzed like an electric fence. He should have felt something. Their connection had saved Ted's life. Together they'd banished Níðhöggur back to Hel. Now there was nothing. Why wasn't their bond trying to force its way through his disguise the same way his tattoos had? He didn't know if that *lacking* was because of his disguise, or something else. Something Loki had done. Something Tilda had done.

She'd know, if he could stand to ask her. Tilda's "gift" was as much a curse as a blessing. Seeing inevitable doom. Never being free of mistakes of the past. No fucking thanks.

Tilda hesitated a moment. Her fingers brushing the leather bag that held her rune stones.

"Checking the future?" Ted asked. "Seeing how badly I screw today up?"

"What gave me away?"

"That distant look you get. A million miles away and looking right through me all at once."

"Guilty. But that's not what I was looking for."

She flipped her braid over her shoulder to fall down her back. That iron-grey hair of hers, once so curious, so incongruous with her youthful face. Tilda's face didn't seem so youthful anymore. She seemed to have grown into that hair.

She smiled as if he was a child who'd told her he'd grow up to be prime minister, or an astronaut, or Superman. A reminder of what was gone. Hel had said what was taken could be won back—if he was worthy—but Ted wasn't so sure. He didn't feel worthy. It hadn't been a calm couple of months of living together—Ted had tried to pass it off as them finally getting to know one another. Figured they'd work through it. But he wasn't so certain he wanted to. Magical connection or not, fated lovers or not.

"I have to believe we can win. I have to believe we have a future. "

Tilda sighed a contented sound. He wondered how long it had been since she'd uttered it. Not that she needed him for happiness. Hell, she'd probably been better off without him.

"I've missed this," she said.

"Me too."

"But this wasn't all we had, was it?"

"Fire and blood. Hard choices and grim futures. Doom."

He wondered about Jenny. They had a connection too. Not a magical one, like he shared with Tilda, but one of shared friends and family. Shared experiences and memories. It was great to be able to share this new life with someone from his old life. To not have to lie. About anything. Ted had no answers.

He didn't think Tilda did, either.

She played idly with her bag of rune stones. Ted lit another cigarette. She motioned at him with her chin, and he passed her one, lit it.

"What'll you tell Jennifer?" she asked. "About this? About us?"

"The truth," Ted said. "That we talked. That we tried to figure out what to do."

"Will that satisfy her?"

Ted shrugged. "I don't know. I don't know if we'll work out. If there's time for that."

"You don't think the two of you will work out, but you still slept with her?"

"I'm not made of fucking stone. And it's not like I believed you and I would 'work out' when I picked you up on the highway."

Her cheek twitched.

Shit.

Ted rubbed at his eyes. Things weren't supposed to be like this. "This visit was supposed to be a quick check-in. A last goodbye to the family."

"You thought that was wise?"

"Knowing what my life is now, I took great pains to hide myself. I buried my powers for fuck's sake. All I wanted was to send my oldest friend off in style. I was supposed to be here a weekend. Tops. *None of this was supposed to happen yet.*"

"But it did. And it's not going to stop because you have a wedding to attend."

She had him there, but he didn't know what to do.

Tilda smiled as if she'd beaten him at a hand of poker. "When we've dealt with his followers, at least you'll be able to piss on his bones."

"Yeah, I might do that."

Something that Tilda had said stirred at him.

Bones.

Build a cage from his bones.

"I think I figured something out."

"**A first, I believe,**" the ravens said together.

Ted readied a mental middle finger when Tilda added her voice to the chorus with, "That has to be a first. So what is it that you've figured out?"

"I know why those suicides and arsons happened where they did."

"There's a pattern?"

"All over old coal mines. Most of which have been closed up for decades, but the river valley is riddled with the tunnels. Coal dust is explosive. They're trying to get Surtur out of the patch."

Tilda considered. "That's not good."

"It's sure as shit not." Ted looked away from her. His next request would be hard to make. It might cost him her help. Or his life. "I need you to work with Loki."

Tilda gripped the table edge. It cracked. "Why?"

"Because the three of us started this fight together, and we'll need to finish it together."

The angry cast to her face softened, as if he'd said something that made sense. "It won't change a thing."

"You've been wrong before."

It was a cruel thing to say. And Tilda knew what he was getting at. But sometimes that was the only way to make someone understand. It had to be said. If they couldn't accept that Tilda might be wrong about his fate, and the world's, then they all might as well lie down and die. Her eyes went distant again.

"Fine," she said, as if pulling teeth, "We need Loki."

"I'll let her know."

Looks like we're getting the band back together.

"Do you think this is the best time for you to be in disguise?"

"It's gotta be done."

"The greater doom hanging over Edmonton makes divining the future difficult. Fire is burning into the present, and past. I don't have the warning I should, but I do know this: by the time three days have passed, Ted Callan will be dead."

"Shit."

She arched an eyebrow. "Shit? That's all you have to say?"

Her eyes no longer held that strange wolf light that had filled them the first time they'd made love. That was gone. In its place, her pupils seemed like skulls.

"I'm sorry, Ted."

Tilda *had* been wrong before. But not often.

His phone buzzed. He checked the incoming text. He forced a smile.

"Time for the stag party."

"Ted—"

"If I'm gonna die this weekend, I'm not facing it sober."

15. Beer Drinkers and Hell Raisers

Rye's stag party was a few hours in, and the guys were all past a case of beer deep. Ted was glad some of the men he and Rye had partied with were still alive. Kent "Doc" Nielsen, Adam "Hammer" Tanner, Brent "Shitty" Smith, and Darren 'Bull' Cook: "The Four Horsemen," four of the rowdiest roughnecks around. They'd give Thor a run for his money when their minds turned to demolition.

Ted had shown up pretending to have pre-gamed, and been spilling more than he drank. Tonight, of all nights, Rye would never let him off without getting destroyed, but Ted figured if he cut loose with the whiskey, he'd end up cutting loose on Edmonton, and he wanted the city to stand long enough for the wedding to go down without a hitch.

Or rather, *with* a hitch.

Everyone else was drunk enough they'd stopped caring whether Ted was wrecked, instead seeing to maintaining their own inebriation. So long as Ted hollered out when they did, his disguise was bulletproof. Both of them.

Rye had bought them all cowboy hats to wear out tonight. So Ted really felt like a jackass. He was no cowboy. Hadn't sat a horse in years. At least Rye hadn't bought them the boots to match.

While Rye may have arranged to have his wedding on an away weekend for the Eskies—a shame, because Ted wanted to see the High Level Bridge lit up all green and gold one more time—at least his future brother-in-law had included watching the game as a part of the plan for the night. The game was a shit-show, but the Esks had squeaked out a victory over the reborn-for-the-third-time Ottawa franchise.

They'd made a drinking game out of the ridiculous new name. Drink when an announcer says "Redblacks," chug when someone says "Rough Riders." The game had been boring, but the simple act of watching football with friends was one Ted had missed. No one he knew in Winnipeg followed sports.

With Ottawa back in the league, Winnipeg had been shuttled back to the Western Conference, which meant Ted's new hometown would be up against his old team. Both looked strong, and in any case, the ABC Rule applied: "Anyone But Calgary."

Their limo stopped outside of the "gentlemen's" club, which would be hopping, judging from the already-full parking lot.

The crew got a free pat down to the tune of AC/DC's "You Shook Me All Night Long" from an unfriendly looking fucker on security. Ted paid for his cover and Rye's, and left a nice tip for the woman at coat check. She had two tip jars, labelled "Tips" and "Ass."

Things were different now than the first time Ted had gone to a ripper bar. There were lots of women at the club tonight—stagettes, birthday parties. The distribution wasn't fifty-fifty, but it was surprisingly close.

When they finally entered the bar proper, Ted could see the VIP seats they'd reserved near the long, narrow stage. Most of the seats at the stage were empty, but then, the stage was empty too. It had a pole at each end, and a trapeze-style bar that hung from the ceiling, but no dancer.

The dark lights and the red and blue hues of the bar would hide every blemish on the dancers—and the club. Six dancers were lined up by the bar, but Ted didn't get a good look as a waitress was on their group immediately after sitting down.

The server leaned in, cute in her tight black UFC panties and red corseted-top. She flashed her cleavage as she took their drink orders and pointed her ass to the table behind them, reminding them that they might be thirsty too. She knew her clientele, and Ted didn't doubt the tips would be flowing when she returned with their drinks.

Ted was the last to order, and he asked for his Jim Beam on the rocks instead of neat. The ice, while it wouldn't improve the taste, would allow him to nurse his drinks a little longer, and provide the illusion that he was more in the game than he was.

Their drinks arrived—expensive, but then you're paying for atmosphere, not the liquor—as the first dancer of their night was up. The deejay announced her (no doubt fake) name, calling everyone up to the front over "Down with the Sickness." *So she was a metal chick.* Ted would lay money that the next songs in her routine would be either "Dragula" or "More Human than Human."

Some of the guys got up to head for the seats at the stage. Ted stayed put. He preferred to watch the show from a slightly removed distance. More so since Canada had replaced one- and two-dollar bills with coins. It was one thing to hand a dancer a bill. Another thing entirely to try and knock a quarter off her ass with a loonie.

As "Down with the Sickness" was mixed into "More Human than Human" one of the dancers wearing a string bikini and impossible boots sidled into the booth and pressed her bare hip against Ted. She had long hair, a long body, and a long face.

She took a sip of her drink, soda water, maybe, with a lime, and asked, "Can I interest you in a private dance?"

"Try the happy groom," Ted said, pointing to Rye, hooting and slapping the stage with his palm. "Wedding's on Sunday, and we're here to empty his wallet."

"Thanks for the tip," she slid out from the booth. "I'll be back for *you* later."

She didn't get far—the next booth—before she found a taker for her offer, and she led the happy youngster towards downstairs and "The Dungeon" where the pisser and the private booths were kept. Ted knew that kid, even if he'd never met him. He had the look. Downstairs he'd be peeling off twenties with no thought of tomorrow. One of those lucky guys who still had work. He was probably on his way back north to the camps. All expenses paid, no reason to hang on to what was left of his last cheque. He'd been that guy, once.

As you head through the crowd with one of the dancers, everyone knows where you're going and what's gonna happen.

There were some cheers from the guy's buddies. It had been a while since Ted had gone, either to a strip club, or for a private dance, but it was like missing a cigarette for a couple of days, and you wonder why you ever smoked, and then you light up and it's like the first time all over again. The club was a like a fresh breath of sleazy air.

The metal chick was done and Rye returned to the booth with the guys. A few of them who'd abandoned their beers when they'd rushed the stage found their drinks gone, picked up as abandoned by the waitress. Their protests died when she came back with a full tray to top everyone up. The Four Horsemen were well beyond caring about cost. Ted crunched at the ice remaining in his glass and dumped the fresh glass of bourbon into the empty, let the ice water it down.

"So when are you coming back to the rigs?" Kent asked.

Ted shook his head. "Not going to happen."

"Pussy. Afraid of a little fire."

Once those words would have gotten Ted's back up. He no longer gave a shit what the guys thought of him. They'd scrapped before. Sometimes Kent had won, sometimes Ted had won. Usually the tipping factor was who was more drunk that particular night.

"You weren't there. And how fucking little is that fire now?"

Kent went from aggressive to petulant. "You suck now, you know that? Used to be more fun."

"I used to be an asshole."

Rye laughed. "Used to."

Ted snickered too, and the patch camaraderie was back.

He wondered who would dance next. It was the Techno chick. After her, Ted expected either the Classic Rock or Country would follow. He hoped Country had the night off—if he heard "Save a Horse, Ride a Cowboy" one more goddamned time, he'd send an engraved invitation to Surtur to kill the song.

It wasn't another dancer that followed. It was the games.

Ted hated the games.

"Who's coming up?" the deejay asked, "Rye and Coke! Get your ass up here!"

Rye jumped out of his seat, threw his arms up in the air, and yelled, "Yeah!"

Which went to show you how far a drunk-out-of-shape guy was willing to debase himself to earn a free round of shooters for his party.

One of the bouncers got on stage to hang up a twined cord of gold and green fabric. *Next dancer must be a local. An Eskies fan.*

"All right, everybody," the deejay hollered, put your hands together for … Loki."

No. Fucking. Way. It couldn't be.

The deejay was still letting the *eeeeeeee* sound hang in the air when a tall, slender woman wearing an elaborate horned helmet and a gold and green costume strutted on stage to Ace Frehley's take on "New York Groove." The same woman who'd offered Ted the private dance.

"Oh shit," Ted said.

The guys took his concern for attraction, and as Ted stared dumbly at Loki, they dragged him to the stage. Loki smiled wide enough to swallow a giant and blew Ted a kiss.

Her routine was pretty standard at first, the slow reveal of her body during the opening song. Which surprised Ted. If ever there'd been a dancer who'd roll out either on fire or juggling ferrets, it was Loki.

The trickster could dance, too. Which was unusual at strip clubs these days. Walking around nude was usually sufficient for the most of the patrons. Ted *did* appreciate someone who could dance. Tilda had been a good dancer. The only time Ted had seen her dance ended in disaster. Susanna could dance, too, although now that was only a fact, there was no memory, no sensation, attached to it. Ted wasn't sure whether Jenny could dance. But he supposed he'd find out on Sunday. If last night was any indication, Jenny could probably move on a dance floor if she wanted to.

Loki had all of her clothes off by the end of the first song, and was clutching the braided green and gold rope the bouncer had hung from the ceiling while spinning in a slow circle. The arm holding the cord was bolt-straight, her other arm drew a line from her shoulder to her extended index finger as she pointed to the crowd.

Rye had taken his seat near to the rope. He was slapping his palm down on the table that ringed the stage, hollering. Loki did an exaggerated kung fu kick in his direction.

The Eurhythmics' "Sweet Dreams" came on and Loki

loosened the knot at the bottom of the rope, splitting it into two separate long lengths of fabric, like scarves, one green, one gold.

Loki wound the scarves around her ankles and wrists and then pulled herself up in the air. A few more steps, a few more wraps, and she was suspended. She alternately revealed and obscured her body as she climbed the fabric. There was nothing supernatural. Ted was close enough to notice the flex of muscle. The tightening of tendons. The sweat dripping from Loki's chin and slicking her entire body. There was joy on her face—exertion too—and pride. Not that Loki had ever been humble, but this look struck Ted as something different, pride in a job well done.

He didn't want to watch any more of Loki's work. Rules or no, he was going outside for a smoke. Loki stretched out to Ted. She leaned in and whispered in Ted's ear, lips brushing him, breath hot against Ted's skin.

"Where're you going? I've got two more songs."

"What the fuck do you think you're doing?" Ted asked.

"I'm giving you an out," Loki whispered. "An excuse to leave without pissing off all of your friends. When I'm done, I'll ask you for a private dance. Then you and I are out of here. Look at them. They'll let you take it."

Ted glanced over Loki's shoulder, and sure enough, the gang egged him on, a couple sliding their index fingers in and out of a circle made of thumb and index finger on their other hands.

"This better be important."

"It is."

Ted left for his cigarette. When he came back, Loki was off the stage and the deejay was spinning "Five to One."

"You missed a hell of a closer," Rye said.

"I'll be seeing it up close as soon as she comes around again."

Rye slapped him on the shoulder. "Good man."

Ted sipped his drink, and watched anxiously for Loki to come back on to the floor. It wasn't a long wait. She wore a gold and green string bikini. A few guys tried to grab her for a private dance, and she slid away from them, slippery as a salmon, to come back to Ted's table.

Ted said, "Let's go."

"I hope you're not always in such a rush," she said, winking theatrically at the table. The Four Horsemen laughed so hard Ted was surprised they didn't fall over.

Loki snatched Ted's hat off his head, put it on, and then took Ted's hand. A loud cry erupted from Ted's table, cheering him on.

Ted wanted to shake Loki's hand out of his, but the trickster was gripping him tightly, and there was no way to do so surreptitiously. Downstairs, Loki led Ted to a stern woman, with graying blonde hair up in a bun. He wasn't sure what they called her, the dungeon master, or mistress, or manager, but she took the money. Paying for Loki's time would eat up the last of Ted's cash, and he was still skittish about putting anything on the Svarta credit card while he was here. Ted counted out the bills, and the woman made a note in her ledger.

Loki took Ted down the hallway past rows of curtained-off booths. They took the one at the end of the hall and Loki drew the curtain closed. She pushed Ted on to the bench.

"You're gonna want to sit down."

"If you've got something to say, fucking say it."

"Not with that attitude, mister."

Loki grooved along with the music. Scissor Sisters. The song opined that the singer snuck up from behind—that, coupled with the song's title, "Whole New Way to Love You" did not strike Ted as a good omen.

"Not my favourite song," she said. "But it will do."

"There's no need for this, I've already seen way too much of you."

"I want you to get your money's worth."

"Loki," Ted said through clenched teeth. "We're never going to sleep together."

Loki grimaced and dropped her head. She let out a dejected sigh.

"Look," Ted said. "I'm sorry—"

"If you tell me it's not you, it's me, I will tie your balls to a goat and start a game of tug-of-war."

It was Ted's turn to grimace. He reached out to Loki, but she drew away.

"You know, the last time you gave me a hug, you threw me out of your city. Maybe *I* shouldn't trust *you*."

Ted didn't want Loki to abandon helping him. Shit, the trickster could also pull off Ted's disguise if she wanted to, revealing him to Surtur and throwing Edmonton to the fiery wolves. It would be a table-flip of epic proportions if Loki stopped liking their game. Ted also didn't like the idea he was only using Loki for her disguise. And he felt bad about how he'd tricked the trickster. At the time it had been his only option, and he'd felt a little pride at getting away with it, but that pride had turned to ash. Looking back made Ted feel pretty fucking low. Not only had he tossed Loki out on her ass, he'd kept Hel behind. Ending their father-daughter reunion before it could begin.

That act had been for Hel's own safety. Tilda was likely to murder the former goddess of death otherwise. Didn't make what he'd done sit any easier.

"C'mon, Irish, let me chase the snake out of your pants." Ted sat in stonefaced denial as Loki tugged at the top button of his jeans. She pouted. "*Fine*. Your loss."

She plopped down on the bench beside Ted.

"What've you found out?" Ted asked. When Loki didn't immediately answer, Ted added what he knew the trickster wanted to hear: "Please."

"Hope for you yet, *kemosabe*."

Ted shook his head. "I can't believe I defended you to Tilda. Said we needed you."

"The Norn is here?"

Ted nodded.

"That'll complicate things."

"How?"

"She's not the only one." Loki paused, waited for the next song to start up—"Little Devil" by the Cult—before saying, "Göndul's in town."

16. The Wound that Never Heals

Göndul.

Leader of Hel's valkyries when the goddess of the dead had come to Winnipeg.

Ted had hoped Tilda had killed her in Hel. Wishful thinking. He'd seen the bodies of the other valkyries, but not Göndul's, so he should've known better. Göndul had given Tilda the kiss of death the first time they'd squared off, and Ted held her to blame for the miscarriage that took Erin.

Göndul was as much to blame for Tilda and Ted's split as anyone else.

Or Tilda.

They'd all made their choices, but the former valkyrie had been the one to kick off that cascading clusterfuck.

If she was in town, and alive, maybe she was the real reason Tilda was in Edmonton. He hoped so. Tilda wanting revenge was far less troubling than facing the end of the world. *Especially if she's not looking for revenge on me.*

No matter how Ted spun it, Göndul being in town was not good.

The lightbulb in the booth burst, and Ted felt a piece of glass nick his cheek. He had to fight his tattoos' desire to come out. He wouldn't be surprised if there was a peal of thunder outside on an otherwise clear night.

"Where?" Ted demanded.

"Where do you think?"

Ted groaned. "She's with Surtur isn't she?"

Loki tapped her nose. "Right in one."

"Fuck me sideways."

"I thought you said no to that option." When Ted didn't smile, Loki asked, "Ready to roll?"

"You seriously think Göndul won't recognize me?" Ted pointed at his chest incredulously. "I look the same."

"No. You don't. Now you have a beard." Loki smiled. "And she knew Ófriður, not Ted Callan."

"We're the same guy, you knob."

"No, you're not. The old you would've taken a swing at me. And at Kent for calling you a pussy. You weren't known for your restraint. This city would already be a smoking crater if—"

"I think you proved my point."

Loki poked Ted in the chest. "Let." Poke. "Me." Poke. "Finish." Ted slapped her hand before she could poke him again. "The dwarves gave those powers to a firecracker. You've changed. You've learned restraint. You've had to. Because you've seen the cost of what happens when you let your temper rule you."

"I did want to tune you up in Saskatchewan."

Loki dismissed Ted's admission with a wave. "That province will bring out the worst in anybody. The point is: you didn't. Göndul could never see Ófriður do that. Thor would've never done that. Besides—" she leaned in and ruffled Ted's shaggy hair— "your disguise is fantastic. Have you considered a ponytail? Maybe a trenchcoat?"

"If we're going, let's go."

On the way up the stairs, Ted passed Rye being led down by two dancers, one short and one tall. Brent was hot on his heels with another dancer.

"Dude, where're you going?"

Ted looked at Loki, who slid in close and tight, gave Ted's ear a nibble.

"We're cutting out early."

Realization sank into Rye's beer-addled brain. "Look, man, I've been known to think with my dick a time or two, but *this* is not a good idea. You're gonna get the herp."

"If you're lucky," Brent added.

Loki didn't take the insult lying down. "I'm clean, unlike you. I saw you scratching at yourself. There's a shampoo for that, hero."

Rye gave himself a surreptitious scratch as he dropped his head.

The smokers outside the club catcalled Loki and congratulated Ted. Ted didn't catch the look Loki shot at them, and given how quickly they shut up, he was glad. He'd seen Loki in the fullness of fury, eyes burning with hate. The ring of smokers probably thought they got off lightly for not being castrated on the spot. He was still a little surprised Loki hadn't enjoyed the attention and instead tugged Ted deeper into the parking lot.

A drunk guy bumped into Ted. He was bearded, glassy-eyed and wearing women's flats. "How am I the only one who got kicked out of the stag party? This fucking *sucks*."

He looked as if he were going to fall down. Ted grabbed the guy to steady him.

"Easy."

Those glassy eyes cleared as he took in Ted's appearance. Then he kneed Ted square in the balls.

Ted's eyes rolled back in his head and his knees wobbled. He put a hand on a car hood to keep from falling. The drunk got in one more shot, a glancing blow off Ted's collarbone. He swung again aiming for Ted's face. Ted ducked and took the shot on the crown of his head. Loki dragged the guy off Ted and threw him to the ground. She squatted on his chest, pinning each of his hands under a stiletto heel.

"Run home," she said softly. "You're out of your league."

She stood and the man got to his feet, stumbled into traffic, and was gone.

Loki pulled Ted to his feet and tossed him a set of keys. Ted snatched them, surprised Loki hadn't lowballed him for the laugh of seeing him drop the keys. "Take the wheel, I hate driving in this city."

Ted was pretty sure he was over the limit. He was shaking. Unspent adrenaline from the fight. Loki didn't seem to care. She waited at the passenger door to the car, tapping her foot. The first time Ted had let Loki drive, the trickster had driven them right into a *jötunn's* illusory trap. At redlined highway speed. That had been in the middle of nowhere on the road to Flin Flon, and Ted had been invulnerable.

He hit the lock button on the key fob and walked towards the flash of headlights. It was a current model, candy-apple-red Dodge Challenger. Wide-bodied. Sleek lines. Hemi engine. Zero to sixty in under six seconds. He'd considered putting one on Svarta's tab. God only knew how dangerous it was to let Loki out in 470 horsepower on a Friday night in downtown Edmonton.

"You like?"

"I do, but if we're talking Dodge, I prefer it in a '72 Charger."

"Noted."

"Colour's nice, though."

"Thanks."

"Who'd you steal it from?"

"No one who'll miss it."

Ted ran a finger lightly over the car's fender. He doubted that.

"You're fine. I switched out your last few with iced tea."

Was Loki only telling him what he wanted to hear? Ted would take his drunk driving over Loki's sober.

"Trust me."

He got in, reached over to pop the lock. When he started the car, there was a different, if satisfying, rumble to the one that had belonged to The Goat. This was no GTO, but it beat the bus.

"We're a little conspicuous in this, you know."

"Maybe, but I doubt a crazy hobo will beat you up inside of it."

Ted looked over at Loki as he eased the car out of the parking lot. "I'm going to hold you to that."

Ted gripped the wheel tight, waiting for cherries to pop in his rearview, Loki's assurances aside. He hated dealing with cops at the best of times. A necessary evil to assure folk didn't eat each other he supposed, but he'd rarely seen eye-to-eye with them. On the other hand, if anyone would be able to get him out of a ticket, it was Loki.

She cranked the AC, and turned every vent she could reach to face her. "I wish you could do something about this damned heat," Loki said, wiping at her brow. "It's like riding around in *jötunn's* pants."

"You'd know," Ted shot back, reclaiming the air from a couple of vents, "I'm the one swimming in ball soup over here."

They stopped for a red light. Ted looked at that red glow. Soon the whole city would be immersed in it.

"I never should've come back here," he said, gripping the steering wheel tightly.

"This isn't you, Ted. You're a fighter. I've never seen you lie down and give up. Never seen you just take a beating. Shit. You walked into Hel and took on two *gods* without your hammer."

"There's gotta be a way to keep this fight from coming. Not now. Not here."

"Maybe. But a fight *is* coming, and you're here now."

"Tell that to the one million people who are gonna die if I fuck up."

"So don't fuck up. They would've died anyway. At least now you have a chance to stop Surtur."

Loki had him there.

"We're here," Ted said.

They slowed down as they passed the Church of the Eternal Flame. There was no sign outside advertising it as such, but the soft glow of candlelight was coming from behind the drawn blinds. Ted circled around the block to park out of sight.

"How are we going to get in? I tend not to blend."

The trickster considered that. "You are a bit of a lout. We could send the ravens in for you."

Not a bad idea. Only one problem: "I don't know where Heckle and Jeckle are right now."

Loki nodded. "Let's ask."

"How're you gonna do that?"

"Oh, you know the trick." Loki pursed her lips together and winked. "Put your lips together and blow."

A high-pitched whistle pierced Ted's ears. *Jesus, they would've heard that in Hel.* There was a flutter of wings. The birds were invisible against the black. Shadows knifing through the streetlights. Three ravens landed at Ted and Loki's feet.

Three?

These were living birds, not inky spirits in borrowed flesh and feathers, not Huginn and Muninn. They cocked their heads, warily watching Ted and Loki and hopping from side to side. To Ted, they looked pissed. But then Huginn and Muninn were usually pissy with him. Maybe it was an inborn raven trait. Ted remembered the ravens had told him—and more than once—that they preferred the day, and to roost at night.

"Give them some food," Ted said.

"What?"

"Bribe them."

Loki furrowed her brow.

"Oh, come on. As if you don't have a stolen apple in your purse. And get me something while you're at it."

"This goes on your tab."

Ted circled his hand in a make-with-the-fucking-bribe motion and Loki reached into her purse. She pulled out a muffin, broke it into chunks and tossed them to the birds.

The ravens waited.

Loki sighed, a put-upon sound, and tore the last remaining morsel in two.

"Nobody trusts me anymore." She handed one piece to Ted and popped the other in her mouth. "Happy?"

"Satisfied might be a better word," Ted said and swallowed his bit of muffin. Not enough to soak up his liquor. But it was fresh as if it had just been baked. Still warm, too.

The birds shuffled closer, comically awkward when not in flight, and interposed themselves between Ted, Loki, and their meal.

Ted knelt down. The birds didn't move. He glanced around, but the street was empty except for a homeless guy a block or two down the avenue. Ted didn't speak raven. But Huginn and Muninn knew English, Icelandic, and who knew what other languages. Ravens could mimic human words. They were supposed to be clever. Without a doubt, the lads had been chatting up the locals. He figured these birds would get his meaning.

"Huginn and Muninn," he said.

The ravens snatched their offering up in their beaks and flew off.

"I should follow them," Loki said. "Make sure they didn't eat and run."

"You'll only make them take longer," Ted said. "They'll backtrack for hours thinking you're going to steal their food."

Loki's eyes glittered. "They'd be right."

"You're staying with me."

Another put-upon sigh. "If I must. Smoke?"

Ted nodded.

Loki lit one for each of them, passed Ted his, and it was moist from the trickster's lips. Ted inhaled deeply, and waited. It had dawned on him that if he weren't hiding his powers, he would've kicked in the door, dragging a thunderstorm behind him, and destroyed the place to get to Göndul. He'd make her talk. He'd make her sorry for everything she'd done.

That plan wouldn't be good for him or for Edmonton.

Ted waited long enough that he was considering lighting another smoke when two ravens came out of nowhere, buzzing Loki, who shrieked and swatted at her hair.

Huginn and Muninn cackled maniacally before ruffling their feathers as if to regain some composure.

"**You called?**" Huginn asked.

Muninn bobbed his head. "**Did you not tell us to keep away?**"

"I need you."

"Nice of you to finally admit it."

"It would be nicer if he said that to me, once in a while," Loki added.

"Ha fucking ha." Ted rubbed at his eyes. "Loki says Göndul is inside and working with the Church, which means she's working with Surtur. I need confirmation—"

Loki slapped Ted's arm. "Hey!"

"—of what she's up to."

The ravens looked startled at the mention of Göndul's name.

"With the renegade valkyrie and Mathilda both in Edmonton, Surtur may not need you to set the spark to his fire."

"To say nothing of the company you keep."

Loki gave the ravens the finger. They in turn looked like they wanted to bite the digit off.

"And if we are discovered?" Huginn asked. "Or *you* are discovered?"

"The time's getting close to when you need to roost anyway. One of you in my head, and the other stays free."

Huginn and Muninn looked from Ted to each other, and back to Ted.

"Can you still talk to each other if you do that?"

Huginn preened himself. "An interesting idea. Who will go?"

"Muninn. Huginn can pull the thoughts from his head."

"Huginn could pull the thoughts from their heads and I could remember them if he dies."

Loki snorted. "What are you, a chicken or a raven?"

Huginn and Muninn looked back and forth at one another.

"**You go then, trickster, if you are so eager.**"

Each raven liked to one-up the other—and Ted and Loki—any chance they got. But Ted could tell neither bird wanted to enter the church. Neither of them wanted to possibly face Göndul. Stuck without his powers, Ted couldn't blame them.

He hated skulking around. It wasn't in his nature. Much as he thought Thor had been a dick, Ted also knew that he had more in common with the Thunderer than Odin, for all that Loki teased Ted about being the new All-Father. As much as Ted's restraint had held—*so far*—he knew he couldn't hold back the storm if he saw Göndul again. She'd beaten him. Mocked him. Tried to kill him. She'd dragged Robin and Aiko into Hel. Tried to kill Tilda. *Had* killed their daughter.

Ted couldn't let that go.

He couldn't trust Loki to go in there, either. He believed the trickster—in a fashion. Loki hadn't betrayed Ted. This time. Yet. That Ted knew of. And she was slick as whale shit when she wanted to be, but would she tell Ted everything, or only what she wanted Ted to know?

Ted knew that answer without thinking.

One of the ravens would be best for this. The mere presence of a raven shouldn't immediately call out his presence. Ravens roosted all over the city now. Ted hoped that wasn't a sign of coming carrion. Ravens and Ófriður, hand in hand. If he fucked this up, they'd glut themselves on the dead he left behind.

"I suggest we step away while your little friend does his business," Loki suggested. "We're a little obvious out here."

"**For once, I agree with the trickster,**" Muninn said.

"Fine," Ted said. "This place gives me the creeps anyway."

Huginn shed his borrowed flesh and drifted into the church, an inky spirit, a shadow in the shape of a bird, as ephemeral as his namesake.

Invisible as thought.

Ted plopped himself down on a bench and rested his head in his hands. It had been mighty fucking peaceful without the birds nattering on at him. He forgot how loud they could be, and how nauseating it was for them to share another's memory with him so directly. He'd never split them like this. He'd had one in his head and the other in the world, but that was after one of the birds had lost their flesh to an *álfur* and had to return. Seeing what Huginn saw, filtered through Muninn directly, and into Ted's brain, was vertigo-inducing.

Maybe it is the bourbon.

Well it isn't helping.

17. Truth Comes Out

Huginn slid through the dingy building that looked more like a bus station than a church. The room was lit solely by candlelight. Dozens upon dozens of candles, covering every flat surface that wasn't the floor. A nod to fire and Surtur, no doubt. Or was Göndul too clueless to pay her utility bills?

The candles cast lots of shadows, so there were lots of places for Huginn to hide. Each of those flames held power, drawn from Muspelheim. Drawn from Surtur himself. Ted could feel the power. A phantom twitch on his back, where Yggdrasill wanted to reach out through his connection with Huginn, and snuff those flames. Ted ignored that itch. If he scratched it, it couldn't be undone.

Instead, he reached into his jacket. He could feel his zippo getting hotter through his shirt. He felt the metal against his palm. A smoke. A smoke would settle him. He flicked the lid of the lighter open.

Ted, no!

Ted heard the raven's voice and felt Loki's hand on his wrist. He wasn't sure who stopped him. Muninn or Loki.

"Loki," Ted said, his voice sounding small and distant to his own ears. "Could you light me one?"

Fire, at this particular moment—in any instance—might be a bad idea.

The fucking bird was right.

"Thanks," Ted said, to raven and trickster.

The fires are tied to Surtur, Huginn. Stay to the shadows. Be careful.

I am not a dolt, Huginn shot back. **Göndul is here. I sense her thoughts. I cannot touch them more than lightly or she will sense me. And you. She is different. Altered.**

Anything else?

She hates you.

Anything else that I don't already know?

She is not alone.

Who's with her?

I do not know. A new player perhaps. Or an old one, so changed that I can no longer recognize her.

Get closer. I want to see who she's with.

It will be dangerous, Huginn said.

Do it. Please.

Be careful, Muninn said.

Huginn chuckled, but sounded nervous. **You are the one being careful.**

The raven slid over the walls of the church. Ted could only follow Huginn's movement because Muninn knew exactly where his brother bird was.

Göndul definitely looked the worse for wear since they'd last fought. She was still tall and athletic, exuding speed and power. She was also leaking greasy, thick smoke from three points of her body. Her belly, under her left breast, and her right eye. It was not the same stuff she'd "bled" before. Ted had seen Hel's valkyries become nothing but mist when he'd killed one and they'd come back fine. This wasn't the cold, crisp fog that filled Niflheim. Instead, the smoke reminded Ted of the fires in the patch when Surtur first rose.

Ted wondered if those holes were where Tilda had stabbed her when the two had fought in Hel. Ted would've liked to have seen that fight. Tilda never had shared what she was doing as he and Loki made their way to Hel's hall.

Huginn's thoughts were so vivid, Ted could taste the stink of sulfur.

"Surtur," he whispered.

Yes, Huginn said. **I believe the giant is filling what she lost, replacing her substance with the stuff of Muspelheim.**

But you can't heal a wound from a valkyrie's spear. The giant had to be replacing the loss as fast as it happened.

The second woman looked familiar. Similar to someone Ted remembered from a fever dream, after Thor had stolen Mjölnir, and Ted had escaped, crippled and half-dead, waiting for the magic of his sun tattoo to recharge so he could heal himself. In his dream, Ted had been back at Grey Ladies, the Norns' tea shop in Gimli. He'd seen someone who could have been this woman's daughter.

She looked dangerous—more dangerous than Göndul. Ted was surprised he felt that way about her, knowing what Göndul was capable of, but he did. The stranger was middle-aged, but she had aged well. She wore a simple dress that ended above her knee, with a low scooped neck, showing strands of woven gold, like braids of hair that she wore around her neck, ending in the largest fucking diamond Ted had ever seen. Her heels had wraps that went up to her knees. She didn't need the extra lift the heels provided to be taller than Göndul. Her hair was ash-grey, similar to Tilda's. A trio of cats wound their way in between and around her legs. They kept their backs to Göndul, tails swishing, but at all times at least one kept a wary eye on the former valkyrie.

Göndul turned and her remaining eye burned and flickered like a tiny bonfire was housed in the socket.

The valkyrie asked, "Is it safe?"

The other woman didn't speak immediately, and when she did, she didn't answer Göndul's question. "Is your house in order? Have you done as you promised?"

Smoke billowed out of Göndul's eye. "You have no power over me. Not anymore."

The strange woman smiled. "So certain are you?"

"You only play along because Surtur has your daughter."

"You would know about taking daughters, wouldn't you?"

The stranger said it with such venom, Ted couldn't help but feel the sting. Göndul was responsible for Erin's death. Ted was sick of hiding. He'd hidden too long.

"I'm coming in," Ted said to Huginn. "They need to see me."

What?

"I don't care."

Muninn shrieked in protest. **Do not do this. Not now. Not yet.**

"Gonna let them know," Ted said. "Let them know I remember what they've done."

"Ted," Loki said. "Stop it."

Ted could feel the trickster's hands on his shoulders, holding him down on the bench. Her slender fingers sank into his collarbone, holding him in place. So surprisingly strong. Loki was stronger than Ted now. But Ted knew he *could* be stronger.

"Let them know that *I am fucking here.*"

The storm cloud was moving under Ted's chest. When it burst free of his disguise, Göndul would have that fight she wanted. And she would regret it.

"Jenny," Loki whispered in Ted's ear, stopping him short. "Your parents. Mike and the kids. Rye and Lisa. If you do this now, they'll all die. You'll die. I'll die. *Everyone* will die."

Ted could smell the change in the air. The fresh scent that promised rain. A wall of clouds would swallow the stars. Somewhere, nearby, there was lightning. Mjölnir wanted that lightning here. Ted wanted that lightning here. He wanted to call every bolt that danced through the skies all over the world to this one place. To leave nothing but a smoking crater of the house that Göndul and Surtur had built in this city. *In my home.*

"My home," he repeated aloud. "Mine. They don't belong here."

Muninn dredged up memories, what happy memories he could find, of what Ted would lose. Ted didn't care. Muninn also remembered what the valkyrie had done—as if Ted would ever forget—and that was all he was willing to see. The Nine Worlds had taken too much from him. He was going to take something back. He was going to get his city back.

"My city. My rules."

"It's not your city, Ted," Loki said. "And you know the goddamned rules."

Ted let out a defeated breath. Loki's grip changed, softened, an embrace.

"Soon," she said, running her fingers through his hair. "I promise. Soon, you can let the storm out. Hold on a little longer. We can do this. We *can* stop Surtur without damning the city. Or the world."

Ted grunted something noncommittal. Saving the world. Stopping Surtur. Both seemed too big to be real. Killing Göndul seemed real. Something tangible. Something he could get his fingers around, and when he had his strength back, something he could destroy. He wanted to shove Loki away. He didn't. If he let himself become a destroyer, he was no better than Surtur. His shoulders slumped, and he dropped his head. He was fucking sick of being powerless.

"Are we good?" Loki asked.

"We're good," Ted muttered.

Thank Odin, Huginn said. **If I had been wearing feathers I would have shit myself.**

Ted forced his concentration, and Huginn's, back to the women's conversation. He still wanted to throw up. He wasn't sure whether it was from relief at what he'd avoided doing, or disappointment he hadn't followed through.

"I will have what is mine," Göndul said.

"And again, I say, so certain are you?"

"Hel told me Ófriður's death: 'He will die by a valkyrie's spear.'"

That stopped Ted cold, nausea churning his stomach. He'd heard his own death. Tilda had never told him any such thing—was she the one that was supposed to kill him? The valkyries were dead. Tilda had one of their spears now.

"You are not a valkyrie anymore."

"Neither are you. Neither is the Norn, but we each have a spear. Which of us will give Ófriður his death? *That* is the only question."

The unnamed woman asked a question of her own. "Have you done as commanded?"

"It is done."

"If it is *done*, where is Surtur?"

"Nearly, then. This city will burn from its bones up." Göndul's words. Bones. "The fires will spread. Muspelheim will fully join with Midgard, and then all will burn. Now answer me. Is. It. Safe."

The woman paused, and smiled. Ted expected her to dodge the question, even if he didn't know what "it" was.

"He will never find it."

Göndul barked a laugh. "That one cannot solve anything. He is a thug for the dwarves."

The stranger smiled. "He and Loki solved Thor neatly enough."

Göndul conceded a curt nod. "Loki doesn't worry me."

The stranger stared death at the valkyrie. "He should."

A snort. "It is Ófriður and the Norn we need to worry about. Loki has the tricks, but they have the power."

"You think so small. Tricksters change the world. How long did things remain unchanged in the Nine? How long did we fight and feast and fuck until Loki got *bored*? Ignore him at your peril."

"And what have you done since then? Hidden away, pining for what was lost instead of taking something new."

"I had my task."

"Yes, the Bright Sword."

That perked Ted up. The Bright Sword. That was the mysterious "it."

"You should have brought Laevateinn with you. Let Ófriður have it. I'd love to see him face Surtur."

So the Bright Sword had another name too.

"The blade is broken," said the valkyrie.

Ted's heart fell. It was all over. If the blade was broken, the first part of Hel's riddle was pointless. He could build eight cages out of Surtur's bones, but what use was a broken magic sword?

Göndul wasn't done rubbing the shitty situation in his face. "It's broken, and soon, so shall he be. When his city is in flames. When his world burns, Ófriður will realize he is only a man. Not a god. Not a hero. *A man*.

"And men die."

The stranger smiled.

"What?" Göndul demanded.

"He has not been a man for some time. He has faced our master. He has beaten gods. He has his own followers. People he has saved are marking themselves with tattoos, the same images the *dvergar* inscribed in his flesh. He is closer to us than you think. He is more myth now, than man."

Göndul waved the other's words away. "He will die easily

enough. He does not know how close his city is to going up in flames. How close Surtur is to burning this world to ash."

"I think he does."

The stranger turned to face where Huginn was hiding. As he'd listened to their conversation, Ted had lost track of the god-damned cats. The three of them stared into the shadows, eyes glittering like bonfires, tails undulating.

Huginn, get out of there.

I am missing something important.

Now is not the time. She's going to find you. And if she finds you, she finds me.

There may not be another opportunity.

"Sinmara, if Ófriður were here, we would know. The city would already be in flames. When he comes, and we will either coax him, or bludgeon him into doing so, Surtur will know."

"Not if he buries his power."

"He would not. *Could* not. We would see through any disguise. Anyone heavily tattooed is being targeted and harassed until he shows his hand."

Sinmara said, "Everyone has tattoos now."

Göndul snorted. "So a few innocents die. Their fate will be a dream compared to what will follow."

"Your plan won't work. There are other ways to hide than changing one's appearance."

Göndul rolled her eyes. "Again with the trickster. He won't be able to resist the storm. You haven't fought him. I have. We will draw him here and the city will light up. Surtur will come. And the end will begin."

"And if his spies are already here?"

"We would know that also."

"I have seen many ravens since I arrived. Odd, don't you think?"

"It doesn't matter what he knows. His doom is set. It will be done."

"Ófriður has his plan. So does Surtur. We shall see whose sets the world afire."

Göndul did not appear to like those words.

"What plan?"

The stranger smiled and walked over to her cats. "I would not be here, were it otherwise." She scratched one behind the ears, and its purr sounded as if a lion were trapped in that tiny body. When the stranger spoke again, she whispered, "Isn't that right, Ted?"

Huginn!

Her hand darted into the shadows. Ted felt her grasp hold of the raven. Felt him struggle to stay hidden away in the darkness, but she had him. Ted didn't know how, but she forced the raven into flesh and feathers, and held Huginn up to the light, and to Göndul.

"Ófriður's spy," she said. "I wonder what he heard? What else might he know?"

Göndul snarled.

Sinmara asked, "Are you Thought, or Memory, little bird?"

The raven sank his beak into her flesh, but she bled only fire, and his new body was consumed. The fire did not stop there. As

Huginn's spirit turned to mist, he was penned in by the smoke leaking from the valkyrie's eye. The fire grew hotter.

Ted felt Huginn's pain. They screamed as one. The cloud was gone, and Ted fell forward.

18. Get What You Need

Ted woke in his old bed. His head pounded as if he'd drunk enough whiskey to float the bed, but he hadn't been that drunk. His head flopped back on his pillow. He winced. From the shot of pain, he may as well have been resting his head on a cinder block. He couldn't think. Couldn't remember how he'd gotten home.

What the fuck had happened last night? He and Loki had left the bar. Gone to spy on Göndul. They'd sent for the ravens. The ravens—

Shit! Huginn. Muninn.

Muninn answered first. **Must you be so loud?**

You're good?

Far from good, but neither Huginn nor I are deceased.

Although I wish that I were, Huginn said.

Do you remember what happened last night?

About that ... Muninn said.

A woman rolled over and threw her arm over Ted's chest. She was wearing Ted's shirt from last night, and Ted was wearing … not much at all. The woman murmured and Ted recognized her as she shifted and her hair fell away from her face. Loki.

Loki was in Ted's bed.

Ted hoped he hadn't fucked Loki. They were friendly again.

He'd hate to have Tilda be right, and to have to beat the shit out of the trickster.

Please tell me I didn't fuck Loki.

The door opened before Muninn could answer. It was Ted's mother.

"I don't know how you got in last night without waking up Sam, but I hope you're feeling up to breakfast."

Loki yawned and stretched as she sat up. "Oh, thank you. I'd love some breakfast."

"Oh!" Ted's mom said. She quickly attempted to hide her surprise at Ted not being alone by saying, "Yes, well. I'll let you two get … cleaned up. And dressed."

She closed the door behind her.

Ted turned to Loki and hissed through clenched teeth, "What the hell, Loki?"

"I had to get you somewhere safe."

"And you had to fucking undress me and stick around?"

"I wanted you to stay safe."

Ted scowled.

"Oh, nothing happened, you big baby. You still have your gonch on." She pulled up Ted's shirt—her makeshift nightshirt—to reveal her thong. "Me too. Your trickster cherry remains unpopped."

She laughed but Ted didn't find the situation very fucking funny.

"C'mon," she said. "Get dressed. Big day today."

Loki peeled out of the nightshirt and Ted looked away.

"I didn't figure you for such a prude."

"I don't want to see any of my friends' kits," Ted said.

"You saw everything last night."

Ted rubbed at his temples. "Don't remind me."

Loki tossed a t-shirt and a pair of jeans on to the bed. Ted eased his way out from under the covers, and swooned as soon as he stood. He grabbed at the dresser, but his fingers slid off and he hit the floor. He hissed as his knee slammed into the cement floor that a thin layer of carpet did nothing to cushion. Loki was beside him in a flash. Those wiry, but surprisingly strong stripper arms hauled him back to his feet.

"You okay?"

"Yeah." Once, waking up like this would've thrown him into a rage. Last year, he would've tried to beat Loki's ass into oblivion. No threat or promise would've been enough to stop Ted. Thinking with his dick or his fists were the two most common sources of his troubles. Neither was the right answer today. Ted scowled at Loki, and shook her grip. "I've felt better."

She forced a smile, clearly wanting to say something, perhaps, "You're fucking welcome," but didn't. Instead, she said, "Waffles should help get you back to normal."

Ted's stomach gurgled. He wasn't sure if that rolling was hunger, or a desire to vomit.

If it makes you feel better, Muninn said, **You did not have relations with Loki last night. She also prevented—**

—Helped prevent—

—Yes, yes. Helped prevent you from reclaiming your powers last night and issuing an open challenge to Surtur in front of his minions.

Oh.

As much as it pains me, Huginn said, **perhaps you owe Loki an apology and thanks for your still being alive. And for Edmonton's continued existence.**

Ravens were right. Goddamn them. They were right.

"Loki," Ted said.

The trickster turned around, her arms behind her back closing the clasp on her bra. "Yes."

"Thanks for keeping me from doing something stupid last night."

She flashed him a smile that was worryingly free of guile. "You're welcome."

"And I'm sorry I assumed the worst."

"Not the first, you won't be the last," Loki said, reaching into Ted's closet and pulling out a dress that Ted knew damned well shouldn't be hanging up in there. "But I appreciate the sentiment."

Ted pulled on his jeans, and snorted at the image on the t-shirt. It was emblazoned with a rooster and read "cock."

"Cute."

"Glad you like it."

Ted let out a long breath and sat back down on the bed. "I don't know what the fuck I'm doing here. I don't know how to beat Surtur."

"You'll figure it out," Loki said as she stepped into her dress.

"In time? Shit, maybe it would've been better if you hadn't stopped me last night. Save everyone the misery of my eventual failure."

"Maybe. But Surtur is coming, and you're here now." Loki walked over, scowling. She took Ted's head in her hands. "This would've happened anyway. At least now you have a chance to stop him."

Ted looked away and muttered, "Snowball's chance in hell."

She pinched Ted's nose. "That's still a chance, big guy. And better than Freyr had when he fought Surtur."

"I don't have a magic sword, either."

"Details. But Mjölnir beats a set of antlers." Loki slapped his cheek playfully. "Let's go upstairs and face the music."

"Oh God," Ted said. "Don't remind me."

Loki flashed him a smile. "I hope your mom likes me."

Samson growled as Ted exited the basement. The moment Loki cleared the stairs, the growls stopped. Samson's tail *fwapped* against one of the chairs and Ted's leg. Fucking dog couldn't wait to slather Loki with sloppy kisses.

"Who's a good boy?" Loki asked, scratching Samson under his collar. "Who's a good boy?"

Samson sat on his hind legs and put his forepaws on Loki's shoulders while she rubbed his belly. Ted reached out and Samson's delighted murmurs turned to a growl.

He sighed and went to get a cup of coffee. The cat was on the windowsill, keeping its eye on a magpie squawking in the yard, its tail swishing in interest. His mother took a mug down from the cupboard for him and set it next to the coffee maker. Ted filled his cup and sat at the table. Ted's mom had set an extra place, and was pouring the remains of the coffee into a carafe. She set it on the table and brewed another pot.

Ted was gonna need that coffee.

Knowing Loki, after this breakfast Ted was also going to need a whiskey chaser.

Ted followed his mom's side-eye to Loki and took another look at her new body. Outside of the club, and in the daylight, she looked younger. She was smiling obliviously while she petted Samson. The dog loved her.

Because of course he fucking did.

"Ted," Helen said. "Why don't you get your … guest a cup of coffee?"

Ted was embarrassed not to know how Loki took her coffee. She knew his foibles well enough. Asking would also reinforce to his mom that Ted had brought a complete stranger into her house for sex.

"Two cream, two sugar," Loki said, either trying to save him or damn him.

"I remember," Ted said.

He tried not to groan when he got up to get the trickster her coffee. He made it for her and set Loki's cup down at the table. Loki took her seat, and Samson parked himself next to her, between Loki and Ted. Perfect. He could simultaneously growl at Ted while being spoiled by Loki with table scraps.

Helen set a plate down in front of Loki, who applied enough

syrup to her waffles to make Ted's teeth ache. She dug in with gusto.

"These are wonderful, Mrs. Callan," Loki said.

Ted's mom smiled, and seemed happy that the stranger in her kitchen at least knew Ted's last name.

"Thank you," Helen said, sitting across from Loki. "You have a lovely smile, dear. It looks familiar. Have we ever met?"

Ted shot Loki a look.

The trickster smiled broadly. "I must have one of those faces."

Ted was still picking at his food while Loki had cleared her plate.

"May I use your washroom?"

"Of course," Helen said, gesturing. "Down the hall."

"Thanks."

Ted felt a change in the room the moment Loki was away from the table, and presumably, out of earshot. Ted's mom unloaded. "I cannot *believe* you."

He was surprised that she'd waited until Loki had left. He'd seen the anger bubbling under the surface, but Helen Callan's anger had always been cold. A glacier to her husband's more volcanic temper. There had been no cutting remarks. Nothing that anyone who didn't know her would perceive out of the ordinary. At least Loki had been on her best behavior.

Helen shook her head. "You're lucky you didn't wind up with someone who'd leave you in an alley somewhere, with your pockets turned out and a kidney missing."

Ted had ended up with exactly the sort to do that, but there was no percentage in telling his mother that, either.

"I don't know what happened. I don't remember."

"I thought you were past getting black-out drunk. You're not nineteen anymore."

It was a familiar accusation. She'd said that to him when he'd been twenty-six. And thirty-six. He'd probably hear it again at forty-six, if he lived that fucking long.

"Somebody must've slipped me something at the stag. I didn't have that much—"

"Don't lie to me, Ted. You got drunk before every interview you had after college. You could've had a government job in an office, not been working in the patch."

She had him there.

Helen rubbed at the bridge of her nose. "At least tell me she's not a prostitute."

Ted wasn't sure he could make that promise. He had no idea what the hell Loki had been up to since they'd got into town. "Unless she lifted my wallet on her way to the washroom, I sure as shit didn't pay her."

Helen scowled at his profanity. Ted normally *tried* not to swear in front of his mom. She lived with his father; he had no idea how it could bother her so fucking much.

His head still pounded. He may as well have drunk two bottles of whiskey, judging by the way he felt. No nausea, at least. Puking was the part of a hangover he hated most. Ted needed to get out, and soon. Heading for a cigarette wouldn't do him any favours with his mother, but it beat staying in the kitchen. Let Loki deal with whatever Ted's mom wanted to say to her in private after the trickster returned from doing God only knew what in the washroom.

He'd no sooner pushed his chair away from the table when his mom said over her shoulder, "Where do you think you're going?"

"Out."

"Out? Is there someone else you want to bring home and introduce me to?"

"Jesus, Mom."

"You will watch your mouth in my house."

"I'm just grabbing a fucking smoke."

That didn't help.

His mother didn't answer, and Ted headed out to the porch. His father leaned against the brick retaining wall separating the porch from the flowerbed, staring at his lawn.

Ted lit a cigarette and joined him.

At least his mom hadn't brought up going to church again, thank Christ. Any other time, Ted probably would've sucked it up and gone along to make her happy—NFL schedule dependent—but caught between Rye's wedding and the end of the world, he'd been hoping to sleep in on Sunday.

"Fireworks over yet?" the Sergeant asked.

"Round One, anyway," Ted answered, joining his father at the wall.

"How'd you do?"

Ted snorted. "How do you think? I'm out here."

The Sergeant chuckled under his breath. "You look like ten gallons of shit in a five-gallon pail, but you didn't need to be carried out. Small victories, kiddo."

Ted looked out over his parents' street. Children rode bicycles.

Trees gave shade. It wasn't a bad place. It was a good place. *The best place.* But it wasn't his. Not anymore. He looked for a place to ash his cigarette. If his mom found ashes on her flowers, and butts in the beds, she'd lay into him again. Wordlessly, his dad slid an ashtray over to Ted. He and the Sergeant had never been much for talking. Ted was confronted with the fact that this visit might be the last time they ever saw one another. He had no idea what to say.

"Choice piece of ass you brought home. She legal?"

Ted groaned. "Yes. And other than that, I'd rather not talk about her."

"Too bad," the Sergeant said. "You've guaranteed that I'm going to have to talk about it the minute you're gone."

"Sorry."

His dad shrugged. "Won't be the first time. Your mom was never fooled by those 'long drives' you took with *whatsher-name*—Eva?—Eva. Or that you were only listening to that shit you called music downstairs. I always got an earful about you."

"You never said anything."

"Didn't see the need. Figured you were smart enough to wear a rubber, or you'd join the army to pay for raising the kid."

"Thanks." *I think.*

"The cops called us last fall, you know."

Ted nodded. They'd called Susanna too.

"You were in some trouble?"

"Yeah," Ted said.

The Sergeant took a sip of his coffee. "You should've fucking called."

"I can fight my own battles."

"I know," Ted's father said.

The silence drew out.

"It's been hard..." Ted paused, what the hell could he say? "All that's happened since I left Alberta. Nothing makes any sense. Feel like I've been fighting nonstop. Not getting anywhere either."

"Don't tell your mother you've been fighting. It'll upset her. Mike's doing enough of that."

"What the hell is his problem? He was more of an asshole to me than usual."

"Mike's been having a hard time since he's been back."

"Mike *is* a hard time."

The Sergeant took a long breath. "He's different now, Mikey is. Since he got back from Afghanistan. I get the feeling ... maybe he did something he's not too proud of. Maybe he saw some things he wishes he hadn't."

"They're not lobbing nerf footballs around over there."

"No, they're not," the Sergeant agreed. "There's no honour in war. There's mud, fear, blood, and death."

"How do you deal with losing people?"

"Keep sight of the goal. Remember them when you've got it. Until then, squash it down, deal with it later."

As hard as the Sergeant was on those he deemed "pussies," he never thought less of a fighting man who didn't want to fight anymore. Someone who didn't want to try to fight, yes, but if you've seen real war, you tried. Period.

"Ted?"

Loki eased the front door closed with the kind of care she'd never shown to anything Ted had owned, back when Loki had been a he.

"We need to get rolling to take care of that business from last night."

The Sergeant raised an eyebrow, and smirked. "Take care of business, kiddo."

"I'm trying."

Loki tossed Ted the keys to the Challenger. He caught them and popped the locks, but didn't use the autostart. He liked to turn the key himself, feel the engine rumble.

They got into the car, and Ted started it. As the engine turned over, he said, "Tilda told me I'm going to die this weekend."

"Man she *is* pissed."

Ted didn't believe for a second that Tilda would be the one to kill him. At least, he didn't want to believe it. The Norn had plenty of opportunity in the last nine months to show up when his defences were down. Any time that one of the monsters he'd cleared out of Winnipeg nearly killed him.

She could've stabbed him through the heart any time he'd been on the shitter too. That would've been a surprise. And an ugly end.

He definitely believed she *could* do it. He didn't want to believe that she would.

The bones of the city.

Ted knew what she meant.

Coal can burn and smoulder underground for decades. Longer. That was something the followers of Surtur could use. They might not need Ted to be here at all to unleash their master. If they used magic to kick off those fires and set enough explosions in those mines, Surtur would come. Ted was sure of it.

And if he tried to do something to stop them, Surtur would show. If he did nothing, the same result.

Fucked whichever way I wriggle.

That was what it must feel like to be Loki. Are you responsible? Yes? Fix it. No? Fix it anyway. At least, that's how Loki told it. How could Ted go into an old mine and stop them without his powers?

"If Göndul and her crew have gone underground, we'll need dwarves."

Loki groaned. "They hate me."

"Rightly so."

"Well sure, if you're going to bring *right* into it," Loki said, flashing a brilliant smile and changing her shape. "They may hate me, but they *love* Freyja."

Ted looked at him. "Your funeral if they catch on."

"If anyone can put the 'fun' in 'funeral,' it's me."

Ted snorted a laugh.

Loki asked, "Why worry about dealing with them? Let's do what needs to be done."

"I have enough enemies, thank you very much."

Loki pursed her lips, considering. "Fair."

"I'm also not able to throw down the way I'm used to."

"You asked for it."

"I know, and thanks again for the sore jaw, the bruises, and getting to live in constant fear of monsters again."

Loki beamed at him. “You’re welcome,”.

“What’s your plan? *Dvergar* are a territorial bunch. It might be better to get Andvari and the Svarta boys to set up a meeting for you.”

Ted asked, “You think that moustached fucker will get here on time?”

Loki shook her head. “Doubtful.”

“Besides, I know where to find dwarves in Edmonton.”

19. Fight Fire With Fire

The dwarves at 'Wolf's had looked familiar. They'd reminded Ted of something. He'd seen dwarves before he'd known there *were* dwarves. They had a table at the Westmount Super Flea Market selling mechanical gewgaws.

His phone buzzed with an incoming text. Loki checked it. "Message from Tyler," she said. "Groomsman breakfast. 7 a.m. Sunday. High Level Diner."

Fuck's sakes. The wedding wasn't until the afternoon. That was his whole day gone. Which would've been fine—fun, even—if Göndul weren't trying to set the city on fire.

The Flea Market was one of Ted's favourite places in Edmonton. You could find anything there if you were willing to spend the time and dig. It was a bewildering mix of every street sale, antique shop, and gypsy merchant all thrown under one roof and serving hotdogs. Winnipeg didn't have anything like it. Not that Ted had any time for shopping these days.

His route took him past the Edmonton Petroleum Club, where Ted and Susanna had had their reception. Ted couldn't figure out why the fuck Rye wanted to go back there. After Thursday night with Jenny, maybe he could start looking at the place more fondly.

The market was in an old mini mall that had been gutted.

People lingered outside one of the rear entrances, smoking. Ted and Loki joined them. Better not to be on edge when he was dealing with dwarves. He'd gotten used to his powers and didn't hate Andvari—not anymore—but Ted still hadn't forgiven the Flin Flon dwarves for how they'd brutalized him on his first night in Winnipeg. He was willing to work with the fuckers. And take their money. But there'd never be Wednesday beers for shits and giggles in their future.

It took him a few flicks to get his disposable lighter to go, but he didn't want to use his Zippo after last night. He cupped his hand to shield the flame and lit his cigarette, taking a deep drag and closing his eyes to the crackle of the paper being consumed.

The Westmount Super Flea Market advertised fifty-cent coffee and fifty-cent hot dogs. The North End one was newer, and looked less sketchy, but bikers and gangbangers still used it for their drops sometimes. It was so congested, and with so many different things there, it was easy for them to hand off weapons or drugs.

He couldn't remember where in the building he'd seen the dwarves last. The market was like a damned maze and it had been over a year since he'd last been there. The booths changed up from week to week, depending on who decided not to renew their leases. The layout could've changed completely in the time Ted had been in Manitoba, and his former landmark vendors could've moved on—or died.

Ted shrugged, butted out his smoke and headed in. He'd never gone in looking for something specific and had picked up the occasional part or tool he'd needed. Usually he was there to root through the CDs. If you were hunting down something specific, odds were, you'd never find it. But for the browser, you'd always discover something. Today, Ted wondered whether the dwarves would be gone because he was looking for them.

Because he needed them.

He'd blow up that bridge when he came to it.

He walked the outskirts of the market before diving into its guts. The place was filled with a weird mix of people. Ted passed a bank of fortune tellers—palm readers, tarot cards. From the look of it, there was no rune caster. Maybe they all shared the spot. He wondered what Tilda would think of them. They were pretty tightly packed in the corner. Ted remembered when he used to snort at them. Today, he eyed them warily. They were probably fakes, but if not…

He'd always assumed fortune tellers were frauds. That anyone with that kind of power would keep it hidden, use it to their own advantage. In a way, he'd been correct. Knowing that magic was real, and had been hidden from most people, put those earlier suspicions into sharp contrast. People have all sorts of motivations. Ted had previously only considered the selfish ones. That someone would use their gift, not for profit, but for altruism, had been inconceivable.

Not that he'd taken a fucking dime from anyone he'd saved from a giant. Robin and Aiko weren't paying for their rune tattoo powers on the instalment plan. The City of Winnipeg hadn't been sent an invoice for dealing with Hel and Thor.

It is more likely the city would send you the invoice, Muninn said with a chuckle.

The raven was probably right.

Maybe there were seers who wanted to help people.

Ted thought Tilda would have been one of those.

Rose-coloured glasses, Muninn said. **For all her protests of being different from her grandmother, Mathilda was always more like Urd than Verdandi. Vera was the one with the softest heart. And if Urd was stone, Tilda is now steel.**

Ted looked back over his shoulder. The palm reader stared at him. She had her client's hand cupped, index finger touching the palm, but her eyes bored into Ted. She stood, releasing her customer, and backed away from the table. Ted couldn't make out the other person's protests over the general din of the market, but when the palm reader reappeared, she had a bag slung over her shoulder and was walking for the exit.

"Hey," the client yelled.

The fortune teller's posture made it clear that not only was she not coming back for the reading, she wasn't coming back, period.

"That can't be a good sign," Loki muttered.

"You think?"

He couldn't blame the fortune teller. With Göndul here—and working for Surtur—the future didn't look too fucking bright. Still, he wondered what she'd seen in him. Was it the fires of Muspelheim? Or what he'd worried the dwarves had made him. Tilda had seen him that way, in the dreamy world of their *seiður* bonding. He'd been a scaled beast then, in her eyes—and his own.

A monster.

Any idea about that palm reader's vision?

The back of Ted's neck itched. He could almost feel Huginn shaking his head. **I am locked in your mind, at the moment. If you wish I will find out when you next release me.**

Don't bother. I've got a pretty good idea.

Ted moved deeper into the market. People stared—not at him, which was a welcome change—but at the screaming woman who'd chased after her palm reader.

Next to the fortune tellers were hairdressers who offered waxing. A man with an Indian accent talked to a potential customer about his time selling T-shirts in Barcelona next to a wall of old electronics and appliances. Ted found the exact same make of dishwasher as the one he'd had that had decided to piss all over the floor of his old house.

The guy who sold airport seizure knives was still around. His table sported plastic buckets filled to the brim with pocket knives of all sorts. Plain single-blade folding knives, Swiss Army knives. A folding knife hidden in an elaborate belt buckle. Ted already had a pocket knife. He also had never been stupid enough to leave it in his pocket when he'd gone to an airport.

Displayed neatly behind the plastic buckets were some larger blades that were harder to miss. Ted had to wonder what dumbass had tried to bring those to an airport, let alone get them through security.

He still had his *álfur* stiletto, but given its origins and power, it wasn't something he wanted to be waving around—or have taken from him.

Knick-knacks and junk. Novelty panties emblazoned with innuendo. An older woman, a North Edmonton mom by the look of her, was next to a Sikh and chatting across from a stand selling Luchadore masks. There was an adult-sized Flash costume.

"You should buy it," Loki said with a wink. "It suits you. What with the lightning bolt and all."

Ted barked a laugh. It had been Loki who'd told him he didn't have the six-pack for spandex. He wouldn't give the trickster the satisfaction. Instead, he breathed in that old mothball smell that seemed to permeate the market, and kept going past booths of used movies and old books. A guy could spend hours there.

Today wasn't that day.

Tomorrow didn't look good either.

The Flea Market's resident conspiracy nut still had a booth selling World War II paraphernalia and German Army surplus.

Half the items in the market today were bongs, or looked like they should be. Ted saw all the things he remembered being here. What he wasn't seeing were dwarves.

I have them, Muninn said.

Thank Christ. Where?

Where they used to be.

The directions that Muninn offered weren't quite GPS, but they got the job done.

Got it, thanks.

If you deem it necessary, "little pebble" would be an appropriate insult for this bunch.

Why would you assume I was going to insult them?

The ravens' silence spoke volumes.

Ted headed for where the Edmonton dvergar were. His phone buzzed. *Goddamn it. If this is about the fucking wedding…*

It wasn't. At least, he hoped not. It was a text from Jenny. That he could deal with.

—Heard you left the bar with a stripper last night.

Ted stopped so that he could text her back; he hated people who texted and walked. They always got in his way. He wished she'd called instead. Jenny, he wanted to talk to. And he hated texting. He could feel Loki reading over his shoulder, something Ted hated more than having to text.

Before Ted had typed, "That was Loki," Jenny asked, —Should I be worried?

—No.

—Ah.

—Will fill you in.

—You'd better. ;)

"Done talking with your girlfriend?" Loki asked. Before Ted could answer, she peered at Ted's phone and added, "And I'm a *dancer*, not a stripper."

"You're not in the same body as last night, so how about you let it go?"

"Fair enough." The trickster's eyes twinkled. "This time."

"Can you do me a favour?"

Loki poured syrup on her answer. "*Anything*."

"Hang back while I talk to the *dvergar*," Ted said.

"You're sure?"

"They'll recognize your fucking mouth a world away."

He found the dwarves right where Muninn had said they'd be, in the dead centre of the mall, nestled between a toy booth selling classic and more recent Star Wars and GI Joe action figures, and a vendor selling rugs that looked like black velvet paintings. There were three dwarves behind the table of their booth.

Of course there were three of them.

Ted supposed that was better than there being nine of them. The other magic fucking number ruling his life.

Each was either noisily eating a hot dog, slurping coffee, or flipping through a magazine. Each also seemed to be getting more food and drink on their faces than into their mouths. They didn't give Ted more than a cursory *go fuck yourself* glance, the same look they shared with anyone walking by, and—presumably—not spending money at their table.

Ted approached the table, but they ignored him. When he got closer, he realized that two were women. Ted assumed they were, anyway. They didn't have beards. A quick glance, and then back to their food. The male *dvergur* was looking at a skin mag.

When they didn't look up again, or otherwise acknowledge him, Ted cleared his throat.

A gravelly chorus of "Go fuck yourself!" was the *dvergar's* response.

Ted's first desire was to flip their table. Quickly followed by the pleasant thought of slapping some manners into them. Neither were going to get Ted what he needed, so he sucked a breath in through clenched teeth and said, "I need your help."

The bearded dwarf said, "I thought we told you to go fuck

yourself," licked his fingers, and flipped another page of his magazine.

"I can pay you."

"You can't afford our help."

Ted dug his Svarta gold card out of his wallet, but didn't hand it over.

"We don't take credit," one of the women said.

"Cash only," the other added.

"How about you look again?" Ted made sure they saw the type. He hated to use it—worried this would single him out to creatures of the Nine while he was in Edmonton. But he had little choice.

Their bushy eyebrows rose as one. The bearded dwarf asked, "Where did you steal this?"

"Freely given."

"Bullshit and trickster promises."

"Call Andvari," Ted said.

The dwarf's eyes narrowed, nearly buried under his bushy eyebrows. Big Beard asked, "And what makes you think this 'Andvari' is any friend of ours?"

Ted shrugged. "You're dwarves."

Over her car magazine, the woman on the right said, "What a small-minded thing to say."

Ted grimaced. She was right. He had assumed they'd all be pals. He should've known better. People were people the Nine Worlds over, whether they were *jötnar*, *álfar*, *dvergar*, or human:

Assholes.

"I'm sorry," he said.

"We don't get paid in apologies."

"I'm pretty sure Andvari's good for the difference."

"If you lie—"

"You'll give me a blood eagle?" Ted asked.

The dwarf looked startled that Ted had mentioned the torturous execution.

"Just fucking try it."

They smiled. The women cracked their knuckles. Big Beard said, "Good. You know how to bargain."

One of the women asked, "Out of curiosity, what do you need?"

Ted looked over the crowd, but no one appeared to be listening. He lowered his voice anyway. "Help shutting down the Church of the Eternal Flame."

"Impossible."

"I do impossible before breakfast. You can't do this?"

"It would cost you," one of the dwarf women said.

The other added, "Not just in gold."

It was Big Beard who gave the final word. "It can't be done."

"Can't or won't?"

Big Beard doubled down. "There is nothing we can do for you."

Ted placed his hands on the table, leaning forward into Big Beard's face. "Nothing, Little Pebble?"

The insult seemed ludicrous. But it worked. One of the women grabbed Ted's hand. She was faster than she looked. The dwarf's giant mitt was a like a vise. That grip reminded Ted of how helpless he'd been when Andvari and his Beards had ambushed him back in Winnipeg. Without his powers, Ted knew these dwarves were stronger than him.

"I will beardfuck the life out of you," Big Beard said, a hug gob of spit running into his beard when he pronounced the "B." "Little pebble."

Someone brushed up against Ted from behind. Loki whispered, "Here if you need me."

Ted regarded the dwarf's face, and stroked his own beard. "Not with that scraggly thing. I can sneeze and grow a better beard than that."

The dwarf's eyes looked fit to bug out of his head. Ted had seen plenty of Loki's shit-eating grins. He threw one at the dwarf who was sputtering but not getting a coherent word or threat out.

One raised an eyebrow and sang.

The *álfur* stiletto leapt from were Ted had it stashed in his boot, and spun rapidly on its hilt. Blade and handle became a blur. The dwarf stopped her song and the knife stopped its spinning—with its blade pointed directly at Ted's crotch.

"You come here with this? You seek to treat with us while you carry *álfur* filth?"

Ted took a step back and raised a hand up. He hoped Loki was here to help him instead of just to get a better view of his imminent beatdown with added castration. Unlike her, Ted couldn't grow them back. The thought of the dwarves having a knife to his crotch again made his entire body itch.

A hissing caw from Muninn worried Ted more. The dwarves were using magic. In front of him. Loki had done so too, but Ted was pretty sure rules of any sort didn't apply to the trickster. What if this use made him vulnerable again? What if Göndul and her mystery partner could use this to find him? What if the dwarves had broken his disguise? They could kill him while he slept.

Ted knew the valkyrie wouldn't be satisfied with only him. Her vengeance would take his family too.

Mjölnir stirred. It would be so simple. Answer their threat with action.

You are still safe, Muninn said, before the raven amended the statement with: **As safe as you ever are.**

How the fuck would you know?

I can feel the tie to the Nine sliding away from you. The connection is being deflected.

To where?

Huginn said, **I cannot say. Ricochets are unpredictable.**

He also didn't like that someone else might be taking a magic bullet meant for him.

Goddammit.

The dwarf must have noticed something was up too. He squinted. He took the reading glasses from atop his bald head and fixed them on his nose; squinted again.

"How?" he asked. "You know to seek us out. You know of the Church. You know Andvari. I sense no connection to the Nine. How are you doing this?"

"None of your fucking business. You'll do as I say."

A snort of derision. "And if we don't?"

"The god of thunder and the goddess of death made threats too. They lost their jobs."

Three sets of eyes went wide.

"Ó—"

"Don't say it. He's not here." The dwarves looked ready to jump up and rush him. "But he can be." Ted snapped his fingers. "Like that."

"Andvari would send his weapon against us?" Big Beard asked.

"He didn't send shit. But that doesn't mean I won't tear through all of you like you're Kleenex."

"Why do you hide? You were not meant for this."

"I'd rather people not know I'm here."

One of the women asked, "Which people?"

"The kind who are too fond of fire, if you feel me."

"Ah…" the other said.

"They're no friends to us. I think we can come to an arrangement. If you will do us a favour."

"A favour?" Ted's eyes narrowed. "What kind?"

Ted was running out of time for side trips. He also wasn't winning any friends with threats, so he went back to a currency they'd care about.

"I'd rather give you Andvari's money."

The dwarven women's eyes glittered and Big Beard's smile cut through the hair of his beard like an axe splitting kindling.

"Gold is for goods, but a favour for a favour."

"Well, shit."

"We have a door in the rock, under the High Level Bridge, we will meet you there. Perhaps we can help you after all."

Ted nodded and he and Loki left the Flea Market. After three steps outside, he started sweating in the heat and humidity. He lit himself a cigarette and offered one to Loki. Ted let out a long exhale of smoke that joined the billowing cloud from the other smokers by the door.

"Well, that went better than expected."

"I can't believe they didn't kill you after you called that one 'little pebble,'" Loki said.

Ted shrugged. "Sun's gotta shine on a dog's ass someday."

20. Play with Fire

Ted looked over his shoulder, trying to see whether anyone was watching them scramble down the riverbank. Loki stopped and Ted slammed into her back.

She staggered and turned, throwing a scowl at him and slapping her shoes against his chest. "I told you we were good." With a look across the river, Ted ducked under the bridge. Tilda was waiting for them. The Norn ran a disdainful eye up and down Loki.

Loki pursed her lips, and gave a slight nod, as if impressed that Tilda had seen through the disguise. She shot a stink-eye right back at Tilda. "Are we going to do this, or what?"

Tilda's hand tightened over her spear.

To her credit, Loki didn't look concerned by the apparent threat. "If you really wanted me dead, you'd have killed me already, and Ted's chances be damned. You *saw* something. And that vision said you needed me. And *you* don't like it."

As Loki jabbed a finger at Tilda's breast, the Norn grabbed her wrist, stopping it. Loki's hand was smaller and Tilda smiled as she clenched hers over it. Loki clearly didn't want to give Tilda the satisfaction of admitting her hand was being crushed.

Tilda smiled grimly. "I don't like *you*."

"I don't like you either." The trickster managed to worm her hand free and dropped it to her side without giving it a shake.

"Your dislike has always been obvious. Not that you give a shit about Ted or his friends either. That's why you left."

"I left because of *you*."

"Do you two mind calling off your pissing contest on account of the weather?"

They both shot Ted a look that would flatten a giant. He took a step back. Unless he woke his powers, there was nothing he could do to stop them from scrapping; and *with* his powers, he'd only make things worse.

Tilda turned her back. Ted felt as if he'd taken a punch in the gut. "I thought I could do this," Tilda said. "That I could stand being around Loki. But Ted, it's hard constantly being reminded that Loki's friendship *still* means more to you than me, or our child."

"Our child is dead."

Slap, right across Ted's face.

The name barely came out as a whisper. *Erin*.

Ted rubbed his jaw. It felt as if she'd loosened a few teeth. He clenched his fist. He'd hit the valkyries plenty, but this … this wasn't right.

The future was clear in Tilda's electric blue eyes. Ted could feel the storm moving across his chest, trying to break out.

"Fine," Tilda said. "I can always kill the trickster another time."

Ted let out a sigh of relief. "Well, it looks like the band's back together."

"You really want me to work with her?" Loki asked, incredulous.

"Only way we win," Ted said, hoping that assumption was correct. The only thing the Norn's expression, and stance, gave away was that she wanted to run the trickster through.

Loki shuffled behind Ted, placing one hand on his shoulder, the other on his bicep. Ted hoped Tilda wasn't so far gone she'd stick them both, just to get to Loki. Loki peered past him, eyeing the Norn.

"If we're going to work together, I need assurances," Loki said. "Assurances that she won't harm me. Or my family."

Ted grimaced. This was not going to be as easy as he had hoped.

"You need to make up for what *you've* done first," Tilda said.

"Now you're bitching about Ragnarök? Will you bring up Baldur next? I *paid* for those sins, believe me. I died on Heimdall's blade. Don't blame me because I was smart enough to come back."

Tilda laughed. "Cheated your doom, and you call it payment."

"You only *think* you know death."

Tilda tightened her grip on her spear. Ted expected Loki to step further behind him, but she didn't. She stepped around him, fixing Tilda with the stare of a hunting hawk.

"Oh, I am *full* of death."

Their argument flared again, each talking over the other so fast, so loud, that Ted couldn't make out what they were saying.

"Stop it. Both of you. Or *I* will stop you. With lightning. Let Surtur pick up the pieces."

Tilda and Loki *did* stop then. They both looked at him.

"You can't bluff me," Tilda said.

"You can't bluff at all," Loki added.

Tilda shot the trickster a dirty look, but continued, "I know what you'll do."

"That so?" Ted cracked his knuckles. "Fucking try me. The both of you."

"You'd be dead before Mjölnir returned to your hand," Tilda said.

"You're not going to kill me. And you're not going to kill Loki."

Tilda asked, "Since when do *you* see the future?"

"Since we have a city to save, and a monster to stop."

Tilda chuckled under her breath. "I never thought *you* would be the voice of reason."

Loki nodded. "I've got a *bad* feeling about this."

Ted poked Loki in the shoulder. "You are one goddamned *Star Wars* joke away from me jumpstarting the end of the world."

"Fine," Tilda said. "We'll deal. We'll barter peace. But it is on Loki to make reparations for the past."

"If I agree to *that*, I'll have a line a thousand thousand deep."

"No," Tilda said. "Let's assume Ragnarök washed your old sins clean. You've paid for *those* actions. You haven't paid for what you did to Ted and to me. And you *will* pay."

Loki considered her words. "I'm open to discussing terms."

"First: you will *never* wear my shape again."

Loki shrugged. "I can live with that." Then she muttered, "Was getting tired of it anyway."

Ted sighed.

Tilda continued. "Second: if I believe you have betrayed Ted, any agreement we make is void."

"Whoa, whoa, whoa," Loki said, holding up her hands. "That's bullshit."

"Not if you don't plan on turning on him," Tilda said smugly.

"You see the future. *Poorly*. What if you misinterpret something I do?"

Tilda snarled. "Unlikely."

"Nevertheless," Ted said. "Since it's my future ass on the line here too, I'm content to say that if Loki *does* fuck me over, all bets are off."

Loki slapped Ted's arm. "Thanks for the vote of confidence. Dick."

Ted furrowed his brow. "I said 'if.'"

Tilda smiled. "Only a matter of time."

"I have a condition of my own," Loki said. "You will allow my daughter to live out her new life."

Tilda crossed her arms, cradling her spear. "No."

"Jesus, Tilda!" Ted said.

"I want her to pay. I will take everything from her."

Loki shook her head, and turned as if to leave. "If my sins are washed clean, so are hers forgiven."

"Not so fast," Tilda cut her off, snapping her spear straight out to block Loki's departure.

"I said that your sins prior to Ragnarök were washed clean, *nothing* you or Hel have done since is forgiven. And since we are talking about what your darling daughter has done...What, *exactly*, would encourage me to spare her thrice-damned life?"

The trickster looked chastened. When she spoke, it was in quiet, measured tones. "She told Ted how to kill Surtur."

Tilda snorted. "She told him a riddle."

"That's more than you told him."

"Hardly problem fucking solved," Ted grumbled.

Loki continued on as if it were. "After Ted kicks the big guy's lava-dripping ass, she will have contributed to saving everyone in each of the Nine Worlds. What the Hel is *that* worth to you?"

"She's hardly the person doing the heavy lifting on that one."

"I didn't say she was responsible or that it was her victory. I said she would have *contributed.* As I have contributed, the ravens have contributed, and *you* have contributed to Ted's eventual victory."

Ted snorted a laugh. "Eventual."

"Think positive, Teddy Bear."

"I'm not sure if I should be more surprised you think I'll win or that you're willing to share credit," Ted muttered.

"People change. You did." Loki turned to Tilda. "And you did. Why is it so hard for you to believe that Hel could? That I could?"

"Oh, I believe it," Tilda said. "But I also believe you'll quickly change right back."

"We began this together," Ted said. "I want to end it the same way."

"I knew you first," Loki said.

"Pretending to be my dog doesn't count and don't interrupt me or I'll sew your lips shut again."

Loki did keep quiet, but she didn't stop smiling.

Ted went on. "From the moment I came to believe that all this viking and Nine Worlds bullshit was real, you both had my back. It hasn't been easy, and mistakes were made—by all of us. I'm hardly fucking innocent, but we got the job done. First against Rungnir and Urd, then Hel and Th—" Ted stopped before he said the name, and Loki smiled. Uttering Thor's name could summon him. And Ted didn't want to chance dragging the god back from his second death. "We need to put all of our disagreements aside. Stopping Surtur has to matter most. If we still can't live with one another afterwards—if we win—"

Loki coughed.

"*After* we win," Ted said.

"Thank you."

"Then, if we still can't stand each other, we go our separate ways. But we go in peace. No feuds. No wars. No killing."

Tilda looked back and forth between Ted and Loki. "Odin made peace between the Aesir and the Vanir. And at times with the *jötnar*, *álfar*, and *dvergar*. I think that the *dvergar* made something more dangerous than they anticipated when they forged Ted Callan into Ófriður."

"I am *not* the All-Father."

Loki smiled and held up Ted's pocket knife. "Not yet."

She opened the folding blade, and drew it across her palm. She winced as the blood oozed up from the cut.

"I've only ever cared about my family," Loki said. "You'll never trust me unless you join it."

Tilda looked at Loki's bleeding hand as if the trickster were waving a dick in her face.

"Be a part of my family. A new family. New gods. New protectors."

"You mean to make us your blood family, your wish-kin," Tilda said. "As you and Odin were long ago."

Loki nodded.

"You expect me to share blood with you."

If Ted hadn't been looking at Tilda, he would've sworn those words had been spoken by Urd. The eldest of the Norns had no love for the trickster, though Ted had no idea why—other than Loki being Loki.

"I know all about the Greenland Affair," Tilda said.

"That was a long time ago."

Tilda tapped at her temple. "Not for me."

Loki rolled her eyes.

"This ceremony," Ted said. "Is it a magic thing?"

Tilda and Loki both stared at him as if he were a moron.

Ted shrugged. "What if it doesn't work?"

Loki asked, "Why wouldn't it work?"

"Because of my disguise," Ted answered.

"It's not magic, Ted," Tilda said. "Though I suppose there is a *sort* of magic in adopting one another, in choosing a new family."

Ted nodded. "Okay."

"It's been a long time since anyone loved you enough to claim you as family, Loki," Tilda said. "Do you remember what to do?"

"You're not the only one with a long memory, Norn."

"Great," Ted muttered. "I'm sucking hind tit here with no fucking clue of what to do next."

No, you are not, Muninn said.

The raven had been there, with Odin, the first time Loki had done this ritual. He knew how. Now, so did Ted.

"Before I commit to this," Ted said: "One question."

"Shoot."

"Did you and Odin ever have sex after you did this ritual?"

Tilda stared at him. "*That's* your question?"

"A gentleman never asks, and a lady never tells," the trickster said.

Ted snorted. "You are neither of those things."

Loki smiled. "Would it make you feel better if I said yes?"

"That's no answer."

"Only one you're getting."

"If the answer is yes, don't tell me," Tilda said. "I know Odin slept with my grandmother. We're getting into transitive property territory that I don't want to consider."

Loki sang. Her voice had a Delta blues sound. Strange, but then, if anyone knew suffering—whether it was causing it, or enduring it—Ted supposed it was Loki.

I remember bygone days
I mixed my blood.
All-Father Odin said
He'd drink from no cup
Not brought to both of us.
I say this to Ted Callan,
To Mathilda Eilífsdóttir
What was done in ancient

Past is now past.
There will be no beer
Not served to us three.
Never will I wear
Your countenance
Nor speak as you
Without your leave.
I swear that war with one
Shall be war with all.
We will speak no words
Of blame.
We will not repay debts
With hatred.
We are wish-kin.
We are blood.

Loki passed the knife to Ted. Ted wasn't sure if that was because it was his turn, or because the trickster wasn't quite ready to believe that Tilda wouldn't use the knife to stab her. Muninn prompted Ted with the words Loki had spoken, and he realized he had no idea what he wanted to say. He might be a better singer now, but he was no poet. He couldn't speak in rhyme, or meter; everything Loki had said, felt a little too "high-fallutin," as the Sergeant would say, to come out of Ted's mouth. He slashed his palm, and took Loki's hand. Nothing to do but wing it.

I remember the good old days
Chasing a dog under a tree
Drinking stolen beer.
I remember living free.
I remember blaming you.
I remember hate.
I remember what I owe.
What was done is done.
Past is now past.
There will be no beer
Not served for three.
Any who brings war
Will know fucking war.
No blame.
No debts.
No hate.
We're a team.
We're wish-kin.
We're blood.

"A little rambly," Loki said, "but a nice first effort."

"Let's hope it's a last effort," Ted said as he passed Tilda the blade.

She held it gingerly at first, pausing long enough to make Ted wonder whether his suspicions and Loki's worries had been valid. Finally, Tilda stuck her spear in the dirt. She sliced her palm, and placed her hand over Ted's and Loki's, mingling her blood with theirs.

I remember bygone days
When Lie-Father,
Ever my enemy,
Became my friend,
Became my enemy.
What was done in ancient
Past is now past.
There will be no beer
Not served to us three.
Death-Father's family is
My own.
Wolf-Father's family is mine.
I swear that war with one
Shall be war with all.
We will speak no words
Of blame.
We will not repay debts
With hatred.
We are wish-kin.
We are blood.

Together, Ted, Tilda and Loki spoke the words that would seal the deal.

This will be so.
May we never feast.
This will be so.
May we never drink.

This will be so.
Until flames burn us,
Even then we will meet
Doom with hands clasped
Spears drawn and teeth bared.

Ted didn't feel any different, not like he had after the *seiður* connection he'd formed with Tilda. But this was no less real because their arrangement didn't have some magic forces binding it. They had chosen this. It was a marriage of sorts, though he'd never admit that to Loki. He had a hard enough time admitting it to himself. His last divorce had gotten messy. It might have been better if they could have gone forward without this ceremony, but Ted knew that wouldn't have happened. Thinking of their bond souring would only spoil it all the faster.

"You can let go of my hand now," Tilda said.

They separated, and Loki reached into her purse, pulling out some strips of cloth. Ted wondered whether Loki had planned for this. He shook his head; now wasn't the time for accusations or suspicions. It was done. He tied the cloth over his palm.

The three of them looked at one another, if not with new eyes then with new understanding. But it was strange to be standing there as traffic drove over the High Level Bridge and an LRT train came out a tunnel below.

"If you are through?" said a gruff dwarven voice from the darkness under the bridge. It was impossible to tell if the voice belonged to a man or a woman.

When the dwarf stepped out of the shadows she wasn't one of the two dwarf women Ted had spoken with at Westmount. She was somewhere in the vicinity of five foot, but didn't have the wide-as-she-was-tall look that *dvergar* men seemed to sport, appearing curvaceous rather than carved out of a single block of stone. Her blonde hair was in a short bob, and she was dressed simply, in blue jeans and a snug fitting Oilers t-shirt. She gave the three of them the stink-eye.

"I was told there would be only two."

Ted crossed his arms over his chest. "Now there's three."

"Pray we don't alter the deal any further," Loki said.

Ted shot her a look. Now was *not* the fucking time for *Star Wars.*

Perhaps you should have included something regarding that film in your blood-bond ceremony, Muninn said.

Thanks. Where were you earlier, jackass?

"I believe I will be welcome," Tilda said. "And if I am not…" she bounced her bag of rune stones in her palm. "Perhaps I will see your doom."

The dwarf gulped and bent low, gesturing towards the door in the rock. "Forgive me, Norn. Of course the weavers of fate are ever welcome in our halls."

Tilda's smile held no warmth. "Of course."

The dwarf hesitated, as if she feared offering anything to Tilda, and added, "My name is Dvala."

Dvala led them underground. She wore an old miner's helmet to light her way—looked like a carbide lamp. Ted wondered whether she needed it, or if the light was for his benefit. Since it only illuminated what was in front of her, and not Ted, it did him little fucking good. There were low-hanging wooden beams, but they were swallowed by the darkness as he came to them.

"Goddammit!" Ted yelled as his head rang off a beam. It was hard to tell who laughed loudest—Tilda, Loki, or the dwarf.

The mine shaft, while leaving ample room for the five-foot dwarf woman, left much to be desired in accommodating Ted's six-four frame. He cracked his head more than a few times on the wooden beams that kept the tunnel from collapsing down upon them. The timbers smelled of freshly cut wood, faintly discernable against the stink of coal dust and sweaty dwarf.

"Why are you complaining?" Loki said cheerfully. "You've got the hardest head in the West."

The trickster had taken the form of the woman Ted had met on the road by Saskatoon, smiling at the amazing clearance she now enjoyed. Loki snickered and was no doubt flashing that brilliant smile. "You should have seen the look on your face."

"Try it again and you'll get a real close-up look at that expression. And then you won't have a face."

"I love it when you threaten me. It shows you still care."

Distracted by Loki, Ted managed to hit his head again. There was a lesson in there somewhere.

"Dammit."

"We are close," Dvala said.

The rest of the trip Ted managed to duck as needed. They entered the mine proper. It was maybe twenty feet wide across the entrance, but no taller than the earlier tunnel.

"A far cry from the days of old," the dwarf said, running her thick-fingered hand over the timbers, "when my family toiled in Niðavellir."

She led them through a dizzying array of shafts.

Muninn, keep track of the path, in case Dvala means to strand us down here.

The tunnels followed the size of the coal seams. Some of them would have had Ted crawling on his belly. He supposed he could live with a little back pain.

Done, Muninn said.

Smart of you to ask, Huginn noted.

I would have done so in any case, Muninn retorted.

It is good he has finally learned to rely upon our help.

Just fucking do it, Ted shot back.

There was an indignant ruffled-feather sound.

Please and thank you.

They went deeper, and Ted began to sweat. His breathing grew heavier, and faster. It was as if they were running out of air. Tilda touched his back. He felt a fresh, cool breeze blow over him. He shivered as the cool air met his sweat.

Dvala turned around, her lamp blinding Ted.

"Take care with your magic," the dwarf said, as Ted shielded his eyes. He couldn't make out any of her features, but from the way she bobbed her head, she nodded to Tilda. "If you please."

The breeze died, and the oppressive heat returned. Ted wiped at his brow, dust and sweat stinging his eyes. Dvala had stopped them at a wide entrance to a tunnel. There was a fierce orange glow coming from far down the path. The timbers shoring up the way in were carved so full of runes that Ted could not make out any original wood grain. It looked ominous as hell.

"Through this path is the payment we demand for our assistance."

Of course it fucking was.

Ted asked, "What's down there?"

Dvala shook her head. "That is not for me to say."

Of course it fucking wasn't.

Dvala continued to march them deeper into the hill. Ted tried to guess how long they'd been walking, and how far they'd gone. He figured he could be grabbing a donair on Jasper by now, assuming they'd been going in a straight line.

Ted felt a tingle at the back of his neck. Dvala had led them to a dead end. The tunnel was blocked by a series of stacked tree trunks; all were still covered in bark.

"Be still, Ted," Tilda said. "It's not a trap. It's a door."

"The Norn speaks true," Dvala said.

"Yeah," Loki muttered. "A door to a trap."

Ted snorted a laugh.

Dvala touched the wall and the entire tunnel seemed to shudder as the door opened. Dirt fell in Ted's hair and he eyed the ceiling suspiciously. Whatever was through that door, he had to hope it looked sturdier than this tunnel.

And had more headroom.

They followed Dvala inside and she closed the door behind

them. There was a soft *whoosh* of air, as if the room sighed outward. It happened again, and again, as if a great bellows worked behind the scenes. The air inside this room was crisp and clear, free of the stink of coal.

Doors which, on the outside, had been chopped, rough timber in a rough-hewn tunnel, were, on the inside, solid iron and set in cut stone blocks. In the light of Dvala's miner's hat, bits of rust flaked around the edges of the doors. Ted ran his hands over the wall. It seemed like the same kind of stone that had been used to build the Leg.

Sounding far off, a deep voice said, "Lights for our guests, daughter."

Light sprung up from sconces set in the walls, giving the room an even, if dim, light. Ted, Loki, and Tilda stood in a great square room with tapestries and rugs and taxidermied animal heads on the walls.

Big Beard was there, standing to the immediate right of the door, flanked by the two female dwarves who'd been with him at the Flea Market. Two dwarven men, who Ted recognized from Howling Wolf's, stood on either side of a dwarf woman Ted didn't recognize.

"Follow me," Dvala said, leading them deeper into the room.

Ted, Loki, and Tilda followed and the other six dwarves fell in behind.

On the opposite end of the room, sitting side by side on a simple stone bench on a raised platform, their hips touching, were two richly dressed *dvergur* women. From the number of gold chains the duo had around their necks, they may has well have had golden beards. *Maybe that was the point.* In any case, they gave Mr. T a run for the bling title.

Dvala knelt on one knee, pressing her palm against the stone floor. She did not incline her head, but met the stares of the women on the bench. She looked over her shoulder at Ted, pissed that none of the guests had followed her lead.

When she stood, Dvala said, “The leaders of Edmonton’s *dvergar*: my mothers, Jorunn and Thorunn.”

Jorunn spoke first. “What an odd assortment of visitors the day brings us. A weapon dressed as a man, three Norns dressed as one, and an old enemy dressed as a friend.”

Thorunn nodded in Big Beard’s direction. “We are told that you have a favour you wish to ask of the *dvergar*.”

“Yes,” Ted said.

Jorunn leaned forward, a smile on her face. “Apparently the *dvergar* have not bestowed enough gifts upon Ófriður.”

“Well this is the first one that I asked for.”

Dvala gasped, and Ted worried he was pushing his luck, but Jorunn and Thorunn laughed; so he kept pushing. “And I’m told I’ll be paying for this one anyway.”

“Yes,” Jorunn said. “Gold is for goods.”

Ted knew what was coming next, and said it in time with Thorunn. “But a favour for a favour.”

Thorunn smiled. “Name your favour, Ófriður.”

“Surtur has followers in your city.”

Jorunn and Thorunn nodded. Ted wasn’t surprised they knew, only that they tolerated the fuckers.

“They plan on turning the city above into a funeral pyre,” Tilda said.

Jorunn asked, "And how would they do this?"

"The old coal mines," Ted said. "All of their arsons and suicides have been located around one old coal site or another. They're going to magically ignite them."

"We know," Thorunn said. "They plan to summon their master."

"If you know this," Tilda said, "why haven't you stopped them?"

"What would you have us do, Norn?" Jorunn asked. "They would sense what we have done. They are led by one of the choosers of the slain. She could choose us for sword-sleep if she knew we were here."

"And there is nothing we could do to stop her," Thorunn said. "*Dvergar* survived Ragnarök by digging deep, away from Surtur's flames, and the floods that followed. We *might* survive … if we do not get involved."

Tilda's eyes narrowed. "You believe that?"

"No," Jorunn said. "But it is something of a comfort to those who do not know the truth."

"And what truth is that?" Ted asked.

"That Surtur's power extends here, to our domain," Thorunn said. "Dvala led you past it, in bringing you to meet us."

Tilda's fingers moved, kneading the leather pouch that held her rune stones. "A finger of Muspelheim, running like a vein of ore. Directly into the heart of your lands."

"Yes," Jorunn said. "Down that tunnel is an ever-burning seam of coal, ignited in some ancient day before Andvari and his people came to Midgard. Since before our clan split from his."

"We have been feeding this flame for all of our time here. It will burn until our bones are dust," Thorunn said. "Until the mountains are taken by the sea."

"Why would you do that?" Ted asked.

Jorunn sighed. "When we first stumbled on that seam of Muspelheim it felt like a gift. We used it to make our forges burn hotter, hot enough to do real crafting. The coal in this part of the world is shit. Barely good enough to warm our tunnels, let alone heat steel."

Ted felt his hammer hand clenching. Mjölnir had burned a lightning bolt from the sky and into the hall of Hel. It could find a way to strike here. "So you're the ones who woke Surtur up. *You're* the reason this happened to me."

The dwarves shook their heads.

"That was not us," Jorunn said.

"Look to your friends for *reasons*," Thorunn said. "We thought that by bleeding his fires away, Surtur would sleep. Sated with what he had already destroyed."

Bleeding Surtur. Pulling away from Edmonton, cutting him off from Muspelheim—it sounded a lot like what Ted and Loki had done to the giant in Flin Flon. It would be fucking wonderful if Ted could find a way to get Surtur out of Alberta entirely.

"Is it wise to keep an eye on Surtur like this?" Tilda asked.

"Wiser than being surprised by him," the dwarf answered. "As Ófriður well knows."

"I do, indeed."

"If you enter the chamber, you may glimpse the giant without alerting him," Jorunn said. She looked pointedly at Ted. "You may see more than that."

Thorunn added, "And if you sever the connection to Muspelheim, we will ensure that the coal mines Skyburner's church seeks to kindle will remain buried. Lost in Niðavellir."

"That's a big risk," Ted said.

"A fair trade," Jorunn said.

"You would use us against Surtur," Thorunn added. "Only fair that we do the same. If we are to protect your city, the giant cannot be allowed to strike us in our halls."

It was fair. Not that that made Ted like it any more.

"This seems a small thing to ask of Ófriður," Jorunn said.

"The flames would not burn Ófriður," Thorunn said. She leaned forward and looked at Ted's arms, covered in tattoos, but bare of dragon-scale. "But he is not here, is he?"

"Yeah well, even if he was, he'd still need to breathe."

"I can cover that," Tilda said. The air rune shifted to hover over Ted's head. He felt cool and pleasant in its radius, and strangely comforted, as if in Tilda's embrace. Which was strange— she'd always run on the hot side, not the cold.

Loki grunted something unintelligible.

"What was that, Wolf-Father?" Thorunn asked. "Do you fear that more of our crafts could bind you, as we bound your son?"

"Every time I get involved with you folks, I tend to get my mouth sewn shut. You don't like me. I don't like you." Loki shrugged. "Hoping to make the deal go smoother for Ted, I guess."

Thorunn and Jorunn chuckled. "Wise," they said together.

Ted let out a deep breath. "I'll do it."

"How?" Tilda asked.

"I have an idea," Ted said. "Seal the mines from Surtur's followers, and I'll take care of your problem."

"A favour for a favour, Ófriður," Jorunn said.

"And you have done nothing yet," Thorunn added.

Well, shit.

Ted ground out, "Fine."

"You'll honour your bargain," Tilda said. It was no question. It was a threat.

Dvala seemed insulted. "You question my mothers' honour?"

Jorunn raised a hand. "The Norn was not questioning anything. Of course we will honour our deal."

Tilda smiled. "I know."

"Since we are agreed," Thorunn said. "Dvala will take you where you need to go."

"No need," Ted said. "I remember the way."

Jorunn and Thorunn nodded. "We will know when it is done."

"No pressure," Loki muttered.

"How are you going to pull this off?" Loki asked Ted.

"Here," Ted said, pulling out his Zippo and bouncing it on his palm. He didn't want to light it. Not in this tunnel. Not until he was close enough to steal Surtur's flames.

Tilda eyed the Zippo. "Is that what I think it is?"

Ted nodded. "Fire stolen from Surtur's minions. Bound by runes and locked into my Zippo."

"Impressive."

"Most impressive," Loki agreed. "But he's not a Jedi yet."

Ted bristled. But then he burst out laughing at the *Star Wars* reference. He couldn't help himself.

Loki smiled. "I knew I'd wear you down."

"I'm not the sneakiest guy in town," Ted said, staring into tunnel, and running his hand over the rune-carved timbers. He thought he saw a woman's shape, beckoning him in.

"No, but you know her," Loki said.

Ted ignored the trickster and continued on. "I'm not sure how the hell I'm going to get deep enough in there to do this."

"Walk quietly," Loki said. "And try not to swing that big stick."

"Who said you're going in there?" Tilda said. "That's insane. You'll *die*."

Ted smiled. "I'll be fine. The weekend isn't over yet."

"Be serious, for one. Fucking. Minute. I know it pains you, but try."

Tilda may have warned Ted of his forthcoming death, but he tended to forget she'd already watched it happen. He looked down the tunnel at the orange glow. It seemed to stretch closer as he stared. There was a flicker cast by the far-off flames that resembled the curves of a woman, dancing.

"I *am* being serious, Til. If you go in there, Surtur will know."

"Since when are you an expert?"

Jorunn had said Ted might find more than Surtur in the

flames of Muspelheim. What if Sinmara were down there? Maybe he could get the Bright Sword from her.

"I can seal the link to Muspelheim from here."

"That's not why it has to be me."

Tilda didn't say "Why the fuck not?" With the shade she was throwing his way, she didn't need to.

Ted felt more sure now. "Sinmara is in there."

Tilda eyed him quizzically. "Who?"

He was surprised she didn't recognize the name. Sinmara had felt like a big-time player. Shit, Ted had only been in the Nine Worlds a year and it seemed everybody knew the name Ófriður. Except he wasn't Ófriður now. Loki had trapped him in Ted Callan.

Ted shrugged. "She claims to have the Bright Sword. What I need to finish off Surtur."

"She's also pals with Göndul," Loki said, eliciting an angry growl from Tilda. "I don't think it's a good idea to send you in there alone. Especially since your dragon scales are buried."

Tilda nodded, evidently still surprised to be agreeing with Loki. "You're not fireproof anymore. It should be me and Loki."

"No offence, sister," Loki said. "But I'd like a little more time before we have a girls' night out."

"So our words meant nothing?"

"They mean we haven't killed each other yet. And that you don't want to do the deed in front of Ted."

"Stop," Ted said.

Tilda and Loki turned to look at him, both had faces full of thunder. He had their attention, but didn't know how to keep it. He was no peacemaker. He was the goddamned Un-peace.

"If I can get Surtur out of Alberta, I know how to trap him. I know where to build his cage." He held up his bloody hand. "I'm taking this seriously, even if you're not."

Tilda's scowl told Ted how seriously she might take what he said next.

"How?"

"I'll trap him in his own name."

It wasn't much, but it was something. It might work. It *had* to work.

Tilda asked, "How will you pull that off?"

"Surtur's death is only for Ted," Loki said. "And I trust him."

That ringing endorsement was almost sure to set Norn and Trickster back to bickering. Instead, Tilda nodded.

"Loki had every right to worry. And Tilda had every right to revenge. *Had*. That is the fucking important word. *Had*. That time is over. You all said it, now stick to it, or I'm going in there without you and saving you both the trouble."

"That'll kill you," Loki said softly.

Ted shrugged. "Maybe Sinmara will want to talk."

"You can't survive Muspelheim, Ted. Not even this tiny shard of it."

She touched his temple, where Muninn's tattoo should be.

"You still need to breathe," Tilda reminded. "And you *will* burn."

"Don't I know it. Got any ideas?"

"I can probably work something out."

She summoned the *Algiz* rune, rune of air, one she'd used to hold Jormungandur's poisonous breath at bay, so long ago, and the *Isa* rune that she'd used to cool her tent at the Fringe. They hung over her head, orbiting like two tiny, glowing moons. Tilda carved a pebble and breathed upon it. She kissed Ted then, before popping the rune stones into his hand "Don't lose these. You and I will share breath."

Loki asked, "No kiss for me?"

"You use up too much air for me to spare, trickster. I've promised not to kill you. Don't push your luck."

"Fair enough." Loki winced. "This is not going to feel good."

Her body changed in an eye blink, and one of Surtur's servitor giants stood before Ted. Even knowing it was Loki, it was enough of a surprise that Ted cocked his fist back, ready to strike. For all the good it would've done.

He was short for a giant, but then Loki's natural *jötunn* form was a little runty. Assuming what Ted had seen had been Loki's natural form—or that Loki even *had* one. The trickster had to hunch over in the short, dwarven tunnels, and was walking on his knees, knuckles dragging like a gorilla's. With his soot-black skin, he was invisible. The only thing that remained were the trickster's flame-filled eyes, smouldering with mischief rather than malice.

"Are you certain you want that form?" Tilda asked. "What if Surtur can control you in it?"

Loki let out a disgusted sigh, steam squealing past his lips. "I'm more than the bloody skin I wear. Do you think I can be compelled to so something I do not wish to?"

Ted cracked his knuckles. "Sometimes."

"Bugger me for being a survivor then—but you can count on me."

"I know."

You can count on Loki to be Loki, Muninn muttered.

Enough chatter. He's my friend. He'll be solid.

He had better be.

"Ted wait," Tilda said, grabbing his shoulder. He winced. He'd forgotten her strength. If she clenched her fingers, she'd dislocate his arm. "If you do meet Sinmara down there, don't bargain with her."

"Is that prophecy, or advice?"

"Whatever it is," Loki said. "I'd listen to the lady."

They headed down into the tunnel. The air was foul—barely breathable. Before long, there was no air at all. Ted could feel the link to Tilda with every laboured breath he took, it echoed in his blood and bones. He'd hardly started, and was already at half speed. Tilda was in better shape than he was, even with his strength and invulnerability taken into account. The dwarves had decided to screw him on the cardio side of the magical gift department. Tilda was breathing for two, and while she might be fine if Ted needed to fight, if she found herself in danger also, would their divided lifeline doom them both?

A wall is only a door I haven't made yet.

21. Fire Woman

Loki led Ted deeper into the dwarven dark, and while Tilda's rune magic kept Ted alive and breathing, it couldn't keep him comfortable. The *Isa* rune clung to him, giving him a sheath of protective cold that was starting to remind Ted of an air conditioner rattling in its death throes.

And he thought he'd been sweating balls topside in the Edmonton summer.

The carved tunnel didn't feel like a tunnel anymore. Ted couldn't place why, but it felt both more, and less, oppressive the further they walked. At least it grew taller the closer he and Loki got to Muspelheim, and Ted no longer had to hunch. He rotated his shoulders, wincing at the *snap, crackle, pop* they made.

The dwarves had said this was a finger of Muspelheim. If the plan went off as envisioned, they'd be giving Surtur the finger all right. Ted hoped it didn't backfire. The queens of Edmonton's *dvergar* seemed pretty confident they could lock the old mines away from Göndul and her church of Surtur. Ted had seen confidence go sideways in a hurry. He'd been that cocky when he'd faced Thor the first time. *And how had that turned out?*

You usually say "I got my fucking ass handed to me," Muninn said.

Ted had to give Muninn credit. The raven had nailed his Ófriður impression.

Now would be a good time to ask Loki about the picture, Muninn said.

Ted nodded to himself. There wasn't anywhere for Loki to wriggle away.

"I can feel your stare," Loki said over his shoulder.

"You were in a picture at my parents' house," Ted said. "Cozied up to my mom."

Loki gave Ted a side-eye. "Now? You want to talk now?"

"Where else do you have to be?"

Loki sighed. "A girl needs a reason to catch a football game?"

"What the fuck were you doing at *my* football game?"

"I don't know what you're talking about."

Loki wasn't the only one who could use manipulation to get what they wanted. "Fine, be that way. I thought my new *sister* would be willing to tell me the truth. Maybe enlighten me as to why she was hanging around my family decades before I'd ever heard of the Nine Worlds."

Loki stopped, his expression pained. It was weird, on the monstrous, *jötunn* face the trickster wore. "You know how to stick it in and break it off, don't you?"

Ted smiled. "I guess I learned from the best."

Loki smiled, as if taking Ted's words as a compliment. "At first I was messing around. Pranking either side. Then you made that winning catch. Everyone was calling you a hero. I thought it was funny, that something so small, that winning *a game* made you a hero. I wanted to see if you could *be* one."

"So you fucked up my life out of curiosity?"

"Oh, please," Loki said. "You fucked up your own life plenty."

A low blow, but Loki was correct. Ted couldn't lay everything that went wrong in his life at the feet of the Nine Worlds.

"You also kept wishing for a life that mattered, but didn't seem to be doing anything to make it happen."

Ted couldn't be mad the trickster *was* responsible for his life getting entwined with the Nine Worlds. There had been some shitty times in the last year—*lots* of shitty times—but when it had been good … he'd never felt more real.

"So you helped me along?"

"Why do you think *you* lasted so long after Surtur's arrival?"

Ted shrugged. "Good luck, bad luck."

Loki smiled his best *you're welcome* smile. "Did you know I got Ryan to switch shifts with you?"

That was news to Ted. He remembered Rye wanted to trade that weekend. Vaguely. Things had been awful with Susanna by then, so Ted had leapt at the chance to be away. Rye had caught an earful from home because his folks had thought he'd been working the site and among the missing or the dead.

"I knew that Surtur would wake up. It was as inevitable as Ragnarök. So I hung around, and I kept my ear to the ground for a way to stop him for good."

"So why me?"

"Odin's hairy balls, Ted. Are we back to the 'why me' shit? I thought you were past all of that. I kept you alive afterwards until I could get the right things in place. Urd's plan for Mimir and the *dvergar* seemed as good as any."

"So the job?"

"Me, not Svarta," Loki said. "I thought it would be easier to keep an eye on you in Manitoba, and away from Surtur's hearth. Didn't count on one of the Norns butting in and claiming you for her own."

"Wanted me all to yourself, eh?"

Loki shrugged. "It's better this way. Much as Tilda pisses me off, much as she hates me, she adds a certain something."

"I don't know if we could pull this off alone."

"Yeah," Loki said, sounding dejected. "But don't *tell* her that."

Ted tapped at his temple. "She knows."

"Of course she does," Loki said sourly, squinting against the glow further down the tunnel. "I think we're getting closer."

Ted took the Zippo out of his pocket. The old metal lighter felt strangely heavy in his hand, its weight trying to settle through Tilda's *Isa* rune. Trying to burn him. He would've felt better if Jorunn and Thorunn had sealed the mines up before he had to do this. Better for Edmonton, if he should fail. Surtur might've known he was coming that way, but then Ted could still be found out.

Much as Ted hated to delegate anything, he couldn't be everywhere in Edmonton. The local *dvergar* might be all he had, but the dwarves had the numbers and know-how to keep Göndul out. Even with his powers, he couldn't protect every potential summoning site. Not alone. And he couldn't bring in help—outside of Tilda and Loki, *all* his current help—without warning Surtur he was in town. But if he had to choose any two people to see him through his fight with Surtur, he had the right two. The only other option was Ted sending Surtur an engraved invitation to destroy downtown Edmonton.

He still couldn't shake the feeling he'd made a bad decision. He sighed. Even that took effort. This running-on-half-a-lung business sucked. He really wished he had his power.

"Stop that," Loki said, in the rumbling voice of a giant.

"Stop what?" Ted said, breathless.

"Wishing for your powers back."

"You can feel that?"

Loki cocked the giant's head, and despite being a fire giant, threw an icy glare in Ted's direction.

"Yes. And if you're not careful, it'll happen. I did some of my best work, and Andvari's tattoos are *still* trying to come out." Loki shook his head. "I don't know whether to buy that dwarf a drink or kick his ass."

"Soften him up with the beer first," Ted suggested. "And warn me, so that I can tag in for the ass-kicking."

"How's it going in there?"

Ted jumped at the sound of the voice. It was a strange mix of Tilda and Huginn. Where the ravens usually sounded as if they were whispering—or yelling—in Ted's ears, Tilda's voice appeared to be coming from directly behind him. Ted glanced over his shoulder in case the Norn had decided to go her own way and follow them down.

"We're close," Ted said. "I think."

Ted hoped they were close. Every step forward was as exhausting as trying to fuck in a sauna.

The stone glowed orange all over. Great plumes of fire burst from walls, burning yellow, orange, and blue. Rocks cracked and broke from the heat. Steam hissed as molten rock enveloped slightly cooler, and still solid, stones.

Ted and Loki found themselves in a tiny corner, looking in on the immensity of Muspelheim—an entire world. He had a feeling he knew what Neil Armstrong had felt looking at Earth from the Moon; the wonder tempered by fear, the uncertainty he would ever see his home again.

Surtur was there. *Holy shit. Right. Fucking. There.* The giant was so far away that he looked small. He had built a throne for himself from the twisted wreckage of Ted's old rig. A shaft of flame flickered with Göndul's face. Ted clenched his fist tight over the Zippo. It seared his skin.

"Easy, bud," Loki said. "She'll get hers."

From the safety of their tunnel, there was light enough to see, but no more than arm's length on either side of Ted and Loki was an unnatural darkness. Not the darkness of being underground, but the void of space. The nothingness of Ginnungagap.

Ted smelled smoke and the sour reek of methane. Smaller flames, maybe the size of a man, were mostly left alone or had tiny—in comparison to the rest of the giants—man-sized bodies curled around them. The larger fires held crouched giants, some similar to the shape Loki now wore, others more closely resembling animals. Vapour ghosts hissed through the air. Ted tried not to look at them. He was afraid if he looked too closely he'd recognize guys from the patch—friends lost to the Nine. Instead he scanned for Sinmara. But she could be anywhere in those flames. Or not there at all.

Ted rubbed at the bridge of his nose. So far, this had been all for nothing.

"You okay, bud?" Loki asked.

"Let's do this and get the hell out of here."

"*You're there,*" Tilda said. "*Collapse the tunnel and get the hell out.*"

Ted nodded absently. But he was looking for the Bright Sword. If Sinmara were here, it had to be here somewhere too. There were all kinds of swords, all forged of black metal, with blades as wide as a man and tall as a building. They seemed to eat the light. There was nothing bright about them. If he could just find Sinmara. She knew where the sword was.

And she'd fucking tell him.

There, Huginn said.

Ted followed the raven's prodding. Sinmara was well-hidden amid the fires. She turned and they locked eyes. She beckoned to him, a woman made of nothing but fire. Embers popped where her body hair would be. She danced in and out of the flames.

A cloak of crackling flames was spun over her shoulders—fastened in place by two great blackened antlers, their tips sharpened to fine points—and trailing off to merge into the other fires of Muspelheim. She wore only the fire, and walked like a warrior, like one of the valkyries, a scabbard resting on her hip. The scabbard the same molten-gold as her hair.

The Bright Sword.

Ted shook his head.

Sinmara had it.

But who was she?

The blade was broken. She'd told Göndul so. She could've been lying, but Ted didn't think so. That sword was what he needed to kill Surtur. Hel's words flickered through his thoughts. "When you build a cage for him from his bones, only then will the Bright Sword appear."

Ted had his cage. It had been his mistake to believe the Bright Sword would've shown up in his hand, right then and there, pulled from thin air as if he'd drawn Excalibur from the stone. But it was here now. And he might not get another chance to take it.

What do we know about her?

We have never met her, Muninn said. **Before she spoke to Göndul at the church.**

I thought you two knew everything.

While I appreciate your confidence, that is not so. This one has always hidden from us. She was nothing but this, a shape in the fire, a glimmer of future doom, when Odin would send us to spy upon Surtur and Muspelheim.

And we were never so close as this.

Too dangerous? Ted asked, half to himself, remembering the ravens' reaction to getting close to Surtur's flames back in Flin

Flon, when one of Ted's inadvertent lightning strikes had called the giant from the patch.

There's nothing for it, Ted said. *When you want to talk to someone, you walk over and say hello.*

No.

Ted stood and walked towards the flames, wondering how to play this. Ravens clicking their discontent all the while.

There was no turning back now. Whoever Sinmara was, she'd seen him. Her shape appeared closer now, flickering from tongue of flame to tongue of flame, staring. She had the same acetylene eyes as Surtur. Her hair, woven tongues of fire, was a braided pattern of yellow, orange, and red.

Her appearance changed, from a creature of fire, to that of the woman who had spoken to Göndul in Surtur's church. Changed again. A woman Ted remembered well. She wore one of Loki's recent favourite forms. She could be Freyja's twin.

Göndul was talking with their master. If that bitch noticed him, it would be fucking game on.

Sinmara walked over, bold as balls. Three fiery mountain lions the size of grizzlies left their flaming seats, and stalked over in her wake. They stared at Ted with hungry eyes. Sinmara stopped at the edge of the tunnel; her cats turned their backs to Ted and blocked his view of Göndul. He wasn't sure whom they were protecting from the former valkyrie. Sinmara didn't seem the type to need the help, but Ted doubted they had any feelings toward him.

She cocked her head, taking Ted's measure, eyeballing his every visible tattoo.

Everyone in the Nine Worlds seemed to know Ted Callan by reputation, even before he'd started forming one. Sinmara was no different. She called him by the name the dwarves had given him:

Ófriður. Unsightly One. Warbringer. Un-peace.

The name wasn't a good icebreaker, given its meaning. So instead, he introduced himself simply: "I'm Ted."

She laughed, and in contrast to Surtur's booming, villainous rumble, her laugh was the crackle of a campfire. It was inviting. Sensuous. It set him entirely at ease.

Be careful, Tilda's voice warned.

I don't think she's sucking me in, Ted shot back. Still, touch a campfire and you'll get burned.

"So humble," she said. "I like that. Ted. Not Ófriður. You have not come to me seeking war."

"It tends to follow me, but this time, no, I'm not looking for a fight."

"What *are* you seeking … Ted?"

There didn't seem to be any reason to lie. "The Bright Sword."

"You would match your lightning and storm against my husband's flames and rage?"

Husband?

Ted didn't want to think about the logistics of *that*. He was surprised—and grateful— Loki hadn't brought it up.

"Somebody has to stand up to Surtur, and I got drafted."

"Better men then you have been doomed to fight the giant. You think to try…" She stared at Ted's right hand and arched an eyebrow. "Your hand against the Lord of Muspelheim?"

Flame shot from her palms, and Ted jumped back, crashing into Loki. The woman smiled. The flames coalesced into an image of Surtur's fiery advance. Fire spun into a globe in her hand. Blue flame for ocean, white hot for mountaintops, yellow flickering flames for landmass. Ted saw Alberta, and the red storm consuming the north of the province. Rivers of fire spread from there over North America, flaring up in Yellowstone, spreading further still, crawling under the oceans until Hawaii was engulfed, spreading until the entire globe was nothing but Surtur's fire. With a soft *whump*, the flames were extinguished and there was nothing but Sinmara.

"Get out of there, Ted!"

Sinmara cocked an ear, as if she were trying to listen to Tilda inside of Ted's skull.

"Do I sense one of the Norns?"

Ted's eyes narrowed. He could feel Sinmara trying to sift around his brain, but in the same way that the *dvergar* magic had slid off him, Ted was pretty sure she didn't get any purchase there. Loki's disguise doing its job again.

"Familiar conjurings, but I don't recognize the conjuror. Since the two of you are bound by sex, I'll assume it's not Urd. Regardless, I'd rather not be eavesdropped upon."

A lattice of flaming runes sprung up behind Ted and Loki. Ted felt Tilda's presence disappear from his mind. He could still feel her, somewhere, through their *seiður* connection, and could hear her if he strained his mind, but it was like a fierce wind was carrying her voice away from his ears.

Sinmara smiled. "There. Now we won't be interrupted."

Ted felt a trickle of sweat run down his forehead dropping from the tip of his nose to sizzle against the tunnel floor.

Sinmara turned to his companion and grinned like a wolf baring its teeth. "Ah, Loki. So good to see you again."

"Wait," Ted said, turning to Loki. "You fucking *know* her?"

Loki's giant face had a sour look. "Oh, *everyone* from Asgard to Niðavellir knows her, intimately. She slept with Odin. With the dwarves. She fucked everyone who happened by on her never-ending quest to find her lost husband. I think she enjoyed the hunt more than the catch, if you feel me." Loki turned to Ted. "Sorry, I would've placed her when we walked in, but for the wrinkles. And the sagging."

Sinmara was unbothered by his insults. "You are one to talk, horsefucker."

Or maybe not. For someone made of fire there was ice in her voice.

"I did that so you didn't have to be traded to that giant in exchange for Asgard's walls," Loki said scratching his nose with his middle finger. "And you know, it occurs to me, that you never once thanked me for the deed. I'm still walking funny, thank you very much."

"Perhaps those thanks you feel I owe you are tempered by every trespass you made against my person, and my hall, and my family. What blame shall I lay at *your* feet?"

"Oh, please," said Loki. "If you mean that necklace of yours, Odin told you not to whore yourself for *dvergur* gold."

"The death of my brother?"

"That was Freyr's own damned fault. If he hadn't been

thinking with his dick, and kept that shiny sword, Surtur would be dead now and you wouldn't be bending over for him. Tell me, does it burn when you piss? Or can you even tell anymore?"

Sinmara said nothing, but then neither did the trickster.

For Ted, the pieces didn't quite fit. "Wait, Freyr was your brother?"

"Sinmara *is* Freyja. Try to keep up, Ted." Loki rolled his *jötunn* eyes, as if to say: *typical.* "She was as gifted at magic as Odin. Hell, she taught him a bunch of what he knew, though we all mocked him for it. Just not to his face."

"We do not have time to play at flyting today, Loki." Freyja said. "You will yelp wicked things no more."

Gleipnir slithered off Loki's wrist, racing upwards until his mouth was sealed shut by the glowing cord. Sinmara smiled, and so did Loki, though tears dripped from his eyes. The pained smile of one who didn't wish to concede a victory to an old opponent.

"Okay, now that I can get a word in edgewise," Ted said, "Let her go."

Freyja scowled. "It wasn't wise to bring Loki down here."

"He got you talking."

A thin smile creased Freyja's face. "Yes, I suppose he did."

"If you wanted me dead, you would've killed me by now. Or given me to Surtur. So that tells me you have no love for him."

Her smile creaked a bit wider. "Does it?"

"Give me the Bright Sword, and I can avenge your brother."

Freyja cast a glance at either shoulder, regarding the antlers on which she'd fastened her cloak of fire. "You want his sword. Perhaps I should give you his last weapons instead. Why should you be better armed than my Freyr?"

"Because giving me your jewellery won't get you what you want."

She sighed and drew the blade from its scabbard. "This is what you are looking for?"

The sword was the same gold he remembered seeing in his fever dream, after Thor had kicked his ass. So bright it shone, it could have been the sun. But that golden glow was only a reflection of the fires of Muspelheim. As she pierced the veil between Surtur's realm and the *dvergar* tunnel, the Bright Sword's blade became a blue so pale it appeared white. It was as if the sun in Ted's palm had been replaced by a shining moon. The fires closest to them dimmed in the broken sword's presence, and Surtur stirred. Freyja slammed the blade back into its scabbard.

The Bright Sword holds the cold of Jötunheim. Freyr was a summer god, but his sword was as cold as if every winter's chill were stored in the blade.

It was also broken. She hadn't lied to Göndul.

Ted couldn't believe it. The sword was *right fucking there.* And it was broken. It had been broken before Hel had ever made her prophecy. Had she been playing him all along? Had Tilda been right? He'd say it wasn't fair, but he knew by now how little fairness had to do with anything.

"Can you fix it?" Ted asked. "Reforge it?"

She smiled sadly. "It would never be the same. You are not Sigurd, and I am not Regin."

"So, we're fucked." Ted asked, "How'd you end up siding with Surtur?"

Freyja laughed and said, "Fight to the death? For the Aesir? Why would I do that when they offered me up to appease every giant who roamed too close to Asgard? Why would I fight for those who gave me no aid in finding my lost husband? Who gave my brother *antlers* to stave off the end of all of us? To Hel with them, and good riddance.

"I tried to avenge my brother. I drove my chariot at Surtur, in my fury thinking I could ride him down." Freyja shook her head. "He couldn't be bothered to kill me. His first task for me was to find Freyr's sword and to bring it to him. Skirnir was still alive, thanks largely to my brother's sword, but he thought me a friend." She hung her head. "I killed him on the fields of Vígríðr and took it. I thought with his blade I could do what Freyr had been unable to. But it was not my doom to face the giant. Surtur broke Laevateinn and left it with me as a reminder he couldn't be stopped. Our world would burn. All of them would. And so I serve him. It was the only way to live long enough to see him dead."

"I can beat him."

"So sure, are you?"

"Give me my shot and I'll show you."

"You can't hold two things in one hand, Ófriður. You have Mjölnir in your right, the sun of Baldur in your left. What will you release? Try to clutch them both and the world's fate will run through your fingers like a handful of water."

"You're saying it's impossible?"

Freyja shook her head sadly and said, "Your body is full up of gifts, Ófriður. There is no room for me to give you the Bright Sword were it whole. And your scaly armour was sealed. How could I carve another into your body?"

Ted tried not to think of the *álfur* dagger. He was glad he didn't have it on him. "There's a way."

A slight incline of her head. "Perhaps there is, but I cannot give you the sword. Today."

Ted tried to keep his smile on his face, but felt it slip. *Cocksucker*. Loki's disguise. Had to be.

"No need to wail, or gnash teeth, Ófriður. The sword can still be yours."

"How?"

"In everything there is a price. And if I do this for you, what will you do for me?"

"What do you need?"

"If anyone or anything can bring back my brother, it's the power of the Lord of Light."

Baldur.

"The *dvergar* crafted you well. You are bursting with magic and war, but none of your gifts will avail you against Skyburner."

"Sheath the bright sword in me," Ted said to Freyja. "And when it is done, and Surtur is caged, I'll draw it free and kill him."

"A mighty thing you ask of me, Ófriður," Freyja said.

Ted thought of his friends and family; his mom and dad deserved to enjoy retirement. His brother deserved to see his children grow and have children of their own. Cam and Carrie deserved to live, dammit. Rye deserved a great wedding. Robin and Aiko too, if Robin would ever get around to popping the fucking question. Jenny sure deserved better than Ted. She'd probably have a chance to find it, too. Tilda *had* told him he'd die, soon. She'd made such a prophecy before, the first night that they'd met. It didn't scare or disturb him this time. If his death bought them life, it was more than worth it.

"I'll do whatever it takes."

"I know you will." The goddess smiled. "But not yet. We cannot do this now. With a foreign trickster's magic twisting you. You will need to be yourself. You will need to be Ófriður."

"And that will bring Surtur running."

She nodded. "Yes."

So much for anything. "I can't do that. Not yet."

"You will not have much choice. You will face him soon. He will sense you if you return to yourself. I am surprised you have hidden this long."

"After Sunday."

You're worried about the wedding? Huginn asked.

I'm worried that if we don't wait until the dvergar seal off the mines, the entire city will light up the moment I touch that sword. And Surtur's got the home field advantage to boot.

"You think you have the time? Göndul will try to slay all you hold dear."

"She'll fucking try."

"So bold. Even now. You are naught but flesh and blood. I could dismiss the Norn's conjuring instead of blocking it. She has power to rival mine, but not my experience. And your hair would burn. And your blood would boil. And your skin would cook. And the *jötnar* would feast. Loki's work runs too deep. He tried playing on two sides. It ended poorly. It ended everything."

"And yet here we are."

Freyja reached out to touch Ted, and he flinched away.

"Sacrifice is needed for power. And yours is not yet complete. Still you cling to the ragged remnants of your mortal life. Your family. Your friends. Your lovers."

Across the gulf of space separating them, Ted could feel Tilda tense at that last comment. For the moment of that reaction, his own breath skipped, as if he'd been snorkelling and she'd plugged his air hole.

"Maybe my new life wasn't worth living without them," Ted asked.

"And how much of your life have you devoted to them? Clinging to the idea of something that you are not in fact prepared to honour or give the respect and due they deserve."

Ted opened his mouth to protest, but knew she was right.

"You are a stranger to your family. A ghost to your friends. A vagabond to your lovers. Until you decide which world you belong in, you are nothing. And it will take more than an empty hand to defeat Surtur.

She speaks truth, Huginn said.

Nothing you have not heard before, Muninn added.

I know, Ted shot back.

But it was so damned hard. He wanted it all. Christmas with the folks. Introduce Tilda and their daughter to her cousins.

Beers with Rye and Loki. Basketball games with Jenny. More with Jenny.

He tried not to think of Jenny, not while Tilda was riding around in his head.

Focus, Huginn said.

He wanted it all, but that's not what would happen. It would be giants opening the top of the Callan house like it was a present. Loki would probably sleep with Rye, who'd get his ass killed trying to clean the imagined smirch on his manhood and honour. Jenny—if she wanted to see him again—would they ever be able to post up in the faded key of her backyard court, and play basketball, sweating and laughing? The choice had been made for Ted when he'd been gifted by the *dvergar*, but then, the ultimate choice did still belong to him. Painful as it would be to say goodbye, it was the choice that had to be made. Ted Callan could not defeat Surtur. Ófriður could.

Maybe.

But there was a price for the lives of his loved ones.

They would live those lives without Ted Callan.

"You have chosen," the fire woman said.

"You know I have."

She smiled. "I still need you to say it. It is necessary," she said, sounding oddly like Tilda.

Ted looked at his hands, at the soft indent still on the finger where his wedding ring had once sat. There was still gold on that hand, but now it was the sun on his palm. He looked back at Freyja. "I choose the Nine Worlds."

"Your choice is made, but now you must go," she hissed, the

words sounding like steam escaping a kettle. "He is nearly done with Göndul, and if he sees you here…"

Freyja disappeared, leaving only a tiny flame behind where she had stood. Ted and Loki slipped deeper back into the tunnels. The cats watched them leave, not moving a hair. Ted checked over his shoulder as he and Loki crept out of Muspelheim; the cats had not moved, not an inch. Ted watched them until he could no longer make out any details beyond the soft glow they shared with their burning home.

The trudge back up the tunnel was more exhausting than the way down. Ted was sweating bullets, and not from the heat. He half-expected all the hordes of Muspelheim to come roaring up after him and Loki like a fiery tornado.

"I think we're good," Loki said.

Evidently, Freyja had taken her shard of Gleipnir with her. Ted nodded and pulled out his Zippo. He flicked the lid open, surprised at how much he'd missed that metallic *clink*, when Tilda's presence slammed into his mind like a suckerpunch to the gut.

"*Kenaz!*" she yelled. Ted's lips moved without his volition, speaking the name of the rune alongside the Norn as he ignited the lighter.

He held the Zippo firm in his hand while a long trail of flame shot from the wick to disappear down the tunnel. Ted ground his teeth against the searing heat of the lighter burning in his hand. There was a backdraft of heat, slapping against him in a great *whoosh* and then the flame on the Zippo was normal, and the tunnel was silent except for Ted and Loki's heaving breaths.

Ted snapped the Zippo shut and hurled it at Loki, who caught it deftly.

Ted shook his hand, yelling, "Fuck, fuck, fuck, fucking shit, fuck!"

"Let me see," Loki said, crouching with his back brushing the ceiling of the tunnel. The trickster's giant hand fully engulfed Ted's. He blew softly against the skin. "Better?"

Ted shook his head. "My lighter, please."

"Done," Loki said, a woman again, and Ted felt the familiar weight in his pocket.

"Let's get out of here."

Sweating, exhausted, and spent, they hustled back to the *dvergur* mine. Ted was feeling pretty chuffed. He'd arranged to get the Bright Sword. Managed to enlist the local dwarves to protect the city. He'd even managed not to die.

Yet, Muninn said.

Loki, however, was not as pleased. "Didn't Tilda tell you not to bargain with Sinmara?"

Ted nodded.

"Wasn't that the one gods-damned thing she told you *not* to do?"

Ted smiled. "I didn't bargain with Sinmara. I bargained with Freyja."

Loki's furious demeanour quickly turned quizzical, and then a Joker-wide grin cut across her face. "Oooh, Mama like."

"I thought you'd appreciate the distinction."

"You know, Ted," Loki said, shaking her head, "you still need a good lawyer. Midgard is still one of the Nine Worlds. You should be able to have the girl and screw her, too."

"Surtur won't be stopped by half-measures," Ted said. "And if you want to try to fuck the big guy into submission, I'd like to see you try."

Ted *didn't* want to see that and idly worried Loki might take him up on it.

Never challenge a trickster. Not to anything.

Tilda was even less pleased than Loki.

"What the Hel were you thinking?"

"We improvised," Loki said.

Tilda's eye twitched.

"We're alive," Ted said. "And Sinmara is Freyja."

"What?"

"She's going to give Ted the Bright Sword."

Tilda obviously didn't like being kept out of the loop. He hoped she wouldn't kill him before Freyja could hand over the sword.

"I'll fill you in on the way out."

They got out of the tunnels and Ted squinted at the sun glinting off the river. It was in the east. That didn't make any sense … unless…

Oh fuck.

Ted's phone buzzed. There was a text from Rye.

—Where are you?

The text from Ryan was quickly followed by a text from Tyler.

—Groomsmen breakfast reminder. Did you sleep in?

The fucking groomsmen breakfast.

—Stripper keeping you busy?

Ted rubbed at the bridge of his nose. "Jesus Christ. I've got to grab my tux and meet the guys."

22. You Dress Up For Armageddon

They made their way from St. Joseph's Basilica to the Edmonton Petroleum Club without incident. Photos were done. Everything had been perfect. Ted wasn't ready to breathe a sigh of relief yet, but once he made it through the reception, Ted Callan could disappear and Ófriður could take over.

It was weird to think of himself as two different people. And Ted felt as if there were a third person, one he didn't know yet, caught between his two identities. He had no idea how Loki kept all her roles straight. But trying to live as Ted again, after what he'd experienced in the Nine Worlds, had given him an idea of what Tilda must have struggled with, trying to live with her mother's and grandmother's memories rolling around in her brain.

What kind of identity crisis would *that* lead to?

Tyler's speech went over well. Ted thought it was shit. Too bland. Too fucking safe. Too much mention of Lisa for a speech that was supposed to be for Rye. It meant nothing to the guy giving the speech, and nothing to the guy it was supposed to celebrate. The only people crying happy tears were Lisa and Tyler's mom, proud of what a great job her boy was doing. Ted considered getting up there and blurting out every stupid thing Rye had ever done that Tyler didn't know—but he didn't. Rye was his friend, one of the oldest he had. *Warts and fucking all.*

It would've been funny, though. The Four Horsemen, sequestered at the back tables where traditionally the rowdiest, drunkest, and sluttiest of friends end up, would have expected no less. They'd seen him do it before. They'd tried calling him out, chanting his name while Tyler walked from his seat to the podium. If he hadn't been in the wedding party, Ted knew where he would've been seated tonight. He was quite used to being seated at one of those two tables.

There had been many good things Rye had done, too. And Tyler said none of those, either, which was why the toast to the groom had been bullshit.

The tables had been cleared away and the first dance was in the books. The Four Horsemen didn't try to kick his ass. They shared a smoke outside instead. True to Rye's fucking world, the first dance had been to Aerosmith's too-sugary love theme from *Armageddon*, but with Jenny's arms around him, that didn't matter to Ted.

If felt like a lifetime ago that Rye had stood for Ted at his wedding. It was good to return the favour. And to have a chance to give Rye shit about having sloppy seconds when it came to wedding venue. Ted had been to tons of functions at the EPC, though not once since he and Susanna had split. There were several rooms in the Edmonton Petroleum Club. Multiple parties could occur simultaneously, and there was some fun to be had in switching parties. Especially when one was trading a cash bar for an open bar.

Given Rye's Mennonite parents, Ted wasn't expecting too much of that rampant partying. There'd probably be no table dancing, only a few broken glasses. Or at least, not until the elders went to bed.

He bumped into Rye at the bar.

"Let me buy you a drink, brother," Ted said, holding up two fingers to the bartender, a pretty brunette with a round face and a huge smile. "Whiskey."

Rye laughed. "You'll owe me a bottle or three by night's end."

Ted shook his head. "Still can't believe you picked this place."

"I like it."

Ted whispered, "It's cursed."

Rye rolled his eyes. "You can*not* still blame EPC for your marriage breaking up. Besides—you got fifteen years. That's more than most people get. Fifteen years will take me to my early retirement and then my mid-life crisis. That seems fair."

"Mid-life?" Ted snorted. "If you think you're going to live to be a hundred and ten, you're dreaming."

They clinked glasses. Rye drained his, Ted took a sip. Rye glanced over at the dance floor. Lisa was beckoning.

"Gotta fly, man."

Ted nodded. "Hey. It was an honour to stand up for you."

"Thanks for coming. It meant a lot."

Rye ordered another drink, probably for courage if he was going to be dancing.

He gave Ted a rough slap on the back, and said, "Time to make an ass of myself."

"At least you have a calling."

The dance floor wasn't quite in full swing, but if they played "The Chicken Dance" to call people out, Ted would be ready to drop his disguise and give Surtur a call. He sipped his bourbon, and tried to avoid looking for Susanna. The whiskey burned its way down his throat. Rich and hot. Rye had shelled out for some top-shelf shit for his groomsmen. Ted would've been happy with plain old Jim Beam, but everyone in the wedding party had their own bottle held in reserve from the regular supply.

It was a nice gesture, and Tyler was being cagey, ordering his scotch when no one else was in line, presumably so he wouldn't have to share. Ted didn't see what the big deal was. No one would be able to pronounce that mouthful correctly anyway. Ted considered getting a glass to fuck with him, but Tyler's brand smelled like peat and barbecue farts, so his good side won out. Instead, he grabbed a Grey Goose vodka for Jenny, who was dancing up a storm with the other bridesmaids. Rye's mom snagged Ted on the way to the dance floor, and held him hostage through "You're Nobody Til Somebody Loves You."

He hadn't seen Susanna yet. But if having an awkward handshake and a bit of a "should we hug? Are we okay to hug?" dance with Susanna was the worst thing to happen to him on this trip, he could count himself lucky.

He was glad Rye had warned him, at least, that his ex-wife would be in attendance, but he wasn't sure he wanted to see her.

He absolutely wanted to see her.

Wanted to see that she'd put on weight. Or that her face had sprouted new lines. And that she seemed haggard without him. He wanted her to be happy. To look great. To smile that huge, natural smile of hers.

Face it, Callan, you don't know what the fuck you want.

Which was why he didn't want to look for her. He'd kept his eyes front as he'd walked down the aisle next to Jenny. Concentrating on the firm grip of her hand on his shoulder. Her beaming smile made even her bridesmaid dress look good.

He didn't have to look for Susanna. She was impossible not to see.

There was no mistaking her. Ted looked up from his bourbon and there was his ex, in a red dress that clung to every curve. And damned if Ted needed Muninn to remember everything beneath that fabric.

He couldn't help but stare, first at her, and then at the table she'd left. Looking for her new guy. The man who'd replaced him.

Susanna had a drink in each hand. She offered one to him and he took it. Had a sip.

"You remembered."

A quirk of a smile. Ted knew that smile. That was her half-in-the-bag-and-ready-to-get-all-the-way-in smile. "How could I forget? You drank enough of it to float our house away."

She circled him, before grabbing a seat next to him. She crossed her legs. Her knee brushed his as she did so.

Even in the din of the reception, the silence between them weighed heavily on Ted. She'd approached him. Ted figured he'd wait for her to say her piece.

"I wasn't sure you'd come."

That wasn't what he'd imagined her saying.

"Where else would I be?"

"Jail?"

Ah, there it is.

"That was a mistake."

She smiled. "That time, maybe."

"Yeah. That time." Ted took a breath, considered his next words over a sip of his drink. "Kinda surprised to see you head over here after your last message."

"That message is why," Susanna said. "After I heard you'd been attacked and it was a misunderstanding….You probably didn't need to hear that."

Ted waved off the oncoming apology. Susanna hated apologizing. Admitting being wrong. Ted wasn't keen on it, either. And Suze had been more right than wrong when they'd been together. He'd hated that. And that they'd kept track.

There was no stopping her, though, when she'd wanted her way. "I'm sorry about that message. I didn't know what to say—and when I did, you were always out of the service area."

"I had other things on my mind."

"Still, I half-expected you to call back and tell me to go fuck myself."

"What good would that've done?" Ted asked. "I was glad to be gone."

Silence again.

"Where's your new guy?" Ted asked. "I didn't see him with you in the receiving line."

"Who told you about Vince?"

The god of lies and trickery, why do you ask?

"I have my sources. I didn't burn *every* bridge when I left the province."

She winced at that. He'd said it more harshly than he'd intended.

"He's up north."

Ted snorted. "You sure didn't learn your lesson, did you?"

Susanna took a deep breath and Ted wondered whether he'd gone too far. She could fucking bellow when she wanted to. Loud enough to knock you down.

"He's not you, Ted."

"Don't I know it."

She swatted his arm. Hard. "That's not what I meant, and you know it."

He smiled wearily. "Hope you're happy."

"Do you?"

"Yeah," Ted said. He wasn't surprised to feel that way. Susanna evidently was.

"I heard you've been playing the field a bit."

"Who told you that?"

"Some twenty-year-old in Winnipeg—"

"She was twenty-three," Ted said. Susanna's tone imbued "twenty" with the tone one would reserve for *whore*.

"Things didn't work out," she said. It was a statement, not a question. If things had worked out, Susanna would probably be avoiding Tilda in the same way that Ted had tried to avoid Susanna.

Ted could've brought up Erin. Could've thrown that in Suze's face, but that would hurt her, and he realized he didn't want to do that. He didn't want to think of Erin, or the child that he and Susanna had lost years before.

"Lisa also said you and Jenny cut out of the rehearsal pretty early." What had come next was *definitely* none of Susanna's business, and Ted shot her a look telling her so. If Susanna gave a shit about who he was sleeping with, the time to act was a couple years gone. "And then you left the stag with a stripper?"

"You hear a lot, don't you?"

"What do you expect? I'm here. Our friends are here. You're not."

"Is that why you came over? To see if my dick has fallen off? Have a good laugh?"

"You always get angry, and then you get crude."

Ted bit back his response. "Crude" wasn't the c-word he was thinking of at the moment. He took another sip of his whiskey to calm down. Which wasn't the best plan. Too many more sips and he'd be so buzzed he wouldn't want to calm down. A surefire way for things to end poorly tonight, and for more folks than him and Susanna.

He caught Rye's eye, who mouthed a "need an exit?" Ted shook his head slightly. Rye nodded, but kept watching.

"I am who I am."

"No. You're not who you were," Susanna said. "The old you would've told me to fuck off. Or would've walked out for a smoke when he saw me coming over."

Ted could use a fucking smoke. "You walked over while

I wasn't looking, or I might've." He managed a laugh after the statement, to lighten it. Susanna didn't laugh, but she didn't swat him again, either.

She took in his appearance, leaned in and squeezed at his shoulder.

"You look good. Different, but good. The beard suits you."

Ted turned his head away from her cleavage and scratched at his beard. "Thanks. It's a pain in the ass, most of the time."

"I've heard you're sporting some interesting tattoos."

"Heard that too, did you?"

"Not quite talk of the town, but it made the rounds."

"I imagine it did."

"Mind if I sneak a peek?"

Softly, he answered, "I do."

She leaned back as if he'd yelled.

"I guess that was rude of me."

I guess so. Ted didn't say it, and managed to bite back a grunt that would've made the same point.

"If you hate them so much, why not have them removed?"

Ted bit back a laugh. That had worked real well the first time he'd tried.

"What's so funny?"

"Nothing," Ted said. "I've been thinking of them as a reminder to be more careful where I drink."

And who I drink with.

"Hell of a reminder."

"I've got a pretty thick skull."

"I remember," Susanna said.

"You would."

"C'mon, let's see 'em." She waved her drink. "I'm buying."

Ted smiled. "You always had a way of getting what you wanted."

Susanna turned over Ted's right hand, looking at where Mjölnir had been. Had it been there, there would've been no spark. Magic had gone out of their lives long before Ted knew magic was real.

"There's got to be more than that or everyone wouldn't be talking about them. They made it sound like you belonged in a circus."

"You'll have to buy me more than one drink if you want me to strip down and show you everything."

"So it's true?"

Ted had already stuffed his tie in his tuxedo jacket pocket and popped the top button of his shirt. Another button down and the top of the storm cloud on his chest and the dragon-scales that surrounded it should be visible. Instead, there was a heart-shaped tattoo with "Loki" inside on a banner. An anatomical heart right above Ted's heart.

"That one's new," Ted said. "My first attempt at a coverup." His heart was beating fast. Faster when Susanna reached out to touch the tattoo. He did his best to steady himself. He didn't want the storm to bust free.

"Tip of the iceberg," he said, buttoning back up. "But that's all you see."

She shrugged. "How long are you sticking around? If you'd

like, you could come out to the old house. See where I buried Loki."

Ted didn't want to do that. Besides, was Loki there? Had the trickster dragged his way out of a shallow grave under an apple tree, or had he left a corpse behind when he'd tired of the role? Ted didn't know. He wanted to find out, as much as he didn't want to see the old homestead.

A familiar voice asked. "Mind if I cut in?"

Susanna looked up, Ted chose not to. That voice belonged to the stripper shape that Loki had been wearing on Friday.

"I'm his plus one," Loki added. She had a plate with a juicy slab of ham on top in one hand, and a wine glass in the other. She set the glass down between Ted and Susanna and took a bite of ham without bothering to use a fork. She licked her fingers. "This ham is so good, it tastes like a pig came in my mouth."

"You'd know," Ted shot back.

Susanna shook her head, an "I'm not surprised" expression that Ted had been on the receiving end of many times before crossed her face.

"He's all yours."

Ted took a deep sip of his whiskey and let out a deeper sigh. Loki's skirt was being held up by a wink and a smile. There were a few murmurs from around Ted that he imagined pertained to that.

Across the floor, the Four Horsemen pointed and hooted.

"What the fuck are you doing here?"

"Let's just say I've got a bad feeling about this."

"No jokes. No *Star Wars*. The truth."

"You need to find a way to make a graceful exit."

"Job's not done."

"They're happily married. You've already shagged a bridesmaid—" more murmurs from the table down the way. Loki opened her purse and showed Ted his groomsman bottle inside. "It's time for us to go."

"Why now?"

"Your disguise isn't perfect, you have to realize that."

"Given who made it, I'm not surprised."

Loki's brow furrowed. "Nice."

"Why don't we discuss this outside over a cigarette?"

Ted glanced around. A few too many folks watched their exchange. And damn Loki's eyes, he did want a cigarette.

"Fine. But I'm not leaving without saying goodbye."

Loki looked ready to protest, but wisely chose to say nothing. Ted was in such a rush to get Loki out the door, that he clipped an elderly woman.

She steadied herself on a banquet table. Ted stopped dead when he recognized her.

Mrs. Wiens, Ted's old Sunday school teacher. How old was she? It had to be a miracle she was still alive. She'd seemed ancient when Ted and Rye had been kids. One of those people you'd swear had been born old. But other than her hair going from dark grey to white, she looked much the same as she had when she'd tried—unsuccessfully—to clean up Ted's act.

"I'm so sorry," Ted said. "Are you okay, Mrs. Wiens?" Ted was past the point where he referred to old teachers with any honorific, but he found he couldn't remember her first name. He'd only ever known her as Mrs. Wiens.

"Still asking questions, Ted?" she asked. "Or do you have all the answers now?"

She remembered him. How many years, and she remembered him.

"Yes and no," Ted said.

Loki opened her mouth to say something.

Ted elbowed her in the ribs as he pulled her close. Through a smile, he muttered, "Don't even think about it."

"Is this your lovely wife?" Mrs. Wiens asked. Before Ted could say *Fuck no*, she said, "Beautiful girl. Such a smile. You're trouble."

"That I am, ma'am."

"You two seem in a rush, I'll leave you to it. Take care of him. He's trouble too."

She walked away, snatching someone's wine glass off their table and leaving Ted with his mouth hanging open.

He felt the pressure of Loki's hand on his elbow.

"I like her," the trickster said. "She's fun."

"Leave her alone."

"That's what I'm trying to do, but you keep dawdling. Oh, Christ—"

"What?"

"Look for yourself, *kemosabe*."

It was Tilda.

"What the fuck?"

"I warned you."

She slid through the crowd, dressed all in white, save for her colourful cloak of falcon feathers. Her ash-grey hair was loose, wild. She made no effort to hide herself. And yet she moved past them with the same ease and invisibility that Ve had demonstrated around some cops after Hel's defeat. No one at the reception reacted to her presence. No one except Jenny.

Her eyes were wide.

Oh, shit.

Anyone with a tie to the Nine Worlds could see her. What if she'd led something here?

"What is she doing here, I wonder?" Loki asked.

Whatever it was, it couldn't be good.

"Ófriður," she said.

Ted felt his body light on fire. His dragon-scale tattoos twisted and clawed wanting out of his skin.

"Ófriður," she said.

A storm moved across Ted's chest, winds, hidden under his flesh whipping and tearing at Loki's disguise.

"Ófriður," she said.

With the third uttering of the name the dwarves had given him, Ted dropped to a knee. Static electricity surrounded him, Loki's carefully coiffed hair stood on end. Ted swore he could see the glow of Mjölnir under his skin. It seemed so bright. How could it not be blinding everyone? Ted felt Loki's breath, hot in his ear.

"Breathe, Ted. Breathe."

Would she stop at three? Would she say his name nine times? Ted didn't think he could hold out that long.

He tensed, waiting for Tilda to speak again.

She didn't.

His heart slowed.

"Y'all right, there T-Bag?" Adam asked.

"I'm good. Just … need a smoke. And some air." He'd didn't remember dropping his glass, but he had. "And a drink."

Adam clearly remembered Loki from Thursday. Ted was surprised the guy remembered his own name.

"Have fun," Adam said with a wink. Ted was surprised he didn't slide a finger in and out of the loop of his thumb and index finger when he said it.

They hustled over to Tilda, where Loki ran an appraising eye over the Norn's outfit. "If you're going to crash a wedding, you shouldn't wear white. You're disrespecting the bride."

Ted held up a hand to silence Loki, and was surprised when the trickster obliged.

He asked Tilda, "What are you doing here?"

He'd barely got the first words out when Tilda spoke over top of him.

"It's time, Ófriður."

"You know, he prefers Ted."

The Norn ignored Loki. "Surtur comes."

23. Fight

A drop of sweat formed on Ted's brow and ran down his face. It seemed as if the lights had come up, but the bright glow was burning through the windows. It couldn't be time yet.

He dug his phone out of his pocket and called home. If Surtur was here, he might not get another chance. It rang and rang, as Tilda looked on sternly, and Loki sadly.

His mom answered, "Hello?"

Ted tried to say something. He wanted to say something. These could be his last words to his family, and he had no idea what they should be.

"I—"

"Ted? Is that you?" His mom sounded worried, then upset. "Are you drunk?"

Tilda put a hand on Ted's should and said, "Ófriður."

The words "I love you" wouldn't pass his lips, so instead, Ted said, "See you later," and hung up.

"Let's take this outside before something bad happens," Loki said, forcing a smile, and raising a glass towards Rye.

She led the way out of EPC and Ted was aware of the Norn's stare boring into his back. Corey was hanging around near the Four Horsemen, dressed in a threadbare suit. Corey nodded at

Ted, Ted nodded back. Corey's hand twitched as he held on to his beer. Maybe Rye had felt guilty and decided to give the guy a meal. Nice thing to do.

Ted had a cigarette lit before he was fully out the door and into the parking lot. The heat and humidity, even at 11 p.m., were like being wrapped in a wet blanket. Sweat slicked Ted's back, and ran free down his face from his hairline. Somewhere out in the city, sirens sounded. Ted strained to hear; multiple sirens, multiple locations. He couldn't tell their direction, but it was a safe bet that some other dumb fuckers had lit themselves on fire in Surtur's name. Maybe the cult was riled up because the dwarves had locked them out.

An aurora burned over Edmonton. An aurora in August, at this time of night … not unheard of, but not common. Ted didn't like it. A couple of shooting stars, stragglers from the Perseids, maybe, streaked across the sky, disappearing into the undulating green of the northern lights. Ted would've made a wish—if he believed in that bullshit. His last careless wish, for a life that mattered, hadn't been made on any shooting star.

And how had that *turned out?*

Not as he'd expected.

Tilda eyed Ted's disposable lighter as he slid it back into the pocket that held his Zippo. Ted tapped his cigarette pack, knocking a couple more smokes forward, and held it out to the Norn and the trickster. Loki took one—*of course she took one*—as did Tilda.

Ted remembered promising—and trying—to quit when she'd been pregnant. She'd quit; Ted had been jealous of how easily. He'd tried many times, before then, but it had never fucking took. He inhaled deeply and exhaled the smoke through his nostrils. He figured it never would.

"Light?" Loki asked.

Ted passed her the Bic, but Loki couldn't coax a flame free. Ted flicked the ash from the tip of his cigarette and offered it to her. She puckered her lips, and made noisy inhales as she lit her cigarette from Ted's. Ted couldn't help but notice that the trickster had passed him back her cigarette, moist from her lips, and not the one that Ted had handed her. Tilda's eyes narrowed.

Was she thinking of the time we'd shared this exact moment, when we'd first met?

If she was, she said nothing. At least no one had taken a swing at each other yet.

Ted could feel the weight of his Zippo in his pants pocket. He'd been afraid to leave it behind. It felt warm in Ted's hand. He'd stolen a fair amount of Surtur's flames outside of Saskatoon; even more from the *dvergur* mines. The Zippo was so warm it felt as if it had burned for hours.

"Surtur's followers know you're here," Tilda said. "Word got around. The fires. The attacks on men with tattoos. All attempts to smoke you out."

"Figures." Ted turned to Loki. "At least Tilda's not blaming you."

Loki smiled wanly. "Jenny's been exposed to magic. Tilda's in town. Huginn and Muninn scouting. There is a whole lotta magic in this one giant town."

"You see?" Tilda said. "You are not ready. You cannot stop this."

She took his hand, and he could feel Mjölnir trying to spark. He could feel the connection between him and Tilda, the link that Loki had buried, trying to knot up tight again and draw him to her. Before, her power had washed over him, but this time it broke against him.

"Huginn?"

I am here, Mathilda, Huginn said.

"Get me through Ted's thick skull."

Stop it!

You need to see this.

With the ravens leading the way, she bulled past his defence. Tilda carved through him to his hidden self and seized their *seiður*-born tie. He could see what she saw. God help him, he saw Surtur coming. And he felt the heat and the powerlessness, and choked on the smoke as it blinded him.

Ted had never been at ground zero for one of Tilda's visions.

He'd seen her react to one, but had never felt the visceral reality of what her gift showed her. In an eyeblink, Ted was back inside the EPC, standing still amidst a crowded dance floor.

From somewhere far away, Loki cried, "No!"

Flames exploded into the hall as Ted wrapped his body around Jenny. A rush of air shot melting shards of glass across the room. When he stood there was nothing left but ash.

Effigies that had been his best friend and Ryan's new wife. Ted's ex-wife. The last of his friends from the patch.

They died.

They died in flames.

They died before screams could pass their lips.

They died with smiles on their faces.

The vision was so intense that Ted felt his control over Loki's disguise slipping. This would happen. This was happening. This had already happened. Inevitable. There was only one way to stop it. Ride the lightning. Call the storm. Put boot to ass.

Fire would hit at the wedding. The flames hurt. Burned. This would kill him—unless he unleashed Ófriður. If Surtur was here, then there was nothing left to wait for. The dwarves had made him their instrument of war. Loki had locked that part of him away, so he'd have one last chance at a normal life. Get to say goodbye.

He still hadn't done that. The hope of safety for his loved ones, a security that couldn't possibly be, now, if ever again. A terrible joke. Ted stood and greeted the flames. They couldn't burn him.

Not anymore.

The fires rushed past him and he wanted to call to the winds; he could give them a twist and spin the fire out of the hall and into a funnel. A giant hand tore the roof off the Petroleum Club. Those left alive—*how could any be left alive?*—cried out and were silent.

No shelter, there's no shelter. Here or anywhere. Ted didn't call the storm. He didn't ride the lightning. He put no boot to ass. The fire spread until it was all there was. Ted burned, and he died.

With a shrill caw, Huginn said, Enough.

The vision disappeared from Ted's mind, like the sun behind a cloud. But the memory of what he'd seen, and the pain it caused him, remained. The door to the club clicked shut.

"Hey, Ted," Jenny said. "You okay here?"

Ted turned, Jenny stared at Tilda. Jenny leaned on a sheathed Tyrfing, holding the bridal bouquet in her hand. Ted tried to force a smile.

"I'm good. No worries."

She waggled the bouquet at him. "Looks like I'm next, if you're game."

Jenny had said she hadn't left home without the sword since Hel had come to Winnipeg. He'd considered asking where she'd hidden it under her bridesmaid's dress, but given how they'd left things, he didn't want her to use it on him.

"I think we're good."

"This doesn't concern you," Tilda and Loki said together—and then scowled at each other.

Jenny crossed her arms. "I think I'll stay right here. Lisa's been driving me crazy, I could use a smoke."

Loki and Tilda's lightning stares said, "Don't you fucking dare," but Ted was tired of being pushed around just because he wasn't sporting his tattoos. He didn't remember Jenny smoking, but he tapped one out for her anyway.

"Hold this," she said to Ted, handing him the bouquet and taking a cigarette.

She held the smoke for a moment, regarding it longingly before putting it between her lips. She made no effort to light it herself, nor to ask Ted for his lighter. Instead, she sighed contentedly, took the cigarette from her lips.

"I think I'll stick to drinking. So what's *really* happening?"

Neither Tilda nor Loki said anything.

Jenny arched an eyebrow. "Don't shut up on my account. Ted's told me everything."

Tilda scowled. "I doubt it."

"If you don't believe me, ask Huginn and Muninn," Jenny said. "I've got a magic sword, I can help."

"If you drop that sword of yours, you'll have more to worry about than the flames," Tilda said. "And if Surtur's followers get their hands on you, being burned alive might be a blessing. Giants are a hungry lot, and these ones will cook you as they eat you."

Jenny shot Tilda a glare. The Norn should have known better, given the circumstances, but it *was* exactly what Urd would have said. Blunt. Mean. But the truth. Always horrible truth.

"So you know how to use that thing?" Loki asked Jenny.

"I know everything the previous owners knew."

Tilda sighed. "I hope it's enough."

The door to EPC opened again and Corey stepped out. He had a cigarette in hand, and was trying unsuccessfully to strike a match. His hand shook as he twitched, stumbling.

Ted asked, "You okay, Corey?"

Corey fixed Ted with a glass-eyed stare.

"Are you high?"

His only answer was trying to strike another match.

"Here," Ted said, "Let me get that."

Ted stepped over and lit the Bic, reaching to light Corey's cigarette.

Tilda yelled, "Ted, no!"

"*Bah!*" Corey slapped the lighter out of Ted's hand. He grabbed Ted's wrist in a frenzied grip, yelling, "I have him!"

Loki tried to pull Corey off Ted. Her nails raked over his face. Corey's elbow slammed into Loki. He bit Ted.

Nine guys rounded the corner of the building. Nine dead guys. Ted knew they were dead, because they'd been at the centre of the blast that had woken Surtur. Their skin was grey. Not the black-and-white-movie versions of their past selves that were common to Hel's army and the dead of Niflheim. These men were cigarette-ash grey, and looked as if a single touch would blow them apart to float away on the wind. He'd known they'd been dead, but that was also before he'd known about magic or the Nine.

Jenny snapped her sword free of its scabbard, and she was in front of Ted in a flash. Tilda stood beside her.

"Here," Corey said. "He's the one she wants."

Ted jerked his hand out of Corey's grip. *Sonofabitch! Freyja had fucked them over.*

The nine dead patch workers spoke as one. "Give us the flame."

"We need it."

"We'll take it."

Their voices hissed and popped and crackled over each other, sounding like a raging bonfire. Smoke billowed out of their mouths.

They each sucked in a huge breath, as if taking a deep drag. Their grey bodies glowed and sparked, orange flames burning under their charred-paper skin. Ash caught in the wind and blew off their bodies. Skin split and lava leaked, hardening to stony armour the moment it touched air. They weren't fire giants, or human. They were something in between.

"The *flame*."

The lighter. They wanted his lighter. Ted had brought this—brought *them*—to the wedding. Each of them drew in another deep breath, their bodies glowing once more like lit cherries beneath ashen skin. They rushed Ted.

Ted had seen Robin fight with a sword. Robin had fenced for years, and knew what to do with a blade—but Jenny was on another level altogether.

Her sword slashed out and caught one of the ash-men in the side. It sheared through the body as if it had been smoke. The creature's torso glowed more brightly where the air had touched it, but his body stayed together. Jenny's blade came out of the body glowing forge-hot.

"Oh, shit," Loki said.

"This is what your trickster's ruse has bought," Tilda said.

Loki shot back, "This wasn't the plan."

If things had gone according to plan, Ted would've made it through Rye's wedding and dinner with his folks and no fucking monsters would've shown up. He would've gotten a better idea of the situation, then got the hell out of Dodge.

Plan A was in the shitter. But Ted had a backup plan. And he had backup. But he couldn't call them.

Ted took a step back, though he hated having to. He felt a nagging itch up and down his back where Yggdrasill should be, the runic tree tattoo wanting to respond to their magic. The storm wanted to come, the lightning wanted to strike, Mjölnir wanted to thunder.

So do I.

Instead, Ted scrambled to put himself behind Jenny and Tilda. Surtur knew he was here. That much was clear as day. The giant was trying to force Ted's hammer hand. He wanted the fight, and the destruction it would bring. He wanted the freedom that Ted could give him. In his gut, Ted wanted that fight, too. But damned if he'd let the world burn to get it.

Tilda spun her spear, its shaft clouting one of the ash-men. They still looked as if a stiff breeze could blow them apart, but when the Norn struck it was as though she'd hit sand. Parts of the body scattered, but reformed. She reversed her spear neatly and stabbed another. The spear tip slid into it, but it didn't fall.

"They're already dead," Ted yelled. "I don't think your valkyrie spear is going to do fuck-all."

"I know that," Tilda shot back. "I'm trying to keep you alive until you sack up and start to fight."

"I can't."

"You have to."

"What are they?" Jenny yelled as she cut the legs from one of the ash-men.

Ted wasn't sure whom she was addressing, but Huginn's voice stood out in the din.

"The Nine call to the Nine."

"You're saying this is my fault?"

"**Possibly. Having a Norn, and Loki, here with you cannot be helping.**"

They came for Ted and there were too many of them for Loki, Tilda, and Jenny to hold off. They weren't what the ash-men wanted.

Ted remembered the guy whose shape was now attacking him. He'd always been a total prickbruise, but Ted wouldn't wish this life on anyone. He lashed out at him out of instinct. The ash-man's rocky-looking exterior was paper-thin, and Ted's fist punched right through it.

Plunging his hand into the ash-man's body was like punching a pot of boiling water. His dragon-scales wanted to rise. Ted couldn't let them. He yelled in pain as he jerked his hand free and tried to back off.

It was too late for that.

The ash-man swatted him with the back of its hand. The body felt solid enough when that hit connected. The impact drove Ted to his knees.

Tilda yelled, "Fight!"

He rubbed at his jaw. "I can't."

"What did you do to him?" Her accusation was directed at Loki this time.

"He's in hiding. Surtur will know he's here."

"Surtur *knows* he's here."

"Yeah, but since we sealed off Muspelheim from the old mines, he can't show himself yet. If Ted's too close and using his powers it's all over."

"You think Surtur needs to be here to destroy the city? You think he needs you here to show up?"

"That's how it worked before."

She shook her head, as if she was speaking to ignorant children. "The King of Muspelheim is coming. You can't hide behind a fence or a disguise anymore."

"Goddamn it."

A punch landed. Ted fought his tattoos. They wanted out. He couldn't let the magic out. Not here. He coughed up blood.

Another punch.

Fuck.

His head was ringing. He couldn't stand. Couldn't fight. One more punch would kill him. He knew that. He was going to die. After everything he'd been through, he was going to die in a parking lot.

The ash-man lifted him up and the heat from its body seared his skin. Loki and Tilda turned into pinpricks of flashbulb light. Their voices distant. Ted couldn't tell which yelled "No!" when the cries and yells were lost in the crash of thunder and the smell of ozone.

He burned.

Not sure whether this new heat was from the giant or the lightning. There was no fighting his power's return this time. No battling this instinct. He'd believed he could hold out. Die rather than allow Surtur to force him to call. But Andvari and the *dvergar* had done their work well. They'd made Ted to fight. To struggle. The fight was coming, there was no avoiding it anymore. Now he had to win.

Still burning. The smell of his own flesh cooking filled his nostrils. There was no sound but the ringing in his ears. Dragon-scale armour sprouted like grass breaking ground. New hurt stopped, but the pain of his burns remained. A warm glow, hotter than the August night, enveloped him. This heat didn't burn, it soothed; a balm on his wounds. And they were gone.

Ted could hear again. First Huginn and Muninn's alarmed shrieks. Their squawks were followed by human cries of alarm like thunder following lightning.

Battle.

Sirens.

Screams.

Thunder boomed overhead. Ted was struck again and again. Mjölnir flooded with lightning, a dam ready to burst. He looked up and a drop of rain slapped his forehead. Clouds had swallowed the stars. He took a step before he realized he was standing upon the air. The lightning strikes had blown off his rental shoes.

A ball of lightning, glowing incandescent, surrounded Ted. Tendrils crackled out in all directions as he shot upwards.

Ted stood there, naked in his power.

"Your Zippo, Ted," Tilda yelled. "Where is it?"

He patted his jacket. "Shit!"

His gaze fell on Corey.

The *snap* of the Zippo's lid being flicked open, and the grinding of the striker over flint seemed loud as thunder.

Flame guttered in the wind.

"*Fehu!*" Corey yelled, jumping into the arms of one of the ash-men. "The world will burn."

Fires erupted from the Zippo. The Petroleum Club was engulfed in moments. The smoke and cloud towered high into the sky, taking the shape of a great battle. A blazing trail cut a scar through Edmonton. Like a jet engine roaring down Kingsway, a thick hot cloud slapped Ted, and the clothes that didn't burn like flash paper melted to his invulnerable skin. And as quick as lightning the cloud was gone, leaving Edmonton buried in smouldering sea of ash, with the tree leaves burned away, it looked like a dirty February day. Except for the goddamned heat. And the cries of the dead, and the dying.

Above it all boomed the sound Ted dreaded. The sound of his nightmares. The sound of the end of all things.

Lock, lock, lock.

Surtur was here.

24. There She Goes, My Beautiful World

Surtur's voice rumbled over Edmonton like an avalanche. Out by Fort Saskatchewan and The Park rose a pillar of fire topped by a spreading mushroom cloud. It was so bright Ted had to look away. Ted wasn't certain what was caught in the blast. But it was gone, and that pillar of fire was getting closer.

Smoke and ash were the first forerunners of Surtur's arrival. A hot, stale wind hit the city fast and hard, like a hurricane gale. Leaves burned off their trees. People cried in pain as their skin was seared. The stink of burning hair, cooking skin, and smoking leaves filled Ted's nose. There were three soft *whuumps* as gasoline stations were caught in the blaze and their pumps exploded, adding an oily, acrid smell to the burning mix.

Odin's fence stretched, bending, twisting and squealing, trying to contain the giant. To shove him back into Muspelheim. Like a sharp shank of steel entering his gut, Ted felt the fence break. Humanity's last protection from magic was gone. Nothing held Surtur back. Nothing held *anything* back.

Ted didn't want to believe it. He whispered, "Oh, Jesus. Oh fuck. Oh no."

"The storm, Ted."

Tilda's voice was barely audible over the rain and thunder, the crackle of fire, and the cries of dying monsters.

"You have to be the storm." She stood right beside him. Her shoulder brushed his and the wind whipped her hair into his face. He looked into her eyes, blue as a bolt of lightning.

Her voice was hard. Cold. Not the voice of the woman who'd told him they were destined to be together. This destruction wasn't what he'd wanted. But want had nothing to do with it. What needed to be done, *that* was what mattered.

"*Naudhiz*," she said, speaking the name of the Need-rune. In his ear, she whispered, "You are the storm."

Thunderheads swelled. Their power flooded into Ted as the entire prairie between his two far-flung homes filled with storms. Lightning strobed across the sky.

One supercell on deck after another. He drew on that lightning, waiting to strike, and he sang to the need-rune himself. He sang to Tilda. His vision blurred as bolt after bolt struck him, choking as ozone filled his nose. Gasping for breath, he tore a hole in the sky. His arms crackled with lightning and swirled with storms. He was a hurricane, a tornado made flesh. An avatar whose furious, beating heart was Ted Callan. A walking thunderhead with tornadoes for limbs. Ófriður was the storm.

Ted was the storm.

And Surtur had fucked with the wrong goddamned city. The giant bellowed a challenge. Ted answered with lightning and thunder.

Clouds circled the city, whipping so fast they seemed still in the flashes of lightning. In the centre of that storm, with Ted at its eye, the sky was clear. As meteors died, and stars burned, and the aurora borealis blazed across the sky and then was gone.

Ted hitched a ride on one of the purplish bolts of volcanic lightning that crackled over Surtur's body. Maybe if those bolts met Mjölnir's lightning, Ted could get Surtur out of Edmonton. Into the Badlands, into the ocean, to Iceland, anywhere but here. It was a long shot. Surtur was bigger than anything Ted had moved before, and he doubted the giant would go quietly.

The *Raidho* rune song was one Ted was used to singing. He shouted the travel rune, and bolt after bolt struck the giant, lighting the sky as if it were high noon.

Surtur didn't fucking budge.

Maybe he would have, if Tilda had helped.

Surtur was too vast. Too strong. Too much. The sky couldn't hold enough lightning, but Edmonton had more power than that. Ted drew on every bit of electricity in the city. Every power line. Every cellphone. Every street light. Every volt and every amp, until Mjölnir was full to bursting.

Until Ted felt as if *he* were going to burst. He couldn't see. He couldn't hear. The white afterstroke was blinding, and his ears had filled with a deafening thrum. He smelled ozone, his tongue soured with the acrid taste of a nine-volt battery times a million.

Ted released.

It was as if every bolt of lightning on earth struck Surtur at the same time. A wide, fat scar of light tore open the sky. Thunder pealed, shaking the city like an earthquake. Wind whipped glass around without care or conscience.

Surtur didn't budge a fucking inch.

He laughed while Ted hung spent in the air. And then he swung for the fences.

The flat of Surtur's palm swatted Ted as if he were a fly. Wind whistled past Ted's ears as he hurtled away from the giant. He tried to orient himself, to stop his uncontrolled flight. Instead, he cracked hard into the pavement. The asphalt and rubble piled on top of him like a makeshift cairn.

If I don't get moving, it will be.

Ted kicked some cement out of the way.

Loki stopped him when he was a foot into the sky. "Ted, no."

Ted hadn't seen her arrive. Tilda and Jenny were there too. Surtur's forces were now pouring out of the ruins of Grant McEwen, blazing a line through the night like a fiery brand, pulled from a larger flame.

"You don't have to do this alone. You *can't* do it alone."

"I can't do it at all."

Loki tossed a pair of jeans at him. "Put on your big boy pants and let's get to work."

Ted didn't want to get to work. He'd already failed. The job was over.

I brought him here.

No, Huginn said. **It would have come to this.**

Muninn added, **Regardless of your actions, you knew you would have to face him again.**

Ted had dealt with guilt before, when Hel had come to Winnipeg. He hadn't chosen that fight either, regardless of her and Thor's justifications. He hadn't chosen this fight. He was irrelevant to it. It would've happened. Wherever Ted might have been, this fight would have found him, or he would've found it. That he was here meant that he could try to mitigate the damage and help those newly tied to the Nine Worlds.

Keep telling yourself that.

The guilt was still there. He'd feel it when the fight was over.

Your fight will never be over.

The ashes of friends, their families, of innocents blew over him as the wind rushed over the street. Tilda's vision of the future had turned to present. Smouldering husks were everywhere.

No more worries about anyone seeing magic. Anyone close enough to the fire giant was already dead. It was easy to joke when his own ass was getting kicked. But not now. This was too much. There was no gallows humour, just a gallows drop.

This hadn't been the plan. The Sergeant always said plans weren't worth a shit once you were *in* the shit. Ted wondered what his dad would say about *this.*

"Ted?" It was Jenny's voice. She was on his other side. A softer hand. "What's happening?"

Jenny had seen some things since she'd found that magic sword of hers, and had joined the Nine Worlds. Another pang of guilt that he couldn't keep her out of this. He'd tried. There was no way she'd seen anything like this.

Ted looked at Tilda, forced himself to stand as she said to Jenny, "It's the end of the world."

He didn't want to believe it. But she sounded certain. It was bad luck to argue with a fortune teller. A voice nagged at him.

She'd been wrong before. You never saw the birth of your child. Never held Erin in your arms. You are not *meant to be together. Wrong, wrong, wrong.* Easy to think when Tilda had been wrong. Harder, after all they'd been through, and the hurts they'd suffered, and inflicted, to remember when Tilda had been right.

The life of a hero or a prince.

A short, ugly death.

The end of the world.

Even if by some miracle Ted defeated Surtur, those words would still be true. This wasn't the far north of Manitoba. There was no forest fire to conceal Surtur's appearance. Everyone would know now, whether they believed or not.

End of the world. End of everything.

"Come on!" Loki's voice came from somewhere far away. Ted didn't move.

"You are a gods-damned wrecking ball. Start swinging."

Jenny spun vacantly, tears cutting rivers through the ashen plain of her face as if she were taking in the destruction for the first time. "Everyone. Everyone. Everyone."

Ted lost count of how many times she repeated the word. She may have come to terms with the fact that magic was real. Time had erased some, if not all, of the terror that had descended on Winnipeg back in November. But nothing she'd seen had been as personal as this. There would be no comforting her. Comfort would have to come after.

If the world didn't burn.

A big fucking if.

This was Ted's fight with Thor, Hel's invasion of Winnipeg all over again. Only fire instead of ice. And once again, Ted was way out of his depth.

We need some goddamned blue-sky thinking here.

"Jenny," he said, softly.

She looked at him, as if hunting for the source of the sound.

More firmly, Ted said, "We're gonna need your sword."

Mention of Tyrfing brought Jenny back to the moment. "You want me to fight *that?*"

"City's not gonna save itself."

Jenny considered that.

"Things've gone to shit in a real fucking hurry," Ted said. He gestured at Tilda and Loki. "We need all the help we can get."

Jenny tightened her grip on Tyrfing. Her voice grim as an old gravestone. "We make them pay."

Ted could hear the giant's *lock, lock, lock.* He'd mistaken it for Surtur's laugh. It wasn't a laugh at all. What the giant had been trying to say was:

Ragnarök. Ragnarök. Ragnarök.

"Dumb bastard doesn't know that Ragnarök is over, and he missed it," Loki said. "One-hit wonder."

"Over?" Ted said with a growl. "I'll give him a fucking Ragnarök. I'll burn him to cinders."

It was a stupid thing to say. It didn't make a damned lick of sense. Surtur wouldn't be burned by Ted's lightning, any more than Ted could be burned by his own lightning.

It was enough for Loki.

"That's the spirit, now get dressed."

As Ted rushed into his jeans, and buttoned the fly, there was a screaming sound as metal twisted and bricks crumbled. A nearby roof tore free. As the wind rushed in with tornado force, Ted stepped into the air.

Ted gathered the storm. He'd need to focus it to summon help. It had only been days since he'd felt the pull of the tattoo on his chest. The storm cloud tattoo reacted as if it had been bottled for years instead of minutes.

Thunder boomed.

Lightning flashed.

"Time to turn this up to eleven," he said, and called a bolt to strike Mjölnir. He hitched a ride, and brought everyone with him.

Everyone.

Ted reached for the rune-marked tokens he'd left behind in Manitoba.

"*Raidho!*" Ted yelled the name of the travel rune.

He stretched thin, pulled in a dozen directions at once. Every rune on Yggdrasill itched and tingled as the storm sought out those Ted had marked as his. His vassals. His friends. The only bastards dumb enough to throw their hat in the ring when he said he'd need help against a walking holocaust.

Lightning hit 97th Street in rapid succession. A peal of thunder. Robin and Aiko. Andvari. A troop of the Flin Flon *dvergar* and their rock trolls. Youngnir and his *jötnar*. Jack Flash of the *álfar*.

"You have summoned us here, Ófriður," the *álfur* said. "And we have come."

"We didn't make you for this." Andvari shook his head as he took in Surtur's immensity. "What will the world do if you fall?"

"It will burn," Jack Flash answered.

"No one asked you," Aiko said.

Ted called monsters to fight monsters.

He'd need them.

All across the city, pillars of flame jetted up into the sky like tank fires. Ted knew without Muninn telling him that those were the sites of the suicides and arsons perpetrated by the Church of the Eternal Flame. His back burned as their magic took hold. Through Huginn's eyes Ted saw a pattern in those fires and in the destruction; those jets that formed the shape of the *Fehu* rune. So much for the *dvergur* containment. Maybe the dwarves had kept Surtur's followers from getting in, but they couldn't keep Surtur's fires from getting out.

With a crack like a thunderstroke, Surtur was in Edmonton.

Looking down the empty road, Surtur rose up between the horns of one of the towers of Grant MacEwan University. The giant leaned on the horns, crumbling them and sending bricks thudding into the campus grounds.

Surtur wasn't actively trying to destroy anything. He didn't need to. He'd brought his fires here and they'd do the job for him. His followers were the ones loving their freedom and rampant destruction. Surtur didn't care about Edmonton. The city was beneath him. *We're all beneath him.*

He wanted the world. Worlds. All nine of them. And he wanted them to burn. Edmonton was only the start.

Ted knew he wouldn't beat Surtur with his fists. He needed subtlety. Loki in his corner wasn't enough, Ted needed to *think*. Never his strong suit. He knew a great deal more about magic than he had before, but would it be enough?

Ted had brought everyone he could.

Surtur didn't step over the campus, though as tall as the giant was it should have been easy enough. Instead, the fire giant strode *through* the building as if kicking over a child's sandcastle.

The giant's rumbling laughter rolled over Ted loud as thunder. Louder.

Surtur was not impressed by Ófriður. *And why should he be?* Ted had a ragtag group of allies. Surtur had an army. Surtur was a fucking army. With him were giants, some bent over, running like dogs; others stood as tall as any Ted had fought in Rungnir's hall. Ash-men. Vapour ghosts, hidden in the heat lines from the flames, seeped forward. Surtur's minions were beyond Ted's ability to take in at a glance.

The giant held his arms up and then snapped them down. Flames shot from the tips of MacEwan. Surtur took another step forward, getting ready to crush them all.

Tilda, Jenny, Loki, Huginn, Muninn.

Not enough. *As if anything would be enough when faced with the walking end of the world.*

He'd called his backup, but there was more help he could call. He still had a cavalry. His ace in the hole.

He touched Mjölnir to the Gjallarhorn that wound around

his left arm. The horn wasn't a cry for help. It was a call for vengeance, for blood. And with Tyr waiting on the other side instead of Hel, a call for justice. Surtur knew the sound of that horn. The giant knew its note as well as Ted knew the giant's mocking laugh.

The horn's sweet and mournful song bellowed into the air, an answer to Surtur's laughter. Grey mist filled the street in front of Ted. Ted opened up Edmonton to the icy fog of Niflheim. The cold of the underworld clashed with Surtur's flames. There was a new world being created in their meeting, Ted knew. He could feel it. He hoped everyone survived long enough to see it.

Ted called to the dead.

They came.

Through the sounds of fire, screams, and storm, they marched, every step a tiny thunderclap, marching in unison. Booted feet stomped to a rest, as if they were soldiers snapping to attention. The Honoured Dead. Men that had entered into Callan family legend. *Einherjar*. Warriors who fought on past their time in the grave. They were not armed with axes or swords, but with Lee-Enfield rifles. They wore no mail, dressed instead in the uniforms of the Canadian Expeditionary Force, circa 1917.

What were five more soldiers to a war? But these five never missed, their every shot was fatal, and they couldn't die. They already had.

The Honoured Dead didn't wait to start fighting. They knew who Ted's enemies were. They fired, and showed how giants could die.

"Hold the gate, Ófriður," a voice boomed.

It belonged to Tyr.

The Honoured Dead had answered Ted's call. And they hadn't come alone. Ted sustained the note of the Gjallarhorn, as the fog flooded Edmonton. Tyr, once god of war and justice, once Hel's prisoner, stood beside the army of the dead. The hand he'd lost to Fenrir now made whole, as were the eyes taken from him by Thor. Tyr stood tall and straight, not as gaunt as Ted remembered him. His jaw was set. His long hair bound in a braid. He ruled in Hel now, and he'd brought his army with him too.

They looked as they once must have in life. Not zombies, but leached of colour; greyscale wisps given form from the mist. Tyr had added to his army. Ted didn't want to trust them. He remembered what they'd done when Hel had unleashed them on Winnipeg.

"I owe you an apology, Ófriður," a voice said from within the crowd. "And to you as well, Mathilda All-And-None."

Ted knew that voice too. It had been months since he'd heard it, but he remembered the valkyrie's mocking voice from when she'd attacked him in a club with her sisters. He also knew it wasn't the one he wanted to see. It wasn't Göndul. She'd be out there with Surtur's army. Somewhere. Waiting for her chance.

Tilda and Ted spoke at the same time. "What the fuck is she doing here?"

Svipul answered before Tyr could speak. She inclined her head in the direction of the new god of the dead. "I was the only one willing to forsake our old mistress. Neither Mist nor Kára would serve the line of Odin again."

Tilda didn't seem to give a shit. "I killed you for the second time, I'd be happy to supply the third."

Tyr stepped between Tilda and Svipul. Bold as Tilda was, she stopped short of picking a fight with the former war god and current death god.

Even with the army of the dead at his back, Ted's force was outnumbered. And now he'd have to watch his back for a valkyrie's spear.

"You've added to your forces," Ted said.

"As have you," Tyr said, taking in the assembled line behind Ted. His eyes narrowed when he took in Youngnir and his *jötnar*. "Heroes of all stripes. Of the Heroes Brave, was Freyr the best. The bound from their fetters he frees. Have you the Bright Sword?"

"No."

Tyr glanced up at the approaching fire giant. "Things could be better."

25. Earth Died Screaming

The ground shuddered and buildings shook. The din of breaking glass, sharp against Surtur's booming laugh and heavy footfalls, cut into Ted's hearing. It was as if the earth itself were trying to flee the monster that walked upon it. Surtur's steps would be felt around the world; they'd trigger seismic equipment, a warning no one would know to heed. Unti it was too late. The giant was a tsunami of fire, swallowing Edmonton—a building, a block at a time.

"Huginn, Muninn," Ted said aloud. There was no point in hiding it, didn't matter who heard him now. "I need eyes up."

The ravens tore out of Ted's head, burning his raw skin. Pain throbbed with his every rapid heartbeat. *Good. Pain is good.* It made him want to fight, and sure as shit he had a fight on his hands. The destruction visible through the ravens' eyes was already too much for Ted to bear. But there would be more. Much more. And soon, unless he got his crew on point.

In a moment the forces of Muspelheim would be on them. Bears, cougars, and wolves, all made of rock and fire, ran ahead of the fiery giants, roaring. They were no longer the hunched and broken things that Ted remembered from the explosion in the patch. Not cloying, weakened creatures, but titans.

Cars crashed, honking. One of Surtur's giants picked up what might have been a Cadillac Escalade and hurled it high into the air, laughing.

"Til, we've got to take this fight the hell out of the city."

"Thousands will die if we don't," she answered, finishing his thought. "I'm on it."

Everyone *will die if I don't pull this off.* Moving the fight was only delaying the inevitable. But it was a good start.

A halo of runes flared into existence over Tilda's head. Ted reached out his hand, hoping she'd take it. The last time they'd shared power, he'd used her strength without thought to her wishes. For this to work they'd need to be on the same page. Blood bond or not, he doubted she'd forgiven him yet. He didn't know that she ever would.

The fires at the end of the street, where Grant MacEwan had once stood proud, erupted. Explosions boomed within the flames, plumes of smoke, and the crackle of consumption. Ted looked to Tilda. She reached towards him.

Surtur's force was on them.

"Loose!" Andvari yelled, and the rock trolls behind Ted slammed him out of the way as they burst forward, advancing on the giants of Muspel like an avalanche. Tyr's army of the dead whooped and followed suit. Ted lost sight of Tilda as the *jötnar* got rolling and they were driven further apart. Ted could feel her, but their connection was jumbled, surrounded by too much noise. Too many creatures of the Nine. Too much magic.

The two armies met with a clash. Lee-Enfield rifles boomed. Their reports echoing through history into the present, loud as howitzers, again and again.

Rock trolls rolled forward as large stony spheres. It was as if Andvari had unleashed a horde of autonomous—and deadly—bowling balls. As the spheres reached their targets, they unfolded into rocky humanoid shapes. Ted knew them well. He'd fought one in Flin Flon, when the dwarves had tried to collect him and Tilda.

There was a pocket in the battle. Ted spotted Tilda. Watching her fight stunned him. It wasn't that she moved like lightning, or tossed giants around, the way Ted fought. Instead, her enemies did that for her. It was as if she were outside of time. The *jötnar* swung their weapons where Tilda *had* been, not where she was. Clubs and fists and swords struck allies. Giants who turned to reach for her found themselves in the path of a building or power line that one of their fellows had struck. The ensuing collapse brought them down. While they were on the ground, Ted's human-sized allies could reach vulnerable necks, eyes, ears.

Ted tried to get to Tilda's side. A fifty-foot giant stepped in front of him. It growled and punched down at him. Ted dove to the side as the truck-sized fist slammed into the asphalt.

"Motherfucker, I do *not* have time for you," Ted said. He pointed a finger at the giant and called a bolt of lightning. The giant dropped, but more of them stepped out of Grant McEwen. There was a great crash as dead met flames. Ghosts of cold mist and ghosts of hot vapour met and fused, becoming inert. Towering above it all was Surtur.

Fire won't win this fight. Ted still had his ace. He didn't know if that ace would be there when he threw the card on the table. He was a prickly bastard, and they were hardly friends. Having

Loki at his side wouldn't help either, but the last time they'd met, he'd said that Ted was square. Ted tried not to think of the size of favour that joining *this* fight would require him to pay back.

He felt the storm tattoo twisting on his chest, spinning like a hurricane. He felt the lightning strikes hitting Lake Winnipeg twinned with bolts landing, against nature, on the surface of the North Saskatchewan. He felt the vastness of his target. He'd called. Whether he got an answer, there'd be no way to tell.

At least he had the fucker's attention.

Some of Youngnir's giants and Andvari's trolls had forced their way through the line of Muspelheim giants. Surtur didn't appear to notice anything that engaged him. When his foot landed upon people, Ted didn't see any malice in the act. It was simply a footstep. Ted's army was beneath the giant's notice. The Honoured Dead trained their Lee-Enfields on Surtur, guns he'd never seen deliver anything but a mortal wound. They may as well have been buzzing mosquitoes for all the giant's reaction.

Seeing they had no effect on the giant, the Honoured Dead trained their rifles back on Surtur's forces. They knew their job better than Ted. He'd motivated every corner of the Nine he knew to come to his call. To fight with him. But not enough of them were fighting *for* him. They all had their own agendas and grudges. They'd all been a part of the world longer than him. They all had their own ideas on how this war was to be waged.

That wasn't going to do the trick.

Something kicked Ted through the wall of a building and into a jumble of charred t-shirts and comic books.

"Looks like that one rang your bell," Robin said.

Ted hadn't heard the tattoo artist follow him in. He and Aiko could slide in and out of shadows cast by the fires. Robin had an *álfur* sword in one hand, and Aiko had a pistol loaded with rune-marked bullets. They had strength and speed too, more than that of a normal person. Aiko was on the other side of Robin. They each held out a hand to haul Ted to his feet.

"What now?" Aiko asked. Their swan cloaks glowed in time with every lightning strike.

"We fight," Ted said. "And try not to die."

It wasn't much of an answer, but Robin and Aiko nodded grimly. Ted was sorry they'd ended up in this world with him. He wished they'd been able to live on in ignorance, but if they hadn't been close to him, they might not have have survived Hel's attack on Winnipeg. He'd given them a chance to fight for themselves.

Now their doom was in their own hands.

Through Huginn's eyes, Ted saw Jenny in the thick of the fight. She was juking and weaving through larger opponents with every bit of the grace she'd shown on the basketball court twenty years ago, blazing past taller women. Only now, when she burned a defender, they hit the ground with a severed Achilles tendon, or fell headless.

It was a hell of a thing to see.

He wanted to watch everything. To watch over them all. But he couldn't. He didn't want any of his friends or allies to die, but if that were his only concern, then everyone would die.

Shall I warn you if anyone is in dire peril? Huginn asked.

We're all in dire peril.

Ted cracked his knuckles, thrust Mjölnir into the sky and rode the lightning. Dirty purple bolts of lightning sparked and danced over Surtur's volcano-like body. Ted felt the charge, the power coming from them. He jumped from bolt to bolt. Each time he landed, he pounded the giant with a haymaker from Mjölnir. The giant's rocky hide cracked and broke. Surtur's body wept lava.

The giant's huge mitt was getting closer. Fast. Too fast, but lightning was faster. Ted grabbed another bolt and landed a hundred feet away across Surtur's shoulders. Another strike from Thor's hammer.

Not Thor's. Not anymore.

Mjölnir might not be the weapon that could kill Surtur, but it had the fucker's attention. So long as the giant stayed put, playing flyswatter to Ted's bug, he couldn't kill Ted's friends. He couldn't get deeper into the city. It was the best chance Ted could give to his side.

His next jump took him to the street, and the sky lit up like daylight. It wasn't from the lightning. Or the sun. Ted crossed his arms over his head. With a great stomp, Surtur's foot drove him through the street.

Rubble piled in, as the giant's foot withdrew, burying him.

He tried to shift the slabs of concrete lying on top of him. No dice. Although at least he recognized where he'd landed.

Surtur had driven him through the street and down into Bay Street Station. He saw the incredulous looks of the gathered crowd. He wondered if they'd fled here seeking shelter. Wondered if they had any idea what was going on above. Another booming footfall shook the station, and the shiny tiles that lined the tunnel dropped and fell. Advertisements tumbled onto the tracks. People screamed and clutched at each other.

Rain pounded through the gash in the ceiling, only a trickle of it reaching him under the rubble. He called the lightning. He wasn't certain how many bolts struck Mjölnir, but their force blew some of the debris off his body and Ted dragged himself out of the pile and dusted himself off.

The people on the stand stared at him, slack-jawed. He couldn't blame them. A half-naked man punched through the ceiling, struck by lightning, and he gets up, and dusts himself off?

Crazy.

Ted knew crazy.

There was a tentative, "Are you okay?" that was lost in another booming cave-in.

"Get out of here!" Ted yelled.

He wasn't sure whether he meant the underground, or the city. There was open sky through the hole in the roof of the station. Rain pasted concrete dust to Ted's face. He stuck out his thumb and rode the lightning bolt back into the sky.

Surtur was waiting for him. The king of Muspelheim was starting to get a feel for the personal touch that only he could bring to destruction. He pushed a building at Ted. What looked like the Alberta Place Suite Hotel.

Motherfucker.

Ted reached out with Mjölnir and jerked himself out of the

way of the falling building and onto the giant's back. Punching Surtur hadn't helped Ted so far, but it felt pretty fucking good, and each punch lessened Ted's guilt. For a moment—before the pleasure of hitting something as hard as he could turned to ashes as he realized how useless it was.

The giant would keep flooding the city with fire and fire giants. The sons of Muspel would feed well on these fires and their king was starving. He wouldn't stop until *all* was fire.

Ted needed the Bright Sword, and he needed Freyja to get it. He hadn't seen her anywhere, but given that everyone was showing up for this rodeo, and the Nine called to the Nine, she had to be close.

Huginn! Muninn!

We hear you, the ravens said together.

You need to find Freyja.

Huginn asked, **Why?**

She owes me that fucking sword. And I aim to collect.

The ravens' voices became incredulous squawks. It had been hard as hell keeping Hel's prophecy from the two noisy birds that shared his skull, but their tone told Ted he'd done the job well.

Why–

–Of all times–

–Do you choose to tell us this now?

"Hel warned me the knowledge was for me alone."

Again, I must ask, "Why now?"

Ted wasn't sure why he said it aloud, instead of projecting the thought towards the ravens. They'd never hear his words over the din, but speaking words aloud made them truer. Easier to believe. A thought is ephemeral. And Ted needed to believe these words.

"Hel's prophecy don't mean shit if we're all dead."

In the moment he said Hel's name, Ted noticed the herald of the former goddess of death.

Göndul.

The former valkyrie's flame-filled right eye glowed like a baleful star. She rode the air currents. Instead of a feathered cloak, wings of flame, fastened to her body with bands of white-hot iron, held her aloft.

She might not be an official chooser of the slain any longer, but Göndul was still doing her share of killing, raining hell down upon Youngnir's *jötnar* and Andvari's *dvergar* with javelins of flame.

Hatred twisted at the storm cloud tattoo on Ted's chest. *She was the one.* But whether Erin's death had been natural or not, it had been Göndul who'd given Tilda the kiss of death at Spectres. In Ted's eyes, she'd spurred the miscarriage of their child. Ted wanted her gone. More than gone. She had to be obliterated. Unmade.

He wasn't sure that was in his power. But Ted knew one thing. The only person who hated Göndul more than him was Tilda.

Ted roped the wind and summoned a downburst. The gale slammed into the valkyrie's back, driving her to the ground in line with where Huginn and Muninn had flown. Tilda had beaten Göndul once, she could do so again.

Only he'd lost her in the chaos.

Something big whistled past Ted, snapping his attention back to the fight. Giants lobbed flaming debris from the wreckage of buildings they'd destroyed.

This was how Ted's grandfather must've felt when he'd faced the Kaiser's forces at Vimy Ridge. The constant din. The sound of the long guns. The smell of burning flesh. The stink of death. Somewhere once beautiful turned to madness.

Wherever one of the giant's missiles struck home, the army of the dead would discorporate into their founding element. Surtur's army was fire, Ted's was mist. And his army burned away faster than the giant's.

Robin's and Aiko's cloaks shone white in the afterglow of lightning flashes. They worked together, using their tattoos to hide, sticking to cover and then taking any shot they could make count.

The giant they fought went still, and then Robin and Aiko were gone, hidden by darkness. Ted hoped they made it out of this fight. He didn't have many friends left.

A chain of lightning streaked across the sky. In the burst of light, Ted tucked his feet up and dropped as a long heavy cable snapped past his head. Behind him, metal screeched over metal as the cable crashed into something.

Jesus.

A giant wore the end of a building crane like a hook hand. He held the end of the cable in his other fist, and jerked it back towards him. The cable shot down the street like a snake, taking the legs out from a rock troll.

"You're next, fucker," Ted said, reaching out to grab a bolt of lightning. It didn't come. Something else hit Ted instead. He felt the air driven from his lungs as the impact sent him ass over tits, pinwheeling through the air, whipping so fast he couldn't get his feet under him.

He caught a dizzying glimpse of the Hotel MacDonald, which he'd narrowly missed hitting, and the High Level Bridge, which he wouldn't.

He called a bolt of lightning. It couldn't miss Mjölnir. The bolt changed his trajectory, knocking him out of the sky, and drove him into the water headfirst.

The river's surface hit as hard as a giant. As it slapped Ted's face, he took a gulp of water that burned all the way down his lungs. He sank like a rock. He flailed and kicked, but wasn't sure if he was swimming down or up. His pulse jackhammered in his temples. Bubbles tickled his face. His fingers touched mud. He'd hit the bottom. He tried to right himself and kick up towards the surface but the current caught and dragged him, sent him tumbling sideways. He couldn't see the lightning flashes. He couldn't hear the thunderclaps. But he could feel them.

Every stroke.

Every peal.

Even as his heart pounded, Ted felt the storm. He kicked for the surface as his lungs burned. What little vision he had was tunnelled into two pinpricks of slightly-less-black. Ted bit his lip, forcing his mouth closed. He wanted a breath so bad. He needed to breathe. He'd die if he didn't get air. He'd die if he tried. He didn't want to die. He couldn't die. Too much to do. The fight wasn't over.

Mike and the kids.

Mom and the Sarge.

Tilda.

Jenny.

Loki.

One breath and it wouldn't matter.

One breath and they were on their own.

One breath, and "Un-peace" would find his peace.

Tilda said he'd die today.

Ted's mouth opened. He didn't want to do it. He couldn't help it. His mind was screaming, *no, no, no, no. Not like this.*

Water flooded his lungs. His struggle ceased, and he drifted. Something brushed against him. Ted barely felt it. The force of the water grew tighter. It was as if the river was trying to crush him. Pinpricks of light. They grew brighter by the moment.

What do you know? There is a light at the end of the fucking tunnel.

Ted wondered who he'd see. God? Tyr? Nothing? Would he go where dead gods went? Would he go to the afterlife he hadn't believed in since he was a child? Was humouring your mother enough to get you into Heaven?

Ravens cawed, but Ted couldn't make out Huginn or Muninn's words amid the din. The bright light faded. Returned. A flash. A muffled boom. A sense of weightlessness, as if he were floating instead of drowning.

A siren wailed. Metal squealed. Thunder. And that wasn't all.

Lock, lock, lock.

Surtur's chant cut into him. Ted's eyes opened. He was above water. A great scaled tendril enveloped him. It gave him a squeeze. Ted puked up river water.

Jormungandur's head rose out of the North Saskatchewan River. So vast was the Midgard Serpent, it was if the entire river were his sinuous green body. Sputtering, soaking wet, Ted faced a monster that had tried to kill him once already. Ted hadn't believed the serpent would come to his call, but he had.

Now who was Jorry fighting for?

Though it burned his lungs to do so, and all Ted wanted to do was gulp air like he was draining a shot of whiskey, he held his breath. The Midgard Serpent could spit poison.

"Ófriður," the serpent said, in his nasal, watery voice. "I have come to honour our bargain."

Ted exhaled.

Thank you every god I've yet to meet and piss off.

Horns honked: people trying to leave downtown, coming from the High Level Bridge—some chucklehead had stopped to watch Ted's impact or to see what had happened and whether there were any survivors. Thunder pealed, and Ted imagined the sonic waves shaking the bridge. A pedestrian grabbed the railing.

With Surtur rampaging through downtown, the genie was out of its bottle as far as hiding magic from the public. A walking volcanic skyscraper bellowing a laugh at the sky and swatting away lightning like he was King fucking Kong on the Empire State Building. Good thing Ted had brought Godzilla.

"Jormungandur!" Ted yelled. "Nothing makes it across the river."

He wasn't sure whether the Midgard Serpent smiled, but Jorry did bob his massive head, and his maw opened up, revealing sword-like teeth.

With speed that belied his enormous size, Jormungandur snatched a giant off the bridge. The serpent tossed the screaming fire giant into the air. Its arms and legs flailed as Jormungandur distended his already immense maw and engulfed the giant as if it were a mouse. Smoke billowed out of his nostrils and the giant—a large, still-struggling lump—moved down Jorry's throat. He grabbed another giant, brave—or stupid—enough to chase a car onto the High Level Bridge. He didn't eat this one, instead whipping his neck and sending the giant skipping across the surface of the North Saskatchewan River. The giant sank, and didn't surface.

Jorry let out a wet, gurgling bellow. *He likes to play with his food.*

I have found Mathilda, Huginn cawed.

Ted wasn't sure where the raven was. He couldn't get a sense of the bird's location.

Where are you?

It was Muninn who answered, **Where you left us.**

I'm coming to you, smart ass.

He ran across the water, and back to the fight. He looked through the ravens' eyes. Their flight was too erratic and dizzying, as they dived and dodged amongst *jötnar* and other monsters, to make out much. Ted wasn't able to suss out where in Edmonton's downtown they were. He'd been gone a year. Amazing what can change in only a year. He felt the barely-there sensation of the water as Sleipnir's hooves carried him over the river.

As soon as Ted spotted a street sign, a landmark of any kind that would pinpoint the ravens, he'd jump to their sides.

Maybe it was because he'd nearly died—and Odin had died for knowledge, for wisdom—but Ted had an idea. He wasn't sure whether he'd call it wise. It was crazier than Loki and twice as dangerous. Might work. Might save Surtur the time and effort of killing everyone.

If you're gonna go, go balls out.

Roads and transit were destroyed. Anyone still downtown would be trapped. And downtown was a kill zone.

There. Through Huginn's eyes, Ted saw Tilda lay out a giant in front of a bookstore that had a purple awning.

Huginn, Muninn: I need you to find every person left in the city on the north side of the river.

Huginn squawked. **At the same time?**

Every thought. Every memory. Every fucking body.

The ravens shrieked their displeasure, but Ted didn't care. Voices split his head. Cries of terror, of loss. It was like being at an Oilers game. The buzz and hum of Rexall Coliseum filled to the rafters. Only louder. Sharper.

Ted's footsteps slowed. He put his hands over his ears, though that did nothing to muffle the din.

We have them, Huginn said.

Now get me inside Tilda's head. The same way you showed me Robin's thoughts after Jack Flash erased his memory.

Muninn felt it was necessary to give Ted a reminder. **She is not Robin.**

Do it.

This will hurt, Huginn warned.

Ted thought it would hurt them both. He didn't want to see what Tilda thought of him. Not that she'd ever sugar-coated her feelings on any topic.

Just fucking do it.

There was a brief sensation of being stretched. The ravens' answering petulance disappeared in a comical helium distortion of their voices. Ted felt every rune tattooed on his back start to itch, then burn. Fire ants ate him alive with every second. He barrelled headlong into a latticework wall of runes, butted up tightly against one another like a phalanx. Ted burst through.

For an instant Ted saw everything. Himself. Tilda. He saw the future, and it was nothing.

"Til—"

"Get out of my head."

"Can you—"

"Stay out of my head. I'm busy."

She stepped aside and yelled "*Tiwaz*." A lance of light shot from the rune stone clutched in her fist and a *jötunn* fell dead. One of its flailing arms crushed a fiery bear-shaped giant, the other landed on a burned-out husk of what had been a woman before she'd immolated herself.

Ted felt another flare of the *Tiwaz* rune. It burned bright in his brain, though he was too far away to see it.

"I can get everyone out of downtown."

"What? How?"

"It'll take the four of us, Huginn, Muninn, you and me."

"Let's do it."

Thank Christ. He'd been worried she'd say no.

A tingle ran up Ted's spine. He felt Tilda's halo of runes burning into his back. Her runes synched up with his. Ted had the elder runes tattooed upon his body, but their power was inscribed deeper in Tilda than the skin-deep working of the dwarves. He could access their power. She *was* their power.

He flushed as their power mingled. It felt like sex. She seized his power through their connection. She could take everything from him. She could remake him. Destroy him. Ted sucked air like he was running a marathon. Thunder rolled overhead as lightning burned a bridge between earth and sky.

All that Ted was, the Norn held clenched in her hand. His future, his past, his present, were hers to destroy or save.

Tilda emptied the sky of lightning.

Ted had felt the drain, when Tilda used rune power too close to him before. Necessary. If he couldn't get Surtur out of Edmonton, he had to get the people as far away from here as he could.

Too many people had died already. He looked at the shining sun on his palm. Tilda's words when they'd lost Erin and he'd tried to heal her were a fresh slap in the face. "There's nothing left to heal."

Dead was dead. And dead was gone. Dead was beyond his power.

Rye and his family had made no bargain with Frigga or Hel. No amount of tears was going to bring Ted's buddy back to life.

But someone would weep. Surtur would fucking bawl, when Ted had his way.

Across the river, in Old Strathcona, thousands of people found themselves safer, if drenched by rain and deafened by thunder. The North Saskatchewan didn't seem like much protection, but it would have to do. Attendees at the Fringe would have a hell of story to tell next year.

If there was a next year.

Ted tried to call a bolt of lightning to hurl him back into the fight. It didn't come.

Tilda and the ravens had done as he'd asked. Everyone downtown was now across the river. For all the good it would do them. Ted was exhausted. The last nine months had been a constant trial, pushing the boundaries of his will and his gifts. But he was huffing, bent over with his hands braced on his thighs, sweat pouring down his brow, lost in the rain, trying to catch his breath. It had been too long without fighting alongside Tilda. This escape stunt had drained his batteries dry.

He wanted to lie down. To sleep. To puke.

You don't know how far you can push yourself until you hit your limit.

Coach Dean's words rattled around Ted's exhausted brain.

Then you fucking push harder.

Ted heaved himself upright, letting the rain wash the sweat-sting from his eyes. Coach Dean egged him on.

No rest for the wicked.

A lightning bolt jerked Ted up into the sky. He leaped across the sky, jumping from one flash of lightning to the next. Each trip bringing him close to Surtur. The giant thought Ted was beneath him. Thought humanity were bugs to be stepped on. Time to change the fucker's mind.

Ted bent a lightning bolt towards Surtur. The giant's train-car sized fist was waiting for him. It flowed like lava, moulding around him. Sealing him up tight. *How could something so big be so fucking fast?*

The giant brought his other fist down, as if trying to crack a nut. Stone rang on metal and Ted wondered what Surtur had hit. Then he realized: *You, dumbass. He hit you. That ringing in your ears is because he rang your bell.* Ted's head lolled on his shoulders.

Surtur brought Ted close to his mouth. Ted couldn't breathe. There was no air, only the sulphur stink of Surtur's exhaust. For a moment, Ted thought the giant was going to eat him. Ted wondered whether his invulnerability would keep him alive long enough for Surtur to shit him out. Did Surtur have to shit? At least Loki wasn't there to make a Sarlacc-pit joke.

"Where are your gods? Where is your lightning? Where is your hope?"

Even Surtur's whispers were loud as a twister. Surtur gave him a quick, crushing squeeze. Enough for Ted to feel his bones creak beneath his dragon-scale tattoos. He tried to take a breath, but his lungs were squashed flat. There was nowhere for the air to go. Surtur whipped Ted away as if he were offal, and he sailed through the air and out of the fight.

26. Don't Open 'Til Doomsday

The burning North Saskatchewan River cut a blazing line right back to the patch and on to Muspelheim and to Surtur's power. Right to Hell on Earth. Tilda's vision was flooded with pasts, presents, but only one future. Fire.

It was all she could see.

No, not all. Step here and this one will hit that one. Action leading to reaction. Leading to action. She looked further into the fire. Leading to … she smiled.

Her.

Jormungandur pulled the largest fire giant he could see—and the building it was menacing—into the river. Being summoned to this … *river* pained him. It was not meant to hold his majesty.

He coiled his endless expanse and looped his scaled immensity around the lower of the two bridges and tore it apart. Metal squealed and groaned as it fatigued and died. He hurled the wreckage at a giant who had come too close to the river's edge. The humans were off the bridge, a fact that did not matter to the Midgard Serpent, but for some reason Ófriður cared about their dooms. The water would be barrier enough to keep the forces of Surtur from crossing and following after.

They would make the attempt.

And they would die.

The serpent chuckled, his laugh a coughing wheeze.

The skies were filled with thunder and rain. Ófriður jumped between flashes of lightning. This … *man* had defeated Thor. He wasn't sure whether to love or hate Ófriður for that.

The Midgard Serpent smiled and his forked tongue slithered between sword-like teeth. He could taste the fear of Surtur's army, and it was sweet. The finest Jormungandur had tasted since Loki had woken him from his first death. Odin had made the world of Midgard a prison for Jormungandur, but it was *his*, and Surtur would not take it.

"Not while I live," Jormungandur said.

The giants stepped into the river, and died. Crushed. Swallowed. Poisoned. Drowned. None that faced Jormungandur lived to retreat. The serpent feasted until their master could not drive them into the water. They fled deeper into the city, still burning, still crushing, but that was not Jormungandur's concern.

When the serpent had fought on the same side as the king of Muspelheim they had not fought together, but Jormungandur knew the *jötunn's* power. If he destroyed Surtur, the Midgard Serpent would eclipse all in stature.

None were vaster than him.

The giant stood, proud of the meagre destruction he'd caused thus far, and it rankled Jormungandur. He wanted to face the giant. To show him that any blaze could be extinguished.

Ófriður would not like it.

Battling *that* giant was not the task set to the Midgard Serpent.

Jormungandur found he didn't care what Ófriður thought. He had lost the man's scent amidst the smoke and rain and ozone of the lightning strikes. Judging from the storm, the man still lived. And was obviously incapable of stopping Surtur.

It falls to me, then.

Jormungandur snapped his winding coils straight. The force of the motion shoved a towering wave into the city, and the serpent rode the momentum towards the king of Muspelheim. He passed over and through buildings. Timbers and mortar and bricks fell.

He wrapped his endless coils around Surtur. An undulating river of green swathed the giant. There were the sounds of rock cracking and breaking. The hiss and sizzle of water evaporating from Surtur's fire. The fishy stink of the serpent's body cooking as he constricted Surtur.

Another crack and the giant bellowed a cry.

I have you now.

Surtur's arms fought against Jormungandur's coils. The giant's stony exterior buckled under the serpent's onslaught. Magma sizzled over green scales, a sound quickly lost beneath Jormungandur's pained cries. The Midgard Serpent was vast, unimaginably vast, but Surtur was inevitable. And the serpent did not hold the giant's death. Fists large enough to crush a train car wrapped around the serpent's body. Slowly, inexorably, they drifted outwards against the pull of Jormungandur's tightening coils. There was a wild look in the serpent's eye as he sensed his doom.

Jormungandur's venomous breath met Surtur's and the air exploded. There was an awful tearing sound as the serpent's body was ripped in two. Blood sprayed, fouling the river. For the second time in his existence, the Midgard Serpent expelled his last breath, but the poison that felled Thor hadn't the strength to defeat the king of Muspelheim. Venom killed what trees on the riverbank had not burned, and buildings were gutted as if they'd been burned with acid.

Over Surtur's laugh, over all the ongoing destruction, Loki's cry of despair rang out like a clear bell.

It was the last thing the trickster's son would hear.

Everything was red.

Fires reflected in the steel of Tyrfing. Blood running freely down the blade made Jenny's hands slick.

Out, damned spot.

There'd be no washing this stain free. Ted had warned her. Magic sought out magic. Warned her that this fight was coming. She'd never have come home if she'd known. It was so hard to leave once you were here. Ted *had* known, and he'd still come home. And now she had no home. She had no family. They were all dead.

Deaddeaddead.

Jenny recited their names.

Friends.

The guests at her brother's wedding.

Every name she could remember. A litany of loss. With every swing of Tyrfing, she yelled a name at Surtur's uncaring army. With every giant she cut down, she felt—not better, but *something.*

Tyrfing rang off another enchanted blade.

"He's dead," Robin said.

Jenny shook her head. She couldn't believe Robin was running around in a swan cloak with a magic sword. So different from how he usually looked, scruffy in an army jacket and with a cigarette hanging from his lips. Aiko too, the diminutive teacher, wore a cloak that matched Robin's and had a pistol that looked half as big as she was.

Jenny wondered whether they'd acquired their weapons and cloaks that same crazy night in November when she'd gotten Tyrfing. When she and a group of strangers had fought the dead, and how, one by one, they'd died with *this* sword in their hands, until it was in hers. She'd fought and lived. She wondered whether they'd known about magic all along.

She shoved Robin's sword away with a growl, looking for her next fight.

27. We Take Care Of Our Own

Helen Callen shuddered as thunder shook the house. Ben had his arm around her and they stared mutely at the powerless television. The grandkids played by candlelight, oblivious to the thunderstorm, while Samson whined and pawed at the door to the basement.

Their sons were out in this.

Mike had left like a bat out of hell when the news had reported the explosion at the Petroleum Club. She wished he'd stayed home. Where it was safe. She'd barely kept Ben from leaving with Mike. She wished she hadn't accused Ted of being drunk. God willing, those wouldn't be her last words to him.

Ted was pretty sure he'd crashed through the Delta and Epcor towers. He tried to right himself. Tried to get his feet under him, but he was tumbling so fast he couldn't stand up or slow down.

He slammed into something hard. Metal squealed and groaned. Surtur had hurled him miles across town. He ricocheted off a giant aluminum baseball bat that some asshole had thought was art. It toppled over as Ted bounced amid chewed-up cement and destroyed cars, skidding to a stop in the middle of the street. A car horn bleated, getting closer, then distant, as the vehicle swerved around him. Tires squealed, followed by the crunch of a collision. Then another. Ted stood, half-heartedly brushed off debris, and shook his head. At least he knew where he'd landed.

He couldn't see. The high beams from a big-ass truck shot him right in the eyes. He shook himself, as if it would help him regain his senses. As if it would help common sense reign in a city that had gone absolutely batshit.

It wasn't his ears ringing—the horn of the truck blinding him was blaring. Ted forced himself to his feet. It was a shame. Brand new Dodge V-8. Dualies. Beautiful truck once, less so with its hood and engine block flattened under a giant's foot.

Lying next to him was what had once been the tallest bat in Canada—since topped. He'd wanted to knock that thing down since it had been erected in 2001. He'd like to take a swing at Surtur with that bat. Despite the driving rain, and cloud-choked night, the giant's fires lit up the sky.

Something nagged at Ted. That truck was familiar. He couldn't see anyone inside. The airbag had deployed. Judging from its state, if anyone had been inside, Ted was too late. He hoped they went quick.

They shouldn't have had to go at all.

But dead was dead.

The rear tire, hanging in the air due to the angle of the broken truck, spun idly.

Ted walked past it. He wasn't going to look back. He couldn't. There was too much happening to dwell on someone already gone.

But he looked back.

There was a yellow ribbon bumper sticker on the gate of the truck.

"Oh fuck."

Ted knew where he'd seen that truck now.

It belonged to his brother.

It couldn't be.

Not Mike.

"What are you doing here, you dumb bastard?"

Ted wrenched the door off the truck. Blood coated the deflated airbag and Mike Callan's face from the nose down. Ted tore away the steering column. His brother wasn't moving. The seatbelt buckle wouldn't release. Ted ripped the belt from its moorings. He gently lifted Mike's body from the truck.

Mike stirred. He might have let out a groan. His breathing was so shallow it was barely there.

"Stupid prick," Ted said, breathing a heavy sigh of relief. "You've gotta live. You're too ugly to die."

Ted looked at his palm. The golden sun of Baldur was black. No magical healing for Mikey. The day it would take for the sun to return would be too long. No point in waiting to heal his brother when the city would be gone.

Niflheim's mists spread across the city. The summoning note of the Gjallarhorn held the door open for Tyr and his army, and flooded the streets, shrouding them in an icy fog unheard of for August in Edmonton.

The giant Móðguður had once told Ted that in Niflheim, time flowed as was needed. Ted wasn't sure if this instance counted, but he needed his brother to live.

"*Naudhiz!*"

He looked at his palm. Nothing. The sun was still black.

When Hel's army had attacked Winnipeg, Ted's tattoos had created an empty space in the fog of Niflheim. It had allowed him to see, to move, to fight. It had kept him separated from the true depths of the underworld. He focused again on his need, feeling the pinprick sensation of the runes on his back activating, and he let the fog swallow him.

It was cold. Damned cold. A cold that seeped through protection of his dragon-scale tattoo armour. His teeth chattered and his breath misted out of his mouth.

Fingers numb and shoulders hunched, Ted clenched his left fist and said the need-rune's name again:

"*Naudhiz!*"

Naudhiz; the fire that burned in the night, the rune of the Norns, the rune of Tilda. He opened his fist and the sun tattoo was golden.

"Okay," Ted said, breathing a sigh of relief. "Let's do this."

Footsteps pounded behind him. Ted knew that sound. *Jötunn*. Not a big one, but one with an overly shitty sense of timing. When Ted turned, there was a twelve-foot giant running down the street, chasing a car that was backing up and putting the nuts to it. Steam hissed off the fiery lines that ran up and down the fire giant's body as it cut through the mist. He roared, clawing towards the car.

Ted yelled back, answering the giant's challenge. No words came out, only incoherent rage. The giant turned, noticed Ted. He snorted as if Ted were beneath his attention. Ted called a bolt of lightning to Mjölnir. The street lit up as lightning touched the hammer. Thunder crashed, staggering the giant.

It stopped. Turned. Smiled. So did Ted.

Heavy rain pelted Ted's body as the giant charged him, lightning flaring in the clouds like a strobe light. Ted remembered the first giant he'd fought, and how fear had mingled with excitement. How huge a twelve-footer had seemed. Now, with Surtur laughing in the distance, this giant may as well have been a dwarf. The king of Muspelheim might not be something Ted was able to beat with his fists, but this sonofabitch was.

The *jötunn* had a weapon. Ted hadn't noticed the stop sign the giant had been carrying. He scythed the weapon at Ted, going headhunting. Ted ducked under the swing and closed the distance between the giant's rangy arms and torso, leading with Mjölnir.

Let's see how you like a taste of lightning.

Ted's punch cracked through the giant's rocky skin, spraying him with the magma that served as the giant's blood. The magma quickly cooled into rock-like blobs against Ted's chest.

In a flash of lightning, Ted noticed an odd piece of jewellery strung around the giant's neck like a medal. A pair of stainless steel truck nuts. Ted would've laughed at the ridiculousness of the fire giant getting teabagged by a stupid truck accessory, but it was likely the once-proud owner of those nuts was dead.

Ted tore the nuts off the giant's neck. "Stay. The. Fuck. Out.

Of. Edmonton," Ted said, punctuating each word by beating the giant across the face with his testicular trophy. The metal testicles shattered with the last blow. Ted hurled them aside, panting.

The giant gasped along with him, flames shooting from cracks Ted had beaten into his chest. It was as if there was a furnace inside the giant. Ted dug his nails in where the creature's sternum should have been, and cracked open the chest as if his hands were a rib spreader. The *jötunn's* heart was a hard ball of lava that cracked and split, oozing magma as if it were blood. Ted could feel the *Fehu* rune, emanating its master's power on the organ. Ted dragged his fingernail over the heart, scratching another rune into the organ.

"*Kenaz*," he said, snuffing the flames and the giant.

Its body solidified and didn't look much different from the shattered asphalt where Ted had landed. Ted kicked the rocky remains apart, scattering them. He didn't know whether the giant would find some way to reform its body, but he didn't want to make the job easier.

When the rocks didn't roll back together and reform, Ted ran back to his brother. Mike's life would never be the same after this night. If Ted waited any longer, Mike would die. If he healed his brother, he'd spend the rest of his life running from monsters. And knowing the shape Mike was in, it would be a short run.

28. Her Eyes Are A Blue Million Miles

Tilda watched Jenny go.

She read the confluence of futures that would find the school-teacher-turned-warrior. She would survive the night with Tilda's intervention if—and that was a *big* if—Ted managed to defeat Surtur. The Norn noted with some satisfaction that there was no future in which Jenny and Ted ended up together. Jenny would have a measure of vengeance for what the giant had done to her family, though it would never satisfy her.

There was a flash of white, glowing incandescent against the flames: the white feathers of a valkyrie's cloak.

Tilda smiled as the city burned. Until she found Freyja, she had her own vengeance to seek.

Svipul did not believe they would win. But there was honour in fighting bravely for a lost cause. She had believed that once, before death had chosen *her* at Ragnarök. Göndul, Kára, and Mist. Svipul hoped her lost sisters found peace.

She repeated her hopes aloud.

"Peace," a voice sneered behind her. Mathilda All-And-None.

Svipul turned to face the Norn. She wore Freyja's falcon cloak, and a halo of glowing runes circled above her head like a hurricane.

"Neither you, nor your sisters, deserve peace."

Svipul narrowed her eyes. "We fight for the same cause."

"No," Tilda said sharply. "You fight for a redemption you will never deserve."

The Norn levelled her spear. Svipul made to ready her shield, but her arm wouldn't move. Runes encircled her body, imprisoning her.

She expected the Norn to taunt her. To mock, and tease, before Svipul met a third, and likely final, death. Instead, she simply lunged, and straightened her arm, driving valkyrie spear into valkyrie body.

Svipul put her hand over the wound. The grey mist of Niflheim that Tyr had used to reform her body leaked through her clenched fingers.

"There is a life you can choose to spare," Tilda said, kneeling beside her. "She will be wounded as you are. Ófriður tried to spare her from this. If you find her, we'll call it even. Otherwise, I'll see you in Hel."

Sally yelled, "Jesus Christ, what am I doing here?"

The storm over the city was like nothing Sally had ever seen. This was end-of-the-world weather.

Given what Callan had told her, that description was all too apt. He'd warned her to stay away. To ignore things like this. But how could anyone ignore what has happening?

She had her phone pointed at the giant *thing* that was crashing through downtown. Callan's giant. He really had told the truth.

All the lights were out and it was dark as hell downtown. Across the river too. She needed to get out of here. People fought with swords and axes. A giant had thrown an LRT car! It had flown so far she couldn't tell where it had landed.

She'd been told magic needed to stay secret. That was safer. Sally wondered what Callan thought of that now. *If he was still alive.* Callan be damned. There was no keeping this secret. Not anymore.

Something struck her. She grunted, dropping her phone when her back hit a wall. She tried to step forward, to steady herself. Excruciating pain. She couldn't move. She was pinned to the wall behind her. She didn't want to look. She had to look.

A spear. There was a spear in her guts.

Pull it out! Pull it out! Pull it out! Would that make it worse?

There was no blood. *Shouldn't there be blood?*

She grabbed the spear. Her skin hissed and burned as she touched its grey wood. Frost coated her fingers, not blisters from a burn. And her whole body went cold as Jasper Avenue in January.

She didn't want to die here. She didn't want to *die*. She blinked away tears. Even *that* motion made her cry out.

"Help. Somebody please help me."

No one would hear her over sounds of destruction, over the other screams that filled the night.

Except that someone did.

The woman would have looked like an angel, if it hadn't been for the fire in one of her eyes. Sally had seen her swagger before, it was a weird mix of pro athlete and cop. It said: *I'm better than you, and can kill you, and I'll get away with it too.*

In the light from that eye, Sally felt cold. A strange sensation with so much fire around. The woman held out her hand, and the spear shot from Sally's body and into her grasp.

Sally slumped to the ground. Misty tendrils floated on the wind and seeped into her body from the edge of her wound, spreading, following the line of veins and arteries.

Surtur had laid a mighty blow upon Ófriður. Tyr believed he was gone. Perhaps dead. Could dwarf-forged dragon-scale armour have protected a man from such a blow? How much destruction might the giant wreak before Ófriður returned? Tyr did not know. The Midgard Serpent had already tried to steal the glory of Surtur's death. Tyr did not care for the glory, only the death itself. The last times he had fought in single combat, he had been crippled, his sword hand lost to the wolf's jaws, and then his eyes taken by his fallen brother, Thor.

Tyr clenched his hand tightly against the hilt of his sword.

Death did not frighten him. He had died once already. He would die a thousand times to do what was right and just. Surtur's time was done. Tyr would end him.

Everything had a death, even if Tyr did not know Surtur's. Hel had given it up before he'd assumed her role. Surtur's death did not belong to him, but he had to try.

He yelled at Surtur, "Face a god, Skyburner. Face justice. Face death."

Surtur laughed.

The god gnashed his teeth. Surtur had *laughed*. Hel had laughed. Thor had laughed. Tyr would be mocked no more. He charged the king of Muspelheim. With his nail boots, Tyr could walk on the mists, as Ófriður walked over air and water. He ran into the air, rain pounding his face as the heat of the giant's body slammed into him like a stone wall.

Tyr slashed at Surtur's reaching palm and the giant's hand recoiled, as if he'd been stung. Tyr smiled. That which could be hurt could be killed.

His joy was short-lived. Surtur's hands clapped together, crushing Tyr between them. The force of the impact blew shattered glass and debris into the air as the booming thunder of the strike echoed over the city. Giants screamed and howled. And Surtur laughed.

"Swordsleep is gone," the giant said. "You hold no death but your own."

The mist boiled away from Tyr's body and his world went black. His blade fell, the hand that had held it gone. Surtur hurled Tyr to the street as if he were refuse, no longer a god, only a broken body left gasping in a shattered road.

Hel was left without a ruler.

Svipul's body roiled and smoked, losing cohesion. She shuddered, thinking of the Norn's words, of what they might have meant. The Norn had promised her a chance. Svipul didn't see what it could be.

Until she came upon a mortal woman, dying from a valkyrie's spear. From Göndul's spear. Their wounds were the same. Göndul was no longer a valkyrie. She had chosen to kill this woman, but she was no longer one who chose. The breath of life gone from the woman's body, her eyes still had the last vestige of a mind that could comprehend.

Svipul chose. She chose for the woman to live. The woman gasped and spasmed, breathing in the mist that leaked out of her body, and made up Svipul. They breathed each other in deep, until they became one.

Sally's eyes snapped open.

Tyr rattled out a breath as Tilda approached. His head lolled on a broken neck; the blind-again god heard the sounds of destruction. The crackle of flames. But Tyr also heard the cries of defiance. Of battle. He reached out to Tilda, trying to stand. Tyr's smile was cracked and missing teeth. Where there was defiance, there was still a chance of victory.

However slim.

"Skuld, Urd, Verdandi," Tyr said. "You are here for my doom. As you were when Garm's jaws found my throat, and my spear pierced the Hel hound's belly. You are witness to my end. Again."

Tilda did not correct the dying god. "I am here."

"There is no one in Hel," Tyr gasped. "No one to rule. No one to give justice to the dead."

"I know."

"Take up the mantle," the god said. "Take it, as I took it from Hel, and be better than us both."

Tilda had wanted to destroy Hel, to unmake her name from existence. She had seen that she would succeed, but not how. She shook her head. She would miss Ted. He certainly made life interesting.

She thought there were no surprises left. She'd planned to do all in her power to get around her bargain with Loki, and get her revenge on Hel, whatever she called herself now, but *this* was better.

"I will do as you ask, Tyr," Tilda said. "Someone must keep Níðhöggur in check."

Upon hearing her words of acceptance, Tyr died. His body went grey, and blew away on the winds, joining the fog. Despite

Tyr's words, there was no physical mantle for Tilda to wear, no cloak that would signify her decision. Nothing but the mist. And Tilda's acceptance was enough for it to find purchase in her, body and soul. That fog called to Tilda's spear, and the concentrated death within. It called to some deeper part of her.

A flicker of the present crossed her mind. Svipul had spared a life, and earned her redemption, if not Tilda's forgiveness. Ted would be happy that life wasn't lost.

Tilda, full with death, stepped back into the fray.

29. Brother

Mike Callan's breath guttered as he died under his brother's gaze. Saving him was damning him. Ted thought of Val and the kids. Didn't they deserve one more day with their dad?

I can't give the family much, but I can give them that.

Ted touched Mike, letting his healing power flow through his brother's body. He could sense the wounds now. Cracked ribs. Broken nose. Internal bleeding. Concussion. Cuts and scrapes. So many tiny hurts Ted couldn't list them all.

The sun tattoo was made to save a life, not be a cure-all, and it worked better on Ted than others. He fixed the worst of his brother's wounds before the golden sun turned black, dormant again. Mike's soft groans turned to a grunt of surprise.

"What are you doing here?"

"Saving your ass. You rolled your truck." Ted shook his head, couldn't help adding: "Still can't drive for shit."

Mike looked at the ruin of his truck. The door lying thirty feet from the car.

"How'd I survive that?"

"You won't if you don't get the fuck out of here."

There was a whistling noise getting louder and closer. Ted pulled Mike out of the way and interposed himself as an LRT car crashed to the street, hurled from somewhere, by something. Shards of glass and pieces of metal bounced off Ted. Ted hoped it had been empty.

Mike gaped. "What the hell?"

Ted ignored the train car, and his brother's question. If there had been anyone inside, there was no hope for them. Ted looked at the black sun on his palm. He didn't think he could summon the strength of need necessary to save a stranger. And given the state of the car, he didn't want to see the remains of those innocent passengers.

"What are you doing here, Mike?"

"I came because of you. You're fucking welcome. Whole city's gone bug-fuck nuts."

Ted shook his head. That was so like Mike. Driving into the apocalypse after Ted had taken pains to get everyone else out.

"Why?"

"How should I know?"

"Why'd you come?" Ted clarified. Then added under his breath, "Ass."

Mike shrugged and then winced. "Mom called in a panic. She saw EPC on the news before the power went out. Thought I could—"

"What? What did you think you could do? You're not a fucking fireman."

"No. I didn't think it through. I was worried my brother was fucking dead." Mike let out a peeved breath before throwing Ted's insult back in his face. "*Ass.*"

"I'm glad you're alive."

"Likewise. Rye and the—?"

Ted crushed his eyes shut and looked away, though the rain and fog would hide any tears. When he spoke, his voice was barely a whisper. "Gone, bro. All gone."

In the illumination from the interior light of Mike's truck, Ted could feel his brother taking in his appearance. And lack of clothing.

"You look different. How'd you pull that off?"

"You wouldn't believe me if I told you."

Mike snorted. "I've seen some pretty crazy shit today."

"Magic."

"*Magic.*" Mike's tone imbued the word with all the derision he usually saved for the Toronto Maple Leafs, or hippies. "Fuck off and pull the other one, why don't you."

How could he see what was happening and not believe? Ted shook his head. Mike had always been able to give Loki a run for her stolen money when it came to pissing Ted off. "If you're gonna waste my time, I've got other places to be."

"Other places, like where?"

Ted pointed towards downtown, and alarms, and the screams of monsters that carried over the storm.

"That is some deep shit."

That it was. Ted didn't have a pithy answer. He just nodded.

"You know when I said you looked different, I didn't mean the tattoos. Or the weight loss." Mike rubbed his own bald head. "Or the hair loss."

Ted ran his hand over his scalp. He hadn't noticed that when his powers had come back, the lightning had burned off his hair and beard. “This is the real me.”

“I can see it. It’s a good look.”

Mike looked into the city. Ted followed his eye, seeing another building crumble next to Surtur. “You’re really a magical monster fighter?”

Ted nodded.

Mike grabbed Ted’s shoulder, and shot him a solemn look. “Fuck ’em up.”

“You’re taking this news awfully well.”

Mike barked a laugh. “Beats the alternative.”

“What alternative?”

“That my brother was a dirtbag, alcoholic fuck-up who bailed on his family.”

“Never.” Ted sighed. “Staying away was the only way I could think of to keep you out of this shitshow.”

“How’d you figure that?”

“Magic, man. It’s like the mafia. Once you’re in, you’re all in. Once you see something, there’s no going back.”

“I’m…. Val and the kids. Mom and Dad.”

Ted nodded sadly. “They’re probably in as deep as we are by now, and if they aren’t, they will be soon enough.”

Mike’s legs went boneless and he dropped to his ass, hiding his face in his hands.

“Goddamn it. I can’t leave them.”

“I’m not asking you to.”

Mike looked up. Tears were streaming down his face. He

rubbed some snot on his forearm. "But if I'm only going to endanger them—"

"World's changing. Too many people are caught in this. I don't think there's any going back for anyone now. Too many people have seen magic. I don't think the monsters will have to hide anymore." Ted looked at the destruction. "Not that they've been doing that great of a job of keeping their secrets."

"You should let the army handle this."

Ted snorted. "What'll they do against a three-hundred-foot-tall walking volcano?"

"Airstrike—"

"Surtur wouldn't notice."

"It has a name?"

"He does," Ted said. "I doubt he'd notice anything short of a nuke, and even if the States loaned us one, that would probably make him more powerful. I've got this."

"You?"

Mike sounded incredulous enough, and Ted couldn't believe he was going to say it, but he pulled out one of Loki's old favourites. "Trust me."

Mike did not look ready to trust Ted on this.

"I'm an army of one."

"This all seems impossible," Mike said, craning his head around to take in the fires, storms, and destruction.

Ted slapped the storm tattoo on his chest as it moved in time with the storm. "Does any of this look like it should be possible?"

Ted couldn't spare any more time for Mike. He had to get his brother home and make him able to keep their family safe.

There was no time to tattoo him the same way he'd done with Robin and Aiko. But there might be something else.

As he listened to the song of the Gjallarhorn, Ted could feel the Honoured Dead, out in Edmonton, out in the fight. He touched the horn tattoo again, and called them to his side as if there had been no distance between them.

"What the hell," Mike said.

Ted knew his brother would recognize the uniforms. At a glance he'd probably be able to guess their regiment and company. He wondered if he'd suss out what else that meant.

"It can't be."

Mike had seen the black-and-white photos around their parents' house as many times as Ted had. He knew his family.

Bits of Niflheim smoke clung to the boots of the Honoured Dead as they broached the hole in the fog that Ted's tattoos created, and approached their descendants. The *einherjar* stopped, brought their heels tight together, and pulled a salute. After a moment Mike returned the gesture. It wasn't quite as crisp as Ted remembered, but his brother had drawn a short straw on a shitty day.

Ted took a Lee-Enfield rifle from his grandfather. The gun turned solid in his hands. Like valkyrie spears, these weapons were the stuff of Niflheim, concentrated death. Ted shuddered. Another rifle formed out of the mist in their grandfather's dead hands.

"I own lots of guns," Mike said as Ted passed him the rifle. "Newer guns. *Bigger* guns."

"Not like this one," Ted said.

He scratched the *Tiwaz* rune on the back of Mike's right hand with his fingernail.

"*Ow!*" Mike yelled as if Ted had ripped a finger off. Ted drew a second rune, *Raidho*, on Mike's head in his brother's blood. It should get his brother home. *Please let it get him home.* "Won't be a shot you take that's not lethal. There's no flesh wounds with this. Straight to the fucking boneyard."

Mike looked at the single clip in the rifle, no doubt he was estimating how many rounds the gun would take. He asked, "Ammo?"

Their grandfather spoke. "The rifle draws on the mists of Niflheim." Ted and Mike both shivered. His voice was made of smashing tombstones and exploding mortar shells. "They are endless. You will never run out of bullets."

Mike hefted the rifle and shot past Ted. A giant tumbled to the street. Ted could always take Mike in the ring, but Mike had always been the better shot. When they had gone hunting with the Sergeant, it was usually Mike who bagged the deer.

"This is what I do, Mikey. This is why I can't be around. Why I don't call. Would you want this—" Ted waved his hand to take in the destruction—"for Cam and Carrie? 'Cause I fucking don't! Give the kids a kiss from Uncle Ted." He took a deep breath. "Because I'm not gonna see them again."

"You're going to break their hearts. They love your dumb ass."

Ted nodded, but making them sad meant they'd still be alive.

"What about Mom and Dad?"

"Tell them .... I don't know. You'll think of something. Just make it good."

"Why me?"

Ted laughed. He couldn't help it. He'd "why me'd" enough since the Nine Worlds had come calling. "Because you've always been full of shit, bro."

Ted stepped into the air and he felt the static charge building. He breathed in deep, waiting for the lightning strike.

"'Bye, bro."

Lightning electrified Ted. He felt it surge through his body, charging the storm-cloud tattoo, filling Mjölnir. He didn't warn his brother he'd be hitching a ride. The lightning forked and hit Mike. Let him ride home on a bolt of lightning. *Try not to shit yourself.*

30. Outlaw

In the hollowed ruins of an Irish pub, Tilda saw her mother. She hadn't seen her among Ted's other allies—as if Vera were trying to hide from her daughter.

"What are you doing here?"

Vera ducked behind a smashed car as a giant stomped by. "Fighting."

The *jötunn* didn't notice Tilda at first. Then its steps slowed, and it turned. A valkyrie spear stabbed up into its groin and it fell screaming.

"You don't have any magic," Tilda said. "You could die here."

Vera shook her head sadly, as if trying to reconcile what her daughter had become, what the world had become, with what their lives had been in Gimli before Urd had started to play her game with the worlds' doom.

"We could all die here."

"*Tiwaz!*" Tilda yelled, and a globe of arrow-shaped runes surrounded her and her mother.

"It's been a year since Urd cost me my powers," Vera said. "I've learned new ones. I'm not helpless."

Tilda watched her mother conjure as she struck out at a distant giant. Crude, compared to what Verdandi had once been capable of, but Verdandi was gone, and only Vera Eilífsdóttir remained.

"Amma?"

"Would be here if I'd let her. Stubborn old ox."

Tilda searched for all the ways death might find her mother today. She denied them all. That much was in her power, now. Unless the entire world burned in Surtur's flames, her mother would live. And, in that worst case, Tilda and Vera would face Surtur in Hel. They would fight until his fires burned Niflheim away as if it were naught but morning mist.

Jenny killed her way through City Place Mall, every level of the shopping centre lousy with giants. Despite the stamina Tyrfing lent her, she was tiring. But she'd fight until the monsters were gone.

Or she was.

"Hello again, Mathilda."

Göndul. Tilda would recognize that voice anywhere.

The other gestured at Tilda's spear. "You have something that belonged to my sister."

The valkyrie's once-milky-dead eyes bubbled and smoked; the reek coming off her was awful. She smiled.

"You want it?" The Norn narrowed her eyes. "Take it."

The wings of her falcon cloak caught the wind, and Tilda shot into the sky, aiming for Göndul. She grabbed her and drove her into the sidewalk. Concrete shattered. Tilda gave her another crack with her fist. She didn't stop there. Göndul was born to battle, but every move she'd made, could make, was as easy to read as the patterns in the runes.

Today would be the last time they met. She could kill the valkyrie. She *should* kill her. Göndul's body smoked, and the concrete rubble surrounding her liquefied.

From behind her, Loki yelled, "Kill her!"

Tilda turned and Göndul hit her, knocking her aside.

"I have other plans for her," Tilda growled, rubbing her jaw. Turning back to the valkyrie, she said, "You'll be sorry Ted showed me the value of mercy."

Flames burned in Göndul's empty eye socket. She spread her arms, taking in the expanse of Surtur's destruction. Her voice sizzled like meat on a griddle. "Did your visions show you this, Norn?"

Tilda smiled. "I've been waiting for you to show yourself. And since I'm blood-bound not to seek revenge upon the trickster or his daughter, I'll take my satisfaction where I can get it."

Göndul attacked her. Tilda didn't move to block. Instead she sidestepped the mere inches necessary for the weapon to miss and stepped into Göndul's reach.

Tilda plucked out Göndul's remaining eye like a grape from a bowl. The valkyrie dropped. She kicked and pawed at the earth, screaming imprecations at the impassive Norn. When Göndul had screamed herself hoarse, Tilda knelt at her side. She jerked Göndul's head up by the hair.

"You doomed Ófriður's child. *My* child. Doomed her to Hel. And all the days until the end of the universe are not enough to punish you. So *this* day will have to suffice."

Tilda tossed the eye backwards and Loki caught it, fumbling, and shuddered.

"The last thing you will ever see is your defeat. There is no one who will take you now. You are *outlaw*. These hands struck out at me and mine." Tilda smashed each with the butt of her spear. "They will never hold sword nor spear again. I have foreseen it. You are no longer a valkyrie, and choose no one's death. Not even your own. Live out what semblance of a life you have, but do it far from my sight."

Tilda drew *Raidho*, the rune of travel, from her pouch of stones, and spoke its name. Its image hovered over Göndul as Tilda sang for a shard of Bifröst.

The Norn's awareness stretched far beyond Alberta. Odin's great, ancient fence around Midgard was gone. Ófriður had finally succeeded. New world was becoming old, was becoming new again. Tilda felt the lightning. There was a storm brewing far away. She touched Göndul and sent her away into it.

Jenny left the ruined mall behind her, dragging Tyrfing. Its blade felt heavy now, for the first time. She clutched at a gash in her side, but couldn't tell where monsters' blood ended and hers began. Her dress was in rags. Her life was in tatters.

A woman walked out of a burning building. It seemed as if her clothes were fire. A crown of fiery symbols orbited her head. A rock monster approached, but she batted it aside as if it were a toy. Her eyes fixed upon Jenny, and she stalked forward like a hunting cat.

Jenny grimaced and raised Tyrfing, ready for the end.

At the entrance to a half-collapsed mall, Tilda found the one they needed to end the fight. To end Surtur.

Jennifer had Tyrfing bared, its steel dripping blood that sizzled like acid against the cracked asphalt of Edmonton's broken streets. Freyja wore a crown of runes, not unlike the one above Tilda's head, but Freyja's were scripted in red flames, rather than the Norn's electric blue.

There was no way Jennifer could win this fight. But Tilda knew the look of a berserk, and Jenny wasn't going to listen to reason—she had murder in her heart. And to her, Freyja, wreathed in flame, was responsible for the deaths of her family. Tilda couldn't disagree. But Freyja, holding a scabbarded blade in one hand and a sword of fire in the other, was fighting against Surtur's forces, not with them.

It would break Ted's heart for Jenny to die in the street. Freyja and Ted needed to be together so their bargain could be completed, and so Ted could take up the Bright Sword against the king of Muspelheim. If Jenny died at Freyja's hands, knowing Ted, he'd let the world burn. That loyalty hurt. It surprised her how much.

She yelled, "Jennifer, stop!

The teacher-turned-warrior appeared not to hear her over the din of battle, even with a rune-driven wind blowing the words to her ears.

"There is a chance that your family still lives," Tilda said. The words were quiet, barely a whisper, but Jenny stopped as if Tilda had slapped her.

"How?" she demanded, gesturing at a burning building with Tyrfing. "How could they have survived this?"

Tilda lowered her eyes. It had been a difficult decision. Once she could never have made such a choice. "It was necessary for Ted to believe them gone. He needed this fight to be personal. He always does. He's many things, but he's not a big-picture guy."

Jenny's hand tightened on the hilt of Tyrfing. "You let it happen. *You let my family die.*"

Tilda worried she'd played her hand too hard. That she'd made an enemy she didn't want.

"I am not heartless, Jennifer. Ted had to *believe* they died. They did not *have* to die. I warded the wedding with runes to protect them from the fire. They will live so long as I live."

Jenny looked up at Surtur. *Good, there was still some reason left in her.*

"You'd best hurry if you want to be with them before the end of all things."

"But the fight."

"Only one sword matters in this battle, and it's not yours."

Jenny looked again at the fire giant, as if weighing duty and love.

"*Raidho*." A rune appeared between them, a rainbow extending away from it.

Jennifer stepped onto the multicoloured bridge and was gone.

"Touching," Freyja said. "But I did not need you to save me from her."

Tilda snorted. "She's more than she appears, and her doom is not yours."

Freyja laughed, as she looked up and rain sizzled against her flaming cloak.

Tilda smiled. "Did you bring it?"

Freyja's eyes narrowed. But she held up the golden scabbard of the Bright Sword. Tilda could feel the doom swirling around that blade, as if all the fates of every life were contained within. True, in a fashion.

"I keep my bargains, Norn."

"Good," Tilda said. "Because letting the world burn would be a poor way to honour your brother's bravery."

Huginn and Muninn landed on Tilda's shoulders.

"**You have found her,**" Huginn said.

Muninn inclined his head toward Freyja. "**Lady Freyja.**"

Freyja returned the nod, slightly.

Tilda asked, "Ted?"

"**Alive. We will lead you to him,**" Huginn said.

"Not necessary," Tilda answered. Her eyes flickered back in her skull and she called for another shard of Bifröst. She grabbed those who would be necessary, and left the fight to win the war.

31. Just the Right Bullets

Surtur's booming laugh rose over the yells and sirens and car alarms.

No peace for the Un-Peace.

"Ted!" Tilda yelled.

He shook his head, looking around for the Norn. There was a rainbow shimmer of light, and Tilda, Loki, and Andvari appeared before of him. And they weren't alone. Freyja was with them. Huginn and Muninn landed on Ted's shoulders.

How's the fight going?

He half-expected the ravens to say, *how do you think?* But instead, he was hit with a rash of images and memories. Ted couldn't believe—didn't want to believe. It was awful. Jenny drenched in blood. Sally. Tyr facing Surtur alone. Svipul. Tilda blinding Göndul. He heard the doom she'd given Göndul, and he shuddered at her voice. It was so fucking cold.

Tilda's eyes were no longer blue. They were as grey as her hair, as grey as the land of the dead. Her eyes were Hel. *God, what had happened to her?*

"Ófriður," Freyja said from behind him.

He whirled around. "You. This is on you."

"Hardly." The goddess said. "I offered you the sword. You were the one who wanted to wait."

"You told Surtur where to find me."

She gestured at the burning downtown. "This was not me."

He looked back at the city. His army might still be fighting, but his friends were already dead, and there was no helping *them*. Anything Ted did without the Bright Sword would only be a delaying tactic.

He dropped his head and fists, defeated. "Okay. Let's do this."

Freyja spun a hut out of the mist and fog of Niflheim that permeated the city. It looked no bigger than a large camping tent. Ted pressed his fingers against it; the fog was solid as stone, and so cold it burned his fingertips.

He hissed and jerked his hand away, sucking at his fingers. "Motherfucker."

"You cannot do this," Andvari said to Freyja. "*Do not do this.*"

She looked at him. "We must. Ófriður wills it."

"The weapon was perfect," Andvari's normally gruff voice sounded more like that of a petulant child.

Loki snorted, as did Tilda. And while Ted couldn't disagree with their response, it *did* sting.

"Your craftsmanship was as impressive as always," Freyja said, "But your weapon was not made to fight *this* war."

Andvari scowled, but nodded.

Freyja gestured for Ted to enter the hut. He did. Andvari followed. The inside was larger than it had appeared, as the Grey Ladies' rune-reading room was back in Gimli. It appeared to be a long, timbered hall, a bench table running its entire length.

Shields hung on the walls at regular intervals. Fires burned in braziers on either side of an ornate wooden chair, carved to resemble two hunting cats.

Ted walked the entire length of the hall, hardly taking notice of his steps.

"We will begin," Freyja said, gesturing with the Bright Sword at the head of her table. "Ófriður, if you please?"

He passed her the *álfur* stiletto.

"It will kill you." Andvari shot a warning look towards Freyja. "You are going to let her kill you."

"Then we all go, her included," Ted said. "And I don't think she wants that."

"I do not." Freyja smiled and turned to Ted. "Have you given thought to what you will trade for the sword? Hammer or Sun?"

Ted clenched his fists. He sighed. "The sun. Take the sun."

"To wield the Bright Sword will burn away Ted Callan forever," Freyja said. "There will be nothing left but Ófriður. It will be as if you died when Surtur rose over the city."

Ted thought of his mom, and dad. Mikey and the kids.

"Better that than my family and friends die for real." He nodded. "Do it."

"Only those of us in this place will remember Ted is Ófriður."

"And I said: *Let's fucking do this.*"

Freyja smiled. "Strip."

"What?"

"This is an ancient thing," she said. "You can't be wearing castoff jeans."

Ted rubbed at his eyes. "Goddammit."

"Ted," Loki said. "It's nothing any of us haven't seen before. And except for Freyja, we've all seen yours in particular."

Muttering as he undresssed, Ted hurled the jeans at Loki to shut her up. And sat on the chair. He shivered when it touched his flesh. It looked warm within Freyja's constructed hall, but she had made everything here out of icy fog, and the chair was so damned cold it felt as if Ted had been tossed into an ice bath.

He thrust out his left arm, palm up. He looked away, not wanting to watch her cut. Andvari bound Ted to the chair with a long thread of Gleipnir, chanting, holding him in place. Ted's heart pounded, and sweat ran from his forehead, chilling as it dripped over his skin. The fear from his first night in Winnipeg was something he'd never forget. He wasn't powerless anymore, he knew that. But it still came roaring back.

Tilda laid her hand on his back, over the tattoo of Yggdrasill. Loki took his right hand. The trickster shaking hands with Mjölnir, Ted smiled. Wherever Thor had ended up after his second death, *that* would drive the prick crazy.

The blade bit into his palm and Ted's smile vanished. Loki's grip seemed to envelop Ted's hand. Ted wanted to grind Mjölnir into a fist against the burning pain of the stiletto sliding under his skin.

His breath hissed past clenched teeth as the goddess carved around the outline of Baldur's sun. He could feel the blade's dragon-blood poison seeping into his body. Ted's stomach roiled, as if he'd chugged a two-six of whiskey. He wanted to puke, but the poison wasn't in his stomach. No amount of retching would make him feel better.

Only the sun.

There would be no healing this time. If things were done right, Freyja would have the sun. Its gift would be hers, and Ted would have to trust her to heal him. If this was a trap, Tilda and Loki would kill the goddess. Small comfort to Ted. He'd be pushing daisies.

Tilda sang in his ear. The sound was comforting. It had been too long since the last time.

There was a new pain. Not the burning of the poisonous dagger, or the sharpness of a blade being drawn against skin. This was more like a scab being picked at. Ted looked. He shouldn't have.

Freyja held one edge of the sun between her fingertips. She tugged the skin away from the meat of Ted's hand. He was sure she was trying to be gentle, but it hurt like a motherfucker. Loki grunted as Ted tried to grind the trickster's hand to powder.

Once Freyja had teased a corner free, she slid the blade under the tattoo, flensing the golden-inked skin away from Ted's body. Blood oozed out of his palm, spilling over the sides of his hand to spatter on the ground.

No matter how much it hurt, he had to remember: *This is why you're here. This is what you asked for. This is what you need.*

She offered him her strength this time without being asked. He couldn't see her. He didn't want to.

Sweat stung his eyes. He clenched them shut.

All other sounds disappeared until his ears were filled with the wet *shuck* of his skin coming free.

"It is done."

Ted opened his eyes. Despite the soothing presence of Tilda's palm on his back, and Loki clenching Mjölnir, when Ted looked at the ruin of his left hand he still felt sick. Freyja poured liquor over the wound and neither Loki and Tilda's combined strength, nor Gleipnir, could keep him seated. He shot to his feet, shredding the tether, blood and whiskey dripping from his hand.

The rapid motion hit him and Ted swooned, falling forward. Someone grasped him around the throat to keep him from face planting. His vision narrowed, and his gorge rose. Ted vomited.

"I thought I made you of sterner stuff," Andvari said.

Between retches, Ted said, "Go fuck yourself."

Gravel dug into his wounded hand. Pain shot up Ted's arm but he didn't care. In that pool of vomit was the remnants of his last supper.

Might be the last thing I ever *eat.*

Food he'd shared with his dead best friend.

Loki knelt next to him. "C'mon, Ted. Nearly there."

His head rolled on his neck as the trickster pulled him back to his seat. Freyja took Ted's palm and pressed it between her breasts. Her skin felt hot. He left a bloody handprint behind.

She shrugged and the flaming cloth that made up her shirt was snuffed with the sound of a furnace pilot light being extinguished.

"You may begin your task," she said to Andvari.

The dwarf pinned the skin of Ted's palm to Freyja's chest. Her lips twitched as each pin pierced her body, but otherwise she gave no sign of discomfort. The needle and thread looked comical in the dwarf's meaty hand, but Ted was too sick to laugh.

Ted's left arm was numb. When the venom reached his heart and lungs, his rapid breaths would stop. His pounding heart would slow. And he'd be gone. Did the poisoned go to Hel? Ted pressed his bloody palm to Mjölnir. If he was going to go out, he wanted to go out swinging.

"Ófriður."

Ted couldn't place where Freyja's voice was coming from. He was jerked up and dragged. Loki steadied him as Tilda placed his raw palm between Freyja's breasts, against his own flayed skin.

Warmth spread from her body to his. Feeling returned to his fingertips. He wanted to flex them. The warmth turned scalding. He tried to tear his hand away from Freyja's body, but she covered his hand with both of hers, and held him.

When the glow faded, Ted felt no more pain. The imprint of his red hand rested between Freyja's breasts, and in that field of blood, Baldur's sun faded from golden to black.

"Too long has the light from Odin's brightest son been imprisoned. He belongs in the world and the world needs him." Freyja looked at Andvari, and her voice dropped to a whisper. "And I will bring his light back into the world."

"You cannot give life back to the dead," Tilda said. She sounded like she dearly wanted to try. Ted understood. He felt the same.

"True," Freyja agreed. "But it is Baldur's doom to be reborn."

New skin covered Ted's left palm, the flesh made whole. It seemed pink and fresh, like that left behind when a scab came off.. Nine months since Andvari and his two dwarves had put

Baldur's sun there, and seeing his palm bare didn't seem real. He'd finally gotten used to what they'd done to his body, and now it was changing. Again.

Freyja drew the broken sword from its scabbard. The steel glowed blue like a bright winter sky. Shining halos spread from the edge of each sharp point, tiny sundogs surrounding the shards of Laevateinn the Bright Sword.

Andvari took the sword from Freyja. He cast a queer look at it. Ted wasn't sure whether the dwarf was impressed with the Bright Sword's crafting, or dismissing it for not being dwarven work.

"We will need something older than this blade to make the image."

Tilda produced a twig of ash wood. The dwarf nodded.

It was a branch from Yggdrasill.

Freyja jerked a banner from her wall, and laid it down on the table in front of Ted. In Andvari's hands the bonds of the steel dissolved and fell to powder on top of the banner. Andvari mixed the powder with blood until it had the consistency of ink.

"Are you ready?" the dwarf asked. He produced a rusted iron bit.

"You put that fucking thing in my mouth again, and you'll be the first one I stab with the Bright Sword."

Andvari smiled. "This will hurt."

"I remember."

Ted sat there, bare-assed, as Freyja began the third, and final, part of the operation, imprinting the power of the Bright Sword into Ted's body with a new tattoo.

The branch of Yggdrasill was a stick the size of a pen. It looked so simple compared to the complexity of the tattoo machine that Ted had used to ink Robin and Aiko. Only a stick with needles bound into a groove with thread.

He braced himself for the first stab. It shouldn't bother him. It shouldn't hurt. He shouldn't feel anything, but they'd need to get around his dragon-scale invulnerability, and so he had suspected it would.

The worst part was the noise. He could *hear* the needles penetrating his skin. Freyja stitched new magic into Ted's left arm, and with every prick of the needle he felt the urge to give Andvari a sock in the jaw. For old times' sake.

Freyja held the instrument as if she were cutting a steak, not drawing; but her work was as beautiful as Andvari's. Funny how far away it felt, the time when Ted would have given anything to be able to look away from what was happening to him. Now, eyes open, he watched a part of his new world unfold before him.

Ted regarded his new tattoo. On the palm of his left hand was the hilt and pommel of a sword, its quillons bending around the meat of his hand to stop short of touching the bell of the Gjallarhorn.

Ted cracked his knuckles. Mjölnir sparked with lightning and the Bright Sword glistened with frost. Outside, thunder crashed.

"Time to tell that fucker I'm coming."

Loki nodded. "You're gonna want your pants."

32. Shake the World

Ted dropped from the sky and crashed down to the street. Fire erupted from within a high-rise, blowing the building apart. He straightened, stood tall, and tried not to grimace at the cracking macaroni sound his knees made. Ted faced Surtur. The giant hadn't seen him yet.

He closed his left hand into a fist, and the Bright Sword appeared there. It felt solid, as if his hand were clutching a leather-wrapped hilt. Its grip was long enough that Ted could hold the weapon in both hands if he chose. Its pale glow bathed him in cool blue light. It was surprisingly easy to wield for a blade as long as Ted was tall.

Ted didn't know anything about swordfighting. Robin had tried to show him a few basic moves, but nothing had stuck. Ted tried to remember the stances and strikes and parries. But then, he wasn't challenging Surtur to a fucking duel.

There was no honour here. It wasn't pistols at dawn. No spilled drink, or slap of glove against cheek. This was life and death. This was dirty, ugly war, and Ted dearly wished it didn't have to be fought. But he finally had an inkling of what his grandfather must have felt after he'd enlisted—when glory and honour turned to rain and mud and blood and death.

The storm on Ted's chest raged more than it ever had. The

thunderheads over Edmonton enveloped the city. Wind and rain buffetted everything, dropping tree limbs on cars, and trees on houses. Mjölnir coaxed lightning across miles of sky to strike any of Surtur's army that Ted could see. So constant were the peals of thunder that Ted could barely make out where one rumble ended and the next began.

Ted gave the sword a spin. It cut through the air with a sharp hum. Snow fell, following the arc of the blade, as if the sky were bleeding cold. He drew in the wind behind him so there was no way that Surtur could miss him.

He shouted, "Hey, fucker. Miss me?"

Wild was the wind that blew his words to the king of Muspelheim. Surtur's laugh stopped mid-lock and the giant turned, slowly, inexorably, towards Ted. Acetylene-blue eyes flared, and went white.

The sky crackled with thunder and in a flash of light Ted was in the sky.

Vapour ghosts surrounded Surtur. Twisted spirits of those the giant had murdered by flame. Those who'd been driven to suicide by his whispers. They enveloped the giant as if he were a planet and they his atmosphere. They'd burned Ted before, scalding him through his dragon-scale tattoos, back when Ted had thought himself invulnerable. They'd given him his first post-gifting taste of real pain. Loki had been able to banish them above Flin Flon. He'd claimed he'd used the last winds of Jötunheim.

Those winds might have been gone. No longer.

Ted spun the sword in a circle above his head and watched

the snow begin to fall. He could feel winter in that blade. As if every flake that had ever fallen was in its metal. The vapour ghosts fled, screeching, from the cold light of the Bright Sword. Their misty forms seeped back into cracks in Surtur's body.

Ted stayed high above the fire giant, jumping from bolt to bolt and cloud to cloud. Ted remembered all too well Surtur's speed. He'd taken his hits, but Ted was still standing, which was more than anyone else who'd fought the giant could say. Gods included.

Surtur seemed to sense when Ted brought the storm to him, so Ted kept the giant distracted by hurling lightning at him. He aimed for the eyes, not that it seemed to do anything. Ted wasn't certain Surtur even used them to see. But it kept the giant's attention on him—and not on stomping his friends into paste.

Ted felt the growing power of the storm tattoo on his chest. The sensation of each lighting strike, replicated by a tiny static shock against his body, Ted had a rough map of where the next one was going to strike. Surtur was one of the tallest things in Edmonton right now. An easy target.

There was no time to think. Another bolt was coming. Ted held up Mjölnir and jumped several blocks, landing in the centre of the blast. For a moment, the ozone stink of the lightning strike masked the smell of the various fires all over the city, and the sulphurous reek of Surtur himself.

Feet thundered behind Ted. He spun and saw one of Surtur's giants. Ted pointed a finger at it and let Mjölnir bring the pain. Lightning split the giant's rocky hide and Ted leapt up to finish the job by extinguishing the giant's heart.

A lance of flame formed in Surtur's hand, the tail end of the fiery weapon seeming to stretch out past the fires in Fort Saskatchewan, as if the fire ran the length of the horizon, as if it originated in Muspelheim and would terminate in the giant's target.

Surtur's fiery spear exploded against Ted's chest, enveloping him in flames. He clamped his jaw shut, worried the fire would sear his lungs and blacken his tongue, dragon scales or no.

Tilda spoke for him. "*Kenaz!*"

Tilda's cloak unfurled, the blue-black falcon feathers holding her aloft, her valkyrie spear aimed at Surtur. Ted didn't think it would do anything to Surtur. Hel had said it was the Bright Sword that was Surtur's death. He needed to figure out *how*.

And fucking soon.

He needed rain now more than lightning, and squeezed the clouds until huge fat drops fell. Ted was already soaked to the skin. He didn't care. Surtur was forming another fiery spear. Ted stepped in front of Tilda. She was tough, but she wasn't fireproof.

"I don't need you to rescue me, Callan."

"I might need you to save me," he shot back.

She snorted, but Ted wasn't sure whether he saw the ghost of smile on her face.

"We need to do something."

"Figure out how to use the Bright Sword to kill him yet?"

"I'm working on it."

Ted hurled lighting at the fire spear. It disappeared in a gout of steam and shards of rock as Surtur's hand exploded. Lava flowed from Surtur's stump; Ted had only delayed the inevitable. Surtur was forming a new hand.

"I can do this all night," Ted yelled at the giant, sending another bolt to strike him. He didn't know whether Surtur could hear him. Didn't matter.

"It's his tie to Muspelheim," Tilda said. "The fires there are endless. Surtur's bound to his world. You're trying to fight an entire world."

When she put it that way, Ted was surprised he hadn't popped a hernia when he'd tried to budge him.

Ted knew he was outmatched. How can you fight an entire world? But Ted had made his own little world in Winnipeg, and he could feel the power he'd left in the ground there, when he'd sunk a fence of his own around the city to keep monsters out. That power was there, waiting. Drawing on the energy he'd sunk into that barrier would weaken it, but strengthen him. He wondered if that's what happened with Odin and the original fence around Midgard. Ted didn't want to leave Winnipeg vulnerable—he'd already pulled all of his allies out of Manitoba to fight *this* fight.

But if Surtur wins, we all lose.

Maybe he could cut off Surtur's connection to Muspelheim. That had been enough to drive him away from Flin Flon. It wouldn't kill Surtur. But it was something. Every second of life they bought was time they had to finish him for good. And Ted would take every second he could get.

Ted felt for his protective fence. This fight was bigger than any one city. Storms gathered, covering the prairies. The runes on his back called out to the runes of protection on the posts of the fence he'd built around Winnipeg. A storm brewed there as well.

It was all-or-nothing time.

He hoped Winnipeg could survive without him. And if trouble came, he'd make it up to them if the world didn't end.

The storm cloud on Ted's chest flowed. It enveloped his entire body. Ted yelled out the name of the *Kenaz* rune, and felt the fires that had burned in Surtur's name. Felt the primal fire that was the giant's bread and butter. Ted wasn't Odin, but he had a fence of his own, and it was time to swing the door shut. Ted had nine times nine ash-wood piles that he had enchanted with runes of protection. He shoved their power into the earth surrounding Edmonton. It was a stretch. Ted wasn't dealing with physical objects and he hadn't walked the road around Edmonton to place them. The power was his. The protection was his.

Surtur roared. It worked. Ted had cut him off from the endless flames of Muspelheim. He felt the giant stretch, trying to tear the barrier.Ted worried it would rip like paper in Surtur's hands.

Hold together. Please.

Surtur threw his will at Ted. It was like staring down a hurricane. But Ted had to hold. His barrier was straining under the onslaught as it was. If Surtur found any weakness, if one link of the nine times nine burned away, they'd be right back where they'd started.

Proper fucked.

"You did it."

Ted had to blink to recognize the speaker.

Tilda. How long since he'd heard pride in that voice at something he'd done?

Surtur's army screamed. Their voices eclipsed the roars of their master. Whereas Surtur cried in rage, his minions wailed in pain. In fear. Vapour ghosts evaporated. Giants dropped to the ground—crawling, moaning, towards the nearest flame. It was as if they were dying. Freezing. As if Surtur were pulling their heat and essence from them.

The king of Muspelheim threw himself at Ted's ad hoc wall. Ted grunted. That time Surtur had hit harder. He was stealing power back from his followers. And what would it matter if he used them up to nothing? They were as nothing to him, distractions. Their fire would fuel him enough to burst Ted's defence, and then Surtur would have all the access he needed to Muspelheim to make new followers.

As if he'd fucking need them at that point.

Ted took to the lightning and leapt for the giant. He slashed at Surtur with the Bright Sword, hoping to end the fight quickly while Surtur was distracted.

The sword rang off Surtur's rocky hide. He thrust instead. The blade of light bent. Ted feared it would shatter. He didn't know what would happen then. Would he have to wait a day before he could call the sword back to his hand? *Could* he call the sword back to his hand?

The Sergeant would have given him shit for taking an untested weapon into combat. Surtur swatted at Ted, but he kicked off the giant's body, catching a lightning bolt to land again on the other shoulder. He'd been here before. Ted's hammer hand had cracked Surtur's rocky body and lava flowed from the wound. It hadn't seemed like much at the time.

But that wound still wept molten rock. It was open.

Vulnerable.

Ted plunged the Bright Sword into it and Surtur howled.

Ted smiled grimly. *Pain, fucker. Let's see how you like it.*

Lightning danced all over the giant's body, and Ted followed. There's a bullshit folk wisdom that lightning never strikes in the same place twice, but Mjölnir remembered every bolt it had laid on Surtur. Muninn remembered. The raven and the hammer pulled Ted from wound to wound.

He stabbed Surtur in each of them. Shoved the Bright Sword as deep as he could, deeper, until his own arm was in up to the fucking shoulder. He didn't know if he was hitting anything vital. He didn't know if there was anything vital to hit.

Everywhere the blade pierced, the cold of Jötunheim took root. Rock solidified, and the giant's movement became less and less fluid. Ted lashed out with a punch that shattered Surtur's rocky exterior, spilling more lava. Punching alone wouldn't do much to his foe, but Ted was running out of spots to stab. Surtur lashed out to grab him, but Ted was already gone, jumping between the purple bolts of volcanic lightning shooting up from Surtur's body. Each time Ted landed on the giant's rocky hide, he pounded Surtur for all he was worth and then disappeared in another flash of light. He'd return to those spots with the Bright Sword soon enough. Surtur was fast for a three-hundred-foot-tall walking volcano, but he'd already lost a step.

It felt good watching the giant flail at him as if he were a mosquito.

Ted unleashed a fresh flurry of thusts. Cracks formed in the great giant's stony skin, and widened as lava oozed. Surtur's obsidian flesh crumbled at the edges of the wounds and fell away from his body. All the while, it seemed as if the giant's body was swelling.

Surtur gave up swiping at Ted. Instead, the giant rubbed up against a building.

"Fuck!" Ted yelped as he caught the next lightning bolt out of there. The *jötnar* and *dvergar* below weren't so lucky. Dwarves could sing to stone, but Ted doubted that would stop the falling tons of bricks from killing them.

The report of the *einherjar's* rifles echoed over the battle and the fires. The only thing that swallowed their sounds was Surtur's howls.

He hoped Mikey didn't need those guns to keep their family safe. Ted had once thought there was no distance on Earth that would prevent him from hearing those spectral Lee-Enfields. Now he wished he had them at his back. But more important than covering his own ass was making sure his mom and dad got to watch their grandchildren grow up.

Ted sank the Bright Sword into one of Surtur's eyes, extinguishing its light. Forever, he hoped. He stared into the roiling maw of the giant as he screamed. Pain shuddered through Surtur's body, rock sliding over rock like tectonic plates.

The giant was going to burst. If Surtur let all of the energy of Muspelheim loose in Edmonton, Ted didn't think being across the river would protect the people there. If they'd had a lick of sense, they would've run for the hills as soon as their feet touched down in Old Strathcona. But Edmontonians were stubborn.

"*Kenaz!*" Ted yelled, trying to bottle the giant's flame. "It has to work."

Ted reached out his hand and called Tilda's name. He wasn't sure if she would take his hand. Wasn't sure if she could do this alone. Her powers had grown in their time apart. Ted hadn't been idle, either.

Her fingers closed over his. Thousands of tiny needles jabbed up and down his spine as she drew on the rune magic that the dwarves had imprinted into his flesh. The intimacy of their *seiður* bond hit him full-force.

Tilda called to Bifröst and opened a path to Surtsey. Ted felt for the cage that he'd had built for Surtur. They'd never get the giant on that bridge to send him away. Ted hadn't been able to budge the giant with his lightning, and Ted doubted even their combined strength could do it.

Together they'd beaten back Níðhöggur, but that was then. Their magical connection had been strained but not shattered. And now, the bond they'd forged to one another felt thinner than hope. But there was more to them than sex. They were family now. *Family*. Ted felt another hand clasp his. Loki's.

Their combined will forced the giant back a step. A step was enough. First the flames that made up the giant's hair and beard were pulled away by Bifröst. His remaining blue eye dimmed.

Surtur's flames broke free form his body. Great jets of fire shot out from every wound Ted had given the giant with hammer fist and sword hand. Surtur's rocky exterior crumbled.

"Too much!" Tilda yelled. "The weight of his power, Bifröst can't hold it. *I* can't hold it together."

"You've got to!" Ted cried.

The bridge was disappearing behind Surtur. Tilda clutched her bag of rune stones and the symbols she'd invoked floated above her head like a halo. "Too much!"

The rainbow shattered.

The world lurched.

Ted felt crushed by the effort, but he stood in the air on the shard of a rainbow. The city below looked at peace, and blessedly normal, except for the rising trails of smoke and the distant wails of sirens. The sounds and sights of Edmonton grew fainter. Shards of the Bifröst bridge, separated into its component colours, fell, glowing, and whipped wildly across the sky.

Still, they fought to hold him. Still, Muspelheim burned its way out of Surtur.

The sky flashed. Ted saw Flin Flon. Minneapolis. St. John's. Reykjavík. Dublin. Cities he couldn't recognize. Cities he'd never set foot in. Muninn had their names, but the ravens' answers were lost in the howl of Surtur's defiance and roaring fire.

Ted burned. He screamed. He shouldn't be able to burn. Dragon-scales couldn't burn. If he was burning, what was happening to Loki and Tilda? The fire filled him, pressing against the inside of his invulnerable hide. His body couldn't contain all that power. But if it didn't, what was left of Surtur would get

Ted to do the giant's destructive job for him. He would die, and when he did, the fires would still consume everything.

Surtur was the end of all things. That was *his* doom. There was no reasoning or arguing with him. Words wouldn't sway a tornado, or an earthquake. No kenning could banish such a force.

Ted funnelled Surtur's destruction to Surtsey. He could feel the island growing with new eruptions. It was a temporary solution. Surtur's power was infinite, and Ted was already tiring.

A quiver ran through the earth. Somehow, he knew dormant volcanoes began to erupt everywhere. Ted had stabbed Surtur with the Bright Sword, but the fires of Muspelheim were the giant's blood. The world would burn.

Fire, unlike Surtur, was neither good nor bad. It was a tool. Fire could destroy as easily as create. Stopping Surtur wouldn't stop the destruction. But a new age of heroes—and damn the dwarves for having the idea to begin with—might.

Muspelheim's fires would not be contained much longer. Surtur was going to pop his fucking top. Nothing could stop that now. But where that energy went—that was something Ted could alter. His cage on Surtsey was imperfect. There was too much energy, and with Ted's luck he'd end up turning the entire island into a brand new Surtur. He wouldn't make the giant somebody else's problem.

Ted's cage wasn't meant to house the giant himself, but that power. Between his dwarven gifts and the friendship of a Norn and a trickster, Ted had power at his disposal. But he couldn't be everywhere. *Superman* couldn't be everywhere. He had already had to choose who to save, and where to go. Choices that had cost him, and his friends, dearly. Shit would fall through the cracks. *People* would fall through the cracks. They'd be hurt. Killed.

The world that was coming didn't need one saviour, it needed more good people trying to make a difference. Enough people had seen magic now. And there was no missing this fight. There was no going back. Maybe those good people would take the chance to join the battle.

Odin had made the world from Ymir's bones and blood. Ted would make his new world from Surtur's flame.

Help me! Ted called out to the ravens.

How? they asked.

For most of the previous year the ravens had been snooping all over the place for Ted. Finding news, finding fights, and bringing them back to Ted. They must have touched or sifted through thousands of minds in that time, as they watched, and listened.

Every soul you've met that could be a hero, that wanted to help, but lacked the power...

Yes?

Find them again. Now. All of them.

Without Odin's fence, monsters would be coming out of their caves like crazy. Let Surtur be *their* extinction, assuming Ted didn't erase all humanity before they had the capacity to dream up new gods.

He pushed Yggdrasill until its runic leaves burnt away. Inky, stinking smoke plumed from his back. As each rune burned off

Ted's world tree tattoo, he felt them seared onto strangers out there in the world. There were hundreds, maybe a thousand. Would it be enough to hold the monsters at bay?

Yggdrasill's trunk and branches, once formed of tightly-packed runes, were now a solid black smudge across Ted's back. The leafy runes across his shoulder blades were gone entirely—except for one. One leaf remained, bearing *Naudhiz*, the need rune, Tilda's rune.

Ted tried to scream. To yell in defiance of the loss, but no sound came out. Distantly he could hear an echoing cry, as if far away. He recognized it as his own voice. There was no Loki. Tilda was gone. His allies in Edmonton were barely a memory.

They'd have to fend for themselves. Hard choices. They had the means. He'd given them that much. Christ, he hoped he had.

Ted drifted in blackness, disturbed only by the light of distant, uncaring stars. He remembered his dream of being an astronaut. As foolish and unattainable as his dream of being a pro football player. A life that mattered, that was all he'd asked for. He had it, for as long as he could keep breathing.

He could walk on the moon.

He could walk *to* the moon if he brought enough food. And if he could only hold his breath long enough to get there. Trying to calculate how long it would take was a fleeting distraction until the numbers flew away from him with everything else. He didn't know where home was. Couldn't feel the Earth. Couldn't sense Surtur's fires.

This had to be enough.

Ted let go, tried to turn back. He saw a pale blue dot, but it was so far away. He didn't know if it was even Earth. There were Nine Worlds. Nine. The world tree tattooed on his back itched and burned. It had to be one of his worlds. A world away, a lifetime away, Tilda and Loki called his name.

It had been fun.

Superpowers. Kicking ass.

It wasn't fun anymore.

It was a job. A calling. Things had changed. Magic came with a price and Ted had to keep paying. The world had to keep paying. It wasn't only Odin's fence that had shattered, but all barriers. Monsters of all stripes burst back into the world.

He let go, and tumbled towards familiar voices, falling like Icarus.

The last thing he heard before everything went black was Huginn's voice.

"You're mixing up your mythologies again."

Tilda was gone.

Loki was gone.

Surtur was gone.

With the last of the giant's fires extinguished, Huginn and Muninn burned away too. A hollow ringing resonated in Ted's ears, an echo of their final pained cry, and then silence. He'd wished for them to be quiet so many times. But not like this.

Not like this.

Surtur's fires burned through the gulf between where they were and where they'd go. Ginnungagap called. Niflheim called.

Nothingness.

Death.

Fire.

Cold.

Creation.

Ted could barely feel his connection to Tilda. To his home. He could barely hear Loki's voice.

In a blur of light, Ted fell.

33. The End of the Rainbow

When Ted opened his eyes, he was on the grounds of the Leg in Edmonton, which, thankfully, was still standing. Destroying one seat of government was enough for anyone. It was pouring rain, but the sky was afire with shades of pink, purple, and red; a small window of sunlight helping far northern fires put brush to canvas. A bright pink rainbow in a purple sky.

Andvari stood, bloody, among the bodies of fallen dwarves and broken rock trolls. He had a faraway look on his face.

"We did it," he whispered, and the wind carried his words to Ted's ears. "The old days are new again."

Where Surtur's body had fallen, sprawled across downtown, there was only a layer of thick, black ash. No bent steel. No broken concrete. No burning cars. No signs of the destruction at all. Only an absence of what had been.

Ted's bare feet rested atop the ash. He took a step and thought he felt it shift between his toes. But when he looked back, his movement had left no trace. He stooped to pick up a handful of dust and let it trickle through his fingers. The wind caught it and it blew away. Where Ted had dipped his hand, the divot had been blown smooth, featureless.

"What do you make of that?" Ted asked.

He'd been addressing the ravens, but a tinnitus ring in the hollow where Huginn and Muninn had roosted was Ted's only answer. He felt their absence like a kick in the gut. They'd always had an answer for him before. Even when he hadn't asked for it. *Especially* when he hadn't asked for it.

Now that Huginn and Muninn were gone, and not coming back, Ted found himself strangely lonely. When the ravens had been silent, which wasn't fucking often, there'd been the flutter of wings, a tickling sensation, as if they'd shifted their talons on a branch. That was gone, along with their voices.

Ted never thought he'd miss them.

They'd been his companions on this road as long as Tilda, as long as Loki. Now, they'd left him alone.

Ted waved at Aiko. She answered the gesture in a perfunctory manner, as if he were a stranger who'd thought he'd recognized her, and it was too late to take back the gesture. She turned her back and hugged Robin. She didn't know him anymore. To her, Ted was dead. He'd forgotten. He dropped his head.

Jenny. God, they'd gotten so close. She wouldn't know him now, either. He could find her, talk to her. Try to explain what had happened. But that wouldn't be fair. He had a lifetime of shared experiences, she would have memories—pain—that he'd be exploiting. Maybe someday, their fate would change. But Ted couldn't be the one to do it.

Still, he couldn't help wondering, would they have found more than a night's happiness? There wouldn't be much of that in her life for a long time now. Her family was dead. Ted wasn't enough to fill that hole. He couldn't be. Had Surtur not arrived, had Ted not made the choice he'd made, would he and Jenny be embracing each other in joy and grief? He wanted to think so. He wanted to follow her. To find a way for her to know him again, but he was a stranger now, and no stranger could help her.

Ted walked until he found Loki. The trickster was kneeling at the side of her monstrous, dead son, Jormungandur, whispering into her palm, as if saying a prayer. Loki leaned forward and dipped her hands into the water of the North Saskatchewan River.

Tilda's hand on Ted's shoulder stopped him from heading over. "You did it."

"My friends," Ted said. "It's like they're on a different fucking planet than me now."

"They are."

"I want to be in their lives. I want them in mine."

"I want that for you too, Ted," Tilda said. "I wanted it for myself too. Once. But I don't see it in the stones. For either of us."

Ted nodded. "I know. They're better off without me."

"Never. But this turn of fate will add to *your* safety as well. They can't be held against you."

When Ted didn't answer, Tilda continued. "Someone would have found them. You have a talent for making big enemies. The Nine came for Jennifer, and for her family, to draw you out. If needed, they'd go for your brother. Your mother. Your father."

It still didn't feel like a fair trade, but Ted was glad Tilda believed his family would be safe. All that had happened to him was worth it, if only for that. Another reminder of Ted's grandpa. He looked down at the Gjallarhorn. At least he hadn't lost *him* too.

"Lonely is the head with the crown."

"You can still have friends. You *have* friends. Friends who can protect themselves. And by extension, protect you."

"Is that what we are? Friends?"

There was a flash of her old blue wolf's eyes. "Always."

Ted put his arm around Tilda. "Where do we go from here?"

She slipped out from under him, gently, but it was still a rebuke. A reminder that they were siblings now. Ted tried not to think of that. "We don't. I'm going to find my own saga. My own way. There will be a lot of people who could benefit from a Norn's wisdom."

"And I wouldn't?" Ted rubbed at his temples. At the absence where Huginn and Muninn had once roosted. "Lord knows I could use some right now."

She smiled at that. "You've already chosen your advisor."

Ted followed her eyes towards Loki, walking back from the river valley.

Tilda kissed his cheek. "That's good luck, not goodbye, you dope. Call me if someone needs their ass kicked. I'll be there."

"Where are you going to go?"

She held up her spear. "Tyr is gone. Hel has no ruler. Someone has to keep Níðhöggur in check."

"You're going to Hel?" That didn't seem a good thing.

She nodded. "I suppose I'll have to find a new name for the place. Nornheim perhaps."

"Call it Tilda. Hel got a lot of fucking mileage out of her name."

Tilda laughed. "No."

"What'll you do down there?"

"I won't be spinning fates. I will find those deserving of an end, and I will end them. Then I will see to it that they do not leave my realm."

"What if you and I disagree on those someones?"

Tilda stamped the butt of her valkyrie spear on the street. "You'd better hope that doesn't happen."

Hel. Whatever its name, it was home to the sick, the cowards, the suicides, those who died in bed. It didn't seem like the place for Tilda.

She must have read his expression. "I'm not dead, and I have no intention of killing myself, Ted," she said. "But someone needs to do this. The dead need someone. Someone better than Hel."

The dead. That was her reason. Her decision made sense now. There was one dead person in particular Tilda had in mind.

"Erin?"

"She needs her mother."

Ted shook his head. "She's gone, Til."

"Not to me." She held out her hand. "You could join me."

Ted hesitated. He was a fighter. He couldn't just … die.

"Can I visit?"

Her eyes glittered. "You'd damned well better. After all, you know the way."

"North and down," Ted said. He'd never forget. "If you rule in Hel, why can't you…?"

Tilda shook her head. "The rules are set. Only if everyone in the Nine Worlds weeps can I release my children from Hel."

Ted clenched his fist and showed off Mjölnir. "Oh, they'll fucking weep."

She smiled and kissed him on the cheek, fondly, but not passionately. "You mean it."

"Fights find me anyway. They may as well do us some good."

Tilda nodded. "They do, indeed. You won't command the same powers you once had. You still have one need-rune on your back, it may allow you to reach such heights, but if you do, it would kill you."

Ted waved as she summoned a rainbow and was gone. It was goodbye. He would visit her, but he knew it wouldn't be soon, or often. There was too much between them.

With Tilda gone, and his friends newly estranged, Ted was left alone with the destruction he and Surtur had caused. He was glad to be alive. Glad that those closest to him had made it through. *Except they hadn't.* He couldn't believe he was going to miss having Huginn and Muninn correct him.

What his short "visit" had done to Edmonton, that much guilt could drive a guy to the grave.

"It's not your fault, Ted," Loki said.

Ted turned, and saw the trickster was right behind him. She'd changed her form again. Red head, late thirties. Great shape. They could be brother and sister. Ted shook his head. He guessed they were. Now.

"How do you figure this isn't my fault?"

"You were made for this," Loki repurposed Andvari's words. "To bring chaos, not hold it back."

"Great. I get to keep fucking people over."

"You are the Un-Peace, Ted. That hasn't changed. Magic may be out of the closet, but you'll still disrupt the lives of anyone close to you."

"So I need to be alone."

"No. Be with someone who not only tolerates chaos, but embraces it."

"You?"

"Don't you friendzone me here, Ted."

"We're family now, Loki." Ted clasped the trickster's hand. The scarred cuts on their palms brushing as they shook. "That would be weird."

"I'm good with weird."

"I know you are," Ted said. "So. What now?"

Loki pulled out the bourbon she'd left in Ted's safe. "Now, we get drunk."

Where does somebody go after they've saved the world? Ted didn't know what he would ever face that could compare with defeating Surtur, but today's challenge seemed a good bet.

"It's a weird damned thing, being at your own funeral," Ted said.

Loki asked, "You okay?"

Ted shrugged. "Wouldn't change things if I wasn't."

Everyone thought Ted was dead after the explosion at EPC. There were no remains, but the fire burned so hot, and there was so much destruction, that there were any number of missing who would never be found. Thankfully, most of Jenny's family, including Rye and their mom and dad, weren't among them.

There had been a mass memorial for those lost in Surtur's attack. Ted was sure his family would have a private service as well. He didn't want to be at that one. He didn't want to see his mom cry, or the Sergeant either. After all he'd put them through, he hoped they still had some tears for him.

It was easier to be lost in the crowd. Awash in the grief of thousands of strangers.

"Seen enough?" Loki asked.

Ted nodded.

He turned around and walked right into his mother. Her eyes were red, rimmed with tears. She and the Sergeant seemed to be leaning on each other to stay upright. There was no recognition on her face. Ted hadn't believed no one would remember his life before Ófriður, or they'd forget Ófriður was once a man named Ted Callan. Hubris. Arrogance. He'd known what the deal was, and still believed he'd be special, and exempt to the cost to be paid.

Ted lost it. Waterworks. Wailing. The whole enchilada. His mother hugged him, a stranger, as if he were her own, as if they shared the same loss. It was enough.

Ted mumbled, "I'm sorry."

He shook the Sergeant's hand, and Mike's as well.

He had to count himself lucky. His family lived. Lots of people hadn't been so blessed. He took one last look over his shoulder at his niece, Carrie, who understood he wouldn't be coming back this time, and his nephew, Cam, who didn't.

And he moved on.

Epilogue
The Red Headed Stranger

It had taken every trick in Loki's book to cheer Ted up over the last year. Every trick, that is, except for the *really* fun ones. Loki shrugged. Disappointing, but he'd made a promise, after all. And it *was* bad form to try to seduce your own blood.

Ted Callan was dead. Gone. Replaced by a myth. The nameless red-headed stranger with more tattoos than clothes. A man who punched out giants. Banished monsters. Fought for the little guy. Edmonton and Winnipeg both claimed him as their own, but it wasn't long before he'd been seen everywhere.

They'd finally made their way back to Winnipeg, hot on the tail of a young get of Fenrir some damned fool was hunting as a werewolf, and Loki insisted they grab a drink in the same spot in Osborne Village where things had really gotten rolling, back when Ted didn't know the Nine Worlds from a hole in the ground. A band called No NDN Princess was playing, which had made Ted inordinately happy. Loki didn't care for punk. Not that what the deejay kept playing was to his liking, either. Ted didn't seem to mind it—he had a penchant for old sad bastard music—but other than his taste in friends, the man wouldn't know a good thing if it was giving him a handjob.

Ted's eyes shifted from his drink to the crowd, as if he were looking for *dvergar*. Maybe he worried they were after him to take his powers back the same way they'd cancelled that no-limit Svarta Mining gold card—now that they'd gotten what they wanted.

If he only knew.

The *dvergar* were looking for them.

Well, for me, at least.

"This place is still a shithole," Ted said, after taking a sip of his bourbon. "But at least they've got a new bartender."

Loki smiled and stroked his long, red goatee. "We fit right in."

With a wave, he beckoned the waitress over. He recognized her from the night he'd introduced himself to Ted. She didn't recognize Loki—understandable, given that he was wearing a different shape. She didn't remember Ted either, which was probably a good thing, given the first impressions the guy tended to make.

Ted had seemed hurt at that. He should know better by now—no one remembered Ted Callan anymore, other than as someone whose life had ended too soon. Ted had learned to pull Loki's disguise over him like a shroud or a coat. When he didn't want to be bothered. But trouble still found Ófriður, and it always would. Besides, as much as Ted bitched, Loki knew he enjoyed a good scrap.

Not as much as he should. But at least he was less of a dick than Thor had been.

Most days.

"Still not sure we did a damned lick of good," Ted said, downing his drink and signalling Sindy the waitress for another.

"Of course we did. Sure, now there are more angel sightings, more Virgin Mary sightings and all kinds of giants and dragons have woken up, but so have heroes. And that's on you, too. Every life one of those new heroes saves, you had a part in that."

"Doesn't feel like enough."

"If you're going to take responsibility for everything bad in the world, I'm going to force-feed you a share of the credit." Loki regarded his fingernails, humming softly. "Whatever I don't feel like claiming for my role in things."

Ted shook his head, but he smiled.

"So … angels?" Ted asked. "Think those sightings are real?"

"*I've* never seen one." Loki said.

"Figures," Ted said. "And it's been a hell of a long time since *I've* seen a virgin."

Loki swatted his shoulder. "Behave."

"You're one to talk," Ted said, as Sindy returned to their table with a fresh whiskey. Ted nodded at Loki, who reluctantly peeled off a bill to cover the drink. "I guess we did do some good after all."

"Are you kidding?" Loki said. "I haven't seen something this fucked since I conceived Sleipnir. But I'll help you fix it."

Ted snorted a laugh. "A classic case of the cure being worse than the disease."

Loki looked across the bar. There was a woman drinking with a large group of people. They were friends, she was the acquaintance, and she looked like she'd rather be drinking alone. He didn't know her name, but she had *some* connection to the Nine Worlds.

Ted asked, "What do you think you're doing?"

"I have no idea what you mean," Loki said.

Ted snorted. "Bullshit. You had that same fucking grin on your face the last time we were both in here."

"Guilty," Loki said, as he put on a sprig of mistletoe and ambled over.

"Leave her alone," Ted called after him.

Loki turned and shot Ted his best shit-eating grin. "She'll talk to me."

She did not want to talk. Ted's laugh brayed across the bar when she slapped Loki. He slunk back to their table, fiddling with his boutonniere.

"Well, that could've gone better."

"You got off light," Ted said. "I would've punched you."

Loki's grin returned in a flash. "Except you didn't, when you were in her place."

"It looks like somebody else wants to," Ted said, nodding towards a table closer to the bar. The bearded guy there was giving them the dirtiest of looks. It was as if Loki had slept with the man's wife. *Not wholly out of the realm of possibility.*

The man chugged his pint of beer and slammed the glass down on the table. Loki sighed. He'd taken Ted's stare for a challenge. Loki knew where this was headed. He pursed his lips. Ted *did* need to blow off some steam. And since the big bastard was heading their way, he was going to get his chance.

"I've heard about you," the bearded man said to Ted.

He was big, bigger than Ted, and had the look of someone who spent too much time at the gym and too much money on hair oil. His long black curly locks were as thick as the hair bursting out of the top of his shirt.

Ted didn't look up from his bourbon, but he did answer the guy. "That's funny, nobody else has."

Loki smiled. *Oh, this should be good. Just the thing to take Ted out of his funk. Maybe a change in music though.*

The song playing, some rubbish about not being the end, abruptly changed to Willie Nelson's "The Red Headed Stranger." Ted smiled, and chuckled.

"You laughing at me?"

"Should I be?"

"Let's see how funny it is when my club smashes that fancy hammer of yours."

Ted raised an eyebrow at Loki. Loki shrugged, perturbed that Ted *still* looked to blame him for the slightest inconvenience.

"Looks like you *have* heard about me."

"C'mon, viking. Let's go. Word has it you know how to throw down."

"I'm German-Irish, for the record," Ted said blandly.

The Greek was working on Ted's last fucking nerve. Loki knew this, because Ted usually reserved that twitching-eyed irritation for Loki. Ted was doing his best to ignore the challenger and pay attention to his drink, which only made the Greek more insistent.

He clamped a sausage-fingered hand over Ted's shoulder. "Outside. *Now*."

Ted sighed. "Tell you what: let me finish my drink, take a piss and I'll then meet you outside."

"NOW!"

"Have it your way." Ted heaved himself to his feet, drained his drink, and asked Loki, "You wanna watch this?"

Loki waved Ted off. "You kids have fun."

Neither Ted nor the Greek wanted to be the first out the door, each probably suspecting a sucker punch. They walked side by side, shouldering their way through the crowd. Loki signalled Sindy for another round. Ted might be gone for a while, considering his challenger was hairy as a lion—maybe he had some invulnerability of his own.

Loki sensed the man the moment he walked through the door, and the fawning reverence the wait staff showed him told Loki he hadn't changed much since the last time they'd crossed words—and spears.

"I see you, Loki," said a tall, lean Aboriginal man said as he sat in Ted's chair.

The man's hair was a mix of black and grey under a Peterbilt baseball cap, and he was dressed like he belonged on the *Western Hour.* He had one dead, milky eye, the other, a pale blue, bored into Loki.

"You see well for a man with only one eye, Blood-Brother. Especially for a one-eyed dead man."

The man's answer was surprisingly light of tone. "Death is a condition we've both shared, old friend."

Loki pushed his seat back from the table, taking a sip of his beer to hide putting his hand on the *álfur* dagger. "We're friends now?"

"We were when we made our wager."

Loki shot a withering glare across the table. "Drop the act. If Raven had come to collect, I'd be dead again."

The man's form shifted, the black and grey hair grew long, past his shoulder and fell over his face, hiding the eye that Loki knew to be missing. A longer beard hid most of the rest of the man's countenance. He straightened his trucker's cap and when he took his hand away, it was a familiar, incredibly abused, wide-brimmed black hat. His flashy clothes became more subdued blues and greys.

Loki asked, "Why are you here, Odin?"

"I want to talk to you," the man said. "Are you going to offer me a drink? For old times' sake?"

"I'm surprised you didn't come to collect your own debt."

Odin smiled. "Should I?"

Loki didn't answer; instead, he looked toward the exit.

"I was wondering when you'd show up," Loki said.

"Was there ever any doubt I'd find you, even if I had to die to do it?"

"You *are* the living embodiment of the bad penny." Loki

asked a question of his own, nodding his head towards the exit. "The Olympian, your doing?"

Odin stroked his beard and shrugged. "Fool. Thinks anyone with a white beard and a bit of flash is his dad. Sky-Father, All-Father, same thing to him."

Loki hid his smile in a sip of his beer. "I suppose you are used to manipulating brutish thugs."

Odin snorted a laugh, leaned back on Ted's chair, and looked to the exit. "And you're not?"

Sindy swung by the table with another beer for Loki and a pint of Guinness for Odin.

"This round's on him," Loki said, pointing at Odin.

"You haven't changed a bit," Odin said to Loki, but nodded to the waitress.

"I don't need to change. I am happy to be me. You were the one who needed to get your shit together."

"To brothers," Odin said, holding up his glass.

Loki sighed and clinked glasses with Odin. "Brothers."

"How did you manage to dodge *your* doom?" Loki asked.

"My spear never misses, and it never gets caught—"

"I remember," Loki said, straightening his moustache so that Odin could see the pinprick scars that ringed his mouth. "I won it for you."

"I followed it right out the wolf's hind end, and came out a story. My friend Snorri kept me alive."

Loki's knuckles tightened over his bottle. "'Wolf's hind end'? That's my son you're talking about."

Odin's brows narrowed, and he leaned over the table. "Do not bring up the topic of *sons* with me."

Loki held up his hands to mollify the crazy old viking. This was a fight he hadn't been expecting, and didn't want. Not unless he had Ted to back him up. As for Odin's story, he *had* drunk deeply of the mead of poetry in times gone by. His story about surviving, as a story, could be true. It *could* also be horseshit.

"Can you forgive me?" Odin asked. "Thoughtless to bring up old hurts here in a new world."

Loki considered, "The last of the Norns told me that Ragnarök washed those past sins away."

"Who am I to argue with her?"

God and giant nodded to each other.

Loki regarded the ceiling. "I suppose you're going to want your old job back."

"No," Odin, answered. "As much as I miss the High Seat, those days are gone. I spent my family upon my rulership. Although I might swing by Gimli to visit Urd. Comfort her in her twilight years."

That was a surprise. Odin had never been one to lightly release power.

The god raised a great bushy eyebrow, the one over his missing eye. "You don't believe me?"

Loki tried not to stare into that hollow socket.

"Ve spreads seeds from a new world ash across the land," Odin said. "Vili is naught but a head in a sack. Let us, you and I, see what new worlds spring from the old. My brothers will not rule, and neither will I."

"If you say so."

"What about him?" Odin asked, gesturing to the rain pelting the windows. He smiled, sadly, when a peal of thunder cracked over the music.

"He's earned a break," Loki said, then grinned. "From dealing with world-shaking problems, at least. Let him fight and fuck and have fun."

"Who's going to rule this new world you helped create, if not him?"

"Rule?" Loki howled a laugh. "Ted? What a glorious disaster that would be! Anyone who came to him with a grievance would be told to 'sack up.' And then he'd punch them in the throat." Loki rubbed a tear from his eye, and then stopped his laughter, as if considering the idea further. "Might be a better idea than I thought."

Odin smiled. "I should go."

"Where?"

"To find someone else to take his place, and mine." Odin shrugged. "This world is better without gods."

Loki smiled. "Speak for yourself."

He watched Odin leave, brushing against Ted as he came back into the bar, soaking wet and smiling. He'd have to tell Ted to check his pockets—Odin was as much a thief as Loki ever was.

He wondered whether Ted was pissed he and Tilda didn't get back together. Or that he'd missed out on an opportunity with Jenny, for that matter. Hel's words to Ted had probably led him to believe that if he were good enough, true enough, brave enough, he'd get the girl.

Instead, he got me.

Loki chuckled. When he'd first spoken to Ted in this exact booth, that had been inconceivable. But looking back on things, Hel hadn't lied. He'd gotten Tilda back in a way, as a friend. Both of Ted's first friends in the Nine would die for him. They were a family. Loki wasn't sure they'd earned their happy ending. And if they had, since when does anyone get what they deserve? He thought of Thor, blind, maimed, dying in Hel for the second time and smiled.

Sometimes.

Even if what they had wasn't what they deserved, it was enough.

Still, Ted could be a morose bastard, and as it was the anniversary of his birth into the Nine tonight, Ófriður was due a gift for his name day. Loki held the cube in his hand, bounced it on his palm and felt its weight. He hoped it was worth the cost. But, after all Ted had been through…

Ted was his friend. His brother. He had stood by Loki. Eventually. He owed the big dumb lunkhead this.

Loki jumped when a hand grabbed the fresh bourbon. It was Ted.

"Don't get too fond of that anonymity of yours," Loki said.

Ted smiled, drained his drink, and slammed the empty glass down on the table. He theatrically dusted his hands off.

"That fight didn't last long," Loki observed.

"No contest," Ted said. "Fucker was all hat and no cattle."

Loki smiled. "Should have known."

"Any idea where we're staying while we're in town?"

"That hotel you were so fond of comes to mind."

"With what money?"

Loki snorted. "I can steal gold from the dwarves any time I want to." He reached into his jacket. "But in the meantime, I got you *this*."

He showed Ted an electric blue metallic cube, with tiny facets all over it, like a monochromatic Rubik's Cube.

It was seamed, like the golden cube that had formed *Skídbladnir*. On one of the faces, the centre square, was a Dodge ram's head. The dwarves had used the bones of Thor's goats to build the chassis of Ted's new Charger. Loki didn't know where they'd gotten those, maybe the same place they'd found Mjölnir. He hadn't bothered asking, he'd been too busy stealing the finished product.

"Is this what I think it is?"

"Thor had two goats, you know. If it gets trashed it'll repair itself. Unfortunately, we won't be able to eat the car in a pinch, but magic can only go so far."

Ted didn't say anything. He watched Loki twirl the cube around in his hand.

"I hope you like the colour."

"What did that cost you?" His voice was breathy. Pleased, but trying to hide it. *Good.*

"Let's just say I won't be going back to Flin Flon anytime soon. Or ever."

"You cheated the dwarves? Again?"

"I gotta be me." Loki shrugged, smiling a small smile. "Hey, you did their dirty work, and Andvari stiffed you on the bill. You paid the cost for them. They owe you far more than this."

"So you stole it."

Loki nodded. "They're gonna be pissed. I think Andvari took a shine to your car, he's been working on this since you left Flin Flon."

Ted's eyes took in the cube, and Loki could see his blood-brother's mental process. Ted was never good at hiding his thoughts. He didn't say "Fuck 'em," but he may as well have.

"Trust me, Teddy. This baby'll *fly*." Loki winked and tossed the cube to Ted. "Let's hit the road."

A new life. A fresh start.

Two things Ted had wanted when he'd left Edmonton for Winnipeg. The new life and fresh start he'd gotten hadn't been what he'd wanted, but it was what he'd asked for. And finally it seemed like that was good enough.

He smiled.

"Fucking magic."

Appendix

Loki's Guide to the Petty Gods and Monsters, and Fantastical Locales and Artifacts of Norse Mythology

Loki: If you don't know me by now … Trickster, liar, father, mother. I've made some new friends who think this saga is about *them*, but I'm disinclined to play the sidekick. If you're the sort to read endings first: *spoiler alert.*

Ófriður: The power of the gods in the flesh of man. Ófriður. Unsightly One. Troublemaker. Un-Peace. The weapon forged by the dwarves to bring back their glory days. Ófriður prefers the name his mother gave him: Ted Callan.

Theodore "Ted" Callan: A former Alberta oil patch worker who doesn't have quite the stomach for spandex, now a hero with nine magical gifts who's looking for a tenth. He's cross with me for…reasons, and has banned me from Winnipeg. I'll worm my way back into his heart, if not his pants.

The Bright Sword: A magic sword. The one that can cool Surtur's fires, and end his wyrd. There are lots of powerful blades in our sagas, but where Ted is concerned the Bright Sword is *the* magic sword. If only Ted knew how in the Hel he was going to get it.

Hel: Former goddess of the dead, and my only daughter (that I know of). Half-dead, half-alive, then dead, now alive. She has a new name, but no one's shared it with me yet. Ted cut our reunion short.

Hel: The realm where my daughter Hel has built her hall and home (also named Hel). She got her imagination from her mother's side.

Valkyries: The choosers of the slain; but after Ragnarök and Odin's death, those who died found themselves the newest employees of their oldest enemy, and in that they are not alone.

Göndul: Once a chooser of the slain, then a valkyrie in name only, choosing for Hel instead of Odin. She led the attack on Ted and Tilda that cost them their child, and our friendship. She should've chosen to stay dead instead of seeking a third master.

Svipul: They called her "The changeable one." She changed sides from Odin to Hel. She's died twice. Third time's the charm.

Tyr: Once a war god, now ruler of Hel in my daughter's absence. Even with boots made of fingernails, he can't fill her shoes.

Níðhöggur: A dragon who ate the roots of Yggdrasill when not glutting herself on the corpses of criminals. A fate I barely managed to escape—unlike *some.*

Mara: The night *mara*. Nightmares. When the vikings came to the New World, they brought their terrors here and buried them. And not every monster died in Ragnarök.

Thor: Don't believe what you read in comics or see in movies. He's a brute and a killer, like all of Odin's sons. Killed at Ragnarök, and again in Hel. My blood had a hand in both. Good riddance.

Mjölnir: Once the hammer of Thor, now the hammer of Ted. With a hammer like this, every problem can look like a nail, but Ted is learning. Let's hope he's learned enough.

The Goat: Thor's chariot was pulled by the goats Tanngrisnir and Tanngnjóstur. Ted Callan's chariot is a different sort of Goat, in his words his 1968 Pontiac GTO is the "Greatest Of All Time." Pity he let it get trashed.

Skídbladnir: Freyr's golden ship. It was made by the dwarves, and while it was large enough to carry all of the gods, it also folded into a cube so small one could fit it into a pocket. A useful feature when someone with quick hands needs to borrow a ride. Shame Ted wrecked *that* too.

Freyr: Brother to Freyja. He was the one originally doomed to face Surtur, but fools and their swords are soon parted. One of the few things Odin couldn't blame me for. Everything about him was bright and golden. Except his brain.

Freyja: Sister of Freyr. Practitioner of sex magic, and very popular at parties. I've heard it said that she had her own host of valkyries, but I've never seen her prove it. Haven't seen her at all since Ragnarök. She could be hiding in Minneapolis for all I know. We shared some harsh words once—more than once.

Flyting: I have been known to throw an insult or two in my time. But *flyting*, a poetic duel of insulting words, is also a time-honoured art and ritual. Funny that the last time we played at words, Odin and his crew didn't care that I killed a man to get into their hall, only what I said about them once I got inside.

Kenning: A way of talking around what you mean to say that can be playful, poetic, a puzzle, or a put-down. Useful when your audience is heavily armed, drunk, and spoiling for a fight.

Seiður: Sex Magic. Also known as *The Best Magic*. Taught to Odin by Freyja, but no secret this good stays secret for long (especially from me), and I've been known to try it a time or two.

Odin: All-Father, but not my father; was once my blood-brother, then my sworn enemy. I haven't heard a peep from him since Ragnarök. I can almost believe he's gone for good.

Huginn: A meddlesome raven, once provider of Odin's thoughts, now he pecks away offering advice to a thicker, but kinder, skull—Ted's.

Muninn: A quarrelsome raven, once the holder of Odin's grudges, now he advises Ted about the Nine Worlds, and tries to convince him not to trust me.

Sleipnir: The fastest thing on two, four, or eight legs, so naturally he became Odin's steed. Sleipnir's gift to run upon water, air, or land with equal ease now belongs to Ted and I'm filled with a mother's pride every time Ted uses it.

Vili and Ve: Pushed aside so the "All-Father" could also be the "only" father, Odin's brothers travel the New World, one as Johnny Appleseed, the other as a head in a sack.

Baldur: The brightest sun in Asgard's sky. Maybe someday he'll finally rise again.

Heimdall: Watcher of the rainbow bridge to Asgard, sounder of the Gjallarhorn, son of Odin, and Holmes to my Moriarty.

Gjallarhorn: The horn of Valhalla, used by Heimdall to summon the *einherjar* when I and my brood came calling at Ragnarök. One of Ted's magical gifts, the Gjallarhorn summons Ted's ancestors to fight at his side.

Asgard: One of the Nine Realms, and formerly the greatest, if you believe everything you read.

Valhalla: Land of feasting and fighting, two of the three big "F's" for the vikings. There wasn't nearly enough of that all-important third "F" to be found for my liking.

Einherjar: The bravest souls of warring mortals. The Honoured Dead. Once they were Odin's warriors, pledged eternally to the All-Father's service, now they are Ted's family, lost in the Great War, but still fighting.

Fenrir: The Wolf of Ragnarök. Maimer of Tyr and Gobbler of Odin. Killed for his efforts and then killed again before I found my way back to Midgard.

Jormungandur: My boy, the Midgard Serpent. Jorry will always hold a special place in my heart for ridding all Nine Worlds of that windbag of a Thunder God, Thor.

The Nine Realms: Asgard, Vanaheim, Álfheim, Jötunheim, Midgard, Svartálfheim, Muspelheim, Niflheim, and Hel, connected to one another by the World Tree, Yggdrasill. Nine Worlds, home to gods and giants, dwarves and elves, and of course, humanity. Nine Worlds, and not a one of them safe.

Bifröst: The rainbow bridge that connected Earth to Asgard. Sundered under the weight of our grudges and the auroras are the only remnants of its power.

Ginnungagap: The space between the Nine Worlds, where dark things wait for gods to fall.

Niflheim: One of the Nine Realms, a place of primordial cold and despair.

Álfheim: Land of the *álfar*—elves, and not a place to bring your Fellowship for counsel.

Álfar: Forget Legolas. Forget Keebler. These elves will snap, crackle, and pop your bones and slit your throat as soon as sing you a song about green and growing things.

Jack Flash: A tattooed elf in Winnipeg. First an enemy, and now ally to Ted.

Jötunheim: One of the Nine Realms, home of the giants, and my old stomping ground.

Jötnar: Giants. Mostly brutish and violent, though some (if I do say so myself) are beings of exemplary taste.

Gull: Ted calls him "Youngnir." Son of Rungnir, and the first *jötunn* that Ted kissed with a fist. Another enemy turned ally.

Ted has a way of turning enemies into friends, and friends into enemies. Maybe that's why we get along.

Ymir: The first giant. The first being. The real All-Father. It is his bones that make up Midgard, so show him some respect.

Midgard: Earth—or as I like to refer to it: where the fun happens.

Black Metal: "Shit Metal" according to Ted. It's full of stories of gods and magic, hammers and rainbow bridges, and who'd want to listen to that?

Gimli: The home of the Norns for the last one hundred fifty years or so. This sleepy little lake townnamed for the home built by the survivors of Ragnarök was also the centre of all things Norse and magical in the New World. Until recently, that is.

Winnipeg: This "heart of the continent" is the new heart and hotbed of Norse magic and monsters.

Edmonton: City of Champions. Ted's city, until he found another and made that his. Can Ted live up to his old stomping grounds' rep?

Jennifer Hildebrandt: A woman from Ted's past. She survived Naglfar Night, but hasn't talked to Ted since. I wonder why.

Flin Flon: The city built on rock, and almost scoured down to that same rock. This northern mining community is a hideout for dwarves and giants.

Niðavellir: The kindgom of the *dvergar*. *They* claim it's one of the Nine Realms. They would. I think they're just refusing to acknowledge the *svartálfar*.

Dvergar: Dwarves, forgers of weapons of legend.

Tyrfing: A cursed dwarven sword, always on the hunt for a new wielder.

Rock Trolls: Loose collections of boulders mortared together by *dvergar* with the blood of folks who'd been exposed to the Nine. Dumb, but incredibly strong.

Andvari: The last of the three dwarves who tattooed Ted. Ruler of the *dvergar* of Flin Flon. He and his moustache are lucky Ted is more forgiving than Mjölnir's last wielder (or the bloke who commissioned that hammer in the first place).

Yggdrasill: The World Tree, the World Ash, its branches stretched to Asgard and its roots delved to Niflheim. Odin hanged himself from the tree to learn the secrets of the runes. Secrets now tattooed upon Ted's back.

Runes: Stones with magic symbols on them. Primarily used by the Norns in their magic, but also by fortune tellers and believers.

The Norns: Back in the day, any witch, elf, or giant with a touch of the sight would call themselves a norn, but there were only three "capital N" Norns: Urd, Skuld, and Verdandi, mistresses of past, future and present. Now there's only one.

Urd: She was the eldest of the Norns, and privy to almost as many secrets as yours truly. She still hates me for my role in the Greenland Affair, but now she's too frail to do anything about it.

Verdandi: Mother to Skuld and was the Norn of the present. She doesn't much like me, though with her it's not anything personal, just Urd's stories.

Skuld: The youngest of the three Norns, and the one upon whom Midgard's future will turn. You know her better as Tilda.

Tilda Eilífsdóttir: Former rover and vagabond, once she was Skuld, the youngest of the Norns. Now Tilda is *the* Norn. Present, past, and future all in one, and cold as Hel. Ted uses the runes. Tilda *is* the runes. You'd think I'd mention her sooner, but she wants me dead. I don't like her either.

Ragnarök: The Fate of the Gods. Where I was supposed to die along with all of my slow-witted enemies: Thor, Heimdall, Tyr. I dodged that bullet, thankfully. But not everyone got the memo that Ragnarök was past—or that a fresh one is in the offing.

Muspelheim: A primordial world of fire. Surtur's world. If the big guy gets his way, it'll be the only that's left when all this is over.

Sinmara: One of Surtur's smarter agents. She holds a grudge against me, though I can't fathom why.

Surtur: Skychoker and Earthburner. The End of All Things was Ted's beginning in the Nine Worlds. Let's hope he's not Ted's end too. The big lug has survived meeting Surtur twice, here's hoping third time lucky.

The Greenland Affair: Word travels. My first adventure after waking up from Ragnarök was a source of contention between me and pretty much everyone else who survived. If I live through Ted saving the world (and that's a big if), maybe I'll tell you about it. Some day.

Acknowledgements

There was a moment when I was willing to dedicate this book to whoever was willing to write this last note on my behalf. With each of my books the final acknowledgments were the last words written before the book went to print, and despite doing this a couple times now, I still live in the paranoid fear of forgetting someone important. If you don't see your name below, feel free to write it in and I'll initial it the next time we meet to make it official.

I gratefully acknowledge the support of the Manitoba Arts Council whose financial support helped make *Too Far Gone* a reality. Thanks Team Ravenstone for getting another gorgeous looking book out into the world. My editor Michael Matheson saw exactly what I wanted to do with this book, and made sure my intent matched what I'd typed. David Jón Fuller, thanks, as always, for straightening out my Icelandic and your attention to detail on the copy edits. I would feel remiss if I didn't also mention Wayne Tefs, editor of *Thunder Road* and *Tombstone Blues*—I will remember your advice and always strive to make new mistakes. "High-fallutin'" is for you, sir.

My first readers who tackled the rough drafts (so you don't have to) remain excellent human beings. Steven Benstead, Lee-Anne Berkvens, Michael Friesen, Frank Krivak, Chris Smith, thank you all. Samantha Beiko did a wonderful job of alternately talking me down and riling me up when this book was getting the best of me. Anyone who knows me knows I love to swear, but even I need an "Agent Profaniteur" on occasion, so warm thanks to Jillian Bell for the expression "prickbruise".

A great many good folks have put up with me while I was on tour or research trips, chauffeured me around, created art for the series, introduced me to music for my playlists, or have been amazing in their support, so thank you to Ann Aguirre, Eileen Bell, Jean Cichon, Michael Cichon, Laurel Copeland, Julie Czerneda, Scott Henderson, Patrick Johanneson, Shanleigh Klassen, Janice MacDonald and Randy Williams, Kevin Madison, Billie Milholland, Brad Neufeld, Jocelyne Quane, Robin Righetti, Ron Samborski, Chris Szego, Brent Vandurme, and Tyler Vitt.

Friends and family. Mom and Dad. And Wendy, always Wendy.

Thank you for reading.

Thunder Road
by Chadwick Ginther

In a flash, Ted Callan's world exploded and amid the flames he saw the incomprehensible, the burning figure of the fire giant Surtur. Before long, Ted learns that the creatures of Norse folklore walk among us and his fate is forever tied to them.

Ted wants nothing more than to have his old life back. No more magic. No more smart-ass gods. To get it, Ted is willing to fight his way through any creature of legend. The problem is, if he succeeds, it might just be the end of the world.

Praise for Thunder Road

Chadwick Ginther is a major new talent. His stunning debut novel grabs you by the throat and shakes you mercilessly; his prose is vivid and sharp and his settings are gritty and terrifyingly real. This is serious fantasy for grownups.

—Robert J. Sawyer, Hugo Award–winning author of Triggers

Thunder Road is a gritty, two-fisted action fantasy jammed with Norse mythology and the unique atmosphere of the Canadian prairies. The imagination and attention to detail make this book a compelling and exciting read. By the time I finished I needed a stiff drink, a smoke and a shower. Chadwick Ginther is one of those authors that gets under your skin. I'm looking forward to his next book.

—J.A. Pitts, author of Forged in Fire

Thunder Road / $16.00
ISBN: 9780888014009
Ravenstone

Tombstone Blues

by Chadwick Ginther

After beating back the might of Surtur, Ted Callan is getting used to his immortal powers. The man who once would stop at nothing to rid himself of his tattoos and their power might even be said to be enjoying his new-found abilities.

However, not everyone is happy the glory of Valhalla has risen from the ashes of Ragnarök. With every crash of Mjölnir, Thor, former god of thunder, rages in Niflheim, the land of the dead.

Now that Ted's woken the dead, there's going to be hell to pay.

Praise for Tombstone Blues

"The book's action set-pieces could anchor a Peter Jackson movie, but it's the personal side that adds depth."

—AE –The Canadian Science Fiction Review

Ginther's mythos, bringing Norse gods and magical creatures within Manitoba's borders, is complexly woven…

—Winnipeg Free Press

Ginther has a Bardic authorial voice that aids in weaving a tale of stunning imagery and fast-paced action.

—Rhubarb

Thunder Road / $16.00
ISBN: 9780888014450
Ravenstone

Originally from Morden, Manitoba, Chadwick Ginther is the winner of The Mary Scorer Award for Best Book by a Manitoba Publisher, the winner of The Michael Van Rooy Award for Genre Fiction and twice nominated for the Prix Aurora Awards for *Thunder Road* and *Tombstone Blues*. His short stories have appeared in many speculative fiction publications, and he cohosts the Winnipeg arm of the Chiaroscuro Reading Series. A bookseller for over a decade, Chadwick Ginther lives and writes in Winnipeg.